Walter Savage Landor, Charles G. Crump

The Longer Prose Works of Walter Savage Landor

Volume 2

Walter Savage Landor, Charles G. Crump

The Longer Prose Works of Walter Savage Landor
Volume 2

ISBN/EAN: 9783337313074

Printed in Europe, USA, Canada, Australia, Japan

Cover: Foto ©Andreas Hilbeck / pixelio.de

More available books at **www.hansebooks.com**

THE LONGER PROSE WORKS OF WALTER SAVAGE LANDOR

EDITED WITH NOTES AND INDEX

BY CHARLES G. CRUMP

IN TWO VOLUMES

SECOND VOLUME

LONDON: PRINTED FOR J. M. DENT & CO.,
AND PUBLISHED BY THEM AT ALDINE
HOUSE, 69 GREAT EASTERN STREET.
MDCCCXCIII.

TABLE OF CONTENTS.

PREFATORY NOTE.

THIS volume contains the " Pentameron," five additional Conversations, and the three critical essays on Theocritus, Catullus. and Petrarca. The " Pentameron " was first published in 1837, and again in 1846 and 1876. Four of the additional conversations appeared at various times in the *Examiner*—" Ovid and Prince of the Getæ " on April 7, 1855; " Pio Nono and Antonelli," Dec. 2, 1854; " Nicholas and Diogenes," Feb. 11, 1854; " Nicholas and Nesselrode," June 11, 1853. None of these four conversations have been since reprinted. The fifth, " Ines di Castro," may be found in the form here given in Vol. III. of the first edition, published in 1828. Landor afterwards enlarged it and turned it into verse. The metrical version will be found in the volume of poems published in 1831 and in the collected works, 1846 and 1876. The Critical Essays all appeared in the *Foreign Quarterly Review*—the one on Catullus in July 1842, that on Theocritus in October of the same year, and that on Petrarch in July 1843.

The Index found at the end of the book has been prepared by Lucy Crump. The main object has been to indicate as far as possible allusions to Landor's own life scattered throughout the volumes, and to illustrate his opinions. A word is needful to explain the method adopted in the numbering of the volumes in the Index. For the sake of clearness and brevity Vols. I. and II. of " Poems and Dialogues " are called Vols. VII. and VIII., and Vols. I. and II. of the " Longer Prose Works," Vols. IX. and X. respectively.

THE PENTAMERON.

THE PENTAMERON.

—✳—

THE EDITOR'S INTRODUCTION.

Wanting a bell for my church at San Vivaldo, and hearing that our holy religion is rapidly gaining ground in England, to the unspeakable comfort and refreshment of the Faithful, I bethought myself that I might peradventure obtain such effectual aid, from the piety and liberality of the converts, as well-nigh to accomplish the purchase of one. Desirous moreover of visiting that famous nation, of whose spiritual prosperity we all entertain such animated hopes, now that the clouds of ignorance begin to break and vanish, I resolved that nothing on my part should be wanting to so blessed a consummation. Therefore, while I am executing my mission in regard to the bell, I omit no opportunity of demonstrating how much happier and peacefuller are we who live in unity, than those who, abandoning the household of Faith, clothe themselves with shreds and warm themselves with shavings.

Subsidiary to the aid I solicit, I brought with me, and here lay before the public, translated by the best hand I could afford to engage, "*Certain Interviews of Messer Francesco Petrarca and Messer Giovanni Boccaccio, etc.,*" which, the booksellers tell me, should be entitled "*The Pentameron,*" unless I would return with nothing in my pocket. I am ignorant what gave them this idea of my intent, unless it be my deficiency in the language, for certainly I had come to no such resolution. Assurances are made to me by the intelligent and experienced in such merchandise, that the manuscript is honestly worth from twenty-five to thirty francesconi, or dollars. To such a pitch hath England risen up again, within these few years, after all the expenditure of her protracted war.

Is there any true Italian, above all is there any worthy native of Certaldo or San Vivaldo, who revolveth not in his mind what a surprise and delight it will be to Giovanni in Paradise, the first time he hears, instead of that cracked and jarring tumbril (which must have grated in his ear most grievously ever since its accident, and have often tried his patience), just such another as he was wont to hear when he rode over to join our townspeople at their *festa?* It will do his heart good, and make him think of old times; and perhaps he may drop a couple of prayers to the Madonna for whoso had a hand in it.

Lest it should be bruited in England or elsewhere, that being in my seventieth year, I have unadvisedly quitted my parish, "*fond of change*," to use the blessed words of Saint Paul, I am ready to show the certificate of Monsignore, my diocesan, approving of my voyage. Monsignore was pleased to think me capable of undertaking it, telling me that I looked hale, spoke without quavering, and, by the blessing of our lady, had nigh upon half my teeth in their sockets, while, pointing to his own and shaking his head, he repeated the celebrated lines of Horatius Flaccus, who lived in the reign of Augustus, a short time before the Incarnation :—

> " Non ebur, sed horridùm
> Buccâ dehiscit in meâ lacuna ! "

Then, turning the discourse from so melancholy a topic, he was pleased to relate from the inexhaustible stores of his archæological requirements, that no new bell whatever had been consecrated in his diocese of Samminiato since the year of our Lord 1611 : in which year, on the first Sunday of August, a thunderbolt fell into the belfry of the Duomo, by the negligence of Canonico Malatesta, who, according to history, in his hurry to dine with Conte Geronimo Bardi, at our San Vivaldo, omitted a word in the mass. While he was playing at bowls after dinner on that Sunday, or, as some will have it, while he was beating Ser Matteo Filicaia at backgammon, and the younger men and ladies of those two noble families were bird-catching with the *civetta*, it began to thunder : and, within the evening, intelligence of the thunderbolt was brought to the Canonico. On his return the day following it was remarked, says the chronicler, that the people took off their caps at the distance of only two or three paces, instead of fifteen or twenty, and few stopped who met him :

for the rumour had already gone abroad of his omission. He often rode, as usual, to Conte Geronimo's, gammoned Ser Matteo, hooded the *civetta*, lined a twig or two, stood behind the spinette, hummed the next note, turned over the pages of the music-book of the *contessine*, beating time on the chair-back, and showing them what he could do now and then on the *viola di gamba*. Only eight years had elapsed when, in the flower of his age (for he had scarcely seen sixty), he was found dead in his bed, after as hearty and convivial a supper as ever Canonico ate. No warning, no *olio santo*, no viaticum, poor man! Candles he had; and it was as much as he had, poor sinner! And this also happened in the month of August! Monsignore, in his great liberality, laid no heavy stress on the coincidence; but merely said,

"Well, Pievano! a mass or two can do him no harm; let us hope he stands in need of few more; but when you happen to have leisure, and nobody else to think about, prythee clap a wet clout on the fire there below in behalf of Canonico Malatesta."

I have done it gratis, and I trust he finds the benefit of it. In the same spirit and by the same authority I gird myself for this greater enterprise. Unable to form a satisfactory opinion on the manuscript, I must again refer to my superior. It is the opinion then of Monsignore, that our five dialogues were written down by neither of the interlocutors, but rather by some intimate, who loved them equally. "For," said Monsignore, "it was the practice of Boccaccio to stand up among his personages, and to take part himself in their discourses. Petrarca, who was fonder of sheer dialogue and had much practice in it, never acquired any dexterity in this species of composition, it being all question and answer, short, snappish, quibbling, and uncomfortable. I speak only of his *Remedies of Adversity and Prosperity*, which indeed leave his wisdom all its wholesomeness, but render it somewhat apt to cleave to the roof of the mouth. The better parts of Homer are in dialogue: and downward from him to Galileo the noblest works of human genius have assumed this form: among the rest I am sorry to find no few heretics and scoffers. At the present day the fashion is over: every man pushes every other man behind him, and will let none speak out but himself.

The *Interviews* took place not within the walls of Certaldo, although within the parish, at Boccaccio's villa. It should be notified to the curious, that about this ancient town, small, deserted, dilapidated as it is, there are several towers and turrets yet standing, one of which belongs to the mansion inhabited in its day by Ser Giovanni.   His tomb and effigy are in the church. Nobody has opened the grave to throw light upon his relics ; nobody has painted the marble ; nobody has broken off a foot or a finger to do him honour ; not even an English name is engraven on the face ; although the English hold confessedly the highest rank in this department of literature.   In Italy, and particularly in Tuscany, the remains of the illustrious are inviolable ; and, among the illustrious, men of genius hold the highest rank. The arts are more potent than curiosity, more authoritative than churchwardens : what Englishman will believe it ?   Well ! let it pass, courteous strangers ! ye shall find me in future less addicted to the marvellous.   At present I have only to lay before you an ancient and (doubt it not) an authentic account of what passed between my countrymen, Giovanni and Francesco, before they parted for ever.   It seemed probable, at this meeting, that Giovanni would have been called away first ; for heavy and of long continuance had been his infirmity : but he outlived it three whole years.   He could not outlive his friend so many months, but followed him to the tomb before he had worn the glossiness off the cloak Francesco in his will bequeathed to him.

We struggle with Death while we have friends around to cheer us ; the moment we miss them we lose all heart for the contest.   Pardon my reflection ! I ought to have remembered I am not in my stone pulpit, nor at home.

Prete Domenico Grigi,

Pievano of San Vivaldo.

London, *October* 1, 1836.

THE PENTAMERON.

Boccaccio. Who is he that entered, and now steps so silently and softly, yet with a foot so heavy it shakes my curtains?

Frate Biagio! can it possibly be you?

No more physic for me, nor masses neither, at present.

Assunta! Assuntina! who is it?

Assunta.[1] I can not say, Signor Padrone! he puts his finger in the dimple of his chin, and smiles to make me hold my tongue.

Boccaccio. Fra Biagio! are you come from Samminiato for this! You need not put your finger there. We want no secrets. The girl knows her duty and does her business. I have slept well, and wake better.   *[Raising himself up a little.*

Why? who are you? It makes my eyes ache to look aslant

[1 First Edition has the following note: I am inclined to believe it must have been Assunta Nardi, who was probably at this time the only servant of Ser Giovanni; for we find in the register at Certaldo the marriage of Fiamminga Nardi, daughter of Simplizio Nardi and of Assunta his wife; and, on her tombstone that ' she was erewhile nurse and governess in the house of Ser Giovanni Boccaccio of this Parish.' What her name was before marriage is uncertain. She left behind several sons and daughters: one son, the second, was a plumber; and our account-book informs us that on the 14th of March, 1388, six *lire* and three *soldi* were disbursed to him ' for an entirely new tongue, and red pigments thereunto applied, in the dragon at the market-place ; likewise for iron bars ; likewise for solder round the perforation for keeping the saint (viz. George) upon his horse.' His daughter Lisa married Agapeto Camarelli of Colli ; which Agapeto rose to be sacristan in that burg ; and his great nephew Claudio Neri was sub-librarian in the library of the Duomo at Samminiato. His son-in-law, Simone Mazzuoli, became a most distinguished carpenter, and erected the canopy, still extant, over the episcopal throne in said Duomo. His descendant, in the third degree, was nothing less than page to the Cardinal Uberto degli Albizzi. We may augur from the prosperity of Assunta's descendants, that her life was discreet and irreproachable.—D.G.]

over the sheets; and I can not get to sit quite upright so conveniently; and I must not have the window-shutters opened, they
tell me.

Petrarca.   Dear Giovanni! have you then been very unwell?

Boccaccio.   O that sweet voice! and this fat friendly hand of
thine, Francesco!

Thou hast distilled all the pleasantest flowers, and all the whole-
somest herbs of spring, into my breast already.

What showers we have had this April, ay!   How could you
come along such roads?   If the devil were my labourer, l would
make him work upon these of Certaldo.   He would have little
time and little itch for mischief ere he had finished them, but
would gladly fan himself with an Agnus-castus, and go to sleep
all through the carnival.

Petrarca.   Let us cease to talk both of the labour and the
labourer.   You have then been dangerously ill?

Boccaccio.   I do not know: they told me I was: and truly a
man might be unwell enough, who has twenty masses said for him,
and fain sigh when he thinks what he has paid for them.   As l
hope to be saved, they cost me a *lira* each.   Assunta is a good
market-girl in eggs, and mutton, and cow-heel; but I would not
allow her to argue and haggle about the masses.   Indeed she
knows best whether they were not fairly worth all that was asked
for them, although I could have bought a winter cloak for less
money.   However, we do not want both at the same time.   I
did not want the cloak: I wanted *them* it seems.   And yet I
begin to think God would have had mercy on me, if I had begged
it of him myself in my own house.   What think you?

Petrarca.   I think he might.

Boccaccio.   Particularly if I offered him the sacrifice on which
I wrote to you.

Petrarca.   That letter has brought me hither.

Boccaccio.   You do then insist on my fulfilling my promise, the
moment I can leave my bed.   I am ready and willing.

Petrarca.   Promise! none was made.   You only told me
that, if it pleased God to restore you to your health again, you
are ready to acknowledge his mercy by the holocaust of your
Decameron.   What proof have you that God would exact it?   If
you could destroy the *Inferno* of Dante, would you?

Boccaccio.   Not I, upon my life !   I would not promise to burn a copy of it on the condition of a recovery for twenty years.

Petrarca.   You are the only author who would not rather demolish another's work than his own ; especially if he thought it better : a thought which seldom goes beyond suspicion.

Boccaccio.   I am not jealous of any one : I think admiration pleasanter.   Moreover, Dante and I did not come forward at the same time, nor take the same walks.   His flames are too fierce for you and me : we had trouble enough with milder.   I never felt any high gratification in hearing of people being damned ; and much less would I toss them into the fire myself.   I might indeed have put a nettle under the nose of the learned judge in Florence, when he banished you and your family ; but I hardly think I could have voted for more than a scourging to the foulest and fiercest of the party.

Petrarca.   Be as compassionate, be as amiably irresolute, toward your own *Novelle,* which have injured no friend of yours, and deserve more affection.

Boccaccio.   Francesco ! no character I ever knew, ever heard of, or ever feigned, deserves the same affection as you do ; the tenderest lover, the truest friend, the firmest patriot, and, rarest of glories ! the poet who cherishes another's fame as dearly as his own.

Petrarca.   If aught of this is true, let it be recorded of me that my exhortations and intreaties have been successful, in preserving the works of the most imaginative and creative genius that our Italy, or indeed our world, hath in any age beheld.

Boccaccio.   I would not destroy his poems, as I told you, or think I told you.   Even the worst of the Florentines, who in general keep only one of God's commandments, keep it rigidly in regard to Dante—

Love them who curse you.

He called them all scoundrels, with somewhat less courtesy than cordiality, and less afraid of censure for veracity than adulation : he sent their fathers to hell, with no inclination to separate the child and parent : and now they are hugging him for it in his shroud! Would you ever have suspected them of being such lovers of justice?

You must have mistaken my meaning; the thought never entered my head: the idea of destroying a single copy of Dante! And what effect would that produce! There must be fifty, or near it, in various parts of Italy.

Petrarca. I spoke of you.

Boccaccio. Of me! My poetry is vile; I have already thrown into the fire all of it within my reach.

Petrarca. Poetry was not the question. We neither of us are such poets as we thought ourselves when we were younger, and as younger men think us still. I meant your *Decameron ;* in which there is more character, more nature, more invention, than either modern or ancient Italy, or than Greece, from whom she derived her whole inheritance, ever claimed or ever knew. Would you consume a beautiful meadow because there are reptiles in it; or because a few grubs hereafter may be generated by the succulence of the grass?

Boccaccio. You amaze me: you utterly confound me.

Petrarca. If you would eradicate twelve or thirteen of the *Novelle,* and insert the same number of better, which you could easily do within as many weeks, I should be heartily glad to see it done. Little more than a tenth of the *Decameron* is bad : less than a twentieth of the *Divina Commedia* is good.

Boccaccio. So little?

Petrarca. Let me never seem irreverent to our master.

Boccaccio. Speak plainly and fearlessly, Francesco! Malice and detraction are strangers to you.

Petrarca. Well then: at least sixteen parts in twenty of the *Inferno* and *Purgatorio* are detestable, both in poetry and principle : the higher parts are excellent indeed.

Boccaccio. I have been reading the *Paradiso* more recently. Here it is, under the pillow. It brings me happier dreams than the others, and takes no more time in bringing them. Preparation for my lectures made me remember a great deal of the poem. I did not request my auditors to admire the beauty of the metrical version :

> Osanna sanctus deus Sabbaoth,
> Super-illustrans charitate tuâ
> Felices ignes horum Malahoth,

nor these, with a slip of Italian between two pales of Latin :

> Modicum,* et non videbitis me,
> Et iterum, sorelle mie dilette,
> Modicum, et vos videbitis me.

I dare not repeat all I recollect of

> Pape Setan, Pape Setan, aleppe.

as there is no holy-water-sprinkler in the room : and you are
aware that other dangers awaited me, had I been so imprudent as
to show the Florentines the allusion of our poet. His *gergo* is
perpetually in play, and sometimes plays very roughly.

Petrarca. We will talk again of him presently. I must now
rejoice with you over the recovery and safety of your prodigal son,
the *Decameron.*

Boccaccio. So then, you would preserve at any rate my
favourite volume from the threatened conflagration.

Petrarca. Had I lived at the time of Dante, I would have
given him the same advice in the same circumstances. Yet how
different is the tendency of the two productions ! Yours is somewhat too licentious ; and young men, in whose nature, or rather
in whose education and habits, there is usually this failing, will
read you with more pleasure than is commendable or innocent.
Yet the very time they occupy with you, would perhaps be spent
in the midst of those excesses or irregularities, to which the
moralist, in his utmost severity, will argue that your pen directs
them. Now there are many who are fond of standing on the
brink of precipices, and who nevertheless are as cautious as any
of falling in. And there are minds desirous of being warmed by
description, which without this warmth, might seek excitement
among the things described.

I would not tell you in health what I tell you in convalescence,
nor urge you to compose what I dissuade you from cancelling.
After this avowal, I do declare to you, Giovanni, that in my
opinion, the very idlest of your tales will do the world as much

---

* It may puzzle an Englishman to read the lines beginning with
Modicum, so as to give the metre. The secret is, to draw out *et* into a
dissyllable, et te, as the Italians do, who pronounce Latin verse, if possible, worse than we, adding a syllable to such as end with a consonant.

good as evil; not reckoning the pleasure of reading, nor the exercise and recreation of the mind, which in themselves are good. What I reprove you for, is the indecorous and uncleanly; and these, I trust, you will abolish. Even these, however, may repel from vice the ingenuous and graceful spirit, and 'can never lead any such toward them. Never have you taken an inhuman pleasure in blunting and fusing the affections at the furnace of the passions; never, in hardening by sour sagacity and ungenial strictures, that delicacy which is more productive of innocence and happiness, more estranged from every track and tendency of their opposites, than what in cold, crude systems hath holden the place and dignity of the highest virtue. May you live, O my friend, in the enjoyment of health, to substitute the facetious for the licentious, the simple for the extravagant, the true and characteristic for the indefinite and diffuse.

Boccaccio. I dare not defend myself under the bad example of any: and the bad example of a great man is the worst defence of all. Since, however, you have mentioned Messer Dante Alighieri, to whose genius I never thought of approaching, I may perhaps have been formerly the less cautious of offending by my levity, after seeing him display as much or more of it in hell itself.

Petrarca. The best apology for Dante, in his poetical character, is presented by the indulgence of criticism, in considering the *Inferno* and *Purgatorio* as a string of *Satires*, part in narrative and part in action; which renders the title of *Commedia* more applicable. The filthiness of some passages would disgrace the drunkenest horse-dealer; and the names of such criminals are recorded by the poet as would be forgotten by the hangman in six months. I wish I could expatiate rather on his injudiciousness than on his ferocity, in devising punishments for various crimes; or rather, than on his malignity in composing catalogues of criminals to inflict them on. Among the rest we find a gang of coiners. He calls by name all the rogues and vagabonds of every city in Tuscany, and curses every city for not sending him more of them. You would fancy that Pisa might have contented him; no such thing. He hoots,

"Ah Pisa! scandal to the people in whose fine country *si* means *yes*, why are thy neighbours slack to punish thee? May

Capraia and Gorgona stop up the mouth of the Arno, and drown every soul within thee!"

Boccaccio. None but a prophet is privileged to swear and curse at this rate, and several of those got broken heads for it.

Petrarca. It did not happen to Dante, though he once was very near it, in the expedition of the exiles to recover the city. Scarcely had he taken breath after this imprecation against the Pisans, than he asks the Genoese why such a parcel of knaves as themselves were not scattered over the face of the earth.

Boccaccio. Here he is equitable. I wonder he did not incline to one or other of these rival republics.

Petrarca. In fact, the Genoese fare a trifle better under him than his neighbours the Pisans do.

Boccaccio. Because they have no Gorgona and Capraia to block them up. He can not do all he wishes, but he does all he can, considering the means at his disposal. In like manner Messer Gregorio Peruzzi, when he was tormented by the quarrels and conflicts of Messer Gino Ubaldini's truffle-dog at the next door, and Messer Guidone Fantecchi's shop-dog, whose title and quality are in abeyance, swore bitterly, and called the Virgin and St Catherine to witness that he would cut off their tails if ever he caught them. His cook, Niccolo Buonaccorsi, hoping to gratify his master, set baits for them, and captured them both in the kitchen. But unwilling to cast hands prematurely on the delinquents, he, after rating them for their animosities and their ravages, bethought himself in what manner he might best conduct his enterprise to a successful issue. He was the rather inclined to due deliberation in these counsels, as they, laying aside their private causes of contention in front of their common enemy, and turning the principal stream of their ill-blood into another channel, agreed in demonstrations which augured no little indocility. Messer Gregorio hath many servants, and moreover all the conveniences which so plenteous a house requires. Among the rest is a long hempen cloth suspended by a roller. Niccolo, in the most favourable juncture, was minded to slip this hempen cloth over the two culprits, whose consciences had made them slink toward the door against which it was fastened. The smell of it was not unsatisfactory to them, and an influx of courage had nearly borne away the worst suspicions. At this instant, while shrewd inquisitiveness and incipient hunger were regaining the ascendancy, Niccolo Buonaccorsi, with all the sagacity and courage, all the promptitude and timeliness of his profession, covered both conspirators in the inextricable folds of the fatal winding-sheet, from which their heads alone emerged. Struggles, and barkings, and exhibitions of teeth, and plunges forward, were equally ineffectual. He continued to twist it about them, until the notes of resentment partook of remonstrance and pain: but he told them plainly he would never remit a jot, unless they became more domesticated and reasonable. In this state of exhaustion and contrition he brought them into the presence of Ser Gregorio, who immediately turned round toward the wall, crossed himself, and whispered an *ave*. At ease and happy as he was at the accomplishment of a desire so long cherished, no sooner had he expressed his piety at so gracious a dispensation, than, reverting to the captor and the captured, he was seized with unspeakable consternation. He discovered at once that he had made as rash a vow as Jeptha's. Alas! one of the children of captivity, the trufle-dog, had no tail! Fortunately for Messer Gregorio, he found a friend among the White Friars, Frate Geppone Pallorco, who told him that when we cannot do a thing promised by vow, whether we fail by moral inability or by physical, we must do the thing nearest it; "which," said Fra Geppone, "hath always been my practice. And now," added this cool, considerate white friar, "a dog may have no tail, and yet be a dog to all intents and purposes, and enable a good Christian to perform anything reasonable he promised in his behalf. Whereupon I would advise you, Messer Gregorio, out of the loving zeal I bear toward the whole family of the Peruzzi, to amerce him of that which, if not tail, is next to tail. Such function, I doubt not, will satisfactorily show the blessed Virgin, and Saint Catherine, your readiness and solicitude to perform the vow solemnly made before these two adorable ladies, your protectresses and witnesses." Ser Gregorio bent his knee at first hearing their names, again at the mention of them in this relationship toward him, called for the kitchen knife, and, in absolving his promise, had lighter things to deal with than Gorgona and Capraia.

Petrarca. Giovanni! this will do instead of one among the worst of the hundred: but with little expenditure of labour you may afford us a better.

Our great fellow-citizen, if indeed we may denominate him a citizen who would have left no city standing in Italy, and less willingly his native one, places in the mouth of the devil, together with Judas Iscariot, the defenders of their country, and the best men in it, Brutus and Cassius. Certainly his feeling of patriotism was different from theirs.

I should be sorry to imagine that it subjected him to any harder mouth or worse company than his own, although in a spirit so contrary to that of the two Romans, he threatened us Florentines with the sword of Germans. The two Romans, now in the mouth of the devil, chose rather to lose their lives than to see their country, not under the government of invaders, but of magistrates from their own city placed irregularly over them; and the laws, not subverted, but administered unconstitutionally. That Frenchmen and Austrians should argue and think in this manner, is no wonder, no inconsistency: that a Florentine, the wisest and greatest of Florentines, should have done it, is portentous.

How merciful is the Almighty, O Giovanni! What an argument is here! how much stronger and more convincing than philosophers could devise or than poets could utter, unless from inspiration, against the placing of power in the hands of one man only, when the highest genius at that time in the world, or perhaps at any time, betrays a disposition to employ it with such a licentiousness of inhumanity.

Boccaccio. He treats Nero with greater civility: yet Brutus and Cassius, at worst, but slew an atheist, while the other rogue flamed forth like the pestilential dog-star, and burnt up the first crop of Christians to light the ruins of Rome. And the artist of these ruins thought no more of his operation than a scene-painter would have done at the theatre.

Petrarca. Historians have related that Rome was consumed by Nero for the purpose of suppressing the rising sect, by laying all the blame on it. Do you think he cared what sect fell or what sect rose? Was he a zealot in religion of any kind? I am sorry to see a lying spirit the most prevalent one, in some among the earliest and firmest holders of that religion which is founded on truth and singleness of intention. There are pious men who believe they are rendering a service to God by bearing false witness in his favour, and who call on the father of lies to hold up his light before the Sun of Righteousness.

We may mistake the exact day when the conflagration began : certain it is, however, that it was in summer : * and it is presumable that the commencement of the persecution was in winter, since Juvenal represents the persecuted as serving for lamps in the streets. Now, as the Romans did not frequent the theatres, nor other places of public entertainment, by night, such conveniences were uncalled for in summer, a season when the people retired to rest betimes, from the same motive as at present, the insalubrity of the evening air in the hot weather. Nero must have been very forbearing if he waited those many months before he punished a gang of incendiaries. Such clemency is unexampled in milder princes.

Boccacio. But the Christians were not incendiaries, and he knew they were not.

Petrarca. It may be apprehended that, among the many virtuous of the new believers, a few seditious were also to be found, forming separate and secret associations, choosing generals or superiors to whom they swore implicit obedience, and under whose guidance or impulse they were ready to resist, and occasionally to attack, the magistrates, and even the prince ; men aspiring to rule the state by carrying the sword of assassination under the garb of holiness. Such persons are equally odious to the unenlightened and the enlightened, to the arbitrary and the free. In the regular course of justice, their crimes would have been resisted by almost as much severity, as they appear to have undergone from despotic power and popular indignation.

Boccacio. We will talk no longer about these people. But since the devil has really and *bonâ fide* Brutus and Cassius in his mouth, I would advise him to make the most of them, for he will never find two more such morsels on the same platter. Kings, emperors and popes would be happy to partake with him of so delicate and choice a repast : but I hope he has fitter fare for them.

Messer Dante Alighieri does not indeed make the most gentle use of the company he has about him in hell and purgatory.

* Des Vignolles has calculated that the conflagration began on the 19th of July, in the year 64, and the persecution on the 15th of November.

Since, however, he hath such a selection of them, I wish he could have been contented, and could have left our fair Florentines to their own fancies in their dressing-rooms.

"The time," he cries, "is not far distant, when there will be an indictment on parchment, forbidding the impudent young Florentines to show their breasts and nipples."

Now, Francesco, I have been subject all my life to a strange distemper in the eyes, which no oculist can cure, and which, while it allows me to peruse the smallest character in the very worst female hand, would never let me read an indictment on parchment where female names are implicated, although the letters were a finger in length. I do believe the same distemper was very prevalent in the time of Messer Dante; and those Florentine maids and matrons who were not afflicted by it, were too modest to look at letters and signatures stuck against the walls.

He goes on, "Was there ever girl among the Moors or Saracens, on whom it was requisite to inflict spiritual or *other* discipline to make her go covered?"

Some of the *other* discipline, which the spiritual guides were, and are still, in the habit of administering, have exactly the contrary effect to make them go covered, whatsoever may be urged by the confessor.

"If the shameless creatures," he continues, "were aware of the speedy chastisement which Heaven is preparing for them, they would at this instant have their mouths wide open to roar withal."

Petrarca. This is not very exquisite satire, nor much better manners.

Boccacio. Whenever I saw a pretty Florentine in such a condition, I lowered my eyes.

Petrarca. I am glad to hear it.

Boccacio. Those whom I could venture to cover, I covered with all my heart.

Petrarca. Humanely done. You might likewise have added some gentle admonition.

Boccacio. They would have taken anything at my hands rather than that. Truly they thought themselves as wise as they thought me: and who knows but they were, at bottom?

Petrarca.   I believe it may, in general, be best to leave them as we find them.

Boccaccio.   I would not say that, neither.   Much may be in vain, but something sticks.

Petrarca.   They are more amused than settled by anything we can advance against them, and are apt to make light of the gravest. It is only the hour of reflection that is at last the hour of sedateness and improvement.

Boccaccio.   Where is the bell that strikes it ?

Petrarca.   Fie ! fie ! Giovanni !   This is worse than the indictment on parchment.

Boccaccio.   Women like us none the less for joking with them about their foibles.   In fact, they take it ill when we cease to do so, unless it is age that compels us.   We may give our courser the rein to any extent, while he runs in the common field and does not paw against privacy, nor open his nostrils on individuality. I mean the individuality of the person we converse with, for another's is pure zest.

Petrarca.   Surely you cannot draw this hideous picture from your own observation : has any graver man noted it ?

Boccaccio.   Who would believe your graver men upon such matters ?   Gout and gravel, bile and sciatica, are the upholsterers that stuff their moral sentences.   Crooked and cramp are truths written with chalkstones.   When people like me talk as I have been talking, they may be credited.   We have no ill-will, no ill-humour, to gratify ; and vanity has no trial here at issue.   He was certainly born on an unlucky day for his friends, who never uttered any truths but unquestionable ones.   Give me food that exercises my teeth and tongue, and ideas that exercise my imagination and discernment.

Petrarca.   When you are at leisure, and in perfect health, weed out carefully the few places of your *Decameron* which are deficient in these qualities.

Boccaccio.   God willing ; I wish I had undertaken it when my heart was lighter.   Is there anything else you can suggest for its improvement, in particular or in general ?

Petrarca.   Already we have mentioned the inconsiderate and indecorous.   In what you may substitute hereafter, I would say to you, as I have said to myself, do not be on all occasions too ceremonious in the structure of your sentences.

Boccaccio. You would surely wish me to be round and polished. Why do you smile?

Petrarca. I am afraid these qualities are often of as little advantage in composition as they are corporeally. When action and strength are chiefly the requisites, we may perhaps be better with little of them. The modulations of voice and language are infinite. Cicero has practised many of them; but Cicero has his favourite swells, his favourite flourishes and cadences. Our Italian language is in the enjoyment of an ampler scope and compass; and we are liberated from the horrible sounds of *us, am, um, ant, int, unt,* so predominant in the finals of Latin nouns and verbs. We may be told that they give strength to the dialect: we might as well be told that bristles give strength to the boar. In our Italian we possess the privilege of striking off the final vowel from the greater part of masculine nouns, and from the greater part of tenses in the verbs, when we believe they impede our activity and vigour.

Boccaccio. We are as wealthy in words as is good for us; and she who gave us these, would give us more if needful. In another age it is probable that curtailments will rather be made than additions; for it was so with the Latin and Greek. Barbaric luxury sinks down into civic neatness, and chaster ornaments fill rooms of smaller dimensions.

Petrarca. Cicero came into possession of the stores collected by Plautus, which he always held very justly in the highest estimation; and Sallust is reported to have misapplied a part of them. At his death they were scattered and lost.

Boccaccio. I am wiser than I was when I studied the noble orator, and wiser by his means chiefly. In return for his benefits, if we could speak on equal terms together, the novelist with the philosopher, the citizen of Certaldo with the Roman consul, I would fain whisper in his ear, " Escape from rhetoric by all manner of means: and if you must cleave (as indeed you must) to that old shrew, Logic, be no fonder of exhibiting her than you would be of a plain, economical wife. Let her be always busy, never intrusive; and readier to keep the chambers clean and orderly than to expatiate on their proportions or to display their furniture."

Petrarca. The citizen of Certaldo is fifty-fold more richly endowed with genius than the Roman consul, and might properly——

Boccaccio. Stay! stay! Francesco! or they will shave all the rest of thy crown for thee, and physic thee worse than me.

Petrarca. Middling men, favoured in their lifetime by circumstances, often appear of higher stature than belongs to them; great men always of lower. Time, the sovran, invests with befitting raiment and distinguishes with proper ensigns the familiars he has received into his eternal habitations: in these alone are they deposited: you must wait for them.

No advice is less necessary to you, than the advice to express your meaning as clearly as you can. Where the purpose of glass is to be seen through, we do not want it tinted nor wavy. In certain kinds of poetry the case may be slightly different; such, for instance, as are intended to display the powers of association and combination in the writer, and to invite and exercise the compass and comprehension of the intelligent. Pindar and the Attic tragedians wrote in this manner, and rendered the minds of their audience more alert and ready and capacious. They found some fit for them, and made others. Great painters have always the same task to perform. What is excellent in their art can not be thought excellent by many, even of those who reason well on ordinary matters, and see clearly beauties elsewhere. All correct perceptions are the effect of careful practice. We little doubt that a mirror would direct us in the most familiar of our features, and that our hand would follow its guidance, until we try to cut a lock of our hair. We have no such criterion to demonstrate our liability to error in judging of poetry; a quality so rare that perhaps no five contemporaries ever were masters of it.

Boccaccio. We admire by tradition; we censure by caprice; and there is nothing in which we are more ingenious and inventive. A wrong step in politics sprains a foot in poetry; eloquence is never so unwelcome as when it issues from a familiar voice; and praise hath no echo but from a certain distance. Our critics, who know little about them, would gaze with wonder at anything similar, in our days, to Pindar and Sophocles, and would cast it aside, as quite impracticable. They are in the right: for sonnet and canzonet charm greater numbers. There are others, or may be hereafter, to whom far other things will afford far higher gratification.

Petrarca. But our business at present is with prose and Cicero; and our question now is, what is Ciceronian? He changed his style according to his matter and his hearers. His speeches to the people vary from his speeches to the senate. Toward the one he was impetuous and exacting; toward the other he was usually but earnest and anxious, and sometimes but submissive and imploring, yet equally unwilling, on both occasions, to conceal the labour he had taken to captivate their attention and obtain success. At the tribunal of Cæsar, the dictator, he laid aside his costly armour, contracted the folds of his capacious robe, and became calm, insinuating, and adulative, showing his spirit not utterly extinguished, his dignity not utterly fallen, his con-sular year not utterly abolished from his memory, but Rome, and even himself, lowered in the presence of his judge.

Boccaccio. And after all this, can you bear to think what I am?

Petrarca. Complacently and joyfully; venturing, nevertheless, to offer you a friend's advice.

Enter into the mind and heart of your own creatures: think of them long, entirely, solely: never of style, never of self, never of critics, cracked or sound. Like the miles of an open country, and of an ignorant population, when they are correctly measured they become smaller. In the loftiest rooms and richest en-tablatures are suspended the most spider-webs; and the quarry out of which palaces are erected is the nursery of nettle and bramble.

Boccaccio. It is better to keep always in view such writers as Cicero, than to run after those idlers who throw stones that can never reach us.

Petrarca. If you copied him to perfection, and on no occa-sion lost sight of him, you would be an indifferent, not to say a bad writer.

Boccaccio. I begin to think you are in the right. Well then, retrenching some of my licentious tales, I must endeavour to fill up the vacancy with some serious and some pathetic.

Petrarca. I am heartily glad to hear of this decision; for, admirable as you are in the jocose, you descend from your natural position when you come to the convivial and the festive. You were placed among the Affections, to move and master them, and gifted with the rod that sweetens the fount of tears. My nature leads me also to the pathetic; in which, however, an imbecile writer may obtain celebrity. Even the hard-hearted are fond of such reading, when they are fond of any; and nothing is easier in the world than to find and accumulate its sufferings. Yet this very profusion and luxuriance of misery is the reason why few have excelled in describing it. The eye wanders over the mass without noticing the peculiarities. To mark them distinctly is the work of genius; a work so rarely performed, that, if time and space may be compared, specimens of it stand at wider distances than the trophies of Sesostris. Here we return again to the *Inferno* of Dante, who overcame the difficulty. In this vast desert are its greater and its less oasis; Ugolino and Francesca di Rimini. The peopled region is peopled chiefly with monsters and moschitoes: the rest for the most part is sand and suffocation.

Boccaccio. Ah! had Dante remained through life the pure solitary lover of Bice, his soul had been gentler, tranquiller, and more generous. He scarcely hath described half the curses he went through, nor the roads he took on the journey: theology, politics, and that barbican of the *Inferno*, marriage, surrounded with its

Selva selvaggia ed aspra e forte.

Admirable is indeed the description of Ugolino, to whoever can endure the sight of an old soldier gnawing at the scalp of an old archbishop.

Petrarca. The thirty lines from

Ed io sentj,

are unequalled by any other continuous thirty in the whole dominions of poetry.

Boccaccio. Give me rather the six on Francesca: for if in the former I find the simple, vigorous, clear narration, I find also what I would not wish, the features of Ugolino reflected full in Dante. The two characters are similar in themselves; hard, cruel, inflexible, malignant, but, whenever moved, moved powerfully. In Francesca, with the faculty of divine spirits, he leaves his own nature (not indeed the exact representative of theirs) and converts all his strength into tenderness. The great poet, like the original man of the Platonists, is double, possessing the further advantage of being able to drop one half at his option, and to resume it. Some of the tenderest on paper have no sympathies beyond; and some of the austerest in their intercourse with their fellow-creatures, have deluged the world with tears. It is not from the rose that the bee gathers her honey, but often from the most acrid and the most bitter leaves and petals.

> Quando legemmo il disiato viso
>   Esser baciato di cotanto amante,
> Questi, chi mai da me non fia diviso!
>   La bocca mi baciò tutto tremante . . .
> *Galeotto* fù il libro, e chi lo scrisse . . .
>   Quel giorno più non vi legemmo avante.

In the midst of her punishment, Francesca, when she comes to the tenderest part of her story, tells it with complacency and delight; and, instead of naming Paolo, which indeed she never has done from the beginning, she now designates him as

> Questi chi mai da me non fia diviso!

Are we not impelled to join in her prayer, wishing them happier in their union?

Petrarca. If there be no sin in it.

Boccaccio. Ay, and even if there be . . . God help us!

What a sweet aspiration in each cesura of the verse! three love-sighs fixed and incorporate! Then, when she hath said

> La bocca mi baciò, tutto tremante,

she stops: she would avert the eyes of Dante from her: he looks for the sequel: she thinks he looks severely: she says,

" *Galeotto* is the name of the book,"
fancying by this timorous little flight she has drawn him far enough from the nest of her young loves. No, the eagle beak of Dante and his piercing eyes are yet over her.

" *Galeotto* is the name of the book."

" What matters that ? "

" And of the writer."

"Or that either?"

At last she disarms him: but how?

"*That* day we read no more."

Such a depth of intuitive judgment, such a delicacy of perception, exists not in any other work of human genius; and from an author who, on almost all occasions, in this part of the work, betrays a deplorable want of it.

Petrarca. Perfection of poetry! The greater is my wonder at discovering nothing else of the same order or cast in this whole section of the poem. He who fainted at the recital of Francesca,

> And he who fell as a dead body falls,

would exterminate all the inhabitants of every town in Italy! What execrations against Florence, Pistoia, Siena, Pisa, Genoa! what hatred against the whole human race! what exultation and merriment at eternal and immitigable sufferings! Seeing this, I can not but consider the *Inferno* as the most immoral and impious book that ever was written. Yet, hopeless that our country shall ever see again such poetry, and certain that without it our future poets would be more feebly urged forward to excellence, I would have dissuaded Dante from cancelling it, if this had been his intention. Much however as I admire his vigour and severity of style in the description of Ugolino, I acknowledge with you that I do not discover so much imagination, so much creative power, as in the Francesca. I find indeed a minute detail of probable events: but this is not all I want in a poet: it is not even all I want most in a scene of horror. Tribunals of justice, dens of murderers, wards of hospitals, schools of anatomy, will afford us nearly the same sensations, if we hear them from an accurate observer, a clear reporter, a skilful surgeon, or an attentive nurse. There is nothing of sublimity in the horrific of Dante, which there always is in Æschylus and Homer. If you, Giovanni, had described so nakedly the reception of Guiscardo's heart by Gismonda, or Lorenzo's head by Lisabetta, we could hardly have endured it.

Boccaccio. Prythee, dear Francesco, do not place me over Dante: I stagger at the idea of approaching him.

Petrarca.   Never think I am placing you blindly or indiscriminately. I have faults to find with you, and even here. Lisabetta should by no means have been represented cutting off the head of her lover, " *as well as she could* " with a clasp-knife. This is shocking and improbable. She might have found it already cut off by her brothers, in order to bury the corpse more commodiously and expeditiously. Nor indeed is it likely that she should have intrusted it to her waiting-maid, who carried home in her bosom a treasure so dear to her, and found so unexpectedly and so lately.

Boccaccio.   That is true : I will correct the oversight. Why do we never hear of our faults until everybody knows them, and until they stand in record against us ?

Petrarca.   Because our ears are closed to truth and friendship for some time after the triumphal course of composition. We are too sensitive for the gentlest touch ; and when we really have the most infirmity, we are angry to be told that we have any.

Boccaccio.   Ah Francesco ! thou art poet from scalp to heel : but what other would open his breast as thou hast done ! They show ostentatiously far worse weaknesses ; but the most honest of the tribe would forswear himself on this. Again, I acknowledge it, you have reason to complain of Lisabetta and Gismonda.

Petrarca.   They keep the soul from sinking in such dreadful circumstances by the buoyancy of imagination. The sunshine of poetry makes the colour of blood less horrible, and draws up a shadowy and a softening haziness where the scene would otherwise be too distinct. Poems, like rivers, convey to their destination what must without their appliances be left unhandled : these to ports and arsenals, this to the human heart.

Boccaccio.   So it is ; and what is terror in poetry is horror in prose. We may be brought too close to an object to leave any room for pleasure. Ugolino affects us like a skeleton, by dry bony verity.

Petrarca.   We can not be too distinct in our images ; but although distinctness, on this and most other occasions, is desirable in the imitative arts, yet sometimes in painting, and sometimes in poetry, an object should not be quite precise. In your novel of Andrevola and Gabriotto, you afford me an illustration.

> Le pareva dal corpo di lui uscire una
> cosa oscura e terribile.

This is like a dream: this *is* a dream.   Afterward, you present to us such palpable forms and pleasing colours as may relieve and soothe us.

> Ed avendo molte rose, bianche e vermi-
> glie, colte, perciocche la stagione era.

Boccaccio.   Surely you now are mocking me.   The roses, I perceive, would not have been there, had it not been the season.

Petrarca.   A poet often does more and better than he is aware at the time, and seems at last to know as little about it as a silkworm knows about the fineness of her thread.

The uncertain dream that still hangs over us in the novel, is intercepted and hindered from hurting us by the spell of the roses, of the white and the red; a word the less would have rendered it incomplete.   The very warmth and geniality of the season shed their kindly influence on us; and we are renovated and ourselves again by virtue of the clear fountain where we rest. Nothing of this poetical providence comes to our relief in Dante, though we want it oftener.   It would be difficult to form an idea of a poem, into which so many personages are introduced, containing so few delineations of character, so few touches that excite our sympathy, so few elementary signs for our instruction, so few topics for our delight, so few excursions for our recreation.   Nevertheless, his powers of language are prodigious; and, in the solitary places where he exerts his force rightly, the stroke is irresistible.   But how greatly to be pitied must he be, who can find nothing in paradise better than sterile theology! and what an object of sadness and of consternation, he who rises up from hell like a giant refreshed!

Boccaccio.   Strange perversion!   A pillar of smoke by day and of fire by night; to guide no one.   Paradise had fewer wants for him to satisfy than hell had; all of which he fed to repletion.   But let us rather look to his poetry than his temper.

Petrarca.   We will then.

A good poem is not divided into little panes like a cathedral window; which little panes themselves are broken and blurred, with a saint's coat on a dragon's tail, a doctor's head on the bosom of a virgin martyr, and having about them more lead than glass, and more gloom than colouring. A good satire or good comedy, if it does not always smile, rarely and briefly intermits it, and never rages. A good epic shows us more and more distinctly, at every book of it we open, the features and properties of heroic character, and terminates with accomplishing some momentous action. A good tragedy shows us that greater men than ourselves have suffered more severely and more unjustly; that the highest human power hath suddenly fallen helpless and extinct; or, what is better to contemplate and usefuller to know, that uncontrolled by law, unaccompanied by virtue, unfollowed by contentment, its possession is undesirable and unsafe. Sometimes we go away in triumph with Affliction proved and purified, and leave her under the smiles of heaven. In all these consummations the object is excellent; and here is the highest point to which poetry can attain. Tragedy has no bye-paths, no resting-places; there is everywhere action and passion. What do we find of this nature, or what of the epic, in the Orpheus and Judith, the Charon and Can della Scala, the Sinon and Maestro Adamo?

Boccaccio. Personages strangely confounded! In this category it required a strong hand to make Pluto and Pepe Satan keep the peace, both having the same pretensions, and neither the sweetest temper.

Petrarca. Then the description of Mahomet is indecent and filthy. Yet Dante is scarcely more disgusting in this place, than he is insipid and spiritless in his allegory of the marriages, between Saint Francesco and Poverty, Saint Dominico and Faith. I speak freely and plainly to you, Giovanni, and the rather, as you have informed me that I have been thought invidious to the reputation of our great poet; for such he is transcendently, in the midst of his imperfections. Such likewise were Ennius and Lucilius in the same period of Roman literature. They were equalled, and perhaps excelled: will Dante ever be, in his native tongue? The past generations of his countrymen, the glories of old Rome, fade before him the instant he springs upward, but they impart a more constant and a more genial delight.

Boccaccio. They have less hair-cloth about them, and smell less cloisterly; yet they are only choristers.

The generous man, such as you, praises and censures with equal freedom, not with equal pleasure : the freedom and the pleasure of the ungenerous are both contracted, and lie only on the left hand.

Petrarca.   When we point out to our friends an object in the country, do we wish to diminish it ? do we wish to show it over-cast ?   Why then should we in those nobler works of creation, God's only representatives, who have cleared our intellectual sight for us, and have displayed before us things more magnificent than Nature would without them have revealed?

We poets are heated by proximity.   Those who are gone warm us by the breath they leave behind them in their course, and *only* warm us : those who are standing near, and just before, fever us. Solitude has kept me uninfected ; unless you may hint perhaps that pride was my preservative against the malignity of a worse disease.

Boccaccio.   It might well be, though it were not ; you having been crowned in the capital of the Christian world.

Petrarca.   That indeed would have been something, if I had been crowned for my Christianity, of which I suspect there are better judges in Rome than there are of poetry.   I would rather be preferred to my rivals by the two best critics of the age than by all the others ; who, if they think differently from the two wisest in these matters, must necessarily think wrong.

Boccaccio.   You know that not only the two first, but many more, prefer you ; and that neither they, nor any who are acquainted with your character, can believe that your strictures on Dante are invidious or uncandid.

Petrarca.   I am borne toward him by many strong impulses. Our families were banished by the same faction : he himself and my father left Florence on the same day, and both left it for ever. This recollection would rather make me cling to him than cast him down.   Ill fortune has many and tenacious ties : good fortune has few and fragile ones.   I saw our illustrious fellow citizen once only, and when I was a child.   Even the sight of such a poet, in early days, is dear to him who aspires to become one, and the memory is always in his favour.   The worst I can recollect to have said against his poem to others, is, that the architectural fabric of the *Inferno* is unintelligible without a long study, and only to be understood after distracting our attention from its inhabitants. Its locality and dimensions are at last un-interesting, and would better have been left in their obscurity. The zealots of Dante compare it, for invention, with the infernal regions of Homer and Virgil. I am ignorant how much the Grecian poet invented, how much existed in the religion, how much in the songs and traditions of the people. But surely our Alighieri has taken the same idea, and even made his descent in the same part of Italy, as Æneas had done before. In the *Odyssea* the mind is perpetually relieved by variety of scene and character. There are vices enough in it, but rising from lofty or from powerful passions, and under the veil of mystery and poetry: there are virtues too enough, and human and definite and practicable. We have man, although a shade, in his own features, in his own dimensions: he appears before us neither cramped by systems nor jaundiced by schools; no savage, no cit, no cannibal, no doctor. Vigorous and elastic, he is such as poetry saw him first; he is such as poetry would ever see him. In Dante, the greater part of those who are not degraded, are debilitated and distorted. No heart swells here, either for overpowered valour or for unrequited love. In the shades alone, but in the shades of Homer, does Ajax rise to his full loftiness: in the shades alone, but in the shades of Virgil is Dido the arbitress of our tears.

Boccaccio. I must confess there are nowhere two whole cantos in Dante which will bear a sustained and close com-parison with the very worst book of the *Odyssea* or the *Æneid;* that there is nothing of the same continued and unabated ex-cellence, as Ovid's in the contention for the armour of Achilles; the most heroic of heroic poetry, and only censurable, if censur-able at all, because the eloquence of the braver man is more animated and more persuasive than his successful rival's. I do not think Ovid the best poet that ever lived, but I think he wrote the most of good poetry, and, in proportion to its quantity, the least of bad or indifferent. The *Inferno,* the *Purgatorio,* the *Paradiso,* are pictures from the walls of our churches and chapels and monasteries, some painted by Giotto and Cimabue, some earlier. In several of these we detect not only the cruelty, but likewise the satire and indecency of Dante. Sometimes there is also his vigour and simplicity, but oftener his harshness and meagreness and disproportion. I am afraid the good

Alighieri, like his friends the painters, was inclined to think the angels were created only to flagellate and burn us; and Paradise only for us to be driven out of it. And in truth, as we have seen it exhibited, there is but little hardship in the case.

The opening of the third canto of the *Inferno* has always been much admired. There is indeed a great solemnity in the words of the inscription on the portal of hell: nevertheless, I do not see the necessity for three verses out of six. After

Per me si va nell' eterno dolore,

it surely is superfluous to subjoin

Per me si va tra la perduta gente;

for, beside the *perduta gente,* who else can suffer the eternal woe? And when the portal has told us that "*Justice moved the high Maker to make it,*" surely it might have omitted the notification that his "*divine power*" did it.

Fecemi la divina potestate;

The next piece of information I wish had been conveyed even in darker characters, so that they never could have been deciphered. The following line is,

La somma Sapienza e 'l primo Amore.

If God's first love was hell-making, we might almost wish his affections were as mutable as ours are: that is, if holy church would countenance us therein.

Petrarca. Systems of poetry, of philosophy, of government, form and model us to their own proportions. As our systems want the grandeur, the light, and the symmetry of the ancient, we can not hope for poets, philosophers, or statesmen, of equal dignity. Very justly do you remark that our churches and chapels and monasteries, and even our shrines and tabernacles on the road-side, contain in painting the same punishments as Alighieri had registered in his poem: and several of these were painted before his birth. Nor surely can you have forgotten that his master, Brunetto Latini, composed one on the same plan.

The Virtues and Vices, and persons under their influence, appear to him likewise in a wood, wherein he, like Dante, is bewildered. Old walls are the tablets both copy: the arrangement is the device of Brunetto. Our religion is too simple in its verities, and too penurious in its decorations, for poetry of high value. We can not hope or desire that a pious Italian will ever have the audacity to restore to Satan a portion of his majesty, or to remind the faithful that he is a fallen angel.

Boccaccio. No, no, Francesco; let us keep as much of him down as we can, and as long.

Petrarca. It might not be amiss to remember that even human power is complacent in security, and that Omnipotence is ever omnipotent, without threats and fulminations.

Boccaccio. These, however, are the main springs of sacred poetry, of which I think we already have enough.

Petrarca. But good enough?

Boccaccio. Even much better would produce less effect than that which has occupied our ears from childhood, and comes sounding and swelling with a mysterious voice from the deep and dark recesses of antiquity.

Petrarca. I see no reason why we should not revert, at times, to the first intentions of poetry. Hymns to the Creator were its earliest efforts.

Boccaccio. I do not believe a word of it, unless He himself was graciously pleased to inspire the singer; of which we have received no account. I rather think it originated in pleasurable song, perhaps of drunkenness, and resembled the dithyrambic. Strong excitement alone could force and hurry men among words displaced and exaggerated ideas.

Believing that man fell, first into disobedience, next into ferocity and fratricide, we may reasonably believe that war-songs were among the earliest of his intellectual exertions. When he rested from battle he had leisure to think of love; and the skies and the fountains and the flowers reminded him of her, the coy and beautiful, who fled to a mother from the ardour of his pursuit. In after years he lost a son, his companion in the croft and in the forest: images too grew up there, and rested on the grave. A daughter, who had wondered at his strength and wisdom, looked to him in vain for succour at the approach of death. Inarticulate grief gave way to passionate and wailing words, and Elegy was awakened. We have tears in this world before we have smiles,

Francesco! we have struggles before we have composure; we have strife and complaints before we have submission and gratitude. I am suspicious that if we could collect the "winged words" of the earliest hymns, we should find that they called upon the Deity for vengeance. Priests and rulers were far from insensible to private wrongs. Chryses in the *Iliad* is willing that his king and country should be enslaved, so that his daughter be sent back to him. David in the *Psalms* is no unimportunate or lukewarm applicant for the discomfiture and extermination of his adversaries: and, among the visions of felicity, none brighter is promised a fortunate warrior, than to dash the infants of his enemy against the stones. The Holy Scriptures teach us that the human race was created on the banks of the Euphrates, and where the river hath several branches. Here the climate is extremely hot; and men, like birds, in hot climates, never sing well. I doubt whether there was ever a good poet in the whole city and whole plain of Babylon. Egypt had none but such as she imported. Mountainous countries bear them as they bear the more fragrant plants and savoury game. Judæa had hers: Attica reared them among her thyme and hives; and Tuscany may lift her laurels not a span below. Never have the accents of poetry been heard on the fertile banks of the Vistula; and Ovid taught the borderers of the Danube an indigenous* song in vain.

Petrarca. Orpheus, we hear, sang on the banks of the Hebrus.

Boccaccio. The banks of the Hebrus may be level or rocky, for what I know about them: but the river is represented by the poets as rapid and abounding in whirlpools; hence, I presume, it runs among rocks and inequalities. Be this as it may: do you imagine that Thrace in those early days produced a philosophical poet?

Petrarca. We have the authority of history for it.

Boccaccio. Bad authority, too, unless we sift and cross-examine it. Undoubtedly there were narrow paths of commerce, in very ancient times, from the Euxine to the Caspian, and from the Caspian to the kingdoms of the remoter East. Merchants in those days were not only the most adventurous, but the most

---

* Aptaque sunt nostris barbara verba modis.
What are all the other losses of literature in comparison with this?

intelligent men : and there were ardent minds, uninfluenced by a spirit of lucre, which were impelled by the ardour of imagination into untravelled regions. Scythia was a land of fable, not only to the Greeks, but equally to the Romans. Thrace was a land of fable, we may well believe, to the nearest towns of northern India. I imagine that Orpheus, whoever he was, brought his knowledge from that quarter. We are too apt to fancy that Greece owed everything to the Phœnicians and Egyptians. The elasticity of her mind threw off, or the warmth of her imagination transmuted, the greater part of her earlier acquisitions. She was indebted to Phœnicia for nothing but her alphabet; and even these signs she modified, and endowed them with a portion of her flexibility and grace.

Petrarca. There are those who tell us that Homer lived before the age of letters in Greece.

Boccaccio. I wish they knew the use of them as well as he did. Will they not also tell us that the commerce of the two nations was carried on without the numerals (and such were letters) by which traders cast up accounts? The Phœnicians traded largely with every coast of the Ægean sea; and among their earliest correspondents were the inhabitants of the Greek maritime cities, insular and continental. Is it credible that Cyprus, that Crete, that Attica, should be ignorant of the most obvious means by which commerce was maintained? or that such means should be restricted to commerce, among a people so peculiarly fitted for social intercourse, so inquisitive, so imaginative, as the Greeks?

Petrarca. Certainly it is not.

Boccaccio. The Greeks were the most creative, the Romans the least creative, of mankind. No Roman ever invented anything. Whence then are derived the only two works of imagination we find among them ; the story of the *Ephesian* * *Matron,* and the story of *Psyche?* Doubtless from some country farther eastward than Phœnicia and Egypt. The authors in which we find these insertions are of little intrinsic worth.

---

* One similar, and better conceived, is given by Du Halde from the Chinese. If the fiction of Psyche had reached Greece so early as the time of Plato, it would have caught his attention, and he would have delivered it down to us, however altered.

When the Thracians became better known to the Greeks they turned their backs upon them as worn-out wonders, and looked toward the inexhaustible Hyperboreans. Among these too she placed wisdom and the arts, and mounted instruments through which a greater magnitude was given to the stars.

Petrarca. I will remain no longer with you among the Thracians or the Hyperboreans. But in regard to low and level countries, as unproductive of poetry, I entreat you not to be too fanciful nor too exclusive. Virgil was born on the Mincio, and has rendered the city of his birth too celebrated to be mistaken.

Boccaccio. He was born in the territory of Mantua, not in the city. He sang his first child's song on the shoulders of the Apennines; his first man's under the shadow of Vesuvius.

I would not assert that a great poet must necessarily be born on a high mountain: no indeed, no such absurdity: but where the climate is hot, the plains have never shown themselves friendly to the imaginative faculties. We surely have more buoyant spirits on the mountain than below, but it is not requisite for this effect that our cradles should have been placed on it.

Petrarca. What will you say about Pindar?

Boccaccio. I think it more probable that he was reared in the vicinity of Thebes than within the walls. For Bœotia, like our Tuscany, has one large plain, but has also many eminences, and is bounded on two sides by hills.

Look at the vale of Capua! Scarcely so much as a sonnet was ever heard from one end of it to the other; perhaps the most spirited thing was some Carthaginian glee, from a soldier in the camp of Hannibal. Nature seems to contain in her breast the same milk for all, but feeding one for one aptitude, another for another; and, as if she would teach him a lesson as soon as he could look about him, she has placed the poet where the air is unladen with the exhalations of luxuriance.

Petrarca. In my delight to listen to you after so long an absence, I have been too unwary; and you have been speaking too much for one infirm. Greatly am I to blame, not to have moderated my pleasure and your vivacity. You must rest now: to-morrow we will renew our conversation.

Boccaccio. God bless thee, Francesco! I shall be talking

with thee all night in my slumbers. Never have I seen thee with such pleasure as to-day, excepting when I was deemed worthy by our fellow-citizens of bearing to thee, and of placing within this dear hand of thine, the sentence of recall from banishment, and when my tears streamed over the ordinance as I read it, whereby thy paternal lands were redeemed from the public treasury.

Again God bless thee! Those tears were not quite exhausted: take the last of them.

SECOND DAY'S INTERVIEW.

Petrarca. How have you slept, Giovanni?

Boccaccio. Pleasantly, soundly, and quite long enough. You too methinks have enjoyed the benefit of riding; for you either slept well or began late. Do you rise in general three hours after the sun!

Petrarca. No indeed.

Boccaccio. As for me, since you would not indulge me with your company an hour ago, I could do nothing more delightful than to look over some of your old letters.

Petrarca. Ours are commemorative of no reproaches, and laden with no regrets. Far from us

> With drooping wing the spell-bound spirit moves
> O'er flickering friendships and extinguisht loves.

Boccaccio. Ay, but as I want no record of your kindness now you are with me, I have been looking over those to other persons, on past occasions. In the Latin one to the tribune, whom the people at Rome usually call Rienzi, I find you address him by the denomination of Nicolaus Laurentii. Is this the right one?

Petrarca. As we Florentines are fond of omitting the first syllable in proper names, calling Luigi *Gigi*, Giovanni *Nanni*, Francesco *Cecco*, in like manner at Rome they say *Renzi* for Lorenzi, and by another corruption it has been pronounced and written Rienzi. Believe me, I should never have ventured to address the personage who held and supported the highest dignity on earth, until I had ascertained his appellation: for nobody ever quite forgave, unless in the low and ignorant, a wrong pronunciation of his name ; the humblest being of opinion that they have one of their own, and one both worth having and worth knowing. Even dogs, they observe, are not miscalled. It would have been as Latin in sound, if not in structure, to write Rientius as Laurentius : but it would certainly have been offensive to a dignitary of his station, as being founded on a sportive and somewhat childish familiarity.

Boccaccio. Ah Francesco! we were a good deal younger in those days; and hopes sprang up before us like mushrooms : the sun produced them, the shade produced them, every hill, every valley, every busy and every idle hour.

Petrarca. The season of hope precedes but little the season of disappointment. Where the ground is unprepared, what harvest can be expected ? Men bear wrongs more easily than irritations ; and the Romans, who had sunk under worse degradation than any other people on record, rose up against the deliverer who ceased to consult their ignorance. I speak advisedly and without rhetoric on the foul depths of their debasement. The Jews, led captive into Egypt and into Babylon, were left as little corrupted as they were found ; and perhaps some of their vices were corrected by the labours that were imposed on them. But the subjugation of the Romans was effected by the depravation of their morals, which the priesthood took away, giving them ceremonies and promises instead. God had indulged them in the exercise of power : first the kings abused it, then the consuls, then the tribunes. One only magistrate was remaining who never had violated it, farther than in petty frauds and fallacies suited to the occasion, not having at present more within his reach. It was now his turn to exercise his functions, and no less grievously and despotically than the preceding had done. For this purpose the Pontifex Maximus needed some slight alterations in the popular belief ; and he collected them from that Pantheon which Roman policy had enlarged at every conquest. The priests of Isis had acquired the highest influence in the city : those of Jupiter were jealous that foreign gods should become more than supplementary and subordinate : but as the women in general leaned toward Isis, it was in vain to contest the point, and prudent to adopt a little at a time from the discipline of the shaven brotherhood. The names and titles of the ancient gods had received many additions, and they were often asked which they liked best. Different ones were now given them; and gradually, here and there, the older dropped into desuetude. Then arose the star in the east; and all was manifested.

Boccaccio. Ay, ay, but the second company of shepherds sang to a different tune from the first, and put them out. Trumpeters ran in among them, horses neighed, tents waved their pennons, and commanders of armies sought to raise themselves to supreme authority, some by leading the faction of the ancient faith, and some by supporting the recenter. At last the priesthood succeeded to the power of the pretorian guard, and elected, or procured the election of, an emperor. Every man who loved peace and quiet took refuge in a sanctuary, now so efficient to protect him; and nearly all who had attained a preponderance in wisdom and erudition, brought them to bear against the worn-out and tottering institutions, and finally to raise up the coping-stone of an edifice which overtopped them all.

Petrarca. At present we fly to princes as we fly to caves and arches, and other things of the mere earth, for shelter and protection.

Boccaccio. And when they afford it at all, they afford it with as little care and knowledge. Like Egyptian embalmers, they cast aside the brains as useless or worse, but carefully swathe up all that is viler and heavier, and place it in their painted catacombs.

Petrarca. What Dante saw in his day, we see in ours. The danger is, lest first the wiser, and soon afterward the un-wiser, in abhorrence at the presumption and iniquity of the priesthood, should abandon religion altogether, when it is forbidden to approach her without such company.

Boccaccio. Philosophy is but the calix of that plant of paradise, religion. Detach it, and it dies away; meanwhile the plant itself, supported by its proper nutriment, retains its vigour.

Petrarca. The good citizen and the calm reasoner come at once to the same conclusion: that philosophy can never hold many men together; that religion can; and those who without it would not let philosophy, nor law, nor humanity exist. Therefore it is our duty and interest to remove all obstruction from it:

to give it air, light, space, and freedom; carrying in our hands a scourge for fallacy, a chain for cruelty, and an irrevocable ostracism for riches that riot in the house of God.

Boccaccio.   Moderate wealth is quite enough to teach with.

Petrarca.   The luxury and rapacity of the church, together with the insolence of the barons, excited that discontent which emboldened Nicola de Rienzi to assume the station of tribune. Singular was the prudence, and opportune the boldness, he manifested at first.   His modesty, his piety, his calm severity, his unbiassed justice, won to him the affections of every good citizen, and struck horror into the fastnesses of every castellated felon.   He might by degrees have restored the republic of Rome, had he preserved his moderation: he might have become the master of Italy, had he continued the master of himself: but he allowed the weakest of the passions to run away with him: he fancied he could not inebriate himself soon enough with the intemperance of power.   He called for seven crowns, and placed them successively on his head.   He cited Lewis of Bavaria and Charles of Bohemia to appear and plead their causes before him; and lastly, not content with exasperating and concentrating the hostility of barbarians, he set at defiance the best and highest feelings of his more instructed countrymen, and displayed his mockery of religion and decency by bathing in the porphyry font of the Lateran.   How my soul grieved for his defection!   How bitterly burst forth my complaints, when he ordered the imprisonment of Stefano Colonna in his ninetieth year!   For these atrocities you know with what reproaches I assailed him, traitor as he was to the noblest cause that ever strung the energies of mankind.   For this cause, under his auspices, I had abandoned all hope of favour and protection from the pontiff: I had cast into peril, almost into perdition, the friendship, familiarity, and love of the Colonnas.   Even you, Giovanni, thought me more rash than you would say you thought me, and wondered at seeing me whirled along with the tempestuous triumphs that seemed mounting toward the Capitol.   It is only in politics that an actor appears greater by the magnitude of the theatre; and we readily and enthusiastically give way to the deception.   Indeed, whenever a man capable of performing great and glorious actions is emerging from obscurity, it is our duty to remove, if we can, all obstruction from before him; to increase his scope and his powers, to extol and amplify his virtues. This is always requisite, and often insufficient, to counteract the workings of malignity round about him. But finding him afterward false and cruel, and, instead of devoting himself to the commonwealth, exhausting it by his violence and sacrificing it to his vanity, then it behoves us to stamp the foot, and to call in the people to cast down the idol. For nothing is so immoral or pernicious as to keep up the illusion of greatness in wicked men. Their crimes, because they have fallen into the gulf of them, we call misfortunes; and, amid ten thousand mourners, grieve only for him who made them so. Is this reason? is this humanity?

Boccaccio. Alas! it is man.

Petrarca. Can we wonder then that such wretches have turned him to such purposes? The calmness, the sagacity, the sanctitude of Rienzi, in the ascent to his elevation, rendered him only the more detestable for his abuse of power.

Boccaccio. Surely the man grew mad.

Petrarca. Men often give the hand to the madness that seizes them. He yielded to pride and luxury: behind them came jealousy and distrust: fear followed these, and cruelty followed fear. Then the intellects sought the subterfuge that bewildered them; and an ignoble flight was precluded by an ignominious death.

Boccaccio. No mortal is less to be pitied, or more to be detested, than he into whose hands are thrown the fortunes of a nation, and who squanders them away in the idle gratification of his pride and his ambition. Are not these already gratified to the full by the confidence and deference of his countrymen? Can siks, and the skins of animals, can hammered metals and sparkling stones, enhance the value of legitimate dominion over the human heart? Can a wise man be desirous of having a less wise successor? And, of all the world, would he exhibit this inferiority in a son? Irrational as are all who aim at despotism, this is surely the most irrational of their speculations. Vulgar men are more anxious for title and decoration than for power; and notice, in their estimate, is preferable to regard. We ought as little to mind the extinction of such existences as the dying down of a favourable wind in the prosecution of a voyage. They are fitter for the calendar than for history, and it is well when we find them in last year's.

Petrarca. What a year was Rienzi's last to me! What an extinction of all that had not been yet extinguished! Visionary as was the flash of his glory, there was another more truly so, which this, my second great loss and sorrow, opened again before me.[2]

Verona! loveliest of cities, but saddest to my memory! while the birds were singing in thy cypresses the earliest notes of spring, the blithest of hope, the tenderest of desire, she, my own Laura, fresh as the dawn around her, stood before me. It was her transit; I knew it ere she spake.*

O Giovanni! the heart that has once been bathed in love's pure fountain, retains the pulse of youth for ever. Death can only take away the sorrowful from our affections: the flower expands; the colourless film that enveloped it falls off and perishes.

Boccaccio. We may well believe it: and, believing it, let us cease to be disquieted for their absence who have but retired into another chamber. We are like those who have overslept the hour: when we rejoin our friends, there is only the more joyance and congratulation. Would we break a precious vase, because it is as capable of containing the bitter as the sweet? No: the very things which touch us the most sensibly are those which we should be the most reluctant to forget. The noble mansion is most distinguished by the beautiful images it retains of beings past away; and so is the noble mind.

The damps of autumn sink into the leaves and prepare them for the necessity of their fall: and thus insensibly are we, as years

[2 First ed. reads:
  " me.
    Nor youth nor age nor virtue can avoid
    Miseries that fly in darkness through the world
    Striking at random irremissibly,
    Until our sun sinks through the waves, until
    The golden brim melts from its brightest cloud,
    And all that we hath seen hath disappeared.
  Verona," &c.]

* This event is related by Petrarca as occurring on the sixth of April, the day of her decease.

close round us, detached from our tenacity of life by the gentle pressure of recorded sorrows. When the graceful dance and its animating music are over, and the clapping of hands (so lately linked) hath ceased; when youth and comeliness and pleasantry are departed,

> Who would desire to spend the following day
> Among the extinguisht lamps, the faded wreaths,
> The dust and desolation left behind?

But whether we desire it or not, we must submit. He who hath appointed our days hath placed their contents within them, and our efforts can neither cast them out nor change their quality. In our present mood we will not dwell too long on this subject, but rather walk forth into the world, and look back again on the bustle of life. Neither of us may hope to exert in future any extraordinary influence on the political movements of our country, by our presence or intervention : yet surely it is something to have set at defiance the mercenaries who assailed us, and to have stood aloof from the distribution of the public spoils. I have at all times taken less interest than you have taken in the affairs of Rome ; for the people of that city neither are, nor were of old, my favourites.

It appears to me that there are spots accursed, spots doomed to eternal sterility ; and Rome is one of them. No gospel announces the glad tidings of resurrection to a fallen nation. Once down, and down for ever. The Babylonians, the Macedonians, the Romans, prove it. Babylon is a desert, Macedon a den of thieves, Rome (what is written as an invitation on the walls of her streets) one vast *immondezzaio*, morally and substantially.

Petrarca. The argument does not hold good throughout. Persia was conquered : yet Persia long afterward sprang up again with renovated strength and courage, and Sapor mounted his war-horse from the crouching neck of Valentinian. In nearly all the campaigns with the Romans she came off victorious : none of her kings or generals were ever led in triumph to the Capitol ; but several Roman emperors lay prostrate on their purple in the fields of Parthia. Formidable at home, victorious over friends and relatives, their legions had seized and subdivided the arable lands of Campania and the exuberant pastures of the Po ; but the glebe that bordered the Araxes was unbroken by them. Persia, since those times, has passed through many vicissitudes, of defeat and victory, of obscurity and glory: and why may not our country? Let us take hopes where we can find them, and raise them where we find none.

Boccaccio. In some places we may; in others, the fabric of hopes is too arduous an undertaking. When I was in Rome nothing there reminded me of her former state, until I saw a goose in the grass under the Capitoline hill. This perhaps was the only one of her inhabitants that had not degenerated. Even the dogs looked sleepy, mangy, suspicious, perfidious, and thievish. The goose meanwhile was making his choice of herbage about triumphal arches and monumental columns, and picking up worms; the surest descendants, the truest representatives, and enjoying the inalienable succession, of the Cæsars. This is all that goose or man can do at Rome. She, I think, will be the last city to rise from the dead.

Petrarca. There is a trumpet, and on earth, that shall awaken even her.

Boccaccio. I should like to live and be present.

Petrarca. This can not be expected. But you may live many years, and see many things to make you happy. For you will not close the doors too early in the evening of existence against the visits of renovating and cheerful thoughts, which keep our lives long up, and help them to sink at last without pain or pressure.

Boccaccio. Another year or two perhaps, with God's permission. Fra Biagio felt my pulse on Wednesday, and cried, "Courage! Ser Giovanni! there is no danger of Paradise yet: the Lord forbid!"

"Faith!" said I, "Fra Biagio! I hope there is not. What with prayers and masses, I have planted a foot against my old homestead, and will tug hard to remain where I am."

"A true soldier of the faith!" quoth Fra Biagio, and drank a couple of flasks to my health. Nothing else, he swore to Assunta, would have induced him to venture beyond one; he hating all excesses, they give the adversary such advantage over us; although God is merciful and makes allowances.

Petrarca. Impossible as it is to look far and with pleasure into the future, what a privilege is it, how incomparably greater than any other that genius can confer, to be able to direct the backward flight of fancy and imagination to the recesses they most delighted in; to be able, as the shadows lengthen in our path, to call up before us the youth of our sympathies in all their tenderness and purity!

Boccaccio. Mine must have been very pure, I suspect, for I am sure they were very tender. But I need not call them up; they come readily enough of their own accord; and I find it perplexing at times to get entirely rid of them. Sighs are very troublesome when none meet them half-way. The worst of mine now are while I am walking uphill. Even to walk upstairs, which used occasionally to be as pleasant an exercise as any, grows sadly too much for me. For which reason I lie here below; and it is handier too for Assunta.

Petrarca. Very judicious and considerate. In high situations, like Certaldo and this villetta, there is no danger from fogs or damps of any kind. The skylark yonder seems to have made it her first station in the air.

Boccaccio. To welcome thee, Francesco!

Petrarca. Rather say, to remind us both of our Dante. All the verses that ever were written on the nightingale are scarcely worth the beautiful triad of this divine poet on the lark.

> La lodoletta che in aere si spazia,
> Prima cantando, e poi tace contenta
> Dell' ultima dolcezza che la sazia.

In the first of them do not you see the twinkling of her wings against the sky? As often as I repeat them my ear is satisfied, my heart (like hers) contented.

Boccaccio. I agree with you in the perfect and unrivalled beauty of the first; but in the third there is a redundance. Is not *contenta* quite enough, without *che la sazia?* The picture is before us, the sentiment within us, and behold! we kick when we are full of manna.

Petrarca. I acknowledge the correctness and propriety of your remark; and yet beauties in poetry must be examined as carefully as blemishes, and even more; for we are more easily led away by them, although we do not dwell on them so long. We two should never be accused, in these days, of malevolence to

Dante, if the whole world heard us.   Being here alone, we may hazard our opinions even less guardedly, and set each other right as we see occasion.

Boccaccio.   Come on then; I will venture.   I will go back to find fault; I will seek it even in Francesca.

To hesitate, and waver, and turn away from the subject, was proper and befitting in her.   The verse, however, in no respect satisfies me.   Anyone would imagine from it that *Galeotto* was really both the title of the book and the name of the author; neither of which is true.   Galeotto, in the *Tavola Rotonda*, is the person who interchanges the correspondence between Lancilotto and Ginevra.   The appellation is now become the generic of all men whose business it is to promote the success of others in illicit love.   Dante was stimulated in his satirical vein, when he attributed to Francesca a ludicrous expression, which she was very unlikely in her own nature, and greatly more so in her state of suffering, to employ or think of, whirled round as she was incessantly with her lover.   Neither was it requisite to say, "the book was a Galeotto, and so was the author," when she had said already that a passage in it had seduced her.   Omitting this unnecessary and ungraceful line, her confusion and her delicacy are the more evident, and the following comes forth with fresh beauty.   In the commencement of her speech I wish these had likewise been omitted,

"E cio sa il tuo dottore;"

since he knew no more about it than anybody else.   As we proceed, there are passages in which I can not find my way, and where I suspect the poet could not show it me.   For instance, is it not strange that Briareus should be punished in the same way as Nimrod, when Nimrod sinned against the living God, and when Briareus attempted to overthrow one of the living God's worst antagonists, Jupiter? an action which our blessed Lord, and the doctors of the holy church, not only attempted, but (to their glory and praise for evermore) accomplished.

Petrarca.   Equally strange that Brutus and Cassius (a remark which escaped us in our mention of them yesterday) should be placed in the hottest pit of hell for slaying Cæsar, and that Cato, who would have done the same thing with less compunction, should be appointed sole guardian and governor of purgatory.

Boccaccio. What interest could he have made to be promoted to so valuable a post, in preference to doctors, popes, confessors, and fathers? Wonderful indeed! and they never seemed to take it much amiss.

Petrarca. Alighieri not only throws together the most opposite and distant characters, but even makes Jupiter and our Saviour the same person.

> E se lecito m' è, o sommo *Giove!*
> Che fosti in terra per noi *crucifisso.*

Boccaccio. Jesus Christ ought no more to be called Jupiter than Jupiter ought to be called Jesus Christ.

Petrarca. In the whole of the *Inferno* I find only the descriptions of Francesca and of Ugolino at all admirable. Vigorous expressions there are many, but lost in their application to base objects; and insulated thoughts in high relief, but with everything crumbling round them. Proportionally to the extent, there is a scantiness of poetry, if delight is the purpose or indication of it. Intensity shows everywhere the powerful master: and yet intensity is not invitation. A great poet may do everything but repel us. Established laws are pliant before him: nevertheless his office hath both its duties and its limits.

Boccaccio. The simile in the third canto, the satire at the close of the fourth, and the description at the commencement of the eighth, if not highly admirable, are what no ordinary poet could have produced.

Petrarca. They are streaks of light in a thunder-cloud. You might have added the beginning of the twenty-seventh, in which the poetry of itself is good, although not excellent, and the subject of it assuages the weariness left on us, after passing through so many holes and furnaces, and undergoing the dialogue between Simon and Master Adam.

Boccaccio. I am sorry to be reminded of this. It is like the brawl of the two fellows in Horace's *Journey to Brundusium.* They are the straightest parallels of bad wit and bad poetry that ancient and modern times exhibit. Ought I to speak so sharply of poets who elsewhere have given me so great delight?

Petrarca. Surely you ought. No criticism is less beneficial to an author or his reader than one tagged with favour and tricked with courtesy. The gratification of our humours is not the intent and scope of criticism, and those who indulge in it on such occasions are neither wise nor honest.

Boccaccio. I never could see why we should designedly and prepensely give to one writer more than his due, to another less. If we offer an honest man ten crowns when we owe him only five, he is apt to be offended. The perfumer and druggist weigh out the commodity before them to a single grain. If they do it with odours and powders, should not we attempt it likewise, in what is either the nutriment or the medicine of the mind? I do not wonder that Criticism has never yet been clear-sighted and expert among us: I do, that she has never been dispassionate and unprejudiced. There are critics who, lying under no fear of a future state in literature, and all whose hope is for the present day, commit injustice without compunction. Every one of these people has some favourite object for the embraces of his hatred, and a figure of straw will never serve the purpose. He must throw his stone at what stands out; he must twitch the skirt of him who is ascending. Do you imagine that the worst writers of any age were treated with as much asperity as you and I? No, Francesco! give the good folks their due: they are humaner to their fellow-creatures.

Petrarca. Disregarding the ignorant and presumptuous, we have strengthened our language by dipping it afresh in its purer and higher source, and have called the Graces back to it. We never have heeded how Jupiter would have spoken, but only how the wisest men would, and how words follow the movements of the mind. There are rich and copious veins of mineral in regions far remote from commerce and habitations: these veins are useless: so are those writings of which the style is uninviting and inaccessible, through its ruggedness, its chasms, its points, its perplexities, its obscurity. There are scarcely three authors, beside yourself, who appear to heed whether any guest will enter the gate, quite satisfied with the consciousness that they have stores within. Such wealth, in another generation, may be curious, but cannot be current. When a language grows up all into stalk, and its flowers begin to lose somewhat of their character, we must go forth into the open fields, through the dingles, and among the mountains, for fresh seed. Our ancestors did this, no very long time ago. Foremost in zeal, in vigour and authority, Alighieri took on himself the same patronage and guardianship of our adolescent dialect, as Homer of the Greek : and my Giovanni hath since endowed it so handsomely, that additional bequests, we may apprehend, will only corrupt its principles, and render it lax and lavish.

Boccaccio. Beware of violating those canons of criticism you have just laid down. We have no right to gratify one by misleading another, nor, when we undertake to show the road, to bandage the eyes of him who trusts us for his conductor. In regard to censure, those only speak ill who speak untruly, unless a truth be barbed by malice and aimed by passion. To be useful to as many as possible is the especial duty of a critic, and his utility can only be attained by rectitude and precision. He walks in a garden which is not his own ; and he neither must gather the blossoms to embellish his discourse, nor break the branches to display his strength. Rather let him point to what is out of order, and help to raise what is lying on the ground.

Petrarca. Auditors, and readers in general, come to hear or read, not your opinion delivered, but their own repeated. Fresh notions are as disagreeable to some as fresh air to others ; and this inability to bear them is equally a symptom of disease. Impatience and intolerance are sure to be excited at any check to admiration in the narratives of Ugolino and of Francesca : nothing is to be abated : they are not only to be admirable, but entirely faultless.

Boccaccio. You have proved to me that, in blaming our betters, we ourselves may sometimes be unblamed. When authors are removed by death beyond the reach of irritation at the touch of an infirmity, we best consult their glory by handling their works comprehensively and unsparingly. Vague and indefinite criticism suits only slight merit, and presupposes it. Lineaments irregular and profound as Dante's are worthy of being traced with patience and fidelity. In the charts of our globe we find distinctly marked the promontories and indentations, and often-times the direction of unprofitable marshes and impassable sands and wildernesses : level surfaces are unnoted. I would not detract one atom from the worth of Dante; which can not be done by summing it up exactly, but may be by negligence in the computation.

Petrarca.   Your business, in the lectures, is not to show his merits, but his meaning; and to give only so much information as may be given without offence to the factious.   Whatever you do beyond, is for yourself, your friends, and futurity.

Boccaccio.   I may write more lectures, but never shall deliver them in person as the first.   Probably, so near as I am to Florence, and so dear as Florence hath always been to me, I shall see that city no more.   The last time I saw it, I only passed through.   Four years ago, you remember, I lost my friend Acciaioli.   Early in the summer of the preceding, his kindness had induced him to invite me again to Naples, and I undertook a journey to the place where my life had been too happy.   There are many who pay dearly for sunshine early in the season: many, for pleasure in the prime of life.   After one day lost in idleness at Naples, if intense and incessant thoughts (however fruitless) may be called so, I proceeded by water to Sorento, and thence over the mountains to Amalfi.   Here, amid whatever is most beautiful and most wonderful in scenery, I found the Seniscalco. His palace, his gardens, his terraces, his woods, abstracted his mind entirely from the solicitudes of state; and I was gratified at finding in the absolute ruler of a kingdom, the absolute master of his time.   Rare felicity; and he enjoyed it the more after the toils of business and the intricacies of policy.   His reception of me was most cordial.   He showed me his long avenues of oranges and citrons: he helped me to mount the banks of slippery short herbage, whence we could look down on their dark masses, and their broad irregular belts, gemmed with golden fruit and sparkling flowers.   We stood high above them, but not above their fragrance, and sometimes we wished the breeze to bring us it, and sometimes to carry a part of it away: and the breeze came and went as if obedient to our volition.   Another day he conducted me farther from the palace, and showed me, with greater pride than I had ever seen in him before, the pale-green olives, on little smooth plants, the first year of their bearing.   " I will teach my people here," said he, " to make as delicate oil as any of our Tuscans."   We had feasts among the caverns: we had dances by day under the shade of the mulberries, by night under the lamps of the arcade: we had music on the shore and on the water.

When next I stood before him, it was afar from these. Torches flamed through the pine-forest of the Certosa: priests and monks led the procession: the sound of the brook alone filled up the intervals of the dirge: and other plumes than the dancers' waved round what was Acciaioli.

Petrarca. Since in his family there was nobody who, from education or pursuits or consanguinity, could greatly interest him ; nobody to whom so large an accumulation of riches would not rather be injurious than beneficial, and place rather in the way of scoffs and carpings than exalt to respectability ; I regret that he omitted to provide for the comforts of your advancing years.

Boccaccio. The friend would not spoil the philosopher. Our judgment grows the stronger by the dying-down of our affections.

Petrarca. With a careful politician and diplomatist all things find their places but men : and yet he thinks he has niched it nicely, when, as the gardener is left in the garden, the tailor on his board at the casement, he leaves the author at his desk : to remove him would put the world in confusion.

Boccaccio. Acciaioli knew me too well to suppose we could serve each other : and his own capacity was amply sufficient for all the exigencies of the state. Generous,* kind, constant soul ! the emblazoned window throws now its rich mantle over him, moved gently by the vernal air of Marignole, or, as the great chapel-door is opened to some visitor of distinction, by the fresh eastern breeze from the valley of the Elsa. We too (mayhap) shall be visited in the same condition ; but in a homelier edifice, but in a humbler sepulchre, but by other and far different guests. While they are discussing and sorting out our merits, which are usually first discovered among the nettles in the churchyard, we will carry this volume with us, and show Dante what we have been doing.

* This sentiment must be attributed to the gratitude of Boccaccio, not to the merits of Acciaioli, who treated him unworthily. [Note added in second ed.]

Petrarca. We [3] have each of us had our warnings: indeed all men have them: and not only at our time of life, but almost every day of their existence. They come to us even in youth; although, like the lightnings that are said to play incessantly, in the noon and in the morning and throughout the year, we seldom see and never look for them. Come, as you proposed, let us now continue with our Dante.

Ugolino relates to him his terrible dream, in which he fancied that he had seen Gualando, Sismondi, and Lanfranco, killing his children: and he says that, when he awakened, he heard them moan in their sleep. In such circumstances, his awakening ought rather to have removed the impression he laboured under; since it showed him the vanity of the dream, and afforded him the consolation that the children were alive. Yet he adds immediately, what, if he were to speak it at all, he should have deferred.

"You are very cruel if you do not begin to grieve, considering what my heart presaged to me; and, if you do not weep at it, what is it you are wont to weep at?"

Boccaccio. Certainly this is ill-timed; and the conference would indeed be better without it anywhere.

Petrarca. Farther on, in whatever way we interpret

Poscia più che 'l dolor potè 'l digiuno,

the poet falls sadly from his sublimity.

Boccaccio. If the fact were as he mentions, he should have suppressed it, since we had already seen the most pathetic in the features, and the most horrible in the stride, of Famine. Gnawing, not in hunger, but in rage and revenge, the archbishop's skull, is, in the opinion of many, rather ludicrous than tremendous.

Petrarca. In mine, rather disgusting than ludicrous: but Dante (we must whisper it) is the great master of the disgusting. When the ancients wrote indecently and loosely, they presented what either had something alluring or something laughable about it, and, if they disgusted, it was involuntarily. Indecency is the most shocking in deformity. We call indecent, while we do not think it, the nakedness of the Graces and the Loves.

[3] [First ed. reads: "*Petrarca.* Come let us proceed with him. Ugolino," &c. (8 lines below).]

Boccaccio.   When we are less barbarous we shall become more familiar with them, more tolerant of sliding beauty, more hospitable to erring passion, and perhaps as indulgent to frailty as we are now to ferocity.   I wish I could find in some epitaph, " he loved so many :" it is better than, " he killed so many."   Yet the world hangs in admiration over this ; you and I should be found alone before the other.

Petrarca.   Of what value are all the honours we can expect from the wisest of our species, when even the wisest hold us lighter in estimation than those who labour to destroy what God delighted to create, came on earth to ransom, and suffered on the cross to save !   Glory then, glory can it be, to devise with long study, and to execute with vast exertions, what the fang of a reptile or the leaf of a weed accomplishes in an hour ?   Shall any-one tell me, that the numbers sent to death or to wretchedness make the difference, and constitute the great ?   Away then from the face of nature as we see her daily ! away from the interminable varieties of animated creatures ! away from what is fixed to the earth and lives by the sun and dew !   Brute inert matter does it : behold it in the pestilence, in the earthquake, in the conflagration, in the deluge !

Boccaccio.   Perhaps we shall not be liked the better for what we ourselves have written : yet I do believe we shall be thanked for having brought to light, and for having sent into circulation, the writings of other men.   We deserve as much, were it only that it gives people an opportunity of running over us, as ants over the images of gods in orchards, and of reaching by our means the less crude fruits of less ungenial days.   Be this as it may, we have spent our time well in doing it, and enjoy (what idlers never can) as pleasant a view in looking back as forward.

Now do tell me, before we say more of the *Paradiso,* what can I offer in defence of the Latin scraps from litanies and lauds, to the number of fifty or thereabout ?

Petrarca.   Say nothing at all, unless you can obtain some Indulgences for repeating them.

Boccaccio.   And then such verses as these, and several score of no better :

I credo ch' ei credette ch' io credessi.
O Jacopo, dicea, da sant Andrea.

Come Livio scrisse, che non erra.
Nel quale un cinque cento dieci e cinque.
Mille ducento con sessanta sei.
Pape Satan, Pape Satan, Aleppè.
Raffael mai *amec, zabe, almî.*
Non avria pur dell orlo fatto *crich.*

Petrarca. There is no occasion to look into and investigate a puddle; we perceive at first sight its impurity; but it is useful to analyse, if we can, a limpid and sparkling water, in which the common observer finds nothing but transparency and freshness: for in this, however the idle and ignorant ridicule our process, we may exhibit what is unsuspected, and separate what is insalubrious. We must do then for our poet that which other men do for themselves; we must defend him by advancing the best authority for something as bad or worse; and although it puzzle our ingenuity, yet we may almost make out in quantity, and quite in quality, our spicilege from Virgil himself. If younger men were present, I would admonish and exhort them to abate no more of their reverence for the Roman poet on the demonstration of his imperfections, than of their love for a parent or guardian who had walked with them far into the country, and had shown them its many beauties and blessings, on his lassitude or his debility. Never will such men receive too much homage. He who can best discover their blemishes, will best appreciate their merit, and most zealously guard their honour. The flippancy with which genius is often treated by mediocrity, is the surest sign of a prostrate mind's incontinence and impotence. It will gratify the national pride of our Florentines, if you show them how greatly the nobler parts of their fellow-citizen excel the loftiest of his Mantuan guide.

Boccaccio. Of Virgil?

Petrarca. Even so.

Boccaccio. He had no suspicion of his equality with this prince of Roman poets, whose footsteps he follows with reverential and submissive obsequiousness.

Petrarca. Have you never observed that persons of high rank universally treat their equals with deference; and that ill-bred ones are often smart and captious? Even their words are uttered with a brisk and rapid air, a tone higher than the natural, to sustain the factitious consequence and vapouring independence they assume. Small critics and small poets take all this courage when they licentiously shut out the master; but Dante really felt the veneration he would impress. Suspicion of his superiority he had none whatever, nor perhaps have you yourself much more.

Boccaccio. I take all proper interest in my author; I am sensible to the duties of a commentator; but in truth I dare hardly entertain that exalted notion. I should have the whole world against me.

Petrarca. You must expect it for *any* exalted notion; for anything that so startles a prejudice as to arouse a suspicion that it may be dispelled. You must expect it if you throw open the windows of infection. Truth is only unpleasant in its novelty. He who first utters it, says to his hearer, "You are less wise than I am." Now who likes this?

Boccaccio. But surely if there are some very high places in our Alighieri, the inequalities are perpetual and vast; whereas the regularity, the continuity, the purity of Virgil, are proverbial.

Petrarca. It is only in literature that what is proverbial is suspicious; and mostly in poetry. Do we find in Dante, do we find in Ovid, such tautologies and flatnesses as these?

Quam si dura silex . . *aut stet Marpessia cautes*
Majus adorta nefas . . *majoremque orsa furorem.*
Arma *amens* capio . . nec *sat rationis* in armis.
   Superatne . . *et vescitur aura*
Ætheria . . *neque adhuc crudelibus occubat umbris?*
Omnes . . cœlicolas . . omnes supera alta tenentes
  Scuta *latentia condunt.*
·Has inter voces . . *media inter talia verba.*
Finem dedit . . *ore loquendi.*
Insonuere cavæ . . *sonitumque dedere cavernæ.*
Ferro accitam . . crebrisque *bipennibus.*
Nec nostri generis puerum . . *nec sanguinis.*

Boccaccio. These things look very ill in Latin; and yet they had quite escaped my observation. We often find, in the *Psalms of David,* one section of a sentence placed as it were in symmetry with another, and not at all supporting it by presenting the same idea. It is a species of piety to drop the nether lip in admiration; but in reality it is not only the modern taste that is vitiated; the ancient is little less so, although differently. To say over again what we have just ceased to say, with nothing added, nothing improved, is equally bad in all languages and all times. [4]

Petrarca.   But in these repetitions we may imagine one part of the chorus to be answering another part opposite.

Boccaccio.   Likely enough.   However, you have ransacked poor Virgil to the skin, and have stripped him clean.

Petrarca.   Of all who have ever dealt with *Winter*, he is the most frost-bitten.   Hesiod's description of the snowy season is more poetical and more formidable.   What do you think of these icicles?—

Œraque [5] dissiliunt vulgo; *vestesque rigescunt !*

Boccaccio.   Wretched falling-off.
Petrarca.   He comes close enough presently.

Stiriaque hirsutis dependent horrida barbis.

We will withdraw from the Alps into the city.   And now are you not smitten with reverence at seeing

Romanos rerum dominos ; *gentemque togatam ?*

The masters of the world . . and *long-tailed coats !*

Come to Carthage.   What a recommendation to a beautiful queen does Æneas offer, in himself and his associates !

Lupi ceu
Raptores ; atrâ in nebulâ, quos *improba ventris*
Exegit cæcos rabies !

Ovid is censured for his

Consiliis non *curribus* utere nostris.

[4 First ed. reads: " times.   Surely you have ransacked," &c. (3 lines below).]

[5 First ed. has the following note:—" These verses are noticed in the treatise ' De usu Latini Sermonis.'   Remarks on the characters of Proteus, Mezentius, &c., may be found in the *Imaginary Conversation* of Tooke and Johnson.   Some who read this volume may never read those."]

Virgil never for

Inceptoque et *sedibus* hæret in iisdem.

The same in its quality, but more forced.[6]

The affectation of Ovid was light and playful; Virgil's was wilful, perverse, and grammatistical. Are we therefore to suppose that every hand able to elaborate a sonnet may be raised up against the majesty of Virgil? Is ingratitude so rare and precious, that we should prefer the exposure of his faults to the enjoyment of his harmony? He first delivered it to his countrymen in unbroken links under the form of poetry, and consoled them for the eloquent tongue that had withered on the Rostra. It would be no difficult matter to point out at least twenty bad passages in the *Æneid*, and a proportionate number of worse in the *Georgics*. In your comparison of poet with poet, the defects as well as the merits of each ought to be placed side by side. This is the rather to be expected, as Dante professes to be Virgil's disciple. You may easily show that his humility no more became him than his fierceness.

Boccaccio. You have praised the harmony of the Roman poet. Now in single verses I think our poetry is sometimes more harmonious than the Latin, but never in whole sentences. Advantage could perhaps be taken of our metre if we broke through the stanza. Our language is capable, I think, of all the vigour and expression of the Latin; and, in regard to the pauses in our versification, in which chiefly the harmony of metre consists, we have greatly the advantage. What, for instance, is more beautiful than your

> Solo . . e pensoso . . i piu deserti campi
> Vo . . misurando . a passi tardi . . e lenti.

Petrarca. My critics have found fault with the *lenti*, calling it an expletive, and ignorant that equally in Italian and Latin the word signifies both *slow* and *languid*, while *tardi* signifies *slow* only.

[6 First ed. reads: " forced. Of all faults, however, the *hypallage* is incomparably the worst and seems Virgil's favourite. Such is

> Odor attulit auras

'The affectation," &c.]

Boccaccio. Good poetry, like good music, pleases most people, but the ignorant and inexpert lose half its pleasures, the invidious lose them all. What a paradise lost is here!

Petrarca. If we deduct the inexpert, the ignorant, and the invidious, can we correctly say it pleases most people? But either my worst compositions are the most admired, or the insincere and malignant bring them most forward for admiration, keeping the others in the background! Sonnetteers, in consequence, have started up from all quarters.

Boccaccio. The sonnet seems peculiarly adapted to the languor of a melancholy and despondent love, the rhymes returning and replying to every plaint and every pulsation. Our poetasters are now converting it into the penfold and pound of stray thoughts and vagrant fancies. No sooner have they collected in their excursions as much matter as they conveniently can manage, than they seat themselves down and set busily to work, punching it neatly out with a clever cubic stamp of fourteen lines in diameter.

Petrarca. A pretty sonnet may be written on a lambkin or a parsnep, there being room enough for truth and tenderness on the edge of a leaf or the tip of an ear; but a great poet must clasp the higher passions breast high, and compel them in an authorative tone to answer his interrogatories.

We will now return again to Virgil, and consider in what relation he stands to Dante. Our Tuscan and Homer are never inflated.

Boccaccio. Pardon my interruption; but do you find that Virgil is? Surely he has always borne the character of the most chaste, the most temperate, the most judicious among the poets.

Petrarca. And will not soon lose it. Yet never had there swelled, in the higher or the lower regions of poetry, such a gust as here, in the exordium of the *Georgics :*

> Tuque adeo, quem mox quæ sint habitura deorum
> Concilia incertum est, urbisne invisere, Cæsar,
> Terrarumque velis curam, et te maximus orbis
> Auctorem frugum? . .

Boccaccio. Already forestalled!

Petrarca.

   . . . tempestatumque potentem.

Boccaccio.   Very strange coincidence of opposite qualifications.
Petrarca.

   Accipiat, cingens maternâ tempora myrto :
   An deus immensi venias maris.

Boccaccio.   Surely he would not put down Neptune ?
Petrarca.

      . . ac tua nautæ
   Numina sola colant : *tibi serviat ultima Thule.*

Boccaccio.   Catch him up ! catch him up ! uncoil the whole
of the vessel's rope ! never did man fall overboard so unluckily,
or sink so deep on a sudden.
Petrarca.

   Teque sibi generum Tethys *emat omnibus undis ?*

Boccaccio.   Nobody in his senses would bid against her : what
indiscretion ! and at her time of life too !

   Tethys then really, most gallant Cæsar !
   If you would only condescend to please her,
   With all her waves would you good graces buy,
   And you should govern all the Isle of Skie.

Petrarca.

   Anne novum *tardis* sidus te mensibus addas ?

Boccaccio.   For what purpose ? If the months were *slow,*
he was not likely to mend their speed by mounting another
passenger.   But the vacant place is such an inviting one !
Petrarca.

   Qua locus Erigonen inter Chelasque sequentes
   Panditur.

Boccaccio.   Plenty of room, sir !
Petrarca.

   . . . ipse tibi jam brachia contrahit ardens,
   Scorpius. . . .

Boccaccio.   I would not incommode him ; I would beg him to
be quite at his ease.

Petrarca.

   . . . et cœli justâ plus parte reliquit.
Quicquid eris (nam te nec sperent Tartara regem
Nec tibi regnandi veniet tam dira cupido,
Quamvis Elysios miretur Græcia campos,
Nec repetita sequi curet Proserpina matrem).

Boccaccio.   Was it not enough to have taken all Varro's invocation, much enlarged, without adding these verses to the other twenty-three ?

Petrarca.   Vainly will you pass through the later poets of the empire, and look for the like extravagance and bombast. Tell me candidly your opinion, not of the quantity but of the quality.

Boccaccio.   I had scarcely formed one upon them before. Honestly and truly, it is just such a rumbling rotundity as might have been blown, with much ado, if Lucan and Nero had joined their pipes and puffed together into the same bladder. I never have admired, since I was a schoolboy, the commencement or the conclusion of the *Georgics ;* an unwholesome and consuming fungus at the foot of the tree, a withered and loose branch at the summit.

Boccaccio.   Virgil and Dante are altogether so different, that, unless you will lend me your whole store of ingenuity, I shall never bring them to bear one upon the other.

Petrarca.   Frequently the points of comparison are salient in proportion as the angles of similitude recede : and the absence of a quality in one man usually makes us recollect its presence in another ; hence the comparison is at the same time natural and involuntary. Few poets are so different as Homer and Virgil, yet no comparison has been made oftener. Ovid, although unlike Homer, is greatly more like him than Virgil is ; for there is the same facility, and apparently the same negligence, in both. The great fault in the *Metamorphoses* is in the plan, as proposed in the argument,

                primaque ab origine mundi
In mea *perpetuum* deducere tempora carmen.

Had he divided the more interesting of the tales, and omitted all the transformations, he would have written a greater number of exquisite poems than any author of Italy or Greece. He wants on many occasions the gravity of Virgil ; he wants on all the variety of cadence; but it is a very mistaken notion that he either has heavier faults or more numerous. His natural air of levity, his unequalled and unfailing ease, have always made the contrary opinion prevalent. Errors and faults are readily supposed, in literature as in life, where there is much gaiety: and the appearance of ease, among those who never could acquire or understand it, excites a suspicion of negligence and faultiness. Of all the ancient Romans, Ovid had the finest imagination; he likewise had the truest tact in judging the poetry of his contemporaries and predecessors. Compare his estimate with Quintilian's of the same writers, and this will strike you forcibly. He was the only one of his countrymen who could justly appreciate the labours of Lucretius.

> Carmina sublimis tunc sunt peritura Lucreti,
>   Exitio terras quum dabit una dies.

And the kindness with which he rests on all the others, shows a benignity of disposition which is often lamentably deficient in authors who write tenderly upon imaginary occasions.

I begin to be inclined to your opinion in regard to the advantages of our Italian versification. It surely has a greater variety, in its usual measure, than the Latin, in dactyls and spondees. We admit several feet into ours: the Latin, if we believe the grammarians, admits only two into the heroic; and at least seven verses in every ten conclude with a dissyllabic word.

Boccaccio. We are taught indeed that the final foot of an hexameter is always a spondee: but our ears deny the assertion, and prove to us that it never is, any more than it is in the Italian. In both the one and the other the last foot is uniformly a trochee in pronunciation. There is only one species of Latin verse which ends with a true inflexible spondee, and this is the *scazon.* Its name of the *limper* is but little prepossessing, yet the two most beautiful and most perfect poems of the language are composed in it—the *Miser Catulle* and the *Sirmio.*

Petrarca. This is likewise my opinion of those two little golden images, which however are insufficient to raise Catullus on an equality with Virgil: nor would twenty such. Amplitude of dimensions is requisite to constitute the greatness of a poet, besides his symmetry of form and his richness of decoration. We

have conversed more than once together on the defects and oversights of the correct and elaborate Mantuan, but never without
the expression of our gratitude for the exquisite delight he has
afforded us.   We may forgive him his Proteus and his Pollio ;
but we can not well forbear to ask him, how Æneas came
to know that Acragas was *formerly* the sire of high-mettled
steeds, even if such had been the fact?   But such was only the
fact a thousand years afterwards, in the reign of Gelon.

Boccaccio.   Was it *then ?*   Were the horses of Gelon and
Theron and Hiero, of Agrigentine or Sicilian breed?   The
country was never celebrated for a race adapted to chariots ; such
horses were mostly brought from Thessaly, and probably some
from Africa.   I do not believe there was ever a fine one in
Italy before the invasion of Pyrrhus.   No doubt, Hannibal
introduced many.   Greece herself, I suspect, was greatly
indebted to the studs of Xerxes for the noblest of her prizes on
the Olympic plain.   In the kingdom of Naples I have observed
more horses of high blood than in any other quarter of Italy.   It
is there that Pyrrhus and Hannibal were stationary : and, long
after these, the most warlike of men, the Normans, took possession
of the country.   And the Normans would have horses worthy of
their valour, had they unyoked them from the chariot of the sun.
Subduers of France, of Sicily, of Cyprus, they made England
herself accept their laws.

Virgil, I remember, in the *Georgics*, has given some directions
in the choice of horses.   He speaks unfavourably of the white :
yet painters have been fond of representing the leaders of armies
mounted on them.   And the reason is quite as good as the reason
of a writer on husbandry, Cato or Columella, for choosing a
house-dog of a contrary colour : it being desirable that a general
should be as conspicuous as possible, and a dog, guarding against
thieves, as invisible.

I love beyond measure in Virgil his kindness toward dumb
creatures.   Although he represents his Mezentius as a hater of
the Gods, and so inhuman as to fasten dead bodies to the living,
and violates in him the unity of character more than character
was ever violated before, we treat as impossible all he has been
telling us of his atrocities, when we hear his allocution to
Rhœbus.

Petrarca. The dying hero, for hero he is transcendently above all the others in the *Æneid,* is not only the kindest father, not only the most passionate in his grief for Lausus, but likewise gives way to manly sorrows for the mute companion of his warfare.

> Rhœbe diu, res si qua diu mortalibus usquam,
> Viximus.

Here the philosophical reflection addressed to the worthy quadruped, on the brief duration of human and equine life, is ill applied. It is not the thought for the occasion ; it is not the thought for the man. He could no more have uttered it than Rhœbus could have appreciated it. This is not however quite so great an absurdity as the tender apostrophe of the monster Proteus to the dead Eurydice. Beside, the youth of Lausus, and the activity and strength of Mezentius, as exerted in many actions just before his fall, do not allow us to suppose that he who says to his horse,

> Diu viximus,

had passed the meridian of existence.

Boccaccio. Francesco ! it is a pity you had no opportunity of looking into the mouth of the good horse Rhœbus : perhaps his teeth had not lost all their marks.

Petrarca. They would have been lost upon me, though horses' mouths to the intelligent are more trustworthy than many others.

Boccaccio. I [7] have always been of opinion that Virgil is inferior to Homer, not only in genius, but in judgment, and to an equal degree at the very least. I shall never dare to employ half your suggestions in our irritable city, for fear of raising up two new factions, the Virgilians and the Dantists.

Petrarca. I wish in good truth and seriousness you could raise them, or anything like zeal for genius, with whomsoever it might abide.

Boccaccio. You really have almost put me out of conceit with Virgil.

Petrarca. I have done a great wrong then both to him and you. Admiration is not the pursuivant to all the steps even of an

---

[7] [First ed. reads : " *Boccaccio.* I shall never dare," &c. (3 lines below).]

admirable poet ; but respect is stationary. Attend him where the ploughman is unyoking the sorrowful ox from his companion dead at the furrow ; follow him up the arduous ascent where he springs beyond the strides of Lucretius ; and close the procession of his glory with the coursers and cars of Elis.

THIRD DAY'S INTERVIEW.

It being now the Lord's day, Messer Francesco thought it meet that he should rise early in the morning and bestir himself, to hear mass in the parish church at Certaldo. Whereupon he went on tiptoe, if so weighty a man could indeed go in such a fashion, and lifted softly the latch of Ser Giovanni's chamber-door, that he might salute him ere he departed, and occasion no wonder at the step he was about to take. He found Ser Giovanni fast asleep, with the missal wide open across his nose, and a pleasant smile on his genial joyous mouth. Ser Francesco leaned over the couch, closed his hands together, and, looking with even more than his usual benignity, said in a low voice,

"God bless thee, gentle soul ! the mother of purity and innocence protect thee ! "

He then went into the kitchen, where he found the girl Assunta, and mentioned his resolution. She informed him that the horse had eaten his * two beans, and was as strong as a lion and as ready as a lover. Ser Francesco patted her on the cheek, and called her *semplicetta !* She was overjoyed at this honour from so great a man, the bosom-friend of her good master, whom she had always thought the greatest man in the world, not ex- cepting Monsignore, until he told her he was only a dog confronted with Ser Francesco. She tripped alertly across the paved court into the stable, and took down the saddle and bridle from the farther end of the rack. But Ser Francesco, with his natural politeness, would not allow her to equip his palfrey.

"This is not the work for maidens," said he ; "return to the house, good girl ! "

She lingered a moment, then went away ; but, mistrusting the

---

* Literally, *due fave*, the expression on such occasions to signify a small quantity.

dexterity of Ser Francesco, she stopped and turned back again, and peeped through the half-closed door, and heard sundry sobs and wheezes round about the girth. Ser Francesco's wind ill seconded his intention ; and, although he had thrown the saddle valiantly and stoutly in its station, yet the girths brought him into extremity. She entered again, and dissembling the reason, asked him whether he would not take a small beaker of the sweet white wine before he set out, and offered to girdle the horse while his Reverence bitted and bridled him. Before any answer could be returned, she had begun. And having now satisfactorily executed her undertaking, she felt irrepressible delight and glee at being able to do what Ser Francesco had failed in. He was scarcely more successful with his allotment of the labour ; found unlooked-for intricacies and complications in the machinery, wondered that human wit could not simplify it, and declared that the animal had never exhibited such restiveness before. In fact, he never had experienced the same grooming. At this conjuncture, a green cap made its appearance, bound with straw-coloured ribbon, and surmounted with two bushy sprigs of hawthorn, of which the globular buds were swelling, and some bursting, but fewer yet open. It was young Simplizio Nardi, who sometimes came on the Sunday morning to sweep the court-yard for Assunta.

"O ! this time you are come just when you were wanted," said the girl.

"Bridle, directly, Ser Francesco's horse, and then go away about your business."

The youth blushed, and kissed Ser Francesco's hand, begging his permission. It was soon done. He then held the stirrup ; and Ser Francesco, with scarcely three efforts, was seated and erect on the saddle. The horse, however, had somewhat more inclination for the stable than for the expedition ; and, as Assunta was handing to the rider his long ebony staff, bearing an ivory caduceus, the quadruped turned suddenly round. Simplizio called him *bestiaccia !* and then, softening it, *poco garbato !* and proposed to Ser Francesco that he should leave the bastone behind, and take the crab-switch he presented to him, giving at the same time a sample of its efficacy, which covered the long grizzle hair of the worthy quadruped with a profusion of pink blossoms, like embroidery. The offer was declined ; but Assunta told Simplizio to carry it himself, and to walk by the side of Ser Canonico quite up to the church-porch, having seen what a sad, dangerous beast his reverence had under him.

With perfect good will, partly in the pride of obedience to Assunta, and partly to enjoy the renown of accompanying a canon of holy church, Simplizio did as she enjoined.

And now the sound of village bells, in many hamlets and convents and churches out of sight, was indistinctly heard, and lost again; and at last the five of Certaldo seemed to crow over the faintness of them all. The freshness of the morning was enough of itself to excite the spirits of youth; a portion of which never fails to descend on years that are far removed from it, if the mind has partaken in innocent mirth while it was its season and its duty to enjoy it. Parties of young and old passed the canonico and his attendant with mute respect, bowing and bare-headed; for that ebony staff threw its spell over the tongue, which the frank and hearty salutation of the bearer was inadequate to break. Simplizio, once or twice, attempted to call back an intimate of the same age with himself; but the utmost he could obtain was a *riveritissimo!* and a genuflexion to the rider. It is reported that a heart-burning rose up from it in the breast of a cousin, some days after, too distinctly apparent in the long-drawn appellation of *Gnor* * Simplizio.

Ser Francesco moved gradually forward, his steed picking his way along the lane, and looking fixedly on the stones with all the sobriety of a mineralogist. He himself was well satisfied with the pace, and told Simplizio to be sparing of the switch, unless in case of a hornet or a gadfly. Simplizio smiled, toward the hedge, and wondered at the condescension of so great a theologian and astrologer, in joking with him about the gadflies and hornets in the beginning of April. "Ah! there are men in the world who can make wit out of anything!" said he to himself.

As they approached the walls of the town, the whole country was pervaded by a stirring and diversified air of gladness. Laughter and songs and flutes and viols, inviting voices and complying responses, mingled with merry bells and with processional hymns, along the woodland paths and along the yellow meadows. It was really the *Lord's Day*, for he made his creatures happy in it,

---

* Contraction of *signor*, customary in Tuscany.

and their hearts were thankful. Even the cruel had ceased from cruelty ; and the rich man alone exacted from the animal his daily labour. Ser Francesco made this remark, and told his youthful guide that he had never been before where he could not walk to church on a Sunday ; and that nothing should persuade him to urge the speed of his beast, on the seventh day, beyond his natural and willing foot's-pace. He reached the gates of Certaldo more than half an hour before the time of service, and he found laurels suspended over them, and being suspended ; and many pleasant and beautiful faces were protruded between the ranks of gentry and clergy who awaited him. Little did he expect such an attendance ; but Fra Biagio of San Vivaldo, who himself had offered no obsequiousness or respect, had scattered the secret of his visit throughout the whole country. A young poet, the most celebrated in the town, approached the canonico with a long scroll of verses, which fell below the knee, beginning,

How shall we welcome our illustrious guest?

To which Ser Francesco immediately replied, " Take your favourite maiden, lead the dance with her, and bid all your friends follow ; you have a good half-hour for it."

Universal applauses succeeded, the music struck up, couples were instantly formed. The gentry on this occasion led out the cittadinanza, as they usually do in the villeggiatura, rarely in the carnival, and never at other times. The elder of the priests stood round in their sacred vestments, and looked with cordiality and approbation on the youths, whose hands and arms could indeed do much, and did it, but whose active eyes could rarely move upward the modester of their partners.

While the elder of the clergy were thus gathering the fruits of their liberal cares and paternal exhortations, some of the younger looked on with a tenderer sentiment, not unmingled with regret. Suddenly the bells ceased ; the figure of the dance was broken ; all hastened into the church ; and many hands that joined on the green, met together at the font, and touched the brow reciprocally with its lustral waters, in soul-devotion.

After the service, and after a sermon a good church-hour in length to gratify him, enriched with compliments from all authors, Christian and Pagan, informing him at the conclusion that, although he had been crowned in the Capitol, he must die, being born mortal, Ser Francesco rode homeward. The sermon seemed to have sunk deeply into him, and even into the horse under him, for both of them nodded, both snorted, and one stumbled. Simplizio was twice fain to cry,

"Ser Canonico! Riverenza! in this country if we sleep before dinner it does us harm. There are stones in the road, Ser Canonico, loose as eggs in a nest, and pretty nigh as thick together, huge as mountains."

"Good lad!" said Ser Francesco, rubbing his eyes, "toss the biggest of them out of the way, and never mind the rest."

The horse, although he walked, shuffled almost into an amble as he approached the stable, and his master looked up at it with nearly the same contentment. Assunta had been ordered to wait for his return, and cried,

"O Ser Francesco! you are looking at our long apricot, that runs the whole length of the stable and barn, covered with blossoms as the old white hen is with feathers. You must come in the summer, and eat this fine fruit with Signor Padrone. You can not think how ruddy and golden and sweet and mellow it is. There are peaches in all the fields, and plums, and pears, and apples, but there is not another apricot for miles and miles. Ser Giovanni brought the stone from Naples before I was born: a lady gave it to him when she had eaten only half the fruit off it: but perhaps you may have seen her, for you have ridden as far as Rome, or beyond. Padrone looks often at the fruit, and eats it willingly; and I have seen him turn over the stones in his plate, and choose one out from the rest, and put it into his pocket, but never plant it."

"Where is the youth?" inquired Ser Francesco.

"Gone away," answered the maiden.

"I wanted to thank him," said the Canonico.

"May I tell him so?" asked she.

"And give him," continued he, holding a piece of silver . . .

"I will give him something of my own, if he goes on and behaves well," said she: "but Signor Padrone would drive him away for ever, I am sure, if he were tempted in an evil hour to accept a quattrino, for any service he could render the friends of the house."

Ser Francesco was delighted with the graceful animation of this ingenuous girl, and asked her, with a little curiosity, how she could afford to make him a present.

"I do not intend to make him a present," she replied: "but it is better he should be rewarded by me," she blushed and hesitated, "or by Signor Padrone," she added, "than by your reverence. He has not done half his duty yet; not half. I will teach him: he is quite a child; four months younger than me."

Ser Francesco went into the house, saying to himself at the doorway,

"Truth, innocence, and gentle manners, have not yet left the earth. There are sermons that never make the ears weary. I have heard but few of them, and come from church for this."

Whether Simplizio had obeyed some private signal from Assunta, or whether his own delicacy had prompted him to disappear, he was now again in the stable, and the manger was replenished with hay. A bucket was soon after heard ascending from the well; and then two words, "Thanks, Simplizio."

When Petrarca entered the chamber, he found Boccaccio with his breviary in his hand, not looking into it indeed, but repeating a thanksgiving in an audible and impassioned tone of voice. Seeing Ser Francesco, he laid the book down beside him, and welcomed him.

"I hope you have an appetite after your ride," said he, "for you have sent home a good dinner before you."

Ser Francesco did not comprehend him, and expressed it not in words but in looks.

"I am afraid you will dine sadly late to-day: noon has struck this half-hour, and you must wait another, I doubt. However, by good luck, I had a couple of citrons in the house, intended to assuage my thirst if the fever had continued. This being over, by God's mercy, I will try (please God!) whether we two greyhounds can not be a match for a leveret."

"How is this?" said Ser Francesco.

"Young Marc-Antonio Grilli, the cleverest lad in the parish at noosing any wild animal, is our patron of the feast. He has wanted for many a day to say something in the ear of Matilda Vercelli. Bringing up the leveret to my bedside, and opening the lips, and cracking the knuckles, and turning the foot round to show the quality and quantity of the hair upon it, and to prove that it really and truly was a leveret, and might be eaten without offence to my teeth, he informed me that he had left his mother in the yard, ready to dress it for me ; she having been cook to the prior.   He protested he owed the *crowned martyr* a forest of leverets, boars, deers, and everything else within them, for having commanded the most backward girls to dance directly.   Where-upon he darted forth at Matilda, saying, ' The *crowned martyr* orders it,' seizing both her hands, and swinging her round before she knew what she was about.   He soon had an opportunity of applying a word, no doubt as dexterously as hand or foot ; and she said submissively, but seriously, and almost sadly, ' Marc-Antonio, now all the people have seen it, they will think it."

"And, after a pause,

" ' I am quite ashamed : and so should you be : are not you now ? '

" The others had run into the church.   Matilda, who scarcely had noticed it, cried suddenly,

" ' O Santissima ! we are quite alone.'

" ' Will you be mine ? ' cried he, enthusiastically.

" ' O ! they will hear you in the church,' replied she.

" ' They shall, they shall,' cried he again, as loudly.

" ' If you will only go away.'

" ' And then ? '

" ' Yes, yes, indeed.'

" ' The Virgin hears you : fifty saints are witnesses.'

" ' Ah ! they know you made me : they will look kindly on us.'

" He released her hand : she ran into the church, doubling her veil (I will answer for her) at the door, and kneeling as near it as she could find a place.

" ' By St Peter,' said Marc-Antonio, ' if there is a leveret in the wood, the *crowned martyr* shall dine upon it this blessed day.' And he bounded off, and set about his occupation.   I inquired what induced him to designate you by such a title.   He an-swered, that everybody knew you had received the crown of martyrdom at Rome, between the pope and antipope, and had performed many miracles, for which they had canonised you, and that you wanted only to die to become a saint."

The leveret was now served up, cut into small pieces, and covered with a rich tenacious sauce, composed of sugar, citron, and various spices. The appetite of Ser Francesco was contagious. Never was dinner more enjoyed by two companions, and never so much by a greater number. One glass of a fragrant wine, the colour of honey, and unmixed with water, crowned the repast. Ser Francesco then went into his own chamber, and found, on his ample mattress, a cool, refreshing sleep, quite sufficient to remove all the fatigues of the morning; and Ser Giovanni lowered the pillow against which he had seated himself, and fell into his usual repose. Their separation was not of long continuance: and, the religious duties of the Sabbath having been performed, a few reflections on literature were no longer interdicted.

Boccaccio. How happens it, O Francesco! that nearly at the close of our lives, after all our efforts and exhortations, we are standing quite alone in the extensive fields of literature? We are only like to *scoria* struck from the anvil of the gigantic Dante. We carry our fire along with us in our parabola, and, behold! it falls extinguished on the earth.

Petrarca. Courage! courage! we have hardly yet lighted the lamp and shown the way.

Boccaccio. You are a poet; I am only a commentator, and must soothe my own failures in the success of my master.

I can not but think again and again, how fruitlessly the bravest have striven to perpetuate the ascendency or to establish the basis of empire, when Alighieri hath fixed a language for thousands of years, and for myriads of men; a language far richer and more beautiful than our glorious Italy ever knew before, in any of her regions, since the Attic and the Dorian contended for the prize of eloquence on her southern shores. Eternal honour, eternal veneration, to him who raised up our country from the barbarism that surrounded her! Remember how short a time before him, his master Brunetto Latini wrote in French; prose indeed; but whatever has enough in it for poetry, has enough for prose out of its shreds and selvages.

Petrarca. Brunetto! Brunetto! it was not well done in thee. An Italian, a poet, write in French! What human ear can tolerate its nasty nasalities? what homely intellect be satisfied with its bare-bone poverty? By good fortune we have nothing to do with it in the course of our examination. Several things in Dante himself you will find more easy to explain than to excuse. You have already given me a specimen of them, which I need not assist you in rendering more copious.

Boccaccio. There are certainly some that require no little circumspection. Difficult as they are to excuse, the difficulty lies more on the side of the clergy than the laity.

Petrarca. I understand you. The *gergo* of your author has always a reference to the court of the Vatican. Here he speaks in the dark: against his private enemies he always is clear and explicit.

Unless you are irresistibly pressed into it, give no more than two, or at most three lectures, on the verse which, I predict, will appear to our Florentines the cleverest in the poem.

Che nel viso degli uomini legge O M O.

Boccaccio. We were very near a new civil war about the interpretation of it.

Petrarca. Foolisher questions have excited general ones. What, I wonder, rendered you all thus reasonable at last?

Boccaccio. The majority, which on few occasions is so much in the right, agreed with me that the two eyes are signified by the two vowels, the nose by the centre of the consonant, and the temples by its exterior lines.

Petrarca. In proceeding to explore the Paradise more minutely, I must caution you against remarking to your audience, that, although the nose is between the eyes, the temples are not, exactly. An observation which, if well established, might be resented as somewhat injurious to the Divinity of the *Commedia*.

Boccaccio. With all its flatnesses and swamps, many have preferred the *Paradiso* to the other two sections of the poem.

Petrarca. There is as little in it of very bad poetry, or we may rather say, as little of what is no poetry at all, as in either, which are uninviting from an absolute lack of interest and allusion, from the confusedness of the ground-work, the indistinctness of the scene, and the paltriness (in great measure) of the agents. If we are amazed at the number of Latin verses in the *Inferno* and *Purgatorio*, what must we be at their fertility in the *Paradiso*, where they drop on us in ripe clusters through every glen and avenue! We reach the conclusion of the sixteenth canto before we come in sight of poetry, or more than a glade with a gleam upon it. Here we find a description of Florence in her age of innocence: but the scourge of satire sounds in our ears before we fix the attention.

Boccaccio. I like the old Ghibelline best in the seventeenth, where he dismisses the doctors, corks up the Latin, ceases from psalmody, looses the arms of Calfucci and Arigucci, sets down Caponsacco in the market, and gives us a stave of six verses which repays us amply for our heaviest toils and sufferings.

Tu lascierai ogni cosa diletta, etc.

But he soon grows weary of tenderness and sick of sorrow, and returns to his habitual exercise of throwing stones and calling names.

Again we are refreshed in the twentieth. Here we come to the simile: here we look up and see his lark, and are happy and lively as herself. Too soon the hard fingers of the master are round our wrists again: we are dragged into the school, and are obliged to attend the divinity-examination, which the poet undergoes from Saint Simon-Peter. He acquits himself pretty well, and receives a handsome compliment from the questioner, who, "*inflamed with love,*" acknowledges he has given "*a good account of the coinage, both in regard to weight and alloy.*"

"Tell me," continues he, "have you any of it in your pocket?"

"Yea," replies the scholar, "and so shining and round that I doubt not what mint it comes from."

Saint Simon-Peter does not take him at his word for it, but tries to puzzle and pose him with several hard queries. He answers both warily and wittily, and grows so contented with his examining master, that, instead of calling him, "*a sergeant of infantry,*" as he did before, he now entitles him "*the baron.*"

I must consult our bishop ere I venture to comment on these two verses:

Credo una essenza, si una e si trina
Che sofferà congiunto *sunt et este,*

as whatever may peradventure lie within them, they are hardly
worth the ceremony of being burnt alive for, although it should be
at the expense of the Church.

Petrarca.   I recommend to you the straightforward course ; but
I believe I must halt a little, and advise you to look about you.
If you let people see that there are so many faults in your author,
they will reward you, not according to your merits, but according
to its defects.   On celebrated writers, when we speak in public,
it is safer to speak magnificently than correctly.   Therefore be
not too cautious in leading your disciples, and in telling them, here
you may step securely, here you must mind your footing : for a
florin will drop out of your pocket at every such crevice you stop
to cross.

Boccaccio.   The room is hardly light enough to let me see
whether you are smiling : but, being the most ingenuous soul
alive, and by no means the least jocose one, I suspect it.   My
office is, to explain what is difficult, rather than to expatiate on
what is beautiful or to investigate what is amiss.   If those who
invite me to read the lectures, mark out the topics for me,
nothing is easier than to keep within them.   Yet with how true
and entire a pleasure shall I point out to my fellow-citizens such
a glorious tract of splendour as there is in the single line,

> Cio ch'io vedevo mi sembrava un riso
> Dell' universo !

With what exultation shall I toss up my gauntlet into the
balcony of proud Antiquity, and cry, *Descend ! Contend !*

I have frequently heard your admiration of this passage, and
therefore I dwell on it the more delighted.   Beside, we seldom
find anything in our progress that is not apter to excite a
very different sensation.   School-divinity can never be made
attractive to the Muses ; nor will Virgil and Thomas Aquinas
ever cordially shake hands.   The unrelenting rancour against the
popes is more tedious than unmerited : in a poem I doubt
whether we would not rather find it unmerited than tedious.
For, of all the sins against the spirit of poetry, this is the most
unpardonable.   Something of our indignation, and a proportion of
our scorn, may fairly be detached from the popes, and thrown on

the pusillanimous and perfidious who suffered such excrescences to shoot up, exhausting and poisoning the soil they sprang from.

Petrarca. I do not wonder they make Saint Peter " redden," as we hear they do, but I regret that they make him stammer,

> Quegli che usurpa in terra il luogo mio,
> Il luogo mio, il luogo mio, etc.

Alighieri was not the first catholic who taught us that the papacy is usurpation, nor will he be (let us earnestly hope) the last to inculcate so evident a doctrine.

Boccaccio. Canonico of Parma! Canonico of Parma! you make my hair stand on end. But since nobody sees it beside yourself, prythee tell me how it happens that an infallible pope should denounce as damnable the decision of another infallible pope, his immediate predecessor? Giovanni the twenty-second, whom you knew intimately, taught us that the souls of the just could not enjoy the sight of God until after the day of universal judgment. But the doctors of theology at Paris, and those learned and competent clerks, the kings of France and Naples, would not allow him to die before he had swallowed the choke-pear they could not chew. The succeeding pope, who called himself an ass, in which infallibility was less wounded, and neither king nor doctor carped at it (for not only was he one, but as truth-telling a beast as Balaam's), condemned this error, as indeed well he might, after two kings had set their faces against it. But on the whole, the thing is ugly and perplexing. That they were both infallible we know ; and yet they differed ! Nay, the former differed from himself, and was pope all the while ; of course infallible ! Well, since we may not solve the riddle, let us suppose it is only a mystery the more, and be thankful for it.

Petrarca. That is best.

Boccaccio. I never was one of those who wish for ice to slide upon in summer. Being no theologian, I neither am nor desire to be sharp-sighted in articles of heresy : but it is reported that there are among Christians some who hesitate to worship the Virgin.

Petrarca. Few, let us hope.

Boccaccio. Hard hearts ! Imagine her, in her fifteenth year, fondling the lovely babe whom she was destined to outlive!

destined to see shedding his blood, and bowing his head in agony. Can we ever pass her by and not say from our hearts :

" O thou whose purity had only the stain of compassionate tears upon it ! blessings, blessings on thee ! "

I never saw her image but it suspended my steps on the high-way of the world, discoursed with me, softened and chastened me, showing me too clearly my unworthiness by the light of a reproving smile.

Petrarca. Woe betide those who cut off from us any source of tenderness, and shut out from any of our senses the access to devotion !

Beatrice, in the place before us, changes colour too, as deeply as ever she did on earth ; for Saint Peter, in his passion, picks up and flourishes some very filthy words. He does not recover the use of his reason on a sudden ; but, after a long and bitter complaint that faith and innocence are only to be found in little children ; and that the child moreover who loves and listens to its mother while it lisps, wishes to see her buried when it can speak plainly ; he informs us that this corruption ought to excite no wonder, since the human race must of necessity go astray, not having any one upon earth to govern it.

Boccaccio. Is not this strange though ; from the mouth of one inspired ? We are taught that there never shall be wanting a head to govern the church ; could Saint Peter say that it *was* wanting ? I feel my catholicism here touched to the quick. However, I am resolved not to doubt : the more difficulties I find, the fewer questions I raise : the saints must settle it, as well as they can, among themselves.

Petrarca. They are nearer the fountain of truth than we are ; and I am confident Saint Paul was in the right.

Boccaccio. I do verily believe he may have been, although at Rome we might be in jeopardy for saying it. Well is it for me that my engagement is to comment on Alighieri's *Divina Commedia* instead of his treatise *De Monarchiâ.* He says bold things there, and sets apostles and popes together by the ears. That is not the worst. He would destroy what is and should be, and would establish what never can nor ought to be.

Petrarca.   If a universal monarch could make children good universally, and keep them as innocent when they grow up as when they were in the cradle, we might wish him upon his throne to-morrow.   But Alighieri, and those others who have conceived such a prodigy, seem to be unaware that what they would establish for the sake of unity, is the very thing by which this unity must be demolished.   For, since universal power does not confer on its possessor universal intelligence, and since a greater number of the cunning could and would assemble round him, he must (if we suppose him like the majority and nearly the totality of his class) appoint a greater proportion of such subjects to the management and control of his dominions. Many of them would become the rulers of cities and of provinces in which they have no connexions or affinities, and in which the preservation of character is less desirable to them than the possession of power.   The operations of injustice, and the opportunities of improvement, would be alike concealed from the monarch in the remoter parts of his territories ; and every man of high station would exercise more authority than he.

Boccaccio.   Casting aside the impracticable scheme of universal monarchy, if kings and princes there must be, even in the midst of civility and letters, why can not they return to European customs, renouncing those Asiatic practices which are become enormously prevalent?   why can not they be contented with such power as the kings of Rome and the lucumons of Etruria were contented with?   But forsooth they are wiser! and such customs are obsolete!   Of their wisdom I shall venture to say nothing, for nothing, I believe, is to be said of it; but the customs are not obsolete in other countries.   They have taken deep root in the north, and exhibit the signs of vigour and vitality.   Unhappily, the weakest men always think they least want help ; like the mad and the drunk.   Princes and geese are fond of standing on one leg, and fancy it (no doubt) a position of gracefulness and security, until the cramp seizes them on a sudden : then they find how helpless they are, and how much better it would have been if they had employed all the support at their disposal.

Petrarca.   When the familiars of absolute princes taunt us, as they are wont to do, with the only apophthegm they ever learnt by heart, namely, that it is better to be ruled by one master than by many, I quite agree with them; unity of power being the principle of republicanism, while the principle of despotism is division and delegation.   In the one system, every man conducts his own affairs, either personally or through the agency of some trustworthy representative, which is essentially the same: in the other system, no man, in quality of citizen, has any affairs of his own to conduct: but a tutor has been as much set over him as over a lunatic, as little with his option or consent, and without any provision, as there is in the case of the lunatic, for returning reason.   Meanwhile, the spirit of republics is omnipresent in them, as active in the particles as in the mass, in the circumference as in the centre.   Eternal it must be, as truth and justice are, although not stationary.   Yet when we look on Venice and Genoa, on the turreted Pisa and our own fair Florence, and many smaller cities self-poised in high serenity; when we see what edifices they have raised, and then glance at the wretched habitations of the slaves around, the Austrians, the French, and other fierce restless barbarians; difficult is it to believe that the beneficent God, who smiled upon these our labours, will ever in his indignation cast them down, a helpless prey to such invaders.

Morals and happiness will always be nearest to perfection in small communities, where functionaries are appointed by as numerous a body as can be brought together of the industrious and intelligent, who have observed in what manner they superintend their families, and converse with their equals and dependents.   Do we find that farms are better cultivated for being large? is your neighbour friendlier for being powerful? is your steward honester and more attentive for having a mortgage on your estate or a claim to a joint property in your mansion?   Yet well-educated men are seen about the streets, so vacant and delirious, as to fancy that a country can only be well governed by somebody who never saw and will never see a twentieth part of it, or know a hundredth part of its necessities; somebody who has no relationships in it, no connexions, no remembrances.   A man without soul and sympathy is alone to be the governor of men!   Giovanni! our Florentines are, beyond all others, a treacherous, tricking, mercenary race.   What in the name of heaven will become of them, if ever they listen to these ravings ; if ever they lose, by their cowardice and dissensions, the crust of salt that keeps them from putrescency, their freedom ?

Boccaccio. Alas! I dare hardly look out sometimes, lest I see before me the day when German and Spaniard will split them down the back and throw them upon the coals. Sad thought! here we will have done with it. We can not help them : we have made the most of them, like the good tailor who, as Dante says, cuts his coat according to his cloth.

Petrarca. Do you intend, if they should call upon you again, to give them occasionally some of your strictures on his prose writings ?

Boccaccio. It would not be expedient. Enough of his political sentiments is exhibited, in various places of his poem, to render him unacceptable to one party ; and enough of his theological, or rather his ecclesiastical, to frighten both. You and I were never passionately fond of the papacy, to which we trace in great measure the miseries of our Italy, its divisions and its corruptions, the substitution of cunning for fortitude, and of creed for conduct. He burst into indignation at the sight of this, and, because the popes took away our Christianity, he was so angry he would throw her freedom after it. Any thorn in the way is fit enough to toss the tattered rag on. A German king will do ; Austrian or Bavarian, Swabian, or Switzer. And, to humiliate us more and more, and render us the laughing-stock of our household, he would invest the intruder with the title of Roman emperor. What! it is not enough then that he assumes it ! We must invite him, forsooth, to accept it at our hands !

Petrarca. Let the other nations of Europe be governed by their hereditary kings and feudal princes : it is more accordant with those ancient habits which have not yet given way to the blandishment of literature and the pacific triumph of the arts : but let the states of Italy be guided by their own citizens. May nations find out by degrees that the next evil to being conquered is to conquer, and that he who assists in making slaves gives over at last by becoming one !

Boccaccio. Let us endure a French pope, or any other, as well as we can ; there is no novelty in his being a stranger. The Romans at all times picked up recruits from the thieves, gods, and priests, of all nations. Dante is wrong, I suspect, in imagining the popes to be infidels; and, no doubt, they would pay for indulgences as honestly as they sell them, if there were anybody at hand to receive the money. But who in the world ever thought of buying the cap he was wearing on his own head? Popes are no such triflers. After all, an infidel pope (and I do not believe there are three in a dozen) is less noxious than a sanguinary soldier, be his appellation what it may, if his power is only limited by his will. My experience has however taught me, that where there is a great mass of power concentrated, it will always act with great influence on the secondary around it. Whether pope or emperor or native king occupy the most authority within the Alps, the barons will range themselves under his banner, apart from the citizens. Venice, who appears to have received by succession the political wisdom of republican Rome, has less political enterprise: and the jealousies of her rivals will always hold them back, or greatly check them, from any plan suggested by her for the general good.

Petrarca. It appears to be the will of Providence that power and happiness shall never co-exist. Whenever a state becomes powerful, it becomes unjust; and injustice leads it first to the ruin of others, and next, and speedily, to its own. We, whose hearts are republican, are dazzled by looking so long and so intently at the eagles, and standards, and golden letters, S. P. Q. R. We are reluctant to admit that the most wretched days of ancient Rome were the days of her most illustrious men; that they began amid the triumphs of Scipio, when the Gracchi perished, and reached the worst under the dictatorship of Cæsar, when perished Liberty herself. A milder and better race was gradually formed by Grecian instruction. Vespasian, Titus, Nerva, Trajan, the Antonines, the Gordians, Tacitus, Probus, in an almost unbroken series, are such men as never wore the diadem in other countries; and Rome can show nothing comparable to them in the most renowned and virtuous of her earlier consuls. Humanity would be consoled in some degree by them, if their example had sunk into the breasts of the governed. But ferocity is unsoftened by sensuality; and the milk of the wolf could always be traced in the veins of the effeminated Romans.

Petrarca. That is true: and they continue to this day less humane than any other people of Italy. The better part of their character has fallen off from them; and in courage and perseverance they are far behind the Venetians and Ligurians. These last, a scanty population, were hardly to be conquered by Rome in the plentitude of her power, and with all her confederates: for which reason they were hated by her beyond all other nations. To gratify the pride and malice of Augustus, were written the verses:

> Vane Ligur! frustraque animis elate superbis,
> Nequicquam patrias tentasti lubricus artes.

Since that time, the inhabitants of Genoa and Venice have been enriched with the generous blood of the Lombards. This little tribe on the Subalpine territory, and the Norman on the Apulian, demonstrate to us, by the rapidity and extension of their conquests, that Italy is an over-ripe fruit, ready to drop from the stalk under the feet of the first insect that alights on it.

Boccaccio. The Germans, although as ignorant as the French, are less cruel, less insolent and rapacious. The French have a separate claw for every object of appetite or passion, and a spring that enables them to seize it. The desires of the German are overlaid with food and extinguished with drink, which to others are stimulants and incentives. The German loves to see everything about him orderly and entire, however coarse and common: the nature of the Frenchman is to derange and destroy everything. Sometimes when he has done so, he will reconstruct and refit it in his own manner, slenderly and fantastically; oftener leaving it in the middle, and proposing to lay the foundation when he has pointed the pinnacles and gilt the weathercock.

Petrarca. There is no danger that the French will have a durable footing in this or any other country. Their levity is more intolerable than German pressure, their arrogance than German pride, their falsehood than German rudeness, and their vexations than German exaction.

Boccaccio. If I must be devoured, I have little choice between the bear and the panther. May we always see the creatures at a distance and across the grating. The French will fondle us, to show us how vastly it is our interest to fondle them; watching all the while their opportunity; looking mild and half-asleep;

making a dash at last ; and laying bare and fleshless the arm we extend to them, from shoulder-blade to wrist.

Petrarca.   No nation, grasping at so much, ever held so little, or lost so soon what it had inveigled.   Yet France is surrounded by smaller and by apparently weaker states, which she never ceases to molest and invade.   Whatever she has won, and whatever she has lost, has been alike won and lost by her perfidy ; the characteristic of the people from the earliest ages, and recorded by a succession of historians, Greek and Roman.

Boccaccio.   My father spent many years among them, where also my education was completed ; yet whatever I have seen, I must acknowledge, corresponds with whatever I have read, and corroborates in my mind the testimony of tradition.   Their ancient history is only a preface to their later.   Deplorable as is the condition of Italy, I am more contented to share in her sufferings than in the frothy festivities of her frisky neighbour.

Petrarca.   So am I : but we must never deny or dissemble the victories of the ancient Gauls, many traces of which are remaining ; not that a nation's glory is the greener for the ashes it has scattered in the season of its barbarism.

Boccaccio.   The Cisalpine regions were indeed both invaded and occupied by them ; yet, from inability to retain the acquisition, how inconsiderable a part of the population is Gaulish ! Long before the time of Cæsar, the language was Latin throughout : the soldiers of Marius swept away the last dregs and stains on the ancient hearth.   Nor is there in the physiognomy of the people the slightest indication of the Gaul, as we perceive by medals and marbles.   These would surely preserve his features ; because they can only be the memorials of the higher orders, which of course would have descended from the conquerors. They merged early and totally in the original mass : and the countenances in Cisalpine busts are as beautiful and dignified as our other Italian races.

Petrarca.   The French imagine theirs are too.

Boccaccio.   I heartily wish them the full enjoyment of their blessings, real or imaginary : but neither their manners nor their principles coincide with ours, nor can a reasonable hope be entertained of benefit in their alliance.   Union at home is all we want, and vigilance to perpetuate the better of our institutions.

Petrarca. The land, O Giovanni, of your early youth, the land of my only love, fascinates us no longer. Italy is our country; and not ours only, but every man's, wherever may have been his wanderings, wherever may have been his birth, who watches with anxiety the recovery of the Arts, and acknowledges the supremacy of Genius. Beside, it is in Italy at last that all our few friends are resident. Yours were left behind you at Paris in your adolescence, if indeed any friendship can exist between a Florentine and a Frenchman: mine at Avignon were Italians, and older for the most part than myself. Here we know that we are beloved by some, and esteemed by many. It indeed gave me pleasure the first morning as I lay in bed, to overhear the fondness and earnestness which a worthy priest was expressing in your behalf.

Boccaccio. In mine?

Petrarca. Yes indeed: what wonder?

Boccaccio. A worthy priest?

Petrarca. None else, certainly.

Boccaccio. Heard in bed! dreaming, dreaming; ay?

Petrarca. No indeed: my eyes and ears were wide open.

Boccaccio. The little parlour opens into your room. But what priest could that be? Canonico Casini? He only comes when we have a roast of thrushes, or some such small matter at table: and this is not the season; they are pairing. Plover eggs might tempt him hitherward. If he heard a plover he would not be easy, and would fain make her drop her oblation before she had settled her nest.

Petrarca. It is right and proper that you should be informed who the clergyman was, to whom you are under an obligation.

Boccaccio. Tell me something about it, for truly I am at a loss to conjecture.

Petrarca. He must unquestionably have been expressing a kind and ardent solicitude for your eternal welfare. The first words I heard on awakening were these:

" Ser Giovanni, although the best of masters . . ."

Boccaccio. Those were Assuntina's.

Petrarca. . . . " may hardly be quite so holy (not being priest or friar) as your Reverence."

She was interrupted by the question, "What conversation holdeth he?"

She answered:

"He never talks of loving our neighbour with all our heart, all our soul, and all our strength, although he often gives away the last loaf in the pantry."

Boccaccio.   It was she!   Why did she say that? the slut!

Petrarca.   "He doth well," replied the confessor.   "Of the church, of the brotherhood, that is, of me, what discourses holdeth he?"

I thought the question an indiscreet one; but confessors vary in their advances to the seat of truth.

She proceeded to answer:

"He never said anything about the power of the church to absolve us, if we should happen to go astray a little in good company, like your Reverence."

Here, it is easy to perceive, is some slight ambiguity. Evidently she meant to say, by the seduction of "bad" company, and to express that his Reverence had asserted his power of absolution; which is undeniable.

Boccaccio.   I have my version.

Petrarca.   What may yours be?

Boccaccio.   Fra Biagio; broad as daylight; the whole frock round!

I would wager a flask of oil against a turnip, that he laid another trap for a penance.   Let us see how he went on.   I warrant, as he warmed, he left off limping in his paces, and bore hard upon the bridle.

Petrarca.   "Much do I fear," continued the expositor, "he never spoke to thee, child, about another world."

There was a silence of some continuance.

"Speak!" said the confessor.

"No indeed he never did, poor Padrone!" was the slow and evidently reluctant avowal of the maiden; for, in the midst of the acknowledgment her sighs came through the crevices of the door: then, without any farther interrogation, and with little delay, she added,

"But he often makes this look like it."

Boccaccio.   And now, if he had carried a holy scourge,

it would not have been on his shoulders that he would have laid it.

Petrarca. Zeal carries men often too far afloat; and confessors in general wish to have the sole steerage of the conscience. When she told him that your benignity made this world another heaven, he warmly and sharply answered,

"It is only we who ought to do that."

"Hush," said the maiden; and I verily believe she at that moment set her back against the door, to prevent the sounds from coming through the crevices, for the rest of them seemed to be just over my night cap. "Hush," said she, in the whole length of that softest of all articulations, "There is Ser Francesco in the next room: he sleeps long into the morning, but he is so clever a clerk, he may understand you just the same. I doubt whether he thinks Ser Giovanni in the wrong for making so many people quite happy; and if he should, it would grieve me very much to think he blamed Ser Giovanni."

"Who is Ser Francesco?" he asked, in a low voice.

"Ser Canonico," she answered.

"Of what Duomo?" continued he.

"Who knows?" was the reply; "but he is Padrone's heart's friend, for certain."

"Cospetto di Bacco! It can then be no other than Petrarca. He makes rhymes and love like the devil. Don't listen to him, or you are undone. Does he love you too, as well as Padrone?" he asked, still lowering his voice.

"I can not tell that matter," she answered, somewhat impatiently; "but I love him."

"To my face!" cried he, smartly.

"To the Santissima!" replied she, instantaneously; "for have not I told your Reverence he is Padrone's true heart's friend! And are not you my confessor, when you come on purpose?"

"True, true!" answered he; "but there are occasions when we are shocked by the confession, and wish it made less daringly."

"I was bold; but who can help loving him who loves my good Padrone?" said she, much more submissively.

Boccaccio. Brave girl, for that!

Dog of a Frate! They are all of a kidney; all of a kennel.

I would dilute their meal well and keep them low.   They should not waddle and wallop in every hollow lane, nor loll out their watery tongues at every wash-pool in the parish.   We shall hear, I trust, no more about Fra Biagio in the house while you are with us.   Ah! were it then for life.

Petrarca.   The man's prudence may be reasonably doubted, but it were uncharitable to question his sincerity.   Could a neighbour, a religious one in particular, be indifferent to the welfare of Boccaccio, or any belonging to him?

Boccaccio.   I do not complain of his indifference.   Indifferent! no, not he.   He might as well be, though.   My Villetta here is my castle: it was my father's; it was his father's.   Cowls did not hang to dry upon the same cord with caps in their *podere;* they shall not in mine.   The girl is an honest girl, Francesco, though I say it.   Neither she nor any other shall be befooled and bamboozled under my roof.   Methinks Holy Church might contrive some improvement upon confession.

Petrarca.   Hush! Giovanni!   But, it being a matter of discipline, who knows but she might.

Boccaccio.   Discipline! ay, ay, ay! faith and troth there are some who want it.

Petrarca.   You really terrify me.   These are sad surmises.

Boccaccio.   Sad enough: but I am keeper of my hand-maiden's probity.

Petrarca.   It could not be kept safer.

Boccaccio.   I wonder what the Frate would be putting into her head?

Petrarca.   Nothing, nothing: be assured.

Boccaccio.   Why did he ask her all those questions?

Petrarca.   Confessors do occasionally take circuitous ways to arrive at the secrets of the human heart.

Boccaccio.   And sometimes they drive at it, methinks, a whit too directly.   He had no business to make remarks about me.

Petrarca.   Anxiety.

Boccaccio.   'Fore God, Francesco, he shall have more of that; for I will shut him out the moment I am again up and stirring, though he stand but a nose's length off.   I have no fear about the girl; no suspicion of her.   He might whistle to the moon on a frosty night, and expect as reasonably her descending.   Never was a man so entirely at his ease as I am about that; never, never. She is adamant; a bright sword now first unscabbarded; no breath can hang about it. A seal of beryl, of chrysolite, of ruby; to make impressions (all in good time and proper place though) and receive none: incapable, just as they are, of splitting, or cracking, or flawing, or harbouring dirt. Let him mind that. Such, I assure you, is that poor little wench, Assuntina.

Petrarca. I am convinced that so well-behaved a young creature as Assunta——

Boccaccio. Right! Assunta is her name by baptism; we usually call her Assuntina, because she is slender, and scarcely yet full-grown, perhaps: but who can tell?

As for those friars, I never was a friend to impudence: I hate loose suggestions. In girls' minds you will find little dust but what is carried there by gusts from without. They seldom want sweeping; when they do, the broom should be taken from behind the house-door, and the master should be the sacristan.

. . . Scarcely were these words uttered when Assunta was heard running up the stairs; and the next moment she rapped. Being ordered to come in, she entered with a willow twig in her hand, from the middle of which willow twig (for she held the two ends together) hung a fish, shining with green and gold.

" What hast there, young maiden? " said Ser Francesco.

" A fish, Riverenza! " answered she. " In Tuscany we call it *tinca.*"

Petrarca. I too am a little of a Tuscan.

Assunta. Indeed! well, you really speak very like one, but only more sweetly and slowly. I wonder how you can keep up with Signor Padrone—he talks fast when he is in health; and you have made him so. Why did not you come before? Your Reverence has surely been at Certaldo in time past.

Petrarca. Yes, before thou wert born.

Assunta. Ah sir! it must have been long ago then.

Petrarca. Thou hast just entered upon life.

Assunta. I am no child.

Petrarca. What then art thou?

Assunta. I know not: I have lost both father and mother; there is a name for such as I am.

Petrarca. And a place in heaven.

Boccaccio.   Who brought us that fish, Assunta? hast paid for it? there must be seven pounds: I never saw the like.

Assunta.   I could hardly lift up my apron to my eyes with it in my hand. Luca, who brought it all the way from the Padule, could scarcely be entreated to eat a morsel of bread or sit down.

Boccaccio.   Give him a flask or two of our wine; he will like it better than the sour puddle of the plain.

Assunta.   He is gone back.

Boccaccio.   Gone! who is he, pray?

Assunta.   Luca, to be sure.

Boccaccio.   What Luca!

Assunta.   Dominedio! O Riverenza! how sadly must Ser Giovanni, my poor padrone, have lost his memory in this cruel long illness! he can not recollect young Luca of the Bientola, who married Maria.

Boccaccio.   I never heard of either, to the best of my knowledge.

Assunta.   Be pleased to mention this in your prayers to-night, Ser Canonico! May Our Lady soon give him back his memory! and everything else she has been pleased (only in play, I hope) to take away from him! Ser Francesco, you must have heard all over the world how Maria Gargarelli, who lived in the service of our paroco, somehow was outwitted by Satanasso. Monsignore thought the paroco had not done all he might have done against his wiles and craftiness, and sent his Reverence over to the monastery in the mountains, Laverna yonder, to make him look sharp; and there he is yet.

And now does Signor Padrone recollect?

Boccaccio.   Rather more distinctly.

Assunta.   Ah me! Rather more distinctly! have patience, Signor Padrone! I am too venturous, God help me! But, Riverenza, when Maria was the scorn or the abhorrence of everybody else, excepting poor Luca Sabbatini, who had always cherished her, and excepting Signor Padrone, who had never seen her in his lifetime . . . for paroco Snello said he desired no visits from any who took liberties with Holy Church . . . as if Padrone did! Luca one day came to me out of breath, with money in his hand for our duck. Now it so happened that the duck, stuffed with noble chestnuts, was going to table at that instant. I told Signor Padrone.

Boccaccio.   Assunta, I never heard thee repeat so long and tiresome a story before, nor put thyself out of breath so.   Come, we have had enough of it.

Petrarca.   She is mortified : pray let her proceed.

Boccaccio.   As you will.

Assunta.   I told Signor Padrone how Luca was lamenting that Maria was seized with an *imagination.*

Petrarca.   No wonder then she fell into misfortune, and her neighbours and friends avoided her.

Assunta.   Riverenza ! how can you smile ? Signor Padrone ! and you too ? You shook your head and sighed at it when it happened.   The Demonio, who had caused all the first mischief, was not contented until he had given her the *imagination.*

Petrarca.   He could not have finished his work more effectually.

Assunta.   He was balked, however.   Luca said,

" She shall not die under her wrongs, please God ! "

I repeated the words to Signor Padrone . . . He seems to listen, Riverenza ! and will remember presently . . . and Signor Padrone cut away one leg for himself, clean forgetting all the chestnuts inside, and said sharply, " Give the bird to Luca ; and, hark ye, bring back the minestra."

Maria loved Luca with all her heart, and Luca loved Maria with all his : but they both hated paroco Snello for such neglect about the evil one.   And even Monsignore, who sent for Luca on purpose, had some difficulty in persuading him to forbear from choler and discourse.   For Luca, who never swears, swore bitterly that the devil should play no such tricks again, nor alight on girls napping in the parsonage.   Monsignore thought he intended to take violent possession, and to keep watch there himself without consent of the incumbent.   " I will have no scandal," said Monsignore ; so there was none.   Maria, though she did indeed, as I told your Reverence, love her Luca dearly, yet she long refused to marry him, and cried very much at last on the wedding-day, and said, as she entered the porch,

" Luca ! it is not yet too late to leave me."

He would have kissed her, but her face was upon his shoulder.

Pievano Locatelli married them, and gave them his blessing : and going down from the altar, he said before the people, as he stood on the last step, " Be comforted, child! be comforted! God above knows that thy husband is honest, and that thou art innocent." Pievano's voice trembled, for he was an aged and holy man, and had walked two miles on the occasion. Pulcheria, his governante, eighty years old, carried an apronful of lilies to bestrew the altar ; and partly from the lilies, and partly from the blessed angels who (although invisible) were present, the church was filled with fragrance. Many who heretofore had been frightened at hearing the mention of Maria's name, ventured now to walk up toward her ; and some gave her needles, and some offered skeins of thread, and some ran home again for pots of honey.

Boccaccio. And why didst not thou take her some trifle?

Assunta. I had none.

Boccaccio. Surely there are always such about the premises.

Assunta. Not mine to give away.

Boccaccio. So then at thy hands, Assunta, she went off not overladen. Ne'er a bone-bodkin out of thy bravery, ay?

Assunta. I ran out knitting, with the woodbine and syringa in the basket for the parlour. I made the basket, . . I and . . . but myself chiefly, for boys are loiterers.

Boccaccio. Well, well: why not bestow the basket, together with its rich contents?

Assunta. I am ashamed to say it . . . I covered my half-stocking with them as quickly as I could, and ran after her, and presented it. Not knowing what was under the flowers, and never minding the liberty I had taken, being a stranger to her, she accepted it as graciously as possible, and bade me be happy.

Petrarca. I hope you have always kept her command.

Assunta. Nobody is ever unhappy here, except Fra Biagio, who frets sometimes : but that may be the walk ; or he may fancy Ser Giovanni to be worse than he really is.

. . . Having now performed her mission and concluded her narrative, she bowed, and said,

" Excuse me, Riverenza! excuse me, Signor Padrone! my arm aches with this great fish."

Then, bowing again, and moving her eyes modestly toward each, she added, " with permission ! " and left the chamber.

"About the Sposina," after a pause began Ser Francesco : "about the Sposina, I do not see the matter clearly."

"You have studied too much for seeing all things clearly," answered Ser Giovanni ; "you see only the greatest. In fine, the devil, on this count, is acquitted by acclamation ; and the paroco Snello eats lettuce and chicory up yonder at Laverna. He has mendicant friars for his society every day ; and snails, as pure as water can wash and boil them, for his repast on festivals. Under this discipline, if they keep it up, surely one devil out of legion will depart from him."

FOURTH DAY'S INTERVIEW.

Petrarca.   Do not throw aside your *Paradiso* for me.   Have you been reading it again so early ?

Boccaccio.   Looking into it here and there.   I had spare time before me.

Petrarca.   You have coasted the whole poem, and your boat's bottom now touches ground.   But tell me what you think of Beatrice.

Boccaccio.   I think her in general more of the seraphic doctor than of the seraph.   It is well she retained her beauty where she was, or she would scarcely be tolerable now and then.   And yet, in other parts, we forget the captiousness in which Theology takes delight, and feel our bosoms refreshed by the perfect presence of the youthful and innocent Bice.

There is something so sweetly sanctifying in pure love.

Petrarca.

> Pure love ? there is no other ; nor shall be,
> Till the worst angels hurl the better down
> And heaven lie under hell : if God is one
> And pure, so surely love is pure and one.

Boccaccio.   You understand it better than I do : you must have your own way.

Above all, I have been admiring the melody of the cadence in this portion of the *Divina Commedia.*   Some of the stanzas leave us nothing to desire in facility and elegance.

Alighieri grows harmonious as he grows humane, and does not, like Orpheus, play the better with the beasts about him.

Petrarca.   It is in Paradise that we might expect his tones to be tried and modulated.

Boccaccio.   None of the imitative arts should repose on writhings and distortions.   Tragedy herself, unless she lead from Terror to Pity, has lost her way.

Petrarca.   What then must be thought of a long and crowded work, whence Pity is violently excluded, and where Hatred is the first personage we meet, and almost the last we part from ?

Boccaccio.   Happily the poet has given us here a few breeezes of the morning, a few glimpses of the stars, a few similes of objects to which we have been accustomed among the amusements or occupations of the country.   Some of them would be less admired in a meaner author, and are welcome here chiefly as a variety and relief to the mind, after a long continuance in a painful posture.   Have you not frequently been pleased with a short quotation of verses in themselves but indifferent, from finding them in some tedious dissertation? and especially if they carry you forth a little into the open air.

Petrarca.   I am not quite certain whether, if the verses were indifferent, I should willingly exchange the prose for them ; bad prose being less wearisome than bad poetry : so much less indeed, that the advantage of the exchange might fail to balance the account.

Boccaccio.   Let me try whether I can not give you an example of such effect, having already given you the tedious dissertation.

Petrarca.   Do your worst.

Boccaccio.   Not that neither, but bad enough.

THE PILGRIM'S SHELL.

Under a tuft of eglantine, at noon.
I saw a pilgrim loosen his broad shell
To catch the water off a stony tongue ;
Medusa's it might be, or Pan's, erewhile,
For the huge head was shapeless, eaten out
By time and tempest here, and here embost
With clasping tangles of dark maidenhair.
   " How happy is thy thirst ! how soon assuaged !

How sweet that coldest water this hot day!"
Whispered my thoughts; not having yet observ'd
His shell so shallow and so chipt around.
Tall though he was, he held it higher, to meet
The sparkler at its outset: with fresh leap,
Vigorous as one just free upon the world,
Impetuous too as one first checkt, with stamp
Heavy as ten such sparklers might be deemed,
Rusht it amain, from cavity and rim
And rim's divergent channels, and dropt thick
(Issuing at wrist and elbow) on the grass.
The pilgrim shook his head, and fixing up
His scallop,
     "There is something yet," said he,
"Too scanty in this world for my desires!"

Petrarca. O Giovanni! these are better thoughts and opportuner than such lonely places formerly supplied us with. The whispers of rose-bushes were not always so innocent: under the budding and under the full-blown we sometimes found other images: sometimes the pure fountain failed in bringing purity to the heart.

    Unholy fire sprang up in fields and woods;
    The air that fann'd it came from solitudes.

If our desires are worthy ones and accomplished, we rejoice in after-time; if unworthy and unsuccessful, we rejoice no less at their discomfiture and miscarriage. We can not have all we wish for. Nothing is said oftener, nothing earlier, nothing later. It begins in the arms with the chidings of the nurse; it will terminate with the milder voice of the physician at the death-bed. But although everybody has heard and most have said it, yet nobody seems to have said or considered, that it is much, very much, to be able to form and project our wishes; that, in the voyage we take to compass and turn them to account, we breathe freely and hopefully; and that it is chiefly in the stagnation of port we are in danger of disappointment and disease.

Boccaccio. The young man who resolves to conquer his love, is only half in earnest or has already half conquered it. But fields and woods have no dangers now for us. I may be alone until doomsday, and loose thoughts will be at fault if they try to scent me.

Petrara. When the rest of our smiles have left us, we may smile at our immunities. There are indeed, for nearly all,

> Rocks on the shore wherefrom we launch on life,
> Before our final harbour rocks again,
> And (narrow sun-paced plains sailed swiftly by)
> Eddies and breakers all the space between.

Yet Nature preserves her sedater charms for us both, and I doubt whether we do not enjoy them the more, by exemption from solicitations and distractions. We are not old while we can hear and enjoy, as much as ever,

> The lonely bird, the bird of even-song,
> When, catching one far call, he leaps elate,
> In his full fondness drowns it, and again
> The shrill shrill glee through Serravalle rings.

Boccaccio. The nightingale is a lively bird to the young and joyous, a melancholy one to the declining and pensive. He has notes for every ear; he has feelings for every bosom; and he exercises over gentle souls a wider and more welcome dominion than any other creature. If I must not offer you my thanks, for bringing to me such associations as the bed-side of sickness is rarely in readiness to supply; if I must not declare to you how pleasant and well placed are your reflections on our condition; I may venture to remark on the nightingale, that our Italy is the only country where this bird is killed for the market. In no other is the race of Avarice and Gluttony so hard run. What a triumph for a Florentine, to hold under his fork the most delightful being in all animated nature! the being to which every poet, or nearly every one, dedicates the first fruits of his labours. A cannibal who devours his enemy, through intolerable hunger, or, what he holds as the measure of justice and of righteousness, revenge, may be viewed with less abhorrence than the heartless gormandiser, who casts upon his loaded stomach the little breast that has poured delight on thousands.

Petrarca. The English, I remember Ser Geoffreddo * telling us, never kill singing-birds nor swallows.

Boccaccio. Music and hospitality are sweet and sacred things

* Chaucer.

with them, and well may they value their few warm days, out of which, if the produce is not wine and oil, they gather song and garner sensibility.

Petrarca.   Ser Geoffreddo felt more pleasure in the generosity and humanity of his countrymen, than in the victories they had recently won, with incredibly smaller numbers, over their boastful enemy.

Boccaccio.   I know not of what nation I could name so amusing a companion as Ser Geoffreddo.   The Englishman is rather an island than an islander; bluff, stormy, rude, abrupt, repulsive, inaccessible.   We must not however hold back or dissemble the learning, and wisdom, and courtesy, of the better.   While France was without one single man above a dwarf in literature, and we in Italy had only a small sprinkling of it, Richard de Bury was sent ambassador to Rome by King Edward.   So great was his learning, that he composed two grammars, one Greek, one Hebrew; neither of which labours had been attempted by the most industrious and erudite of those who spoke the languages: he likewise formed so complete a library as belongs only to the Byzantine emperors. This prelate came into Italy attended by Ser Geoffreddo, in whose company we spent, as you remember, two charming evenings at Arezzo.

Petrarca.   What wonderful things his countrymen have been achieving in this century!

Boccaccio.   And how curious it is to trace them up into their Norwegian coves and creeks three or four centuries back!

Petrarca.   Do you think it possible that Norway, which never could maintain sixty thousand * male adults, was capable of sending, from her native population, a sufficient force of warriors to conquer the best province of France, and the whole of England? And you must deduct from these sixty thousand, the aged, the artisans, the cultivators, and the clergy, together with all the dependents of the church: which numbers, united, we may believe amounted to above one half.

Boccaccio.   That she could embody such an army from her own very scanty and scattered population; no, indeed: but if

* With the advantages of her fisheries, which did not exist in the age of Petrarca, and of her agriculture, which probably is quintupled since, Norway does not contain at present the double of the number.

you recollect that a vast quantity of British had been ejected by incursions of Picts, and that also there had been on the borders a general insurrection against the Romans, and against those of half-blood (which is always the case in a rebellion of the Aboriginals), and if you believe, as I do, that the ejected Romans of the coast at least, became pirates, and were useful to the Scandinavians, by introducing what was needful of their arts and saleable of their plunder, taking in exchange their iron and timber, you may readily admit as a probability, that by the display of spoils and the spirit of enterprise, they encouraged, headed, and carried into effect the invasion of France, and subsequently of England.   The English gentlemen of Norman descent have neither blue eyes, in general, nor fair complexions, differing in physiognomy altogether both from the Belgic race and the Norwegian.   Beside, they are remarkable for a sedate and somewhat repulsive pride, very different from the effervescent froth of the one, and the sturdy simplicity of the other.   Sir Geoffreddo is not only the greatest genius, but likewise the most amiable of his nation.   He gave his thoughts and took yours with equal freedom.   His countrymen, if they give you any, throw them at your head; and, if they receive any, cast them under their feet before you.   Courtesy is neither a quality of native growth, nor communicable to them.   Their rivals, the French, are the best imitators in the world; the English the worst; particularly under the instruction of the Graces.   They have many virtues, no doubt; but they reserve them for the benefit of their families, or of their enemies; and they seldom take the trouble to unpack them in their short intercourse abroad.

Petrarca.   Ser Geoffreddo, I well remember, was no less remarkable for courtesy than for cordiality.

Boccaccio.   He was really as attentive and polite toward us as if he had made us prisoners.   It is on that occasion the English are most unlike their antagonists and themselves.   What an evil must they think it to be vanquished! when, struggling with their bashfulness and taciturnity, they become so solicitous and inventive in raising the spirits of the fallen.   The Frenchman is ready to truss you on his rapier, unless you acknowledge the perfection of his humanity, and to spit in your face, if you doubt for a moment the delicacy of his politeness.   The Englishman is almost angry if you mention either of these as belonging to him, and turns away from you that he may not hear it.

Petrarca. Let us felicitate ourselves that we rarely are forced to witness his self-affliction.

Boccaccio. In palaces, and especially the pontifical, it is likely you saw the very worst of them: indeed there are few in ·any country of such easy, graceful, unaffected manners as our Italians. We are warmer at the extremities than at the heart: sunless nations have central fires. The Englishman is more gratified when you enable him to show you a fresh kindness, than when you remind him of a past one; and he forgets what he has conferred as readily as we forget what we have received. In our civility, in our good-nature, in our temperance, in our frugality, none excel us; and greatly are we in advance of other men, in the arts, in the sciences, in the culture, in the application, and in the power of intellect. Our faculties are perfect, with the sole exception of memory; and our memory is only deficient in its retentiveness of obligation.

Petrarca. Better had it failed in almost all its other functions. Yet, if our countrymen presented any flagrant instances of ingratitude, Alighieri would have set apart a *bolga* for their reception.

Boccaccio. When I correct and republish my *Commentary*, I must be as careful to gratify, as my author was to affront them. I know, from the nature of the Florentines and of the Italians in general, that in calling on me to produce one, they would rather I should praise indiscriminately than parsimoniously. And respect is due to them for repairing, by all the means in their power, the injustice their fathers committed; for enduring in humility his resentment; and for investing him with public honours, as they would some deity who had smitten them. Respect is due to them, and I will offer it, for placing their greatness on so firm a plinth, for deriving their pride from so wholesome a source, and for declaring to the world that the founder of a city is less than her poet and instructor.

Petrarca. In the precincts of those lofty monuments, those towers and temples, which have sprung up amid her factions, the name of Dante is heard at last, and heard with such reverence as only the angels or the saints inspire.

Boccaccio. There are towns so barbarous, that they must be

informed by strangers of their own great man, when they happen
to have produced one ; and would then detract from its merits,
that they might not exhibit their awkwardness in doing him
honour, or their shame in withholding it.   There are such ; but
not in Italy.   I have seen youths standing and looking with
seriousness, and indeed with somewhat of veneration, on the broad
and low stone bench, to the south of the Cathedral, where Dante
sat to enjoy the fresh air in summer evenings ; and where Giotto,
in conversation with him, watched the scaffolding rise higher and
higher up his gracefullest of towers.   It was truly a bold action,
when a youngster pushed another down on the poet's seat.   The
surprised one blushed and struggled, as those do who unwittingly
have been drawn into a penalty (not lightened by laughter) for
having sitten in the imperial or the papal chair.

Petrarca.   These are good signs, and never fallacious.   In the
presence of such young persons we ought to be very cautious how
we censure a man of genius.   One expression of irreverence may
eradicate what demands the most attentive culture, may wither the
first love for the fair and noble, and may shake the confidence of
those who are about to give the hand to a guidance less liable to
error.   We have ever been grateful to the Deity, for saving us
from among the millions swept away by the pestilence, which
depopulated the cities of Italy, and ravaged the whole of Europe :
let us be equally grateful for an exemption as providental and as
rare in the world of letters ; an exemption from that *Plica Polonica*
of invidiousness, which infests the squalider of poetical heads, and
has not always spared those which ought to have been cleanlier.

Boccaccio.   Critics are indignant if we are silent, and petulant
if we complain.   You and I are so kindly and considerate in
regard to them, that we rather pat their petulance than prick up
their indignation.   Marsyas, while Apollo was flaying him
leisurely and dexterously, with all the calmness of a god, shortened
his upper lip prodigiously, and showed how royal teeth are fastened
in their gums : his eyes grew bloodshot, and expanded to the size
of rock-melons, though naturally, in length and breadth, as well as
colour, they more resembled a well-ripened bean-pod.   And there
issued from his smoking breast, and shook the leaves above it, a
rapid irregular rush of yells and howlings.   Remarking so material
a change in his countenance and manners, a satyr, who was much

his friend and deeply interested in his punishment, said calmly,
"Marsyas! Marsyas! is it thou who cries out so unworthily?
If thou couldst only look down from that pleasant, smooth, shady
beech-tree, thou wouldst have the satisfaction of seeing that thy
skin is more than half drawn off thee: it is hardly worth while to
make a bustle about it now."

Petrarca. Every Marsyas hath his consoling satyr. Probably
when yours was flayed, he was found out to be a good musician,
by those who recommended the flaying and celebrated the flayer.
Among authors, none hath so many friends as he who is just now
dead, and had the most enemies last week. Those who were
then his adversaries are now sincerely his admirers, for moving
out of the way, and leaving one name less in the lottery. And
yet, poor souls! the prize will never fall to them. There is
something sweet and generous in the tone of praise, which
captivates an ingenuous mind, whatever may be the subject of it;
while propensity to censure not only excites suspicion of malevolence, but reminds the hearer of what he can not disentangle
from his earliest ideas of vulgarity. There being no pleasure in
thinking ill, it is wonderful there should be any in speaking ill.
You, my friends, can find none of it: but every step you are
about to take in the revisal of your Lectures, will require much
caution. Aware you must be that there are many more defects
in our author than we have touched or glanced at: principally
the loose and shallow foundation of so vast a structure; its un-
connectedness; its want of manners, of passion, of action, consistently and uninterruptedly at work toward a distinct and worthy
purpose; and lastly (although less importantly as regards the
poetical character) that splenetic temper, which seems to grudge
brightness to the flames of hell, to delight in deepening its gloom,
in multiplying its miseries, in accumulating weight upon depression,
and building labyrinths about perplexity.

Boccaccio. Yet, O Francesco! when I remember what Dante
had suffered and was suffering from the malice and obduracy of
his enemies; when I feel (and how I do feel it!) that you also
have been following up his glory through the same paths of exile;
I can rest only on what is great in him, and the exposure of
a fault appears to me almost an inhumanity.

The first time I ever walked to his villa on the Mugnone, I

felt a vehement desire to enter it; and yet a certain awe came upon me, as about to take an unceremonious and an unlawful advantage of his absence. While I was hesitating, its inhabitant opened the gate, saluted, and invited me. My desire vanished at once; and although the civility far exceeded what a stranger as I was, and so young a stranger too, could expect, or what probably the more illustrious owner would have vouchsafed, the place itself and the disparity of its occupier made me shrink from it in sadness, and stand before him almost silent. I believe I should do the same at the present day.

Petrarca. With such feelings, which are ours in common, there is little danger that we should be unjust toward him; and, if ever our opinions come before the public, we may disregard the petulance and aspersions of those whom nature never constituted our judges, as she did us of Dante. It is our duty to speak with freedom; it is theirs to listen with respect.

Boccaccio. History would come much into the criticism, and would perform the most interesting part in it. But I clearly see how unsafe it is to meddle with the affairs of families: and every family in Florence is a portion of the government, or has been lately. Every one preserves the annals of the republic; the facts being nearly the same, the inferences widely diverging, the motives utterly dissimilar. A strict examination of Dante would involve the bravest and most intelligent; and the court of Rome, with its royal agents, would persecute them as conspirators against religion, against morals, against the peace, the order, the existence of society. When studious and quiet men get into power, they fancy they can not show too much activity, and very soon prove, by exerting it, that they can show too little discretion. The military, the knightly, the baronial, are spurred on to join in the chase; but the fleshers have other names and other instincts.

Petrarca. Posterity will regret that many of those allusions to persons and events, which we now possess in the pages of Dante, have not reached her. Among the ancients there are few poets who more abound in them than Horace does, and yet we feel certain that there are many which are lost to us.

Boccaccio. I wonder you did not mention him before. Perhaps he is no favourite with you.

Petrarca. Why can not we be delighted with an author, and

even feel a predilection for him, without a dislike to others? An admiration of Catullus or Virgil, of Tibullus or Ovid, is never to be heightened by a discharge of bile on Horace.

Boccaccio. The eyes of critics, whether in commending or carping, are both on one side, like a turbot's.

Petrarca. There are some men who delight in heating themselves with wine, and others with headstrong frowardness. These are resolved to agitate the puddle of their blood by running into parties, literary or political, and espouse a champion's cause with such ardour that they run against everything in their way. Perhaps they never knew or saw the person, or understood his merits: what matter? No sooner was I about to be crowned, than it was predicted by these astrologers, that Protonotary Nerucci and Cavallerizzo Vuotasacchetti (two lampooners, whose hands had latterly been kept from their occupation by drawing gold-embroidered gloves on them) would be rife in the mouths of men after my name had fallen into oblivion.

Boccaccio. I never heard of them before.

Petrarca. So much the better for them, and none the worse for you. Vuotasacchetti had been convicted of filching in his youth; and Nerucci was so expert a logician, and so rigidly economical a moralist, that he never had occasion for veracity.

Boccaccio. The upholders of such gentry are like little girls with their dolls: they must clothe them, although they strip every other doll in the nursery. It is reported that our Giotto, a great mechanician as well as architect and painter, invented a certain instrument by which he could contract the dimensions of any head laid before him. But these gentlemen, it appears, have improved upon it, and not only can contract one, but enlarge another.

Petrarca. He could perform his undertaking with admirable correctness and precision; can they theirs?

Boccaccio. I never heard they could: but well enough for their customers and their consciences.

Petrarca. I see then no great accuracy is required.

Boccaccio. If they heard you they would think you very dull.

Petrarca. They have always thought me so: and, if they change their opinion, I shall begin to think so myself.

Boccaccio. They have placed themselves just where, if we

were mischievous, we might desire to see them. We have no
power to make them false and malicious, yet they become so the
moment they see or hear of us, and thus sink lower than our force
could ever thrust them.   Pigs, it is said, driven into a pool beyond
their depth, cut their throats by awkward attempts at swimming.
We could hardly wish them worse luck, although each had a
devil in him.   Come, let us away ; we shall find a purer stream
and pleasanter company on the Sabine farm.

Petrarca.   We may indeed think the first ode of little value,
the second of none, until we come to the sixth stanza.

Boccaccio.   Bad as are the first and second, they are better
than that wretched one, sounded so lugubriously in our ears at
school, as the masterpiece of the pathetic ; I mean the ode
addressed to Virgil on the death of Quinctilius Varus.

Præcipe lugubres
Cantus, Melpomene, cui liquidam pater
Vocem cum citharâ dedit.

Did he want anyone to help him to cry ?   What man immersed
in grief cares a quattrino about Melpomene, or her father's fairing
of an artificial cuckoo and a gilt guitar ?   What man, on such an
occasion, is at leisure to amuse himself with the little plaster
images of Pudor and Fides, of Justitia and Veritas, or disposed
to make a comparison of Virgil and Orpheus ?   But if Horace
had written a thousand-fold as much trash, we are never to forget
that he also wrote

Cœlo tonantem, etc.,

in competition with which ode, the finest in the Greek language
itself has, to my ear, too many low notes, and somewhat of a
wooden sound.   And give me *Vixi puellis,* and give me *Quis
multa gracilis,* and as many more as you please ; for there are
charms in nearly all of them.   It now occurs to me that what is
written, or interpolated,

Acer et *Mauri* peditis cruentum
Vultus in hostem,

should be *manci ;* a foot soldier *mutilated,* but looking with
indignant courage at the trooper who inflicted the wound.
The Mauritanians were celebrated only for their cavalry.

In return for my suggestion, pray tell me what is the meaning of

Obliquo laborat
Lympha fugax trepidare rivo.

Petrarca. The moment I learn it you shall have it. *Laborat trepidare ! lympha rivo ! fugax* too ! *Fugacity* is not the action for hard work, or *labour.*

Boccaccio. Since you can not help me out, I must give up the conjecture, it seems, while it has cost me only half a century. Perhaps it may be *curiosa felicitas.*

Petrarca. There again ! Was there ever such an unhappy (not to say absurd) expression ! And this from the man who wrote the most beautiful sentence in all latinity.

Boccaccio. What is that ?

Petrarca. I am ashamed of repeating it, although in itself it is innocent. The words are :

Gratias ago languori tuo, quo diutius sub
umbrâ voluptatis lusimus.

Boccaccio. Tear out this from the volume ; the rest, both prose and poetry, may be thrown away. In the *Dinner of Nasidienus,* I remember the expression *nosse laboro ; I am anxious to know :* this expedites the solution but little. In the same piece there is another odd expression :

Tum in lecto quôque *videres*
Stridere secretâ divisos aure *susurros.*

Petrarca. I doubt Horace's felicity in the choice of words, being quite unable to discover it, and finding more evidences of the contrary than in any contemporary or preceding poet ; but I do not doubt his infelicity in his *transpositions* of them, in which certainly he is more remarkable than whatsoever writer of antiquity. How simple, in comparison, are Catullus *
and Lucretius in the structure of their sentences ! but the most simple and natural of all are Ovid and Tibullus. Your main difficulty lies in another road : it consists not in making explanations, but in avoiding them. Some scholars will assert

* Except "Non ita me divi vera gemunt juêrint." [Note added in second ed.]

that everything I have written in my sonnets is allegory or allusion; others will deny that anything is; and similarly of Dante. It was known throughout Italy that he was the lover of *Beatrice* Porticari. He has celebrated her in many compositions; in prose and poetry, in Latin and Italian. Hence it became the safer for him afterward to introduce her as an allegorical personage, in opposition to the *Meretrice;* under which appellation he (and I subsequently) signified the Papacy. Our great poet wandered among the marvels of the Apocalypse, and fixed his eyes the most attentively on the words,

> Veni, et ostendam tibi sponsam, uxorem Agni.

He, as you know, wrote a commentary on his *Commedia* at the close of his Treatise *de Monarchiâ.* But he chiefly aims at showing the duties of pope and emperor, and explaining such parts of the poem as manifestly relate to them. The Patarini accused the pope of despoiling and defiling the church; the Ghibellines accused him of defrauding and rebelling against the emperor; Dante enlists both under his flaming banner, and exhibits the *Meretrice* stealing from *Beatrice* both the *divine* and the *august* chariot; the church and empire. Grave critics will protest their inability to follow you through such darkness, saying you are not worth the trouble, and they must give you up. If Laura and Fiametta were allegorical, they could inspire no tenderness in our readers, and little interest. But, alas! these are no longer the days to dwell on them.

> Let human art exert her utmost force,
> Pleasure can rise no higher than its source;
> And there it ever stagnates where the ground
> Beneath it, O Giovanni! is unsound.

Boccaccio. You have given me a noble quaternion; for which I can only offer you such a string of beads as I am used to carry about with me. Memory, they say, is the mother of the Muses: this is her gift, not theirs.

DEPARTURE FROM FIAMETTA.

> When go I must, as well she knew,
> And neither yet could say adieu,
> Sudden was my Fiametta's fear
> To let me see or feel a tear.

It could but melt my heart away,
Nor add one moment to my stay.
But it was ripe and would be shed . . .
So from her cheek upon my head
It, falling on the neck behind,
Hung on the hair she oft had twined.
Thus thought she, and her arm's soft strain
Claspt it, and down it fell again.

Come, come, bear your disappointment, and forgive my cheating you in the exchange! Ah Francesco! Francesco! well may you sigh; and I too; seeing we can do little now but make verses and doze, and want little but medicine and masses, while Fra Biagio is merry as a lark, and half master of the house. Do not look so grave upon me for remembering so well another state of existence. He who forgets his love may still more easily forget his friendships. I am weak, I confess it, in yielding my thoughts to what returns no more; but you alone know my weakness.

Petrarca. We have loved; * and so fondly as we believe none other ever did; and yet, although it was in youth, Giovanni, it was not in the earliest white dawn, when we almost shrink from its freshness, when everything is pure and quiet, when little of earth is seen, and much of heaven. It was not so with us; it was with Dante. The little virgin Beatrice Porticari breathed all her purity into his boyish heart, and inhaled it back again; and if war and disaster, anger and disdain, seized upon it in her absence, they never could divert its course nor impede its destination. Happy the man who carries love with him in his opening day! he never loses its freshness in the meridian of life, nor its happier influence in the later hour. If Dante enthroned his Beatrice in the highest heaven, it was Beatrice who conducted him hither. Love, preceding passion, ensures, sanctifies, and I would say survives it, were it not rather an absorption and transfiguration into its own most perfect purity and holiness.

* The tender and virtuous Shenstone, in writing the most beautiful of epitaphs, was unaware how near he stood to Petrarca. Heu quanto minus est cum aliis versari quàm tui meminisse,

Pur mi consola che morir per lei
Meglio è che gioir d'altra.

[Note added in second ed.]

Boccaccio. Up! up! look into that chest of letters, out of which I took several of yours to run over yesterday morning. All those of a friend whom we have lost, to say nothing of a tenderer affection, touch us sensibly, be the subject what it may. When, in taking them out to read again, we happen to come upon him in some pleasant mood, it is then the dead man's hand is at the heart. Opening the same paper long afterward, can we wonder if a tear has raised its little island in it? Leave me the memory of all my friends, even of the ungrateful! They must remind me of some kind feeling; and perhaps of theirs; and for that very reason they deserve another. It was not my fault if they turned out less worthy than I hoped and fancied them. Yet half the world complains of ingratitude, and the remaining half of envy. Of the one I have already told you my opinion, and heard yours; and the other we may surely bear with quite as much equanimity. For rarely are we envied, until we are so prosperous that envy is rather a familiar in our train than an enemy who waylays us. If we saw nothing of such followers and out-riders, and no scabbard with our initials upon it, we might begin to doubt our station.

Petrarca. Giovanni, you are unsuspicious, and would scarcely see a monster in a minotaur. It is well, however, to draw good out of evil, and it is the peculiar gift of an elevated mind. Nevertheless, you must have observed, although with greater curiosity than concern, the slipperiness and tortuousness of your detractors.

Boccaccio. Whatever they detract from me, they leave more than they can carry away. Beside, they always are detected.

Petrarca. When they are detected, they raise themselves up fiercely, as if their nature were erect and they could reach your height.

Boccaccio. Envy would conceal herself under the shadow and shelter of contemptuousness, but she swells too huge for the den she creeps into. Let her lie there and crack, and think no more about her. The people you have been talking of can find no greater and no other faults in my writings than I myself am willing to show them, and still more willing to correct. There are many things, as you have just now told me, very unworthy of their company.

Petrarca. He who has much gold is none the poorer for having much silver too. When a king of old displayed his wealth and magnificence before a philosopher, the philosopher's exclamation was :

" How many things are here which I do not want ! "

Does not the same reflection come upon us, when we have laid aside our compositions for a time, and look into them again more leisurely ? Do we not wonder at our own profusion, and say like the philosopher,

" How many things are here which I do not want ! "

It may happen that we pull up flowers with weeds ; but better this than rankness. We must bear to see our first-born despatched before our eyes, and give them up quietly.

Boccaccio. The younger will be the most reluctant. There are poets among us who mistake in themselves the freckles of the hay-fever for beauty-spots. In another half century their volumes will be enquired after ; but only for the sake of cutting out an illuminated letter from the title-page, or of transplanting the willow at the end, that hangs so prettily over the tomb of Amaryllis. If they wish to be healthy and vigorous, let them open their bosoms to the breezes of Sunium ; for the air of Latium is heavy and overcharged. Above all, they must remember two admonitions ; first, that sweet things hurt diges- tion ; secondly, that great sails are ill adapted to small vessels. What is there lovely in poetry unless there be moderation and composure ? Are they not better than the hot, uncontrollable harlotry of a flaunting, dishevelled enthusiasm ? Whoever has the power of creating, has likewise the inferior power of keeping his creation in order. The best poets are the most impressive, because their steps are regular ; for without regularity there is neither strength nor state. Look at Sophocles, look at Æschylus, look at Homer.

Petrarca. I agree with you entirely to the whole extent of your observations ; and, if you will continue, I am ready to lay aside my Dante for the present.

Boccaccio. No, no ; we must have him again between us : there is no danger that he will sour our tempers.

Petrarca. In comparing his and yours, since you forbid me to declare all I think of your genius, you will at least allow me to congratulate you as being the happier of the two.

Boccaccio.   Frequently, where there is great power in poetry, the imagination makes encroachments on the heart, and uses it as her own.   I have shed tears on writings which never cost the writer a sigh, but which occasioned him to rub the palms of his hands together, until they were ready to strike fire, with satisfaction at having overcome the difficulty of being tender.

Petrarca.   Giovanni! are you not grown satirical?

Boccaccio.   Not in this.   It is a truth as broad and glaring as the eye of the Cyclops.   To make you amends for your shuddering, I will express my doubt, on the other hand, whether Dante felt all the indignation he threw into his poetry.   We are immoderately fond of warming ourselves; and we do not think, or care, what the fire is composed of.   Be sure it is not always of cedar, like Circe's.*   Our Alighieri had slipt into the habit of vituperation; and he thought it fitted him; so he never left it off.

Petrarca.   Serener colours are pleasanter to our eyes and more becoming to our character.   The chief desire in every man of genius is to be thought one; and no fear or apprehension lessens it.   Alighieri, who had certainly studied the gospel, must have been conscious that he not only was inhumane, but that he betrayed a more vindictive spirit than any pope or prelate who is enshrined within the fretwork of his golden grating.

Boccaccio.   Unhappily, his strong talon had grown into him, and it would have pained him to suffer amputation.   This eagle, unlike Jupiter's, never loosened the thunderbolt from it under the influence of harmony.

Petrarca.   The only good thing we can expect in such minds and tempers, is good poetry: let us at least get that; and, having it, let us keep and value it.   If you had never written some wanton stories, you would never have been able to show the world how much wiser and better you grew afterward.

Boccaccio.   Alas! if I live, I hope to show it.   You have raised my spirits: and now, dear Francesco! do say a couple of prayers for me, while I lay together the materials of a tale; a right merry one, I promise you.   Faith! it shall amuse you, and pay decently for the prayers; a good honest litany-worth.   I

---

* Dives inaccessis ubi Solis filia lucis
Urit odoratam nocturna in lumina cedrum.   *Æn.*

hardly know whether I ought to have a nun in it : do you think
I may ?

Petrarca.   Can not you do without one ?

Boccaccio.   No ; a nun I must have : say nothing against her ;
I can more easily let the abbess alone.   Yet Frate Biagio * . . .
that Frate Biagio, who never came to visit me but when he
thought I was at extremities or asleep . . . Assuntina ! are you
there ?

Petrarca.   No ; do you want her ?

Boccaccio.   Not a bit.   That Frate Biagio has heightened my
pulse when I could not lower it again.   The very devil is that
Frate for heightening pulses.   And with him I shall now make
merry . . . God willing . . . in God's good time . . . should
it be his divine will to restore me ! which I think he has begun
to do miraculously.   I seem to be within a frog's leap of well
again ; and we will presently have some rare fun in my *Tale of
the Frate.*

Petrarca.   Do not openly name him.

Boccaccio.   He shall recognise himself by one single expression.
He said to me, when I was at the worst,
" Ser Giovanni ! it would not be much amiss (with permission !)
if you begin to think (at any spare time) just a morsel, of
eternity."

" Ah ! Fra Biagio ! " answered I, contritely, " I never heard
a sermon of yours but I thought of it seriously and uneasily, long
before the discourse was over."

* Our San Vivaldo is enriched by his deposit.   In the church, on the
fifth flagstone from before the high altar, is this inscription :

HIC SITUS EST,

BEATAM IMMORTALITATEM EXPECTANS,

D. BLASIUS DE BLASIS,

HUJUS CŒNOBII ABBAS,

SINGULARI VIR CHARITATE,

MORIBUS INTEGERRIMIS,

REI THEOLOGICÆ NEC NON PHYSICÆ

PERITISSIMUS.

ORATE PRO ANIMA EJUS.

To the word *orate* have been prefixed the letters PL, the aspiration, no
doubt, of some friendly monk ; although Monsignore thinks it susceptible
of two interpretations ; the other he reserves *in petto.*

Domenico Grigi.

"So must all," replied he, "and yet few have the grace to own it."

Now mind, Francesco! if it should please the Lord to call me unto him, I say, *The Nun and Fra Biagio* will be found, after my decease, in the closet cut out of the wall, behind yon Saint Zacharias in blue and yellow.

Well done! well done! Francesco. I never heard any man repeat his prayers so fast and fluently. Why! how many (at a guess, have you repeated? Such is the power of friendship, and such the habit of religion! They have done me good : I feel myself stronger already. To-morrow I think I shall be able, by leaning on that stout maple stick in the corner, to walk half over my podere.

Have you done? have you done?

Petrarca. Be quiet : you may talk too much.

Boccaccio. I can not be quiet for another hour ; so, if you have any more prayers to get over, stick the spur into the other side of them : they must verily speed, if they beat the last.

Petrarca. Be more serious, dear Giovanni.

Boccaccio. Never bid a convalescent be more serious : no, nor a sick man neither. To health it may give that composure which it takes away from sickness. Every man will have his hours of seriousness ; but, like the hours of rest, they often are ill chosen and unwholesome. Be assured, our heavenly Father is as well pleased to see his children in the playground as in the school-room. He has provided both for us, and has given us intimations when each should occupy us.

Petrarca. You are right, Giovanni! but we know which bell is heard the most distinctly. We fold our arms at the one, try the cooler part of the pillow, and turn again to slumber ; at the first stroke of the other, we are beyond our monitors. As for you, hardly Dante himself could make you grave.

Boccaccio. I do not remember how it happened that we slipped away from his side. One of us must have found him tedious.

Petrarca. If you were really and substantially at his side, he would have no mercy on you.

Boccaccio. In sooth, our good Alighieri seems to have had the appetite of a dogfish or shark, and to have bitten the harder the warmer he was. I would not voluntarily be under his manifold rows of dentals. He has an incisor to every saint in the calendar. I should fare, methinks, like Brutus and the Archbishop. He is forced to stretch himself, out of sheer listlessness, in so idle a place as Purgatory: he loses half his strength in Paradise: Hell alone makes him alert and lively: there he moves about and threatens as tremendously as the serpent that opposed the legions on their march in Africa. He would not have been contented in Tuscany itself, even had his enemies left him unmolested. Were I to write on his model a tripartite poem, I think it should be entitled, *Earth, Italy, and Heaven.*

Petrarca. You will never give yourself the trouble.

Boccaccio. I should not succeed.

Petrarca. Perhaps not: but you have done very much, and may be able to do very much more.

Boccaccio. Wonderful is it to me, when I consider that an infirm and helpless creature, as I am, should be capable of laying thoughts up in their cabinets of words, which Time, as he rushes by, with the revolutions of stormy and destructive years, can never move from their places. On this coarse mattress, one among the homeliest in the fair at Impruneta, is stretched an old burgess of Certaldo, of whom perhaps more will be known hereafter than we know of the Ptolemies and the Pharaohs; while popes and princes are lying as unregarded as the fleas that are shaken out of the window. Upon my life, Francesco! to think of this is enough to make a man presumptuous.

Petrarca. No, Giovanni! not when the man thinks justly of it, as such a man ought to do, and must. For, so mighty a power over Time, who casts all other mortals under his, comes down to us from a greater; and it is only if we abuse the victory that it were better we had encountered a defeat. Unremitting care must be taken that nothing soil the monuments we are raising: sure enough we are that nothing can subvert, and nothing but our negligence, or worse than negligence, efface them. Under the glorious lamp entrusted to your vigilance, one among the lights of the world, which the ministering angels of our God have suspended for his service, let there stand, with unclosing eyes, Integrity, Compassion, Self-denial.

Boccaccio. These are holier and cheerfuller images than Dante has been setting up before us. I hope every thesis in dispute among his theologians will be settled ere I set foot among them. I like Tuscany well enough : it answers all my purposes for the present : and I am without the benefit of those preliminary studies which might render me a worthy auditor of incomprehensible wisdom.

Petrarca.   I do not wonder you are attached to Tuscany. Many as have been your visits and adventures in other parts, you have rendered it pleasanter and more interesting than any : and indeed we can scarcely walk in any quarter from the gates of Florence, without the recollection of some witty or affecting story related by you.   Every street, every farm, is peopled by your genius : and this population can not change with seasons or with ages, with factions or with incursions.   Ghibellines and Guelphs will have been contested for only by the worms, long before the *Decameron* has ceased to be recited on our banks of blue lilies and under our arching vines.   Another plague may come amidst us ; and something of a solace in so terrible a visitation would be found in your pages, by those to whom letters are a refuge and relief.

Boccaccio.   I do indeed think my little bevy from Santa Maria Novella would be better company on such an occasion, than a devil with three heads, who diverts the pain his claws inflicted, by sticking his fangs in another place.

Petrarca.   This is atrocious, not terrific nor grand.   Alighieri is grand by his lights, not by his shadows ; by his human affections, not by his infernal.   As the minutest sands are the labours of some profound sea, or the spoils of some vast mountain, in like manner his horrid wastes and wearying minutenesses are the chafings of a turbulent spirit, grasping the loftiest things and penetrating the deepest, and moving and moaning on the earth in loneliness and sadness.

Boccaccio.   Among men he is what among waters is

The strange, mysterious, solitary Nile.

Petrarca.   Is that his verse ?   I do not remember it.

Boccaccio.   No, it is] mine for the present : how long it may continue mine I can not tell.   I never run after those who steal my apples : it would only tire me : and they are hardly worth recovering when they are bruised and bitten, as they are usually.

I would not stand upon my verses: it is a perilous boy's trick, which we ought to leave off when we put on square shoes. Let our prose show what we are, and our poetry what we have been.

Petrarca.   You would never have given this advice to Alighieri.

Boccaccio.   I would never plough porphyry; there is ground fitter for grain.   Alighieri is the parent of his system, like the sun, about whom all the worlds are but particles thrown forth from him.   We may write little things well, and accumulate one upon another; but never will any be justly called a great poet unless he has treated a great subject worthily.   He may be the poet of the lover and of the idler, he may be the poet of green fields or gay society; but whoever is this can be no more.   A throne is not built of birds'-nests, nor do a thousand reeds make a trumpet.

Petrarca.   I wish Alighieri had blown his on nobler occasions.

Boccaccio.   We may rightly wish it: but, in regretting what he wanted, let us acknowledge what he had: and never forget (which we omitted to mention) that he borrowed less from his predecessors than any of the Roman poets from theirs.   Reasonably may it be expected that almost all who follow will be greatly more indebted to antiquity, to whose stores we, every year, are making some addition.

Petrarca.   It can be held no flaw in the title-deeds of genius, if the same thoughts re-appear as have been exhibited long ago. The indisputable sign of defect should be looked for in the proportion they bear to the unquestionably original.   There are ideas which necessarily must occur to minds of the like magnitude and materials, aspect and temperature.   When two ages are in the same phasis, they will excite the same humours, and produce the same coincidences and combinations.   In addition to which a great poet may really borrow: he may even condescend to an obligation at the hand of an equal or inferior: but he forfeits his title if he borrows more than the amount of his own possessions. The nightingale himself takes somewhat of his song from birds less glorified: and the lark, having beaten with her wing the very gates of heaven, cools her breast among the grass.   The lowlier of intellect may lay out a table in their field, at which table the highest one shall sometimes be disposed to partake : want does not compel him. Imitation, as we call it, is often weakness, but it likewise is often sympathy.

Boccaccio. Our poet was seldom accessible in this quarter. Invective picks up the first stone on the wayside, and wants leisure to consult a forerunner.

Petrarca. Dante (original enough everywhere) is coarse and clumsy in this career. Vengeance has nothing to do with comedy, nor properly with satire. The satirist who told us that Indignation made his verses * for him, might have been told in return that she excluded him thereby from the first class, and thrust him among the rhetoricians and declaimers. Lucretius, in his vituperation, is graver and more dignified than Alighieri. Painful ; to see how tolerant is the atheist, how intolerant the catholic : how anxiously the one removes from among the sufferings of Mortality, her last and heaviest, the fear of a vindictive Fury pursuing her shadow across rivers of fire and tears : how laboriously the other brings down Anguish and Despair, even when Death has done his work. How grateful the one is to that beneficent philosopher who made him at peace with himself, and tolerant and kindly toward his fellow creatures ! how importunate the other that God should forego his divine mercy, and hurl everlasting torments both upon the dead and the living !

Boccaccio. I have always heard that Ser Dante was a very good man and sound catholic : but Christ forgive me if my heart is oftener on the side of Lucretius ! † Observe, I say, my heart ; nothing more. I devoutly hold to the sacraments and the mysteries : yet somehow I would rather see men tranquillised than frightened out of their senses, and rather fast asleep than burning. Sometimes I have been ready to believe, as far as our holy faith will allow me, that it were better our Lord were nowhere, than torturing in his inscrutable wisdom, to all eternity, so many myriads of us poor devils, the creatures of his hands. Do not cross thyself so thickly, Francesco ! nor hang down thy nether lip so loosely, languidly, and helplessly ; for I would be a

---

* Facit indignatio versum. *Juv.*

† Qy. How much of Lucretius (or Petronius or Catullus, before cited) was then known ? *Remark by Monsignore.*

good catholic, alive or dead.   But, upon my conscience, it goes hard with me to think it of him, when I hear that woodlark yonder, gushing with joyousness, or when I see the beautiful clouds, resting so softly one upon another, dissolving . . . and not damned for it.   Above all, I am slow to apprehend it, when I remember his great goodness vouchsafed to me, and reflect on my sinful life heretofore, chiefly in summer time, and in cities, or their vicinity.   But I was tempted beyond my strength ; and I fell as any man might do.   However, this last illness, by God's grace, has well nigh brought me to my right mind again in all such matters : and if I get stout in the present month, and can hold out the next without sliding, I do verily think I am safe, or nearly so, until the season of beccaficoes.

Petrarca.   Be not too confident !

Boccaccio.   Well, I will not be.

Petrarca.   But be firm.

Boccaccio.   Assuntina ! what ! are you come in again ?

Assunta.   Did you or my master call me, Riverenza ?

Petrarca.   No, child !

Boccaccio.   O ! get you gone ! get you gone ! you little rogue you !

Francesco, I feel quite well.   Your kindness to my playful creatures in the *Decameron* has revived me, and has put me into good-humour with the greater part of them. Are you quite certain the Madonna will not expect me to keep my promise ?   You said you were : I need not ask you again.   I will accept the whole of your assurances, and half your praises.

Petrarca.   To represent so vast a variety of personages so characteristically as you have done, to give the wise all their wisdom, the witty all their wit, and (what is harder to do advantageously) the simple all their simplicity, requires a genius such as you alone possess.   Those who doubt it are the least dangerous of your rivals.

FIFTH DAY'S INTERVIEW.

It being now the last morning that Petrarca could remain with his friend, he resolved to pass early into his bed-chamber. Boccaccio had risen, and was standing at the open window, with his arms against it. Renovated health sparkled in the eyes of the one; surprise and delight and thankfulness to heaven, filled the other's with sudden tears. He clasped Giovanni, kissed his flaccid and sallow cheek, and falling on his knees, adored the Giver of life, the source of health to body and soul. Giovanni was not unmoved: he bent one knee as he leaned on the shoulder of Francesco, looking down into his face, repeating his words, and adding,

"Blessed be thou, O Lord! who sendest me health again! and blessings on thy messenger who brought it."

He had slept soundly; for ere he closed his eyes he had unburdened his mind of its freight, not only by employing the prayers appointed by Holy Church, but likewise by ejaculating; as sundry of the fathers did of old. He acknowledged his contrition for many transgressions, and chiefly for uncharitable thoughts of Fra Biagio: on which occasion he turned fairly round on his couch, and leaning his brow against the wall, and his body being in a becomingly curved position, and proper for the purpose, he thus ejaculated:

"Thou knowest, O most Holy Virgin! that never have I spoken to handmaiden at this villetta, or within my mansion at Certaldo, wantonly or indiscreetly, but have always been, inasmuch as may be, the guardian of innocence; deeming it better, when irregular thoughts assailed me, to ventilate them abroad than to poison the house with them. And if, sinner as I am, I have thought uncharitably of others, and more especially of Fra Biagio, pardon me, out of thy exceeding great mercies! And let it not be imputed to me, if I have kept, and may keep hereafter, an eye over him, in wariness and watchfulness; not otherwise. For thou knowest, O Madonna! that many who have a perfect and unwavering faith in thee, yet do cover up their cheese from the nibblings of vermin."

Whereupon, he turned round again, threw himself on his back at full length, and feeling the sheets cool, smooth, and refreshing, folded his arms, and slept instantaneously. The consequence of his wholesome slumber was a calm alacrity: and the idea that his visitor would be happy at seeing him on his feet again, made him attempt to get up: at which he succeeded, to his own wonder. And it was increased by the manifestation of his strength in opening the casement, stiff from being closed, and swelled by the continuance of the rains. The morning was warm and sunny: and it is known that on this occasion he composed the verses below:

> My old familiar cottage-green!
> I see once more thy pleasant sheen;
> The gossamer suspended over
> Smart celandine by lusty clover;
> And the last blossom of the plum
> Inviting her first leaves to come;
> Which hang a little back, but show
> 'Tis not their nature to say no.
> I scarcely am in voice to sing
> How graceful are the steps of Spring;
> And ah! it makes me sigh to look
> How leaps along my merry brook,
> The very same to-day as when
> He chirrupt first to maids and men.

Petrarca. I can rejoice at the freshness of your feelings: but the sight of the green turf reminds me rather of its ultimate use and destination.

> For many serves the parish pall
> The turf in common serves for all.

Boccaccio. Very true; and, such being the case, let us carefully fold it up, and lay it by until we call for it.

Francesco, you made me quite light-headed yesterday. I am rather too old to dance either with Spring, as I have been saying, or with Vanity: and yet I accepted her at your hand as a partner. In future, no more of comparisons for me! You not only can do me no good, but you can leave me no pleasure: for here I shall remain the few days I have to live, and shall see nobody who will be disposed to remind me of your praises. Beside, you yourself will get hated for them. We neither can deserve praise nor receive it with impunity.

Petrarca. Have you never remarked that it is into quiet

water that children throw pebbles to disturb it! and that it is into deep caverns that the idle drop sticks and dirt? We must expect such treatment.

Boccaccio. Your admonition shall have its wholesome influence over me, when the fever your praises have excited has grown moderate.

. . . After the conversation on this topic and various others had continued some time, it was interrupted by a visitor. The clergy and monkery at Certaldo had never been cordial with Messer Giovanni, it being suspected that certain of his *Novelle* were modelled on originals in their orders. Hence, although they indeed both professed and felt esteem for Canonico Petrarca, they abstained from expressing it at the villetta. But Frate Biagio of San Vivaldo was (by his own appointment) the friend of the house; and, being considered as very expert in pharmacy, had, day after day, brought over no indifferent store of simples, in ptisans, and other refections, during the continuance of Ser Giovanni's ailment. Something now moved him to cast about in his mind whether it might not appear dutiful to make another visit. Perhaps he thought it possible that, among those who peradventure had seen him lately on the road, one or other might expect from him a solution of the questions, What sort of person was the *crowned martyr?* whether he carried a palm in his hand? whether a seam was visible across the throat? whether he wore a ring over his glove, with a chrysolite in it, like the bishops, but representing the city of Jerusalem and the judgment seat of Pontius Pilate? Such were the reports; but the inhabitants of San Vivaldo could not believe the Certaldese, who, inhabiting the next township to them, were naturally their enemies. Yet they might believe Frate Biagio, and certainly would interrogate him accordingly. He formed his determination, put his frock and hood on, and gave a curvature to his shoe, to evince his knowledge of the world, by pushing the extremity of it with his breast-bone against the corner of his cell. Studious of his figure and of his attire, he walked as much as possible on his heels, to keep up the reformation he had wrought in the workmanship of the cordwainer. On former occasions he had borrowed a horse, as being wanted to hear confession or to carry medicines, which might otherwise be too late. But, having put on an entirely new habiliment, and it being the season when horses are beginning to do the same, he deemed it prudent to travel on foot. Approaching the villetta, his first intention was to walk directly into his patient's room: but he found it impossible to resist the impulses of pride, in showing Assunta his rigid and stately frock, and shoes rather of the equestrian order than the monastic. So he went into the kitchen where the girl was at work, having just taken away the remains of the breakfast.

"Frate Biagio!" cried she, "is this you? Have you been sleeping at Conte Jeronimo's?"

"Not I," replied he.

"Why!" said she, "those are surely his shoes! Santa Maria! you must have put them on in the dusk of the morning, to say your prayers in! Here! here! take these old ones of Signor Padrone, for the love of God! I hope your Reverence met nobody."

Frate. What dost smile at?

Assunta. Smile at! I could find in my heart to laugh outright, if I only were certain that nobody had seen your Reverence in such a funny trim. Riverenza! put on these.

Frate. Not I indeed.

Assunta. Allow me then?

Frate. No, nor you.

Assunta. Then let me stand upon yours, to push down the points.

. . . Frate Biagio now began to relent a little, when Assunta, who had made one step toward the project, bethought herself suddenly, and said,

"No; I might miss my footing. But, mercy upon us! what made you cramp your Reverence with those ox-yoke shoes? and strangle your Reverence with that hang-dog collar?"

"If you must know," answered the Frate, reddening, "it was because I am making a visit to the Canonico of Parma. I should like to know something about him: perhaps you could tell me?"

Assunta. Ever so much.

Frate. I thought no less: indeed I knew it. Which goes to bed first?

Assunta. Both together.

Frate.   Demonio ! what dost mean ?

Assunta.   He tells me never to sit up waiting, but to say my prayers and dream of the Virgin.

Frate.   As if it was any business of his !   Does he put out his lamp himself ?

Assunta.   To be sure he does : why should not he ? what should he be afraid of ?   It is not winter : and beside, there is a mat upon the floor, all round the bed, excepting the top and bottom.

Frate.   I am quite convinced he never said anything to make you blush.   Why are you silent ?

Assunta.   I have a right.

Frate.   He did then ? ay ?   Do not nod your head : that will never do.   Discreet girls speak plainly.

Assunta.   What would you have ?

Frate.   The truth ; the truth ; again, I say, the truth.

Assunta.   He *did* then.

Frate.   I knew it !   The most dangerous man living !

Assunta.   Ah ! indeed he is !   Signor Padrone said so.

Frate.   He knows him of old : he warned you, it seems.

Assunta.   Me !   He never said it was I who was in danger.

Frate.   He might : it was his duty.

Assunta.   Am I so fat ?   Lord ! you may feel every rib. Girls who run about as I do, slip away from apoplexy.

Frate.   Ho ! ho ! that is all, is it ?

Assunta.   And bad enough too ! that such good-natured men should ever grow so bulky ; and stand in danger, as Padrone said they both do, of such a seizure ?

Frate.   What ? and art ready to cry about it ?   Old folks can not die easier : and there are always plenty of younger to run quick enough for a confessor.   But I must not trifle in this manner.   It is my duty to set your feet in the right way : it is my bounden duty to report to Ser Giovanni all irregularities I know of, committed in his domicile.   I could indeed, and would, remit a trifle, on hearing the worst.   Tell me now, Assunta ! tell me, you little angel ! did you . . . we all may, the very best of us may, and do . . . sin, my sweet ?

Assunta.   You may be sure I do not : for whenever I sin I run into church directly, although it snows or thunders; else I never could see again Padrone's face, or any one's.

Frate. You do not come to me.

Assunta. You live at San Vivaldo.

Frate. But when there is sin so pressing I am always ready to be found. You perplex, you puzzle me. Tell me at once how he made you blush.

Assunta. Well then!

Frate. Well then! you did not hang back so before him. I lose all patience.

Assunta. So famous a man! . . .

Frate. No excuse in that.

Assunta. So dear to Padrone . . .

Frate. The more shame for him!

Assunta. Called me . . .

Frate. And *called* you, did he! the traitorous swine!

Assunta. Called me . . . *good girl.*

Frate. Psha! the wenches, I think, are all mad: but few of them in this manner.

. . . Without saying another word, Fra Biagio went forward and opened the bedchamber-door, saying, briskly,

"Servant! Ser Giovanni! Ser Canonico! most devoted! most obsequious! I venture to incommode you. Thanks to God, Ser Canonico, you are looking well for your years. They tell me you were formerly (who would believe it?) the handsomest man in Christendom, and worked your way glibly, yonder at Avignon.

"Capperi! Ser Giovanni! I never observed that you were sitting bolt-upright in that long-backed arm-chair, instead of lying abed. Quite in the right. I am rejoiced at such a change for the better. Who advised it?"

Boccaccio. So many thanks to Fra Biagio! I not only am sitting up, but have taken a draught of fresh air at the window, and every leaf had a little present of sunshine for me.

There is one pleasure, Fra Biagio, which I fancy you never have experienced, and I hardly know whether I ought to wish it you; the first sensation of health after a long confinement.

Frate. Thanks! infinite! I would take any man's word for that, without a wish to try it. Everybody tells me I am exactly what I was a dozen years ago ; while, for my part, I see every-body changed : those who ought to be much about my age, even those . . . Per Bacco !   I told them my thoughts when they had told me theirs ; and they were not so agreeable as they used to be in former days.

Boccaccio.   How people hate sincerity.

Cospetto !   why, Frate !   what hast got upon thy toes ? Hast killed some Tartar and tucked his bow into one, and torn the crescent from the vizier's tent to make the other match it ? Hadst thou fallen in thy mettlesome expedition (and it is a mercy and a miracle thou didst not) those sacrilegious shoes would have impaled thee.

Frate.   It was a mistake in the shoemaker.   But no pain or incommodity whatsoever could detain me from paying my duty to Ser Canonico, the first moment I heard of his auspicious arrival, or from offering my congratulations to Ser Giovanni, on the annunciation that he was recovered and looking out of the window.   All Tuscany was standing on the watch for it, and the news flew like lightning.   By this time it is upon the Danube.

And pray, Ser Canonico, how does Madonna Laura do ?

Petrarca.   Peace to her gentle spirit ! she is departed.

Frate.   Ay, true.   I had quite forgotten : that is to say, I recollect it.   You told us as much, I think, in a poem on her death.   Well, and do you know ! our friend Giovanni here is a bit of an author in his way.

Boccaccio.   Frate ! you confuse my modesty.

Frate.   Murder will out.   It is a fact, on my conscience. Have you never heard anything about it, Canonico ?   Ha ! we poets are sly fellows : we can keep a secret.

Boccaccio.   Are you quite sure you can ?

Frate.   Try, and trust me with any.   I am a confessional on legs : there is no more a whisper in me than in a woolsack.

I [8] am in feather again, as you see ; and in tune, as you shall hear.

April is not the month for moping.   Sing it lustily.

---

[8] [First ed. reads : "woolsack. *Boccaccio.* I am . . . as you shall hear. *Frate.* April," &c.]

Boccaccio.   Let it be your business to sing it, being a Frate;
I can only recite it.

Frate.   Pray do then.

Boccaccio.

> Frate Biagio! sempre quando
> Quà tu vieni cavalcando,
> Pensi che le buone strade
> Per il mondo sien ben rade;
> E, di quante sono brutte,
> La più brutta è tua di tutte.
> Badi, non cascare sulle
> Graziosissime fanciulle,
> Che con capo dritto, alzato,
> Uova portano al mercato.
> Pessima mi pare l'opra
> Rovesciarle sottosopra.
> Deh! scansando le erte e sassi,
> Sempre con premura passi.
> Caro amico! Frate Biagio!
> Passi pur, ma passi adagio.*

Frate.   Well now really, Canonico, for one not exactly one
of us, that canzone of Ser Giovanni has merit: has not it?   I
did not ride, however, to-day; as you may see by the lining of
my frock.   But *plus non vitiat;* ay, Canonico!   About the roads
he is right enough; they are the devil's own roads; that must be
said for them.

Ser Giovanni! with permission; your mention of eggs in the
canzone, has induced me to fancy I could eat a pair of them.

* Avendo io fatto comparire nel nostro idioma toscano, e senza
traduzione, i leggiadri versi sopra stampati, chiedo perdono da chi legge.
Non potei, badando con dovuta premura ai miei interessi ed a quelli del
proposito mio, non potei, dico, far di meno; stanteche una riunione de'
critici, i più vistosi del Regno unito d'Inghilterra ed Irlanda, avrà con
unanimità dichiarato, che nessuno, di quanti esistono i mortali, saprà mai
indovinare la versione.   Stimo assai il tradduttore; lavore per poco, e
agevolmente; mi pare piutosto galantuomo; non c' è male; ma poeta
poco felice poi.   Parlano que' Signori critici riveritissimi di certi poemetti
e frammenti già da noi ammessi in questo volume, ed anche di altri del
medesimo autore forse originali, e restano di avviso commune, che non vi
sia neppure una sola parola veramente da intendersi; che il senso (chi
sa?) sarà di *ateisimo,* ovvero di *alto tradimento.*   Che *questo* non lo sia, nè
palesamente nè occultamente, fermo col proprio pugno.

Domenico Grigi.

The hens lay well now: that white one of yours is worth more than the goose that laid the golden: and you have a store of others, her equals or betters: we have none like them at poor St Vivaldo. *A riverderci, Ser Giovanni! Schiavo! Ser Canonico! mi commandino.*

. . . Fra Biagio went back into the kitchen, helped himself to a quarter of a loaf, ordered a flask of wine, and, trying several eggs against his lips, selected seven, which he himself fried in oil, although the maid offered her services. He never had been so little disposed to enter into conversation with her; and, on her asking him how he found her master, he replied, that in bodily health Ser Giovanni, by his prayers and ptisans, had much improved, but that his faculties were wearing out apace. "He may now run in the same couples with the Canonico: they can not catch the mange one of the other: the one could say nothing to the purpose, and the other nothing at all. The whole conversation was entirely at my charge," added he. "And now, Assunta, since you press it, I will accept the service of your master's shoes. How I shall ever get home I don't know." He took the shoes off the handles of the bellows, where Assunta had placed them out of her way, and tucking one of his own under each arm, limped toward St Vivaldo.

The unwonted attention to smartness of apparel, in the only article wherein it could be displayed, was suggested to Frate Biago by hearing that Ser Francesco, accustomed to courtly habits and elegant society, and having not only small hands, but small feet, usually wore red slippers in the morning. Fra Biagio had scarcely left the outer door, than he cordially cursed Ser Francesco for making such a fool of him, and wearing slippers of black list. "These canonicos," said he, "not only lie themselves, but teach everybody else to do the same. He has lamed me for life: I burn as if I had been shod at the blacksmith's forge."

The two friends said nothing about him, but continued the discourse which his visit had interrupted.

Petrarca. Turn again, I entreat you, to the serious; and do not imagine that because by nature you are inclined to playfulness, you must therefore write ludicrous things better. Many of your stories would make the gravest men laugh, and yet there is little wit in them.

Boccaccio. I think so myself; though authors, little disposed as they are to doubt their possession of any quality they would bring into play, are least of all suspicious on the side of wit. You have convinced me. I am glad to have been tender, and to have written tenderly: for I am certain it is this alone that has made you love me with such affection.

Petrarca. Not this alone, Giovanni! but this principally. I have always found you kind and compassionate, liberal and sincere, and when Fortune does not stand very close to such a man, she leaves only the more room for Friendship.

Boccaccio. Let her stand off then, now and for ever! To my heart, to my heart, Francesco! preserver of my health, my peace of mind, and (since you tell me I may claim it) my glory.

Petrarca. Recovering your strength you must pursue your studies to complete it. What can you have been doing with your books? I have searched in vain this morning for the treasury. Where are they kept? Formerly they were always open. I found only a short manuscript, which I suspect is poetry, but I ventured not on looking into it, until I had brought it with me and laid it before you.

Boccaccio. Well guessed! They are verses written by a gentleman who resided long in this country, and who much regretted the necessity of leaving it. He took great delight in composing both Latin and Italian, but never kept a copy of them latterly, so that these are the only ones I could obtain from him. Read: for your voice will improve them.

TO MY CHILD CARLINO.

Carlino! what art thou about, my boy?
Often I ask that question, though in vain,
For we are far apart: ah! therefore 'tis
I often ask it; not in such a tone
As wiser fathers do, who know too well.
Were we not children, you and I together?
Stole we not glances from each other's eyes?
Swore we not secrecy in such misdeeds?
Well could we trust each other. Tell me then
What thou art doing. Carving out thy name,

Or haply mine, upon my favourite seat,
With the new knife I sent thee over sea?
Or hast thou broken it, and hid the hilt
Among the myrtles, starr'd with flowers, behind?
Or under that high throne whence fifty lilies
(With sworded tuberoses dense around)
Lift up their heads at once, not without fear
That they were looking at thee all the while.

  Does Cincirillo follow thee about?
Inverting one swart foot suspensively.
And wagging his dread jaw at every chirp
Of bird above him on the olive-branch?
Frighten him then away! 'twas he who slew
Our pigeons, our white pigeons peacock-tailed,
That fear'd not you and me . . . alas, nor him!
I flattened his striped sides along my knee,
And reasoned with him on his bloody mind,
Till he looked blandly, and half-closed his eyes
To ponder on my lecture in the shade.
I doubt his memory much, his heart a little,
And in some minor matters (may I say it?)
Could wish him rather sager. But from thee
God hold back wisdom yet for many years!
Whether in early season or in late
It always comes high-priced. For thy pure breast
I have no lesson; it for me has many.
Come throw it open then! what sports, what cares
(Since there are none too young for these) engage
Thy busy thoughts? Are you again at work,
Walter and you, with those sly labourers,
Geppo, Giovanni. Cecco, and Poeta,
To build more solidly your broken dam
Among the poplars, whence the nightingale
Inquisitively watch'd you all day long?
I was not of your council in the scheme,
Or might have saved you silver without end,
And sighs too without number. Art thou gone
Below the mulberry, where that cold pool
Urged to devise a warmer, and more fit
For mighty swimmers, swimming three abreast?
Or art thou panting in this summer noon
Upon the lowest step before the hall,
Drawing a slice of watermelon, long
As Cupid's bow, athwart thy wetted lips
(Like one who plays Pan's pipe) and letting drop
The sable seeds from all their separate cells,
And leaving bays profound and rocks abrupt,
Redder than coral round Calypso's cave.

Petrarca.[9] There have been those anciently who would have been pleased with such poetry, and perhaps there may be again. I am not sorry to see the Muses by the side of childhood, and forming a part of the family. But now tell me about the books.

Boccaccio. Resolving to lay aside the more valuable of those I had collected or transcribed, and to place them under the guardianship of richer men, I locked them up together in the higher story of my tower at Certaldo. You remember the old tower?

Petrarca. Well do I remember the hearty laugh we had together (which stopped us upon the staircase) at the calculation we made, how much longer you and I, if we continued to thrive as we had thriven latterly, should be able to pass within its narrow circle. Although I like this little villa much better, I would gladly see the place again, and enjoy with you, as we did before, the vast expanse of woodlands and mountains and maremma; frowning fortresses inexpugnable; and others more prodigious for their ruins; then below them, lordly abbeys, overcanopied with stately trees and girded with rich luxuriance; and towns that seem approaching them to do them honour, and villages nestling close at their sides for sustenance and protection.

Boccaccio. My disorder, if it should keep its promise of

[9 First ed. reads: "family. What is this at the end? *Boccaccio.* I am not quite certain that the author would have allowed you to read those. Indeed, I had forgotten they were in the same paper. Although he was under no obligation to the house of Este, nor wished nor needed it, he felt at a distance the general joy which announced the destinies of the lady Victoria. This little poem is curious as being the only one upon the occasion, which never left its native place for court or crowd, contented with one solitary aspiration. I think there are only two stanzas. My neighbour was able without a wrench or a pother, to put into four or five verses, what another (yet hardy enough) brought cramps and pot-hooks to protract into a baker's dozen. Come give me your voice again.

> *Petrarca.* I will not look into the sky
> To augur aught of future years:
> Enough the heavens have shown us, why
> Our hopes are sure and vain our fears.
> Victoria! thou art risen to save
> The land thy earliest smiles have blest.
> A brave man's child will cheer the brave,
> A tender mother's the distrest.
> But now," &c.]

leaving me at last, will have been preparing me for the accomplishment of such a project. Should I get thinner and thinner at this rate, I shall soon be able to mount not only a turret or a belfry, but a tube of macarone,* while a Neapolitan is suspending it for deglutition.

What I am about to mention, will show you how little you can rely on me! I have preserved the books, as you desired, but quite contrary to my resolution : and, no less contrary to it, by your desire I shall now preserve the *Decameron*. In vain had I determined not only to mend in future, but to correct the past ; in vain had I prayed most fervently for grace to accomplish it, with a final aspiration to Fiammetta that she would unite with your beloved Laura, and that, gentle and beatified spirits as they are, they would breathe together their purer prayers on mine. See what follows.

Petrarca. Sigh not at it. Before we can see all that follows from their intercession, we must join them again. But let me hear anything in which they are concerned.

Boccaccio. I prayed ; and my breast, after some few tears, grew calmer. Yet sleep did not ensue until the break of morning, when the dropping of soft rain on the leaves of the fig-tree at the window, and the chirping of a little bird, to tell another there was shelter under them, brought me repose and slumber. Scarcely had I closed my eyes, if indeed time can be reckoned any more in sleep than in heaven, when my Fiammetta seemed to have led me into the meadow. You will see it below you : turn away that branch : gently ! gently ! do not break it ; for the little bird sat there.

Petrarca. I think, Giovanni, I can divine the place. Although this fig-tree, growing out of the wall between the cellar and us, is fantastic enough in its branches, yet that other which I see yonder, bent down and forced to crawl along the grass by the prepotency of the young shapely walnut-tree, is much more so. It forms a seat, about a cubit above the ground, level and long enough for several.

---

* This is valuable, since it shows that *macarone* (here called *pasta*) was invented in the time of Boccaccio ; so are the letters of Petrarca, which inform us equally in regard to *spectacles*. Ad *ocularium* (occhiali) mihi confugiendum esset auxilium.   *Domenico Grigi.*

Boccaccio. Ha! you fancy it must be a favourite spot with me, because of the two strong forked stakes wherewith it is propped and supported!

Petrarca. Poets know the haunts of poets at first sight; and he who loved Laura . . . O Laura! did I say he who *loved* thee? . . . hath whisperings where those feet would wander which have been restlesss after Fiammetta.

Boccaccio. It is true, my imagination has often conducted her thither; but there in this chamber she appeared to me more visibly in a dream.

"Thy prayers have been heard, O Giovanni," said she.

I sprang to embrace her.

"Do not spill the water! Ah! you have spilt a part of it."

I then observed in her hand a crystal vase. A few drops were sparkling on the sides and running down the rim: a few were trickling from the base and from the hand that held it.

"I must go down to the brook," said she, "and fill it again as it was filled before."

What a moment of agony was this to me! Could I be certain how long might be her absence? She went: I was following: she made a sign for me to turn back: I disobeyed her only an instant: yet my sense of disobedience, increasing my feebleness and confusion, made me lose sight of her. In the next moment she was again at my side, with the cup quite full. I stood motionless: I feared my breath might shake the water over. I looked her in the face for her commands . . . and to see it . . . to see it so calm, so beneficent, so beautiful. I was forgetting what I had prayed for, when she lowered her head, tasted of the cup, and gave it me. I drank; and suddenly sprang forth before me, many groves and palaces and gardens, and their statues and their avenues, and their labyrinths of alaternus and bay, and alcoves of citron, and watchful loopholes in the retirements of impenetrable pomegranate. Farther off, just below where the fountain slipt away from its marble hall and guardian gods, arose, from their beds of moss and drosera and darkest grass, the sisterhood of oleanders, fond of tantalising with their bosomed flowers and their moist and pouting blossoms the little shy rivulet, and of covering its face with all the colours of the dawn. My dream expanded and moved forward.

I trod again the dust of Posilipo, soft as the feathers in the wings of Sleep. I emerged on Baia ; I crossed her innumerable arches ; I loitered in the breezy sunshine of her mole ; I trusted the faithful seclusion of her caverns, the keepers of so many secrets ; and I reposed on the buoyancy of her tepid sea. Then Naples, and her theatres and her churches, and grottoes and dells and forts and promontories, rushed forward in confusion, now among soft whispers, now among sweetest sounds, and subsided, and sank, and disappeared. Yet a memory seemed to come fresh from every one : each had time enough for its tale, for its pleasure, for its reflection, for its pang. As I mounted with silent steps the narrow staircase of the old palace, how distinctly did I feel against the palm of my hand the coldness of that smooth stone-work, and the greater of the cramps of iron in it !

"Ah me ! is this forgetting ?" cried I anxiously to Fiammetta.

"We must recall these scenes before us," she replied : "such is the punishment of them. Let us hope and believe that the apparition, and the compunction which must follow it, will be accepted as the full penalty, and that both will pass away almost together."

I feared to lose anything attendant on her presence : I feared to approach her forehead with my lips : I feared to touch the lily on its long wavy leaf in her hair, which filled my whole heart with fragrance. Venerating, adoring, I bowed my head at last to kiss her snow-white robe, and trembled at my presumption. And yet the effulgence of her countenance vivified while it chastened me. I loved her . . . I must not say *more* than ever . . . *better* than ever ; it was Fiammetta who had inhabited the skies. As my hand opened toward her,

"Beware !" said she, faintly smiling ; "beware, Giovanni ! Take only the crystal ; take it, and drink again."

"Must all be then forgotten ?" said I sorrowfully.

"Remember your prayer and mine, Giovanni. Shall both have been granted . . . O how much worse than in vain ?"

I drank instantly ; I drank largely. How cool my bosom grew ; how could it grow so cool before her ! But it was not to remain in its quiescency ; its trials were not yet over. I will not, Francesco ! no, I may not commemorate the incidents she related to me, nor which of us said, "I blush for having loved *first ;*" nor which of us replied, " Say *least*, say *least*, and blush again."

The charm of the words (for I felt not the encumbrance of the body nor the acuteness of the spirit) seemed to possess me wholly. Although the water gave me strength and comfort, and somewhat of celestial pleasure, many tears fell around the border of the vase as she held it up before me, exhorting me to take courage, and inviting me with more than exhortation to accomplish my deliverance. She came nearer, more tenderly, more earnestly ; she held the dewy globe with both hands, leaning forward, and sighed and shook her head, drooping at my pusillanimity. It was only when a ringlet had touched the rim, and perhaps the water (for a sunbeam on the surface could never have given it such a golden hue) that I took courage, clasped it, and exhausted it. Sweet as was the water, sweet as was the serenity it gave me . . . alas ! that also which it moved away from me was sweet !

" This time you can trust me alone," said she, and parted my hair, and kissed my brow. Again she went toward the brook : again my agitation, my weakness, my doubt, came over me : nor could I see her while she raised the water, nor knew I whence she drew it. When she returned, she was close to me at once : she smiled : her smile pierced me to the bones : it seemed an angel's. She sprinkled the pure water on me ; she looked most fondly ; she took my hand ; she suffered me to press hers to my bosom ; but, whether by design I can not tell, she let fall a few drops of the chilly element between.

" And now, O my beloved ! " said she, " we have consigned to the bosom of God our earthly joys and sorrows. The joys can not return, let not the sorrows. These alone would trouble my repose among the blessed.

" Trouble thy repose ! Fiammetta ! Give me the chalice ! " cried I . . . "not a drop will I leave in it, not a drop."

" Take it ! " said that soft voice. " O now most dear Giovanni ! I know thou hast strength enough ; and there is but little . . . at the bottom lies our first kiss."

" Mine ! didst thou say, beloved one ? and is that left thee still ?"

" *Mine*, said she, pensively ; and as she abased her head, the broad leaf of the lily hid her brow and her eyes ; the light of heaven shone through the flower."

"O Fiammetta! Fiammetta!" cried I in agony, "God is the God of mercy, God is the God of love . . . can I, can I ever?" I struck the chalice against my head, unmindful that I held it; the water covered my face and my feet. I started up, not yet awake, and I heard the name of Fiammetta in the curtains.

Petrarca. Love, O Giovanni, and life itself, are but dreams at best. I do think

> Never so gloriously was Sleep attended
> As with the pageant of that heavenly maid.

But to dwell on such subjects is sinful. The recollection of them, with all their vanities, brings tears into my eyes.

Boccaccio. And into mine too . . . they were so very charming.

Petrarca. Alas, alas! the time always comes when we must regret the enjoyments of our youth.

Boccaccio. If we have let them pass us.

Petrarca. I mean our indulgence in them.

Boccaccio. Francesco! I think you must remember Raffaellino degli Alfani.

Petrarca. Was it Raffaellino who lived near San Michele in Orto?

Boccaccio. The same. He was an innocent soul, and fond of fish. But whenever his friend Sabbatelli sent him a trout from Pratolino, he always kept it until next day or the day after, just long enough to render it unpalatable. He then turned it over in the platter, smelt at it closer, although the news of its condition came undeniably from a distance, touched it with his forefinger, solicited a testimony from the gills which the eyes had contradicted, sighed over it, and sent it for a present to somebody else. Were I a lover of trout as Raffaellino was, I think I should have taken an opportunity of enjoying it while the pink and crimson were glittering on it.

Petrarca. Trout, yes.

Boccaccio. And all other fish I could encompass.

Petrarca. O thou grave mocker! I did not suspect such slyness in thee: proof enough I had almost forgotten thee.

Boccaccio. Listen! listen! I fancied I caught a footstep in the passage.　Come nearer; bend your head lower, that I may whisper a word in your ear.　Never let Assunta hear you sigh. She is mischievous: she may have been standing at the door: not that I believe she would be guilty of any such impropriety: but who knows what girls are capable of!　She has no malice, only in laughing; and a sigh sets her windmill at work, van over van, incessantly.

Petrarca.　I should soon check her.　I have no notion . . .

Boccaccio.　After all, she is a good girl . . . a trifle of the wilful.　She must have it that many things are hurtful to me . . . reading in particular . . . it makes people so odd. Tina is a small matter of the madcap . . . in her own particular way . . . but exceedingly discreet, I do assure you, if they will only leave her alone.

I find I was mistaken, there was nobody.

Petrarca.　A cat perhaps.

Boccaccio.　No such thing.　I order him over to Certaldo while the birds are laying and sitting: and he knows by experience, favourite as he is, that it is of no use to come back before he is sent for.　Since the first impetuosities of youth, he has rarely been refractory or disobliging.　We have lived together now these five years, unless I miscalculate; and he seems to have learnt something of my manners, wherein violence and enterprise by no means predominate.　I have watched him looking at a large green lizard; and, their eyes being opposite and near, he has doubted whether it might be pleasing to me if he began the attack; and their tails on a sudden have touched one another at the decision.

Petrarca.　Seldom have adverse parties felt the same desire of peace at the same moment, and none ever carried it more simultaneously and promptly into execution.

Boccaccio.　He enjoys his *otium cum dignitate* at Certaldo: there he is my castellan, and his chase is unlimited in those domains.　After the doom of relegation is expired, he comes hither at midsummer.　And then if you could see his joy!　His eyes are as deep as a well, and as clear as a fountain: he jerks his tail into the air like a royal sceptre, and waves it like the wand of a magician.　You would fancy that, as Horace with his head, he was about to smite the stars with it.　There is ne'er such another cat in the parish ; and he knows it, a rogue ! We have rare repasts together in the bean-and-bacon time, although in regard to the bean he sides with the philosopher of Samos ; but after due examination. In cleanliness he is a very nun ; albeit in that quality which lies between cleanliness and godliness, there is a smack of Fra Biagio about him. What is that book in your hand ?

Petrarca. My breviary.

Boccaccio. Well, give me mine too . . . there, on the little table in the corner, under the glass of primroses. We can do nothing better.

Petrarca. What prayer were you looking for ? let me find it.

Boccaccio. I don't know how it is : I am scarcely at present in a frame of mind for it. We are of one faith : the prayers of the one will do for the other : and I am sure, if you omitted my name, you would say them all over afresh. I wish you could recollect in any book as dreamy a thing to entertain me as I have been just repeating. We have had enough of Dante : I believe few of his beauties have escaped us : and small faults, which we readily pass by, are fitter for small folks, as grubs are the proper bait for gudgeons.

Petrarca. I have had as many dreams as most men. We are all made up of them, as the webs of the spider are particles of her own vitality. But how infinitely less do we profit by them ! I will relate to you, before we separate, one among the multitude of mine, as coming the nearest to the poetry of yours, and as having been not totally useless to me. Often have I reflected on it ; sometimes with pensiveness, with sadness never.

Boccaccio. Then, Francesco, if you had with you as copious a choice of dreams as clustered on the elm-trees where the Sibyl led Æneas, this, in preference to the whole swarm of them, is the queen dream for me.

Petrarca. When I was younger I was fond of wandering in solitary places, and never was afraid of slumbering in woods and grottoes. Among the chief pleasures of my life, and among the commonest of my occupations, was the bringing before me such heroes and heroines of antiquity, such poets and sages, such of the prosperous and the unfortunate, as most interested me by their courage, their wisdom, their eloquence, or their adventures.

Engaging them in the conversation best suited to their characters, I knew perfectly their manners, their steps, their voices : and often did I moisten with my tears the models I had been forming of the less happy.

Boccaccio. Great is the privilege of entering into the studies of the intellectual ; great is that of conversing with the guides of nations, the movers of the mass, the regulators of the unruly will, stiff, in its impurity and rust, against the finger of the Almighty Power that formed it : but give me, Francesco, give me rather the creature to sympathise with ; apportion me the sufferings to assuage. Ah, gentle soul ! thou wilt never send them over to another ; they have better hopes from thee.

Petrarca. We both alike feel the sorrows of those around us. He who suppresses or allays them in another, breaks many thorns off his own ; and future years will never harden fresh ones.

My occupation was not always in making the politician talk politics, the orator toss his torch among the populace, the philosopher run down from philosophy to cover the retreat or the advances of his sect ; but sometimes in devising how such characters must act and discourse, on subjects far remote from the beaten track of their career. In like manner the philologist, and again the dialectician, were not indulged in the review and parade of their trained bands, but, at times, brought forward to show in what manner and in what degree external habits had influenced the conformation of the internal man. It was far from unprofitable to set passing events before past actors, and to record the decisions of those whose interests and passions are unconcerned in them.

Boccaccio. This is surely no easy matter. The thoughts are in fact your own, however you distribute them.

Petrarca. All can not be my own ; if you mean by *thoughts* the opinions and principles I should be the most desirous to inculcate. Some favourite ones perhaps may obtrude too prominently, but otherwise no misbehaviour is permitted them : reprehension and rebuke are always ready, and the offence is punished on the spot.

Boccaccio. Certainly you thus throw open, to its full extent, the range of poetry and invention ; which can not but be very limited and sterile, unless where we find displayed much diversity

of character as disseminated by nature, much peculiarity of sentiment as arising from position, marked with unerring skill through
every shade and gradation ; and finally and chiefly, much inter-
texture and intensity of passion. You thus convey to us more
largely and expeditiously the stores of your understanding and
imagination, than you ever could by sonnets or canzonets, or
sinewless and sapless allegories.

But weighter works are less captivating. If you had published
any such as you mention, you must have waited for their accept-
ance.   Not only the fame of Marcellus, but every other,

Crescit occulto velut arbor ævo ;

and that which makes the greatest vernal shoot is apt to make
the least autumnal. Authors in general who have met celebrity
at starting, have already had their reward ; always their utmost
due, and often much beyond it. We can not hope for both
celebrity and fame : supremely fortunate are the few who
are allowed the liberty of choice between them. We two
prefer the strength that springs from exercise and toil, acquiring
it gradually and slowly : we leave to others the earlier blessing of
that sleep which follows enjoyment. How many at first
sight are enthusiastic in their favour! Of these how large
a portion come away empty-handed and discontented! like
idlers who visit the seacoast, fill their pockets with pebbles
bright from the passing wave, and carry them off with rapture.
After a short examination at home, every streak seems faint and
dull, and the whole contexture coarse, uneven, and gritty :
first one is thrown away, then another ; and before the
week's end the store is gone, of things so shining and
wonderful.

Petrarca. Allegory, which you named with sonnets and
canzonets, had few attractions for me, believing it to be the
delight in general of idle, frivolous, inexcursive minds, in
whose mansions there is neither hall nor portal to receive
the loftier of the Passions. A stranger to the Affections,
she holds a low station among the handmaidens of Poetry,
being fit for little but an apparition in a mask. I had reflected
for some time on this subject, when, wearied with the length of
my walk over the mountains, and finding a soft old molehill,

covered with grey grass, by the way-side, I laid my head upon it, and slept. I can not tell how long it was before a species of dream or vision came over me.

Two beautiful youths appeared beside me ; each was winged ; but the wings were hanging down, and seemed ill adapted to flight. One of them, whose voice was the softest I ever heard, looking at me frequently, said to the other,

"He is under my guardianship for the present: do not awaken him with that feather."

Methought, hearing the whisper, I saw something like the feather on an arrow ; and then the arrow itself ; the whole of it, even to the point ; although he carried it in such a manner that it was difficult at first to discover more than a palm's length of it ; the rest of the shaft, and the whole of the barb, was behind his ankles.

"This feather never awakens anyone," replied he, rather petulantly ; "but it brings more of confident security, and more of cherished dreams, than you without me are capable of imparting."

"Be it so ! " answered the gentler . . . "none is less inclined to quarrel or dispute than I am. Many whom you have wounded grievously, call upon me for succour. But so little am I disposed to thwart you, it is seldom I venture to do more for them than to whisper a few words of comfort in passing. How many reproaches on these occasions have been cast upon me for indifference and infidelity ! Nearly as many, and nearly in the same terms, as upon you ! "

"Odd enough that we, O Sleep ! should be thought so alike ! " said Love, contemptuously. "Yonder is he who bears a nearer resemblance to you: the dullest have observed it." I fancied I turned my eyes to where he was pointing, and saw at a distance the figure he designated. Meanwhile the contention went on uninterruptedly. Sleep was slow in asserting his power or his benefits. Love recapitulated them ; but only that he might assert his own above them. Suddenly he called on me to decide, and to choose my patron. Under the influence, first of the one, then of the other, I sprang from repose to rapture, I alighted from rapture on repose . . . and knew not which was sweetest. Love was very angry with me, and declared he

would cross me throughout the whole of my existence. Whatever I might on other occasions have thought of his veracity, I
now felt too surely the conviction that he would keep his word.
At last, before the close of the altercation, the third Genius had
advanced, and stood near us. I can not tell how I knew him,
but I knew him to be the Genius of Death. Breathless as I
was at beholding him, I soon became familiar with his features.
First they seemed only calm; presently they grew contemplative;
and lastly beautiful: those of the Graces themselves are less
regular, less harmonious, less composed. Love glanced at him
unsteadily, with a countenance in which there was somewhat of
anxiety, somewhat of disdain; and cried, "Go away! go away!
nothing that thou touchest, lives."

"Say rather, child!" replied the advancing form, and advancing grew loftier and statelier. "Say rather that nothing of
beautiful or of glorious lives its own true life until my wing hath
passed over it."

Love pouted, and rumpled and bent down with his forefinger
the stiff short feathers on his arrow-head; but replied not. Although he frowned worse than ever, and at me, I dreaded him
less and less, and scarcely looked toward him. The milder and
calmer Genius, the third, in proportion as I took courage to
contemplate him, regarded me with more and more complacency.
He held neither flower nor arrow, as the others did; but, throwing back the clusters of dark curls that overshadowed his countenance, he presented to me his hand, openly and benignly. I
shrank on looking at him so near, and yet I sighed to love him.
He smiled, not without an expression of pity, at perceiving my
diffidence, my timidity: for I remembered how soft was the
hand of Sleep, how warm and entrancing was Love's. By
degrees, I became ashamed of my ingratitude; and turning my
face away, I held out my arms, and felt my neck within his.
Composure strewed and allayed all the throbbings of my bosom;
the coolness of freshest morning breathed around; the heavens
seemed to open above me; while the beautiful cheek of my
deliverer rested on my head. I would now have looked for
those others; but knowing my intention by my gesture, he said,
consolatorily,

"Sleep is on his way to the Earth, where many are calling

him; but it is not to these he hastens; for every call only makes him fly farther off. Sedately and gravely as he looks, he is nearly as capricious and volatile as the more arrogant and ferocious one."

"And Love!" said I, "whither is he departed? If not too late, I would propitiate and appease him."

"He who can not follow me, he who can not overtake and pass me," said the Genius, "is unworthy of the name, the most glorious in earth or heaven. Look up! Love is yonder, and ready to receive thee."

I looked: the earth was under me: I saw only the clear blue sky, and something brighter above it.

PIEVANO GRIGI TO THE READER.

BEFORE I proceeded on my mission, I had a final audience of Monsignore, in which I asked his counsel, whether a paper sewed and pasted to the *Interviews*, being the substance of an intended *Confession*, might, according to the *Decretals*, be made public. Monsignore took the subject into his consideration, and assented. Previously to the solution of this question, he was graciously pleased to discourse on Boccaccio, and to say, "I am happy to think he died a good catholic, and contentedly."

"No doubt, Monsignore!" answered I, "for when he was on his death-bed, or a little sooner, the most holy man in Italy admonished him terribly of his past transgressions, and frightened him fairly into Paradise."

"Pievano!" said Monsignore, "it is customary in the fashionable literature of our times to finish a story in two manners. The most approved is, to knock on the head every soul that has been interesting you: the second is, to put the two youngest into bed together, promising the same treatment to another couple, or more. Our forefathers were equally zealous about those they dealt with. Every pagan turned Christian: every loose woman had bark to grow about her, as thick and astringent as the ladies had in Ovid's Metamorphoses; and the gallants, who had played false with them, were driven mad by the monks at their death-bed. I neither hope nor believe that poor Boccaccio gave way to their importunities, but am happy in thinking that his decease was as tranquil as his life was inoffensive. He was not exempt from the indiscretions of youth : he allowed his imagination too long a dalliance with his passions ; but malice was never found among them. Let us then, in charity to him and to ourselves, be persuaded that such a pest as this mad zealot had no influence over him—

> Nè turbò il tuono di nebbiosa mente
> Acqua si limpida e ridente.*

I can not but break into verse, although no poet, while I am thinking of him.   Such men as he would bring over more to our good-natured, honest old faith again than fifty monks with scourges at their shoulders."

"Ah, Monsignore ! " answered I, "could I but hope to be humbly instrumental in leading back the apostate church to our true catholic, I should be the happiest man alive."

"God forbid you should be without the hope ! " said Monsignore. "The two chief differences now are ; with ours, that we must not eat butcher's meat on a Friday ; with the Anglican, that they must not eat baked meat on a Sunday. Secondly, that *we* say, *Come, and be saved ;* the Anglican says, *Go, and be damned.*"

Since the exposition of Monsignore, the Parliament has issued an Act of Grace in regard to eating.   One article says :

"Nobody shall eat on a Sunday roast, or baked, or other hot victuals whatsoever, unless he goes to church in his own carriage ; if he goes thither in any other than his own, be he halt or blind, he shall be subject to the penalty of twenty pounds.   Nobody shall dance on a Sunday, or play music, unless he also be able to furnish three *écarté* tables at the least, and sixteen wax-lights."

I write from memory ; but if the wording is inexact, the sense is accurate. Nothing can be more gratifying to a true Catholic than to see the amicable game played by his bishops with the Anglican. The Catholic never makes a false move. His fish often slips into the red square, marked *Sunday,* but the shoulder

---

* Nor did the thunderings of a cloudy mind
  Trouble so limpid and serene a water.

of mutton can never get into its place, marked *Friday :* it lies upon the table, and nobody dares touch it. Alas ! I am forgetting that this is purely an English game, and utterly unknown among us, or indeed in any other country under heaven.

To promote still farther the objects of religion, as understood in the Universities and the Parliament, it was proposed that public prayers should be offered up for rain on every Sabbath-day, the more effectually to encompass the provisions of the Bill. But this clause was cancelled in the Committee, on the examination of a groom, who deposed that a coach-horse of his master's, the Bishop of London, was touched in the wind, and might be seriously a sufferer : *"for the bishop,"* said he, *"is no better walker than a goose."*

There [10] is, moreover, great and general discontent in the lower orders of the clergy, that some should be obliged to serve a couple of churches, and perhaps a jail or hospital to boot, for a stipend of a hundred pounds, and even less, while others are incumbents of pluralities, doing no duty at all, and receiving three or four thousands. It is reported that several of the more fortunate are so utterly shameless as to liken the Church to a Lottery-office, and to declare that, unless there were great prizes, no man in his senses would enter into the service of our Lord. I myself have read with my own eyes this declaration, but I hope the signature is a forgery. What is certain is, that the emoluments of the bishopric of London are greater than the united revenue of *twelve* cardinals ; that they are amply sufficient for the board, lodging, and education of *three hundred* young men destined to the ministry ; and that they might relieve from famine, rescue from sin, and save, perhaps, from eternal punishment, *three thousand fellow-creatures yearly.* On a narrow inspection of one manufacturing town in England, I deliver it as my firm opinion that it contains more crime and wretchedness than all the four continents of our globe. If these enormous masses of wealth had been fairly sub-divided and carefully expended, if a more numerous and a more efficient clergy had been appointed, how very much of sin and sorrow had been obviated and allayed ! Ultimately the poor will be driven to desperation, there being no check upon them, no guardian over them ; and the eyes of the

[10 From " There " to " cross " (37 lines) added in second ed.]

sleeper, it is to be feared, will be opened by pincers. In the midst of such woes, originating in her iniquities and aggravated by her supineness, the Church of England, the least reformed church in Christendom, and the most opposite to the institutions of the State, boasts of being the purest member of the Reformation. Shocked at such audacity and impudence, the conscientious and pious, not only of her laity but also of her clergy, fall daily off from her, and resigning all hope of parks and palaces, embrace the cross.

Never since the Reformation (so called) have our prospects been so bright as at the present day. Our own prelates, and those of the English church, are equally at work to the same effect; and the Catholic clergy will come into possession of their churches with as little change in the temporals as in the spirituals. It is the law of the land that the church can not lose her rights and possessions by lapse of time; impossible then that she should lose it by fraud and fallacy. Although the bishops of England, regardless of their vocations and vows, have, by deceit and falsehood, obtained Acts of Parliament, under sanction of which they have severed from their sees, and made over to their families, the possessions of the episcopacy, it can not be questioned that what has been wrongfully alienated will be rightfully restored. No time, no trickery, no subterfuge can conceal it. The exposure of such thievery in such eminent stations, worse and more shameful than any on the Thames or in the lowest haunts of villany and prostitution, and of attempts to seize from their poorer brethren a few decimals to fill up a deficiency in many thousands, has opened wide the eyes of England. Consequently, there are religious men who resort from all quarters to the persecuted mother they had so long abandoned. God at last has made his enemies perform his work; and the English prelates, not indeed on the stool of repentance, as would befit them, but thrust by the scorner into his uneasy chair, are mending with scarlet silk, and seaming with threads of gold, the copes and dalmatics of their worthy predecessors. I am overjoyed in declaring to my townsmen that the recent demeanour of these prelates, refractory and mutinous as it has been (in other matters) to the government of their patron the king, has ultimately (by joining the malcontents in abolishing the favourite farce of religious freedom, and in forbidding roast meat and country air on the Sabbath) filled up my subscription for the bell of San Vivaldo.

Salve Regina Cœli!

PRETE DOMENICO GRIGI.

LONDON, *June 17th*, 1837.

HEADS OF CONFESSION; A MONTHFUL.

Printed and published Superiorum Licentiâ.

March 14.   Being ill at ease, I cried, "Diavolo! I wish that creaking shutter was at thy bedroom instead of mine, old fellow!" Assuntina would have composed me, showing me how wrong it was.   Perverse; and would not acknowledge my sinfulness to her.   I said she had nothing to do with it; which vexed her.

March 23.   Reproved Assuntina, and called her *ragazzaccia!* for asking of Messer Piero Pimperna half the evening's milk of his goat.   Very wrong in me; it being impossible she should have known that Messer Piero owed me four *lire* since . . . I forget when.

March. 31.   It blowing tramontana, I was ruffled: suspected a feather in the minestra: said the rice was as black as a coal.   Sad falsehood! made Assuntina cry . . . . Saracenic doings.

Recapitulation.   Shameful all this month; I did not believe such bad humour was in me.

Reflection.   The devil, if he can not have his walk one way, will take it another; never at a fault.   Manifold proof; poor sinner!

April 2.   Thought uncharitably of Fra Biagio.   The Frate took my hand, asking me to confess, reminding me that I had not confessed since the 3rd of March, although I was so sick and tribulated I could hardly stir.   Peevish; said, "Confess yourself; I won't; I am not minded; you will find those not far off who . . . " and then I dipped my head under the coverlet, and saw my error.

April 6. Whispers of Satanasso; pretty clear! A sprinkling of vernal thoughts, much too advanced for the season. About three hours before sunset Francesco came. Forgot my prayers; woke at midnight; recollected, and did not say them. Might have told him; never occurred that, being a Canonico, he could absolve me; now gone again these three days, this being the fourteenth. Must unload ere heavier-laden. Gratiæ plena! have mercy upon me!

THE TRANSLATOR'S REMARKS.

On the Alleged Jealousy of Boccaccio and Petrarca.

AMONG the most heinous crimes that can be committed against society is the

temerati crimen amici,

and no other so loosens the bonds by which it is held together. Once, and only once in my life, I heard it defended by a person of intellect and integrity. It was the argument of a friendly man, who would have invalidated the fact; it was the solicitude of a prompt and dexterous man, holding up his hat to cover the shame of genius. I have indeed had evidence of some who saw nothing extraordinary or amiss in these filchings and twichings; but there are persons whose thermomenter stands higher by many degrees at other points than honour. There are insects on the shoals and sands of literature, shrimps which must be half-boiled before they redden; and there are blushes (no doubt) in certain men, of which the precious vein lies so deep that it could hardly be brought to light by cordage and windlass. Meanwhile their wrathfulness shows itself at once by a plashy and puffy superficies, with an exuberance of coarse rough stuff upon it, and is ready to soak our shoes with its puddle at the first pressure.

"Thou shalt not bear false witness against thy neighbour" is a commandment which the literary cast down from over their communion-table to nail against the doors of the commonalty,

with a fist and forefinger pointing at it. Although the deprecia-
tion of any work is dishonest, the attempt is more infamous when
committed against a friend. The calumniator on such occasions
may in some measure err from ignorance, or from inadequate
information, but nothing can excuse him if he speaks contemptuously. It is impossible to believe that such writers as Boccaccio
and Petrarca could be widely erroneous in each other's merits;
no less incredible is it that, if they did err at all, they would
openly avow a disparaging opinion. This baseness was reserved
for days when the study opens into the market-place, when
letters are commodities, and authors chapmen. Yet even upon
their stalls, where an antique vase would stand little chance with
a noticeable piece of blue-and-white crockery, and shepherds and
sailors and sunflowers in its circumference, it might be heartily
and honestly derided; but less probably by the fellow-villager of
the vendor, with whom he had been playing at quoits every day
of his life. When an ill-natured story is once launched upon the
world, there are many who are careful that it shall not soon
founder. Thus the idle and inconsiderate rumour, which has
floated through ages, about the mutual jealousy of Boccaccio and
Petrarca, finds at this day a mooring in all quarters. Never were
two men so perfectly formed for friendship; never were two who
fulfilled so completely that happy destination. True it is, the
studious and exact Petrarca had not elaborated so entirely to his
own satisfaction his poem, *Africa*, as to submit it yet to the
inspection of Boccacio, to whom unquestionably he would have
been delighted to show it the moment he had finished it. He
died, and left it incomplete. We have, it must be acknowledged, the authority of Petrarca himself, that he never had read
the *Decameron* through, even to the last year of his life, when he
had been intimate with Boccaccio four-and-twenty How easy
would it have been for him to dissemble this fact! how certainly
would any man have dissembled it who doubted of his own heart
or of his friend's! I must request the liberty of adducing his
whole letter, as already translated.

"I have only run over your *Decameron*, and therefore I am
not capable of forming a true judgment of its merit: but upon
the whole it has given me a great deal of pleasure. *The freedoms
in it are excusable; from having been written in youth, from the*

subjects it treats of, and from the persons for whom it was designed.
Among a great number of gay and witty jokes, there are however
many grave and serious sentiments. I did as most people do : I
paid most attention to the beginning and the end. Your description of the people in the Plague is very true and pathetic : and
the touching story of Griseldis has *been ever since laid up in my
memory, that I may relate it in my conversations with my friends.*
A friend of mine at Padua, a man of wit and knowledge, undertook to read it aloud ; but he had scarcely got through half of
it, when his tears prevented him going on. He attempted it
a second time ; but his sobs and sighs obliged him to desist.
Another of my friends determined on the same venture ; and,
having read it from beginning to end, without the least alteration
of voice or gesture, he said, on returning the book,

" ' It must be owned this is an affecting history, and I should
have wept could I have believed it true ; but there never was and
never will be a woman like Griseldis.' "

Here was the termination of Petrarca's literary life : he closed
it with the last words of this letter ; which are, " Adieu, my
friends! adieu my correspondence." Soon afterward he was
found dead in his library, with his arm leaning on a book. In
the whole of his composition, what a carefulness and solicitude
to say everything that could gratify his friend ; with what
ingenuity are those faults not palliated but *excused* (his own
expression) which must nevertheless have appeared very grievous
ones to the purity of Petrarca.

But why did not Boccaccio send him his *Decameron* long
before ? Because there never was a more perfect gentleman,
a man more fearful of giving offence, a man more sensitive
to the delicacy of friendship, or more deferential to sanctity of
character. He knew that the lover of Laura could not amuse
his hours with mischievous or idle passions ; he knew that he rose
at midnight to repeat his matins, and never intermitted them. On
what succeeding hour could he venture to seize ? with what
countenance could he charge it with the levities of the world ?
Perhaps the Recluse of Arqua, the visitor of old Certaldo, read
at last the *Decameron*, only that he might be able the better to
defend it. And how admirably has the final stroke of his
indefatigable pen effected the purpose ! Is this the jealous

rival? Boccaccio received the last testimony of unaltered friendship in the month of October 1373, a few days after the writer's death. December was not over when they met in heaven: and never were two gentler spirits united there.

The character of Petrarca shows itself in almost every one of his various works. Unsuspicious, generous, ardent in study, in liberty, in love, with a self-complacence which in less men would be vanity, but arising in him from the general admiration of a noble presence, from his place in the interior of a heart which no other could approach or merit, and from the homage of all who held the principalities of Learning in every part of Europe.

Boccaccio is only reflected in full from a larger mass of compositions: yet one letter is quite sufficient to display the beauty and purity of his mind. It was written from Venice, when finding there not Petrarca whom he expected to find, but Petrarca's daughter, he describes to the father her modesty, grace, and cordiality in his reception. The imagination can form to itself nothing more lovely than this picture of the gentle Ermissenda: and Boccaccio's delicacy and gratitude are equally affecting. No wonder that Petrarca, in his will, bequeathed to his friend a sum the quintuple in amount of that which he bequeathed to his only brother, whom however he loved tenderly. Such had been, long before their acquaintance, the celebrity of Petrarca, such the honours conferred on him wherever he resided or appeared, that he never thought of equality or rivalry. And such was Boccaccio's reverential modesty, that, to the very close of his life, he called Petrarca his master. Immeasurable as was his own superiority, he no more thought himself the equal of Petrarca than Dante (in whom the superiority was almost as great) thought himself Virgil's. These, I believe, are the only instances on record where poets have been very tenaciously erroneous in the estimate of their own inferiority. The same observation can not be made so confidently on the decisions of contemporary critics. Indeed, the balance in which works of the highest merit are weighed, vibrates long before it is finally adjusted. Even the most judicious men have formed injudicious opinions on the living and the recently deceased. Bacon and Hooker could not estimate Shakespeare, nor could Taylor and Barrow give Milton his just award. Cowley and Dryden were preferred to both, by a great majority of the learned. Many, although they believe they discover in a contemporary the qualities which elevate him above the rest, yet hesitate to acknowledge it; part, because they are fearful of censure for singularity; part, because they differ from him in politics or religion; and part, because they delight in hiding, like dogs and foxes, what they can at any time surreptitiously draw out for their sullen solitary repast. Such persons have little delight in the glory of our country, and would hear with disapprobation and moroseness it has produced four persons so pre-eminently great, that no name, modern or ancient, excepting Homer, can stand very near the lowest: these are, Shakespeare, Bacon, Milton, and Newton. Beneath the least of these (if anyone can tell which is least) are Dante and Aristoteles, who are unquestionably the next.* Out of Greece and England, Dante is the only man of the first order; such he is, with all his imperfections. Less ardent and energetic, but having no less at command the depths of thought and treasures of fancy, beyond him in variety, animation, and interest, beyond him in touches of nature and truth of character, is Boccaccio. Yet he believed his genius was immeasurably inferior to Alighieri's; and it would have surprised and pained him to find himself preferred to his friend Petrarca; which indeed did not happen in his lifetime. So difficult is it to shake the tenure of long possession, or to believe that a living man is as valuable as an old statue, that for five hundred years together the critics held Virgil far above his obsequious but high-souled scholar, who now has at least the honour of standing alone, if not first. Milton and Homer may be placed together: on the continent Homer will be seen at the right hand; in England, Milton. Supreme, above all, immeasurably supreme, stands Shakespeare. I do not think Dante is any more the equal of Homer than Hercules is the equal of Apollo. Though Hercules may display more muscles, yet Apollo is the powerfuller without any display of them at all. Both together are just equivalent to Milton, shorn of his *Sonnets*, and of his *Allegro* and *Penseroso;* the most delightful of what (wanting a better

---

* We can speak only of those whose works are extant. Democritus and Anaxagoras were perhaps the greatest in discovery and invention. [Note added in second ed.].

name) we call *lyrical* poems.   But in the contemplation of these
prodigies we must not lose the company we entered with.   Two
contemporaries so powerful in interesting our best affections, as
Giovanni and Francesco, never existed before or since.   Petrarca
was honoured and beloved by all conditions.   He collated with
the student and investigator, he planted with the husbandman, he
was the counsellor of kings, the reprover of pontiffs, and the
pacificator of nations.   Boccaccio, who never had occasion to
sigh for solitude, never sighed *in* it : there was his station, there
his studies, there his happiness.   In the vivacity and versatility of
imagination, in the narrative, in the descriptive, in the playful, in
the pathetic, the world never saw his equal, until the sunrise of
our Shakespeare.   Ariosto and Spenser may stand at no great
distance from him in the shadowy and unsubstantial ; but multi-
form Man was utterly unknown to them.   The human heart,
through all its foldings, vibrates to Boccaccio.

IMAGINARY CONVERSATIONS.

IMAGINARY CONVERSATIONS.

——✳——

OVID AND A PRINCE OF THE GETÆ.

Prince. Art thou really so debilitated in body and in spirits, my poor Ovid, as to fear, what even your effeminate Romans rarely do, the approach of Death?

Ovid. Hospitable, brave, compassionate host! my final hour indeed approaches me, but very far am I from fearing it.

Prince. And yet, to die like a woman or an infant, on a bed, without wound and succumbing under a mere malady of the heart, is sorrowful, is terrible. I wish it had been permitted thee, by those who sent thee hither, to fall gloriously on the field of battle. Why smilest thou? What a smile! how faint! how sickly!

Ovid!—Alas my friend! a wish recurred to me very different from yours on the manner of dying; a wish coming with importunity from days long past. Levity in youth is heaviness in age.

Prince. Courage, man, courage! Never talk about age until age is nigh. Thou hast every tooth in thy head yet, and able to cope with stouter things than fish, and chicory, and mallow, and nauseous mulse. In my larder are buck and boar; mother Earth's best benison to her activest and bravest. I have known one hoisted up from the grave's edge by sticking manfully to the neck of a boar. Venison is sheepish; boar for me! I can eat it without honey and vinegar; try whether thou canst do it with such condiments. What sayest thou?

Ovid. Truly I can say little; and nothing to the purpose, unless thanks are my voice, no less than my appetite is failing me.

Prince. I have plenty of both, and would willingly give thee a good share of them if I could. I do think I may help the appetite a little if thou wilt but listen to what I say. The women have been kneading and baking on the stone, ever since sunrise, the finest wheaten flour, sent hither from that ancient city whose walls are washed by their salt river, which separates the two worlds. Moreover its salt came with it, white as snow. Such cakes and so besprinkled, make the mouths of your priests water as they offer them to marble and maple folk, who methinks have weaker appetite and slower digestion than themselves. O, could you but come down for a moment and see our sparkling cakes! each three spans across! white inside as the salt over them; white and thin too, as that hand of thine now lying above the blanket. No danger is here in the eating of them. Here thou art safe, and shalt soon be well again.

Ovid. Illusory the hope but kind the expression, O my friend!

Prince. Wishes won't always do, nor prayers either. I have given our oldest and holiest priest seven new laid goose-eggs to sing seven times for thy recovery.

Ovid. Death often comes at man's invocation, but never keeps away.

Prince. I have no opinion of him. Death may threaten, but Death is cowardly and often stands aloof from those who disdain to fear him. Marvellously hast thou escaped his snares. Poison and strangulation are Roman obituaries: we reserve them for useless hounds, itinerant foxes, and domestic pilferers. But neither such punishments nor elimination from native land, are denounced for seeing unintentionally an old goat, on his hind legs, rushing at aunt, or mother, or daughter.

Ovid. Beware! beware! Augustus is now a god.

Prince. Who made him one? He was a man the other day, and hardly that.

Ovid. At Rome we are in the practice of creating gods. Before long yon Getæ will be compelled to acknowledge his divinity. I feel ashamed of having done it, although but in poetry. Alas I have done worse even there. Wantonness! Idleness at the root of it!

Prince. Nothing is worse than idleness; not even poetry: but don't be vext about it. Did'st thou not undertake to teach me the art? Verily didst thou, setting me copies in my own language, while I was sitting down, pushing one hand into my beard and the other into the bush above it. But neither my verses, nor thine in Getic, ran so glibly as what thou repeatedst in thine own tongue. Thine resembled a car running smoothly over the frozen river; mine the same car jolting upon rough masses of broken ice. After all, a very effeminate language is your Latin. I think our own metres best suit our own poetry.

Ovid. Indeed I think so. But as you and your countrymen heard I was a poet, you desired from me a specimen of our Latin verse, and an attempt to imitate it in the Getic. I was not discouraged nor disconcerted by your laughter; for I love every ingenuous expression of sentiment, and, poet as I am, I smiled at yours, without bitterness and without reserve.

Prince. There is one thing among many which I always have admitted in thee; never have I known thee to undervalue another poet, but, on the contrary, to eulogise even thy contemporaries, and, it may be thy superiors, if there are any in thy walk.

Ovid. Those are the very men to eulogise.

Prince. Horatius Flaccus especially pleases thee.

Ovid. No poet has such variety.

Prince. There is another, who excelled, it seems, in the same measure as thine, and on whose verses thou hast ever dwelt with delight: Albius Tibullus: and yet there is as much difference in your tones as between a lark's and a cushat's; his being low and tender; thine exulting and exuberant. In this hot weather I have been fain to *read*, for want of other occupation; and I am curious to learn how so gentle a heart could be estranged.

Ovid. Gentleness is not always the criterion of stability; nor is it always that men change first. Manly and beauteous in form and features as was Albius, fond too and affectionate and domestic, it may be that Delia, educated in the country, was less indifferent to the flatteries she received at Rome. Inexperienced girls are dazzled by novelty, and the net is drawn over them by a show of deference. True love grows too familiar.

Prince. I should have hated her.

Ovid. Albius tho' he dissembled his resentment; thought her undeserving of the love and immortality he had bestowed on her; providing for daughter and mother, he formed another attachment and without malignity against Delia, and too proud for descending to reproach her, bestowed on his fresh favourite the name of Nemesis the Avenger.

Prince. Wert thou intimate with him ?

Ovid. Had he lived, we might have seen each other oftener.

Prince. How fared he among the lesser in your poultry yard?

Ovid. Avoiding celebrity, admitting few to his friendship, and keeping aloof from the fraternal feuds of poets, he never was near enough the ridge of the ring to look down on, or even to hear the clamour of, their animosities.

Prince. Thou seemest to have known him thoroughly though briefly.

Ovid. I knew him little but loved him much, and praised him unrepiningly. Tender poetry survives heroic. The myrtles of Idalia spring up fresh and fresh, when the oak of Dodonia is shattered root and branch.

Prince. Brave heart! brave and gentle! I know not whether our poetry is better than yours; but our people think it so; and that is enough.

According to thy own account of the matter, ye have brought all yours from another people, and thus older poets. Ye have carried them away with you; and not them only, but also their gods and goddesses, and even their shepherds and shepherdesses.

Ovid. We Romans do indeed take whatever gods we find: some we borrow, others we steal. Never subdue we a city but we capture its gods, women, and children, and we give them new names according to our fancy: the gentlest are Etruscan. These we place round about the hearthstone, for the boys and girls to play with, being nearly of the same height. The Greeks have furnished our temples with grander and costlier.

Prince. I have discovered one neither grand nor costly in my own pasture. A cow was rubbing the dung or fly off her hide against it. By thy description it must be that god Terminus; the best of them and the most palpably useful, though leading an inactive and solitary life. No; perhaps I may be wrong. Yesterday I saw, upon the vest over the bosom of thy serious and innocent daughter, who had been placing it to her lips and would fain have hidden it from me, a small silver image of a huntress, with a bow in her hand, a quiver across her shoulder, and before her feet a noble dog looking up at her.

Ovid. Poor girl! may that goddess, if she hears, protect thee!

Prince. She should have taken her to the chase, for she sadly wants exercise, weak and wan, with broken slumber.

Ovid. Ah me! I am sick at heart that she too should suffer.

Prince. Hush! hither she comes. She carries no smile with her, but at every step, in every place, she lights them up: can she not even in this chamber? answerest thou nothing? gasping only and groaning . . . art thou worse?

Ovid. I am afraid if she sees me, she will think I am.

Prince. Let me tell her thou art weary and slumbering.

Ovid. Thanks for that kind office. Anxious as I am to see her, after her day of praying and night of vigils, I must forbear that until I am more composed.

Prince. I will hasten and tell her she may come back shortly.

Ovid. Infinite thanks!

Prince. It has required of me as little time to comfort her. Perhaps in this interval you really have dozed.

Ovid. Accept my thanks for that also. Tears relieved and refreshed me. In another half hour she will kiss my brow again.

Prince. I have then done some good to-day, and must be rewarded for it. Thou hast reason to be proud of thy daughter, and, if not very proud of thy disciple in poetry, yet be, in some sort contented. I was shy (we poets always are) of reading a few of my verses to thee.

Ovid. If they are few, let me hear them: I could not do justice to many.

Prince. They are thy own favourite metre and manner.

"Give me thy hand pretty maiden, and thine be the sword and the
    sceptre."
Sceptre and sword I renounce; give me but give me thy hand.
Pleasant to slay the old wolf, and to take the young eaglet is pleasant,
Pleasanter far to bring home lamb that would wander away.
Many a morning I clomb to the twin-bearing nest of the ringdove,
O could I clomb by thy help, where thou art sleeping anight.
Gold shall encircle thy arm and in gold shall thy tresses be braided.
When thou hast fastened a clasp richer than gold around me.

I was half inclined to borrow a thought or two of thine on the occasion; but I feared she might imperfectly understand me, and might question me about some of them, insisting to know where, in the wandering of my thoughts, I had picked up such dainty curiosities. Do not sigh after such things. If they are gone, good riddance!

Ovid. If I sighed, at the thought of dying so far from my native land, from the ancient walls of Rome and from the pleasant orchards of Sulmo, its little translucent streams, its meadows of anemones and crocuses, its banks of violets latent in the moss, its narrow sequestered groves, wide enough for one happy pair of doves, and its hill-side brakes, where innumerable nightingales contend in song. O for the quiet grey villa, with various coloured lichens to enliven it. And then the thick wall, knee-high, supporting the long walk, but wanting support itself, with lavender and caper and rosemary springing up out of every crevice, where the lizard is doubtful of the bee, and the bee is apprehensive of the lizard. The gay vine above, from her crooked and decaying trellace, flaps incessantly the dark unyielding bay. Pardon my wandering. It is all a dream: alas, what else is life?

Prince. A man's country is where his friends are. Hast thou none here?

Ovid. Yes, and kind ones.

Prince. The earth is alike the birthplace and the sepulchre of all. But then your gods, forsooth! We can beget as good and serviceable here upon the banks of our Danube. We neither know nor care whether, when they leave the earth, they spring up among the stars, as your two last did. By what we hear from travellers who have lately sailed up our river, your Roman priests have propagated two or three additional of late. Surely they had plenty before. Thou hast catalogued and kalendered them neatly on the notch-stick of thy *Fasti.* Most of them are hearty and their wives and daughters comely and fair-spoken; but there are among these females a few ferocious as polecats with sucklings at the teat. Why ransack east or west for others? a train of bald priests behind them, cursing you unless you stand quietly to be pilfered by them, and doing worse than cursing if you ridicule their prostrations and grimaces.

Ovid. You seem angry.

Prince. No wonder. Our privileges are violated: we poets ought to be the only inventors. I have been attempting to read the songs of one highly prized by thee: songs to be accompanied, it seems, by stringed instruments.

Ovid.   Those of Horatius Flaccus, named just now?

Prince.   The same.   Girl after girl! fie upon him.

Ovid.   They were all or nearly all the creation of his fancy. However, he had Grecian models.

Prince.   Yea verily; and nude as my knuckles.   I do think my own poetry is better.   My reason is, because it is true, and reaches at once its destination.   When I love I call the girl by her name and tell her so.   When I lead my men to battle, I order the loudest voices to sing my warsong; and there is such a clatter of what ye Romans call *consonants* and *alliterations*, ye would imagine them to be clubs and swords against shields and bucklers.   Who is at the door?

Ovid.   I hear the light step of my daughter.   Come in, sweet watcher!   Ah! these two last weary days have worn thee down; paler than ever . . . or my dimness shows thee so.

Daughter.   Yes, my own father, it is that.   I am quite well again.   We both of us were always pale; and this (my flatterers said) made me so like you.

Ovid.   Two long days my heavy eyes have rolled and toiled after thee.   And art thou well again?

Daughter.   Dearest! quite well.

Ovid.   Well enough to carry my bones in their urn to Rome? . . . Support her! support her!   Speak to thy father once more.   What screamed she?   Delay not; I must and will hear.   Dying men may command; speak out.

Prince.   That even thy bones are banished.

Ovid.   Bring her back to my last embrace.

Daughter.   Father! look on me!   Thou lookest hitherward, but seest not thy child.   O father! father! canst thou leave me desolate.

Prince.   Hush! he sleeps.

Daughter.   Sleeps?   Heaven and Earth! it is only in death he could ever find such calmness.

Prince.   Then bid death welcome.   Patience! patience.

Daughter.   Detain me no longer.   Let me but close his eyes while the spirit yet hovers.   Father! hear.   Dost thou feel the pressure of my fingers on those beloved and once loving eyes? Dost thou feel my lips on thine again?   My own are less warm . . . he may.

Prince.   Be comforted, child, be comforted! Thou art in the house of a friend, and shalt be ere winter in thine own. Look up, and through the window.   Lo! the corn is yellow; the moon is large and bright; the winds and waves are tranquil! In this chamber shall be soon no mourner . . . or but one.

INES DE CASTRO, DON PEDRO, AND DOÑA BLANCA.

Pedro.   Ines, in one word, I have ceased to love you.   Loose me girl; let me go.

Ines.   Is it true? can it be? must I believe it?

Pedro.   Yes, my sweet . . . yes, my . . . yes, Inez.

Ines.   And are you still so generous, my Pedro, as to be sorry that you have ceased to love me! to sigh, almost to weep, as you turn away from me.   Take off that hand from above mine then, for I dare not move it; it is my prince's; it was my lover's. Be it my duty to go, not yours.

Pedro.   Whither wilt thou go, unfortunate Ines? Wouldst thou abandon me, O light heart!

Ines.   I would obey you; I have sworn it.

Pedro.   Not yet: would to God it were so.

Ines.   Indeed not yet at the altar: but did you not force me to say I loved you, before you went against the Moors? do you now punish me for this?   It was unmaidenly: so it was to place my arm around your neck: so it was, and worse, not to fly and leave you, and take refuge in a cloister, when you kissed my very lips . . . but you were going, and my heart was faint, and I did not see anything; not you, who might have given me more pride and courage; not an image of her who, in her spotless purity, might have saved me.

Pedro.   I never exacted the promise of your obedience.

Ines.   What else is love?

Pedro.   O Ines, Ines! must we two never know more of it than this!   Forget me, hate me.   I am ungrateful, wild, desperate.

Ines.   If you have ceased to love me, Pedro, I cannot reason with you . . . . I have no power . . . you no need of it: but if you fancy in yourself these blemishes, let me persuade you, O generous and tender Pedro that they do not exist in you, and are not to be feared by you or thought of: they have hearts enough, and room enough in all of them; never will they enter Pedro's.

Pedro.   I cannot marry you.

Ines.   Heaven has decreed it then, my beloved.

Pedro.   Thy hands are marble.   Perfidious wretch !   Woman of sermons, songs and satires not of earth or nature ! this indifference, this immobility, this smile.

Ines.   O Pedro, Pedro ! you relieve my heart before it breaks . . . .   I thought you had said you never more could love me.

Pedro.   I will love no other . . . . . so help me God ! so protect me, O blessed Virgin ! so hear me, Ines !

Blanca (entering abruptly).   The exclamation, I think, was *perfidious wretch,* Infante !   Rightly said.   Accusation of a perfidy is the precursor of one.   Is this your promise to your father, when he pardoned the sorceress ?

Pedro.   Madam, I heard no accusation of sorcery : the threat was enough.   When you protested by the martyrs and angels and confessors, that Ines de Castro should be accused of sorcery before the competent tribunals, if she would not consent to resign me, I placed such reliance on your royal word, and knew so well the meaning of *competency* in tribunals, I swore upon my keees that your wishes should be accomplished.

Ines.   O Pedro ! your love then for me separates us ! and would you not tell me this to make me happy !

Pedro.   Pity her, O merciful queen !   Look with com- passion on those tears, that anguish !

Blanca.   It is against the course of Nature that royal blood should mingle with plebeian.

Pedro.   Madam, I see none such here.

Blanca.   All that is not royal, to royal eyes should appear so. Fie ! the universe cries out aloud in condemnation of you.

Pedro.   I would answer your reproof with calmness, lady, if calmness in such contingencies were not truly the thing most offensive.

Blanca. Speak ; answer you cannot.

Pedro. Against the course of Nature, which you do oppose to me, it is impossible to run, unless we do violence to others or to ourselves. And the universe of princes is a narrow one indeed : court, church, camp, are its three continents ; there is nothing else, above or below or around, but air and sea, quieter or stormier.

Blanca. Rare manhood ! to argue with a woman ! Rare courtesy ! to instruct a queen !

Pedro. Alas, the distracted will reason ! Why will not those who are not so ! Hard as is the alternative, I would rather be wanting to my plighted faith, than ever see the woman I love resign or loosen it. To ask were inhumanity, to contract for it were baseness. If she could think me unworthy of her, she might bear to lose me ; and what care I how many, how great, how unmerited are my sufferings, if her's are less !

Ines. O my prince, let the most unworthy of your father's vassals clasp your knee.

Blanca. In my presence ! what ! and·thou leanest thy forehead on thy keeper's knee !

Pedro. Madam, I have not yet learned Castilian. My royal father has conferred on me no such title for my humble services. I am but Don Pedro.

Ines. O happy father ! happy Portugal ! happy above queens, Dona Blanca ! happy too, too happy, whatever may befall thee, Ines !

Blanca. Has the audacious girl ceased ? Constantia is royal, your equal, your superior, a daughter of Castile. Shall the interest of nations be postponed to the forwardness of boyish appetite ?

Pedro. Never will I while Ines lives . . .

Blanca. Ferocious and insolent and faithless man, enemy to legitimity and religion ! if I am unworthy to seek a proper match for you, if my own daughter is slighted, rejected, and despised, I will at least make your mistress more tractable . . . for her I have found one, and will honour her nuptials this very hour.

No earthly thing is wanting to the bridegroom ; he has youth, estate, rank, person, and court favour. . . .

What ! thankless ! uncompliant, graceless girl, will nothing serve under royalty ?

Ines.   O were there none on earth! I then were happy.

Queen.   Impiety! abomination! treason!

Ines.   I lost my senses to have uttered it.   I might love God . . . I might not love you, Pedro!   And hence the worst and wildest wish that ever distraction wrung from love . . . to draw the sun ('tis nothing less) from heaven for my own warmth. O what were Portugal, or earth without you?   Inanimate, or trampled on, or waste, or self-opprest as one in wicked slumber. Reign, gracious Pedro! teaching first obedience.   Be everything that kings have ever been, unless they should have loved.

Queen.   Sir, loose that hand . . .

Ines.   And . . . yes . . . love too . . . but only not love Ines.   I must not throw myself again before you.   You must not hear those royal words repeated.   They hurt you so, they almost made you angry.   Well do you blush at being moved so soon.   O that I may not touch those cheeks with mine, to catch their modesty and beauteousness!   Where am I! in whose presence! but we part.

Queen.   Mad impudence! am I then but a fly,
Or bird, or idle unobservant air,
That every wish shall strip itself before me?
Again must I command you? loose that hand, sir;
No transports here, no palm to breast or cross,
Unless for grace or pardon; and methinks
Those things are best alone, or with the priest.

Ines.   Into what errors have I led you, Pedro!
Constantia may retrieve you . . . she alone.
Give me my hand . . . O make me take it back.

The princess is mild and lovely, she knows your merits, she is worthy of you . . . obey, yield.   I must not throw myself at your feet again, but let me pray and once more move you.

Blanca.   Does it require an effort, girl, to espouse a princess of Castile, and thy superior in beauty as in birth?

Ines.   O indeed she is, Don Pedro, indeed she is.   I did not think of saying it, but you know it.

Blanca.   Come then, shrink not, resist not, hang not back. Guard!

Ines.   Good soldier, I know you dare not act otherwise . . . the royal word just given as you heard was *strike!*

Pedro.   O God! she has fallen against the door.
Is she hurt?   Open! ho, guard, open!

Blanca.   Would you tread upon her blood? have you no
decency? it runs through, before your feet.   Obdurate, insensate,
who now will pity you?

Pedro.   None! none! She is dead!   My father! you too are
childless.*

PIO-NONO AND ANTONELLI.

Antonelli.   Devil take that dove! he always flies away the
moment I enter.

Pio-Nono.   Antonelli! Antonelli! this exclamation, to a
certain point, is not unlike an oath!   Nay, nay; up, man, up!

Antonelli.   Not before I receive absolution from your
Holiness.

Pio-Nono.   Well then, take it, and now upon your legs again.
Red stockings, and calves uppermost, are unfit to lie horizontally
in that way.

Antonelli.   To see that dove so indocile and unmannerly was
enough to make a saint forget himself, even the blessed Peter.

Pio-Nono.   My worthy predecessor, it is reported, was at

---

* This is not the true story of Ines who was murdered some time
after.

Character is the business of the Dialogue: chronology must be contented to yield a little, in distant ages and countries.   The adventures of
Ines supply two fine subjects for tragedy.   The first when King Alfonso
had resolved to murder her at Corinbra, and desisted from the resolution on
seeing her beauty, and that of her children : the second, when the assassination was accomplishing.   La Moethe and others have composed a drama
on Ines, and her story is the most interesting part in the Lusiad of
Camoens.   This distinguished and admirable poet was not felicitous in
the development of character; which, whatever may be talked of and
repeated on the beautiful and the sublime, is the best and most arduous
part of poetry.   It is this which gives to Homer a large portion of his
glory; it is this which sustains us half-stifled in the Socratic school of
Euripides; and it is this which, even with a third of the poetry, would
have elevated Shakespeare immeasurably above all.

certain times, propense to the choleric. We are all frail creatures.

Antonelli. Excepting your Beatitude, being not only the successor of Peter, to whom none bowed down in worship, but also of Christ, to whom all did.

Pio-Nono. We know this well enough : let it pass. I am vext that the scurvy dove was not better taught : by this time he ought to have learnt his lesson. Should he have descended on my head, or only have fluttered over it awhile ?

Antonelli. Immaterial which; but certainly one of them is necessary.

Pio-Nono. The form of a dove is all we want; the dove himself is supervacaneous.

Antonelli. Per Bacco ! he seems to speak in parables.

Pio-Nono. Now could not one or other of those clever artists, who arrange the lamps on the cupola, contrive, with the preliminary aid of a milliner, to furnish a dove of more tractable materials ? Flesh and blood are unruly, even in doves.

Antonelli. I am afraid we must come to that at last : for, your Holiness wearing no hair upon the crown, there is no place for a pea or a lentil, which would do the business. I never heard of a dove that was not ready at feeding-time.

Pio-Nono. What a dovecote have I then in the Holy College ! and what prodigious flights throughout the country circumjacent !

Antonelli. If I may be permitted to understand the allusion and the smile of your Holiness, I would crave the liberty of remarking that the most pious and devout would hesitate to mortify the flesh in these jubilant days, when your Beatitude is about to enlarge and consolidate the halo of glory which encircles the brow of God's mother.

Pio-Nono. As matters stand we must deliberate what is to be done.

Antonelli. It appears to me that at last, the worst come to the worst, we must suspend an artificial dove at some height over the canopy. If the thing should be suspected, we have only to aver that it is symbolical. In another age there will be schisms on this subject, and the real dove will carry the day.

Pio-Nono. Schisms, schisms . . . on what have there not been ?

Antonelli.   Faith is kept alive by the conflict of spiritual and material.   Some turn their eyes towards symbol, others toward reality.   For instance the Real Presence.

Pio-Nono.   Prythee stop there: do not touch the Real Presence. . . . do not take Christ's body out of men's mouths. The laity has always been on the alert to make an irruption into that larder: it has given us some trouble to keep the cup for ourselves. But the mystery now to be elucidated is equally awful . . . the Miraculous Conception.   The profane dare to ask whether one miraculous conception is not enough; namely the Blessed Virgin of her miraculous child.   They presume to demand of us whether there is any authority in Holy Scripture for Saint Elizabeth's. These are thorny questions which require a dexterous hand, with a tough skin on finger and thumb.

Antonelli.   We must extricate the knot; otherwise the heretical Greek Church will get the start of us; and presently we may lose our hold on the Holy Places.

Pio-Nono.   A bad job that would be.   Indeed I begin to fear that my son in Christ, the Emperor of the French, grows lukewarm.

Antonelli.   The worst of it is, he threatens to withdraw our defenders from us.

Pio-Nono.   Austrians will occupy the vacancy.

Antonelli.   The French are poor, but honest; the Austrians are poorer and rapacious.   The French officer pays and is polite : the Austrian takes without payment and without politeness.   The French are often fierce, the Austrians are always brutal.

Pio-Nono.   You did not formerly think of the French so favourably.

Antonelli.   Formerly I knew them less.   Of the Austrians I always thought and always spoke the same.

Pio-Nono.   Antonelli I have always trusted in your perspicacity, but believe me, it is a property we must conceal as carefully as if it was stolen.   The more we see the less we must let others see.   Certainly the French, generous and improvident, do spend a great deal of money in our city.

Antonelli.   There are murmurs against them from opposite quarters : from the intractable republicans and the long-suffering ecclesiastics.   Officers, bands of martial music, epaulets, medals for valour in the field of battle, draw to them thoughtless girls, readier to approach the barracks than the confessionals. The pious groan profoundly at this backsliding, while the rebellious and the atheistical ask tauntingly whether the fair penitents are the likelier to bring for baptism little heads with moustaches or bald ones *more patrum.*

Pio-Nono. My heart bleeds . . .

Antonelli (aside). Too adipose a covering for that.

Pio-Nono. What were you suggesting ?

Antonelli. A reply to your Holiness, interrupted by unutterable grief.

Pio-Nono. Grief for what ? Faith ! I forgot my injunction. Was it about the prisoners ? I won't have many strangled : mind that. For twenty at Naples I would not punish five capitally. Disobedient sons shall find in me a merciful and clement father. Divine justice demands . . . But we were about to arrange the formulary of the Conception. It should be august. After due invocation of our tutelary saints for nine days in twelve churches, Torlonia must be called in to aid us.

Antonelli. He holds back now that he has lost the farming of the tobacco ; we must apply to Rothschild.

Pio-Nono. Secretly then. Rothschild is a Jew. The Virgin may be indignant, and may confound our counsels.

Antonelli. It appears to me, Holy Father, that our Blessed Lady will be much amused at seeing an infidel Jew the main supporter of the most miraculous claim her advocates ever brought into court. As for that cursed dove pecking his breast on the perch yonder, I would, with permission, have him caught when he is roosting, and given to a chorister for supper.

NICHOLAS AND DIOGENES.

Nicholas. Dost thou know who I am, fellow ? that thou darest to laugh in my face.

Diogenes. Call me not *fellow.*

Nicholas. What art thou else ?

Diogenes.   *Fellow* I am, but no fellow of thine.   I always spoke the truth above ground ; thou didst never.   Desirest thou to know who are my fellows?
Nicholas.   Not I indeed.
Diogenes.   I thought so ; but thou shalt.
Nicholas.   Threatenest thou crowned heads?
Diogenes.   Crowned heads! where are they?
Nicholas.   Mine was.
Diogenes.   It was until the world rose up against thee, and until thy own slave struck off both crown and head together.
Nicholas.   Laughest thou at a vile assassination?
Diogenes.   The gods forbid.   I laugh at a blunderer who attempted to throw down all human laws before him : who succeeded in so doing but was crushed under their fragments. Nobody trys to chain a mad dog up; every man pursues him unto death.   Men and gods unite in one grand hunt against the irreclaimable brute, the breaker of chain and muzzle ; we knock him on the head and sweep his *kennel clean out.*   Assassination is not the word.   But you despots see things inverted, and name them abitrarily.   What is great to others is small to you : what is smallest in the sight of Wisdom is greatest in the sight of Folly. Spider eyed insects your many eyes betray you, and ye are caught at last in the web you have woven for the flies.
Nicholas.   Audacious! and this to me.
Diogenes.   Verily to thee, the latest and most obvious witness of my indictment.   However I am not cited as thy accuser. Thy accusers will come forward, ten thousand at a time ; and the hall, extending over half of these vast regions, must be cleared ten thousand times for them, and many times after, until at last come the Sacred Band of my brave compatriots, forth from the blazing roofs and blood reddened billows of Sinope.
Nicholas.   It was a disaster they brought on themselves.
Diogenes.   Yea, truly, by confiding in any word of thine. Assassination, forsooth! and this was none!   Peradventure I mistook thy meaning, which thou wert always fond of making people do : perhaps it was that ‘ vile assassination ’ is assassination of the vile.   Such a definition would have been bandied about in the grove of Academos, and caught upon perfumed beard and deposited on budding.

Nay, do not let my praises puff thee up afresh, and make thee a bigger and burlier, tho' an empty shade. I will lower a chord of my lyre, as songmen say, and forbear to celebrate him who dispatched thee hither. He may indeed have had no virtue or courage in him: but low as men hold the rat-catcher, they hold the rat lower.

Nicholas. Audacious villain!

Diogenes. I was more audacious in the world above, where my fist could fairly have clutched thee. Miserable phantom! hast thou never been instructed what respect was paid me by the most powerful of kings compared with whom thou art but as a scorpion to a basilisk? I lived in poverty and died in peace. Glorious prerogative! Dost thou fancy that thy raids of slaves can ever make a man greater, wiser, or happier? Quite the contrary. But to reason with a madman is to be one.

Nicholas. What a bladder of gall.

Diogenes. Thou shalt drink it to the last drop. Advance, my countrymen! advance and surround this miscreant. My fellow-citizens! and ye from the Bosphorus, confederates and defenders of Sinope! Turnest thou pale, O murderous dastard! Turnest thou pale, O concrete slime of Styx and Acheron! Men without their limbs are sailing in the air around thee. Look up, ' vile assassin.' He dares not. Surround him ye who have arms and legs and carry him off in the midst of you. Howl, howl after him, ye women, who wailed of late so unavailingly. Fear not ye little children to come nigh: approach, approach, the fire that burnt your entrails is extinguished; for him it never shall be. The gods have condemned your murderer to carry it eternally in his heart.

NICHOLAS AND NESSELRODE.

Nicholas. It seems, Count Nesselrode, that you have not a word to say.

Nesselrode. Your Majesty has not spoken.

Nicholas. Indeed I thought I had.

Nesselrode. Your Majesty seemed preoccupied.

Nicholas. No wonder. Those cursed Turks, Negid at the head of them, affront me. I did believe the young man was effeminate.

Nesselrode. The effeminate are sometimes unwieldy, the weak intractable.

Nicholas. I did believe that the concessions he had already surrendered to me in favour of my protectorate, or rather my headship, of the Greek church, would have alienated him from all devout Mahometans. Instead of which, tolerant and generous as they always are wherever the Government is concerned, the miscreants applaud him for his exercise of these virtues, and are rabid against me for demanding more and greater concessions.

Nesselrode. Certainly they are roused, and even exasperated.

Nicholas. That would be nothing; I might indeed have desired it ; but the voice of Europe is encouraging them in their obstinacy.

Nesselrode. Too true.

Nicholas. Too true ! is that all ? Has a minister of state, a prime minister, to say nothing but *too true ?*

Nesselrode. May it please your Majesty, it seldom has happened that Ministers have been censured for being *too true.*

Nicholas. I do believe thou hast by nature a grain or two of wit in the vortexes of thy brain. The smallest of these quantities is enough to undo a politician. Speak seriously ; for matters and times are serious.

Nesselrode. Sire ! it is in such matters and times that a single thought of less gravity than the rest is a god send.

Nicholas. Worse and worse ! First a witticism, now a reflection. Nesselrode ! I can well believe that you are growing old, but not in a court. What is to be done ? no, I do not ask you what is to be done, but how to do it. I am resolved to execute my design, to continue my operations. Consistency and firmness have always been among my attributes ; never must I lose them in the eyes of my people and of the world.

Nesselrode. It would indeed be disgraceful, and what is worse than disgraceful, it would be difficult and detrimental to retract.

Nicholas. If France had been silent and quiet about the *Holy Places,* I might have been too.

Nesselrode. Louis Napoleon wanted to conciliate the pope, and to bring him for his coronation to Paris round by Jerusalem. Louis Napoleon is long sighted, and never puts out an arm without an object which he is certain he can seize. If the pope refuses him now, he will bring his Holiness by the ear into Notre Dame.

Nicholas. I admire the man's resolute character, and only wish I may never have to deal with it. I ought to have entertained a suspicion that he would directly or indirectly, thwart me in my steps against the Ottoman Empire.

Nesselrode. Sire ! it might have been seen easily and clearly. I was not encouraged by your Majesty to deliver my opinion at full length upon this subject ; military men and nobles of ancient family, your Majesty deigned to assure me, had set their hearts upon it.

Nicholas. Scarcely was there a courtier who had not fixed upon the site of palace and villa and garden round Constantinople.

Nesselrode. This I knew ; but I also knew that those hearts, whether light ones or heavy ones, must be cast down from the pleasant places they were set upon, and that the Turks will contrive to lie along them at full length, or with legs crost under them, for some time yet.

Nicholas. This is vexatious to think of. It may not be. Rather would I hazard a war with half Europe.

Nesselrode. Perhaps your Majesty might encounter more than half Europe at this enterprise.

Nicholas. Impossible, Austria is under my thumb.

Nesselrode. Under the soft part of it, may it please your Majesty. Austria is greatly more interested to prevent the absorption or partition of Turkey than any other power is. The Danube rolls indolently now along her dominions ; it might swell into formidable activity against her under the steam and the fortresses of your Majesty.

Nicholas. France has always turned her eyes toward the east ; England will counteract her interference.

Nesselrode. England has even a greater interest in maintaining the Ottoman Empire than France has. England will never be so insane as to take an active part in hostilities on this question ; but the Catholic Powers and the Protestant Powers will unite, if necessary, in active opposition to your Majesty's progress.

Nicholas.   Has France forgotten that we once spared her? Has Austria that we lately saved her?

Nesselrode.   No, sire, and neither of them will ever forget or forgive it.

Nicholas.   I am not the man to eat my words; and my threats are the least indigestible of any.

Nesselrode.   We may so masticate our words and remove so much by a dexterous use of the fingers, of what is gristle or husk, that the operation is far from difficult or unpleasant.

Nicholas.   France and England can never act together.

Nesselrode.   They did at Navarino.

Nicholas.   It was but for the day.   You are grown over-cautious and somewhat timid; I would not willingly say conscientious; I would not hint at incapacity in a minister who has served me so long and so faithfully.   You seem almost to apprehend a coalition against me.

Nesselrode.   God forbid!   Luckily for us, there is only one vigorous mind among the arbiters of human affairs.

Nicholas.   Nesselrode! Nesselrode! no flattery!   What makes you start?

Nesselrode.   Sire, my incomplete meaning was, that at present there is only one vigorous mind among all the Powers of Europe which could inspire the fear of our humiliation.   Certainly, too certainly, the time is advancing when the chief Continental Powers will unite that confederacy.   Already there is not a single one of them which does not see distinctly that Russia is too formidable for Europe; Persia has long seen it.   While the kings of Christendom bring Greek and Latin close together, Persia and Turkey will unite their sects in one common cause, chaunting "There is but one God, and Mahomet is his prophet."

Nicholas.   You shall never be mine.   You are capable of managing the weak ministers of Potentates round about me, but not me.   Constantinople is already in flames before me.

Nesselrode.   The Greeks deprecate the degradation of their Church in its transfer to Moscow or Petersburgh; and the Muscovite nobility, in the city of their ancestors, are happier round the *Kremlin*, than they ever will be round the *Seven Towers*.

Those fires of Constantinople will crack and split your empire.

CRITICISMS

ON

THEOCRITUS, CATULLUS, AND PETRARCH.

CRITICISMS.

THE IDYLS OF THEOCRITUS.

Within the last half-century the Germans have given us several good editions of Theocritus. That of Augustus Meinekius, to which the very inferior and very different poems of Bion and Moschus are appended, is among the best and the least presuming. No version is added; the notes are few and pertinent, never pugnacious, never prolix. In no age, since the time of Aristarchus, or before, has the Greek language been so profoundly studied, or its poetry in its nature and metre so perfectly understood, as in ours. Neither Athens nor Alexandria saw so numerous or so intelligent a race of grammarians as Germany has recently seen contemporary. Nor is the society diminisht, nor are its labours relaxt, at this day. Valckenaer, Schrieber, Schaeffer, Kiesling, Wuesteman, are not the only critics and editors, who, before the present one, have bestowed their care and learning on Theocritus.

Doubts have long been entertained upon the genuineness of several among his Idyls. But latterly a vast number, even of those which had never been disputed, have been called in question by Ernest Reinhold, in a treatise printed at Jena in 1819. He acknowledges the eleven first, the thirteenth, fourteenth, fifteenth, sixteenth, and eighteenth. Against the arbitrary ejection of the remainder rose Augustus Wissowa in 1828. In his *Theocritus Theocritæus*, vindicating them from suspicion, he subjoins to his elaborate criticism a compendious index of ancient quotations, in none of which is any doubt entertained of their authenticity. But surely it requires no force of argument, no call for extraneous help, to subvert the feeble position that, because the poet wrote his Pastorals mostly in his native dialect, the Doric, he can never have written in another. If he composed the eighteenth Idyl in the Æolic, why may he not be allowed the twelfth and twenty-second in the Ionic? Not, however, that in the twelfth he has done it uniformly: the older manuscripts of this poem contain fewer forms of that dialect than were afterwards foisted into it, for the sake of making it all of a piece. It is easy to believe that the Idyls he wrote in Sicily were Doric, with inconsiderable variations, and that he thought it more agreeable to Hiero, whose favour he was desirous of conciliating. But when he retired from Sicily to the court of Ptolemy, where Callimachus and Apollonius and Aratus were residing, he would not on every occasion revert to an idiom little cultivated in Egypt. Not only to avoid the charge of rivalry with the poets who were then flourishing there, but also from sound judgment, he wrote heroic poetry in Homeric verse; in verse no less Ionic than Homer's own; indeed more purely so.

Thirty of his poems are entitled IDYLS : in short all but the Epigrams, however different in length, in subject, and in metre. But who gave them this appellation? or whence was it derived? We need go up no higher than to εἶδος for the derivation : and it is probable that the poet himself supplied the title. But did he give it to all his compositions? or even to all those (excepting the Epigrams) which are now extant. We think he did not, although we are unsupported in our opinion by the old scholiast who wrote the arguments. "The poet," says he, "did not wish to specify his pieces, but *ranged them all under one title.*" We believe that he ranged what he thought the more important and the more epic under this category, and that he omitted to give any separate designation to the rest, prefixing to each piece (it may be) its own title. Nay, it appears to us not at all improbable that those very pieces which we moderns call more peculiarly Idyls, were not comprehended by him in this designation. We believe that εἰδύλλιον means a *small image of something greater ;* and that it was especially applied at first to his short poems of the heroic cast and character. As the others had no genuine name denoting their quality, but only the names of the interlocutors or the subjects (which the ancient poets, both Greek and Roman, oftener omitted) they were all after a while comprehended in a mass within one common term. That the term was invented long after the age of Theocritus, is the opinion of Heine and of Wissowa: but where is the proof of the fact, or foundation for the conjecture? Nobody has denied that it existed in the time of Virgil; and many have wondered that he did not thus entitle his Bucolics, instead of calling them Eclogues. And so indeed he probably would have done, had he believed that Theocritus intended any such designation for his Pastorals. But neither he nor Calpurnius, nor Nemesian, called by the name of Idyl their bucolic poems; which they surely would have done if, in their opinion or in the opinion of the public, it was applicable to them. It was not thought so when literature grew up again in Italy, and when the shepherds and shepherdesses recovered their lost estates in the provinces of poetry, under the patronage of Petrarca, Boccaccio, Pontanus, and Mantuanus.

Eobanus Hessus, a most voluminous writer of Latin verses, has translated much from the Greek classics, and among the rest some pieces from Theocritus. From time to time we have spent several hours of idleness over his pages; but the further we proceeded, whatever was the direction, the duller and drearier grew his unprofitable pine-forest, the more wearisome and disheartening his flat and printless sands. After him, Bruno Sidelius, another German, was the first of the moderns who conferred the name of Idyl on their Bucolics. As this word was enlarged in its acceptation, so was another in another kind of poetry, namely, the Pæan, which at first was appropriated to Apollo and Artemis, but was afterward transferred to other deities. Servius, on the first Eneid, tells us that Pindar not only composed one on Zeus of Dodona, but several in honour of mortals. The same may be said of the Dithyrambic. Elegy, too, in the commencement, was devoted to grief exclusively, like the *næniæ* and *threnæ*: subsequently it embraced a vast variety of matters, some of them ethic and didactic; some the very opposite to its institution, inciting to war and patriotism, for instance those of Tyrtæus; and some to love and licentiousness, in which Mimnermus has been followed by innumerable disciples to the extremities of the earth.

Before we inspect the Idyls of Theocritus, one by one, as we intend to do, it may be convenient in this place to recapitulate what little is known about him. He tells us, in the epigraph to them, that there was another poet of the same name, a native of

Chios, but that he himself was a Syracusan of low origin, son of Praxagoras and Philina. He calls his mother πεϱίϰλειτη (illustrious), evidently for no other reason than because the verse required it. There is no ground for disbelieving what he records of his temper; that he never was guilty of detraction. His exact age is unknown, and unimportant. One of the Idyls is addressed to the younger Hiero, another to Ptolemy Philadelphus. The former of these began his reign in the one hundred and twenty-sixth Olympiad, the latter in the one hundred and twenty-third. In the sixteenth Idyl the poet insinuates that the valour of Hiero was more conspicuous than his liberality : on Ptolemy he never had reason to make any such remark. Among his friends in Egypt was Aratus, of whom Cicero and Cæsar thought highly, and of whose works both of them translated some parts. Philetas the Coan was another: and his merit must also have been great; for Propertius joins him with Callimachus, and asks permission to enter the sacred grove of poetry in their company.

> Callimachi manes et Coi sacra Philetæ!
> In vestrum quæso me sinite ire nemus.

It appears, however, that Aratus was more particularly and intimately Theocritus's friend. To him he inscribes the sixth Idyl, describes his loves in the seventh, and borrows from him the religious exordium of the seventeenth. After he had resided several years in Egypt, he returned to his native country, and died there.

We now leave the man for the writer, and in this capacity we have a great deal more to say. The poems we possess from him are only a part, although probably the best, of what he wrote. He composed hymns, elegies, and iambics. Hermann, in his dissertation on hexameter verse, expresses his wonder that Virgil, in the Eclogues, should have deserted the practice of Theocritus in its structure; and he remarks, for instance, the first in the first Idyl.

> Ἀδύ τι τὸ ψιθύρισμα καὶ ἁ πίτυς . . αἰπόλε τήνα

This pause, however, is almost as frequent in Homer as in Theocritus: and it is doubtful to us, who indeed have not counted the examples, whether any other pause occurs so often in the Iliad. In reading this verse, we do not pause after πίτυς, but after ψιθύρισμα : but in the verses which the illustrious critic quotes from Homer the pause is precisely in that place.

Πόντῳ μὲν τὰ πρῶτα κορύσσεται .   .   αὐτὰρ ἔπειτα
Χέρσῳ ῥηγνύμενον μεγάλα βρέμει . . ἀμφὶ δέ τ' ἄκρας.

Although the pause is greatly more common in the Greek Hexameter than in the Latin, yet Hermann must have taken up Virgil's Eclogues very inattentively in making his remark. For that which he wonders the Roman has imitated so sparingly from the Syracusan occurs quite frequently enough in Virgil, and rather too frequently in Theocritus. It may be tedious to the inaccurate and negligent ; it may be tedious to those whose reading is only a species of dissipation, and to whom ears have been given only as ornaments ; nevertheless, for the sake of others, we have taken some trouble to establish our position in regard to the Eclogues, and the instances are given below.*

* Ecl. i., containing 83 verses.

Namque erit ille mihi semper deus . . .
Non equidem invideo, miror magis . . .
Ite meæ, felix quondam, pecus . . .

Ecl. ii.   73 verses.

Atque superba pati fastidia . . .
Cum placidum ventis stares mare . . .
Bina die siccant ovis ubera . . .
Heu, heu! quid volui misero mihi . . .

Ecl. iii.   111 verses.

Die mihi, Damœta, cujum pecus . . .
Infelix, O semper oves pecus . . .
Et, si non aliquâ nocuisses . . .
Si nescis, meus ille caper fuit . . .
Bisque die numerant ambo pecus . . .
Parta meæ Veneri sunt munera . . .
Pollio et ipse facit nova carmine . . .
Parcite, oves, nimium procedere . . .

Ecl. v.   90 verses.

Sive antro potius succedimus . . .
Frigida, Daphni, boves ad flumina . . .
Quale sopor fessis in gramine . . .
Hæc eadem docuit cujum pecus . . .

In Theocritus it is not this usage which is so remarkable ; it is the abundance and exuberance of dactyls. They hurry on one after another, like the waves of a clear and rapid brook in the sunshine, reflecting all things the most beautiful in nature, but not resting upon any.

Ecl. vi.   86 verses.

Cum canerem reges et prælia . . .
Ægle Naïadum pulcherrima . . .
Carmina quæ vultis cognoscite . . .
Aut aliquam in magno sequitor grege . . .
Errabunda bovis vestigia . . .
Quo cursu deserta petiverit . . .

Ecl. vii.   70 verses.

Ambo florentes ætatibus . .
Vir gregis ipse caper deerraverat . . .
Aspicio ; ille ubi me contra videt . . .
Nymphæ noster amor Lebethrides . .
Quale meo Codro concedite . . .
Setosi caput hoc apri tibi . . .
Ite domum pasti, si quis pudor . . .
Aut si ultra placitum laudârit . . .
Si fœtura gregem suppleverit . . .
Solstitium pecori defendite . . .
Populus Alcidæ gratissima . . .
Fraxinus in sylvis pulcherrima.

Ecl. viii.   109 verses.

Sive oram Illyrici legis æquoris . . .
A te principium. tibi desinet . . .
Carmina cœpta tuis, atque hac sine . . .
Nascere præque diem veniens age . . .
Omnia vel medium fiant mare . . .
Desine Mænalios jam desine . . .
Ducite ab urbe domum, mea carmina . . .
Transque caput jace : ne respexeris . . .

Ecl. ix.   67 verses.

Heu cadit in quemquam tantum scelus . .
Tityre dum redeo, brevis est via . . .
Et potum pastas age Tityre . . .
Pierides, sunt et mihi carmina . . .
Omnia fert ætas, animum quoque . . .
Nunc oblita mihi tot carmina . . .
Hinc adeo media est nobis via . . .
Incipit apparere Bianoris . . .

Idyl I. Of all the poetry in all languages that of Theocritus is the most fluent and easy; but if only this Idyl were extant, it would rather be memorable for a weak imitation of it by Virgil, and a beautiful one by Milton, than for any great merit beyond the harmony of its verse. Indeed it opens with such sounds as Pan himself in a prelude on his pipe might have produced. The dialogue is between Thyrsis and a goatherd. Here is much of appropriate description; but it appears unsuitable to the character and condition of a goatherd to offer so large a reward as he offers for singing a song. "If you will sing as you sang in the contest with the Libyan shepherd Chromis, I will reward you with a goat, mother of two kids, which goat you may milk thrice a-day; for, though she suckles two kids, she has milk enough left for two pails."

We often hear that such or such a thing "is not worth an old song." Alas! how very few things are! What precious re-collections do some of them awaken! What pleasurable tears do they excite! They purify the stream of life; they can delay it on its shelves and rapids; they can turn it back again to the soft moss amidst which its sources issue.

But we must not so suddenly quit the generous goatherd: we must not turn our backs on him for the sake of indulging in these reflections. He is ready to give not only a marvellously fine goat for the repetition of a song, but a commodity of much higher value in addition; a deep capacious cup of the most elaborate workmanship, carved and painted in several compartments. Let us look closely at these. The first contains a woman in a veil and fillet: near her are two young suitors who throw fierce *words* one against the other: she never minds them, but smiles

Ecl. x.   77 verses.

Nam neque Parnassi. vobis juga . . .
Omnes unde amor iste rogant tibi . . .

Instances of the cadence are not wanting in the Eneid. The fourth book, the most elaborate of all, exhibits them.

" Tempora, quis rebus dexter modus " . .

And again in the last lines, with only one interposed.

" Devolat. et supra caput adstitit
Sic ait et dextra crinem secat "

upon each *alternately*. Surely no cup, not even a magical one, could express all this. But they *continue* to carry on their ill-will. In the next place is an old fisherman on a rock, from which he is hauling his net. Not far from him is a vineyard, laden with purple grapes. A little boy is watching them near the boundary-hedge, while a couple of foxes are about their business: one walking through the rows of vines, picking out the ripe grapes as he *goes along ;* the other devising mischief to the boy's wallet, and *declaring* on the word of a fox that he will never quit the premises until he has captured the breakfast therein deposited. The song is deferred no longer: and a capital song it is: but the goatherd has well paid the piper. It is unnecessary to transcribe the verses which Virgil and Milton have imitated.

> Nam neque Parnassi vobis juga nam neque Pindi
> Ulla moram fecere, neque Aonia Aganippe.

Virgil himself, on the present occasion, was certainly not detained in any of these places. Let us try whether we cannot come toward the original with no greater deviation, and somewhat less dulness.

> Where were ye, O ye nymphs! when Daphnis died?
> For not on Pindus were ye, nor beside
> Penëus in his softer glades, nor where
> Acis might well expect you, once your care.
> But neither Acis did your steps detain,
> Nor strong Anapus rushing forth amain,
> Nor high-brow'd Etna with her forest chain.

Harmonious as are the verses of Theocritus, the Greek language itself could not bear him above Milton in his Lycidas. He had the good sense to imitate the versification of Tasso's Aminta, employing rhyme where it is ready at hand, and permitting his verses to be longer or shorter, as may happen. They are never deficient in sweetness, taken separately, and never at the close of a sentence disappoint us. However, we can not but regret the clashing of irreconcileable mythologies. Neither in a poem nor in a picture do we see willingly the Nymphs and the Druids together: Saint Peter comes even more inopportunely: and although, in the midst of such scenery, we may be prepared against wolves with their own heads and "*maws*" and "*privy paws*," yet we deprecate them when they appear with a bishop's: they are then an over-match for us. The ancients could not readily run into such errors: yet something of a kind not very dissimilar may be objected to Virgil.

Venit Apollo,
"Galle! quid insanis?" inquit.

When the poet says, "Cynthius aurem vellit et admonuit," we are aware that it is merely a form of phraseology: but among those who, in Virgil's age, believed in Apollo, not one believed that he held a conversation with Gallus. The time for these familiarities of gods with mortals had long been over,

Nec se contingi patiuntur lumine claro,

There was only one of them who could still alight without suspicion among the poets. Phœbus had become a mockery, a by-word; but there never will be a time probably when Love shall lose his personality, or be wished out of the way if he has crept into a poem. But the poem must be a little temple of his own, admitting no other occupant or agent beside himself and (at most) two worshippers.

To return to this first Idyl. Theocritus may be censured for representing a continuity of action in one graven piece, where the girl smiles on two young men alternately. But his defence is ready. He would induce the belief that, on looking at the perfection of the workmanship, we must necessarily know not only what is passing, but also what is past and what is to come. We see the two foxes in the same spirit, and enter into their minds and machinations. We swear to the wickedest of the two that we will keep his secret, and that we will help him to the uttermost of our power, when he declares (φατί) that he will have the boy's breakfast. Perhaps we might not be so steadily his partisan, if the boy himself were not meditating an ill turn to another creature. He is busy in making a little cage for the cicala. Do we never see the past and the future in the pictures of Edwin Landseer? who exercises over all the beasts of the field and fowls of the air an undivided and unlimited dominion, καὶ νόον ἔγνω.

We shall abstain, as far as may be, in this review, from verbal criticism, for which the judicious editor, after many other great scholars, has left but little room: but we can not consent with him to omit the hundred and twentieth verse, merely because we find it in the fifth Idyl, nor because he tells us it is rejected in the best editions. Verses have been repeated both by Lucretius and by Virgil. In the present case the sentence, without it, seems obtruncated, and wants the peculiar rhythm of Theocritus, which is complete and perfect with it. In the two last verses are αἱ δὲ χίμαιραι Οὐ μὴ σκιρτάσητε. Speaking *to* the she-goats he could not well say *αἱ*, which could only be said in speaking *of* them. Probably the right reading is ὧδε, although we believe there is no authority for it. The repetition of that word is graceful and adds to the sense. "Come hither, Kissaitha! milk this one: but, you others! do not leap about *here*, lest, &c." The poet tells us he will hereafter sing more sweetly: it is much to say; but he will keep his promise: he speaks in the character of Thyrsis. When the goatherd gives the cup to the shepherd he wishes his mouth to be filled with honey, and with the honey-*comb!*

Idyl II. is a monologue, and not bucolic. Cimætha, an enchantress, is in love with Delphis. The poem is curious, containing a complete system of incantation as practised by the Greeks. Out of two verses, by no means remarkable, Virgil has framed some of the most beautiful in all his works. Whether the Idyl was in this particular copied from Apollonius, or whether he in the Argonautics had it before him, is uncertain. Neither of them is so admirable as,

> Sylvæque et sæva quierant
> Æquora.
> At non infelix animi Phœnissa; neque unquam
> Solvitur in somnos. *oculisve aut pectore noctem*
> *Accipit:* ingeminant curæ, rursusque resurgens
> Sævit amor.

> The woods and stormy waves were now at rest,
> But not the hapless Dido; never sank
> She into sleep, never received she night
> Into her bosom; grief redoubled grief.
> And love sprang up more fierce the more represt.

Idyl III.   A goatherd whose name is not mentioned, declares his love, with prayers and expostulations, praises and reproaches, to Amaryllis.   The restlessness of passion never was better expressed.   The tenth and eleventh lines are copied by Virgil, with extremely ill success.

> *Quod potui,* puero *sylvestri* ex arbore *lecta*
> Aurea mala decem misi, cras altera mittam.

How poor is *quod potui !* and what a *selection* (lecta) is that of crabs ; moreover, these were *sent* as a present (misi), and not offered in person.   There is not even the action, such as it is, but merely the flat relation of it.   Instead of a narration about sending these precious crabs, and the promise of as many more on the morrow, here in Theocritus the attentive lover says, " Behold ! I bring you ten apples.   I gathered them myself from the tree whence you desired me to gather them : to-morrow I will bring you more.   Look upon my soul-tormenting grief !   I wish I were a bee that I might come into your grotto, penetrating through the ivy and fern, however thick about you."   Springing up and away from his dejection and supplication, he adds wildly,

> Νῦν ἔγνων τὸν Ἔρωτα : βαρὺς θεὸς ἦ ῥα λεαίνας
> Μασδὸν ἐθήλαζε, δρυμῷ δέ μιν ἔτρεφε μάτηρ.*
>
> Now know I Love, a cruel God, who drew
> A lioness's teat, and in the forest grew.

Virgil has amplified the passage to no purpose.

> Nunc scio quid sit amor : duris in cotibus illum
> Ismarus aut Rhodope aut extremi Garamantes
> Nec *generis* nostri puerum nec *sanguinis* edunt.

Where is the difference of meaning here between *genus* and *sanguis ?*   And why all this bustle about Ismarus and Rhodope and the Garamantes ?   A lioness in an oak-forest stands in place of them all, and much better.   Love being the deity, not the passion, *qui* would have been better than *quid,* both in propriety and in sound.   There follows,

* We have given not the editor's but our own punctuation : none after θεός : for if there were any in that place, we should have wished the words were βαρὺν θεόν.

Alter ab undecimo jam tum me ceperat annus.

This is among the most faulty expressions in Virgil. The words *jam tum me* sound woodenly: and *me ceperat annus* is scarcely Latin. Perhaps the poet wrote *mihi*, abbreviated to *mi ; mihi cœperat annus.* There has been a doubt regarding the exact meaning: but this should raise none. The meaning is, "I was entering my *thirteenth* year." *Unus* ab undecimo would be the twelfth : of course *alter* ab undecimo must be the thirteenth. Virgil is little more happy in his translations from Theocritus than he is in those from Homer. It is probable that they were only school exercises, too many and (in his opinion) too good to be thrown away. J. C. Scaliger, zealous for the great Roman poet, gives him the preference over Homer in every instance where he has copied him. But in fact there is nowhere a sentence, and only a single verse anywhere, in which he rises to an equality with his master. He says of Fame,

Ingrediturque solo et caput inter sidera condit.

The noblest verse in the Latin language.

Idyl IV. Battus and Corydon.* The greater part is tedious ; but at verse thirty-eight begins a tender grief of Battus on the death of his Amaryllis : Corydon attempts to console him. "You must be of good courage, my dear Battus ! Things may go better with you another day." To which natural and brief reflection we believe all editions have added two verses as spoken by Corydon. Nevertheless, we suspect that Theocritus gave the following one to Battus, and that he says in reply, or rather in refutation, "There are hopes in the living, but the dead leave us none." Then says Corydon, "The skies are sometimes serene and sometimes rainy." Battus is comforted ; he adds but θαρσεω ; for he perceives on a sudden that the calves are nibbling the olives. Good Battus has forgotten at once all his wishes

---

* The close of verse thirty-one is printed ἅ τε Ζάκυνθος; in other editions ἀ Ζάκυνθος. Perhaps both are wrong. The first syllable of Ζάκυνθος is short, which is against the latter reading ; and τε would be long before Ζ, which is against the former. Might not a shepherd who uses the Doric dialect have said Δάκυνθος. We have heard of a coin inscribed Δακυνθιων. In Virgil we read *nemorosa Zacynthos ;* but it seems impossible that he should have written the word with a Ζ.

and regrets for Amaryllis, and would rather have a stout cudgel. His animosity soon subsides, however, and he asks Corydon an odd question about an old shepherd, which Corydon answers to his satisfaction and delight.

IDYL V. Comatas, a goatherd, and Lacon, a shepherd, accuse one another of thievery. They carry on their recriminations with much spirit: but the beauty of the verses could alone make the contest tolerable. After the fortieth are several which Virgil has imitated, with little honour to his selection. Theocritus, always harmonious, is invariably the most so in description. This is, however, too long continued in many places: but here we might wish it had begun earlier and lasted longer. Lacon says,

> Sweeter beneath this olive will you sing,
> By the grove-side and by the running spring,
> Where grows the grass in bedded tufts, and where
> The shrill cicala shakes the slumberous air.

This is somewhat bolder than the original will warrant, but not quite so bold as Virgil's "*rumpunt arbusta* cicadæ." It is followed by what may be well in character with two shepherds of Sibaris, but what has neither pleasantry nor novelty to recommend it: and the answer would have come with much better grace uninterrupted. Comatas, after reminding Lacon of a very untoward action in which both were implicated, thus replies:

> I will not thither: cypresses are here,
> Oaks, and two springs that gurgle cool and clear,
> And bees are flying for their hives, and through
> The shady branches birds their talk pursue.

They both keep their places, and look out for an arbitrator to decide on the merit of their songs. Morson, a woodman, is splitting a tree near them; and they call him. There is something very dramatic in their appeal, and in the objurgation that follows. The contest is carried on in extemporary verses, two at a time. After several, Comatas says, "All my she-goats, excepting two, are bearers of twins: nevertheless, a girl who sees me among them says, 'Unfortunate creature! do you milk them all yourself!'" Lacon, as the words now stand, replies, "*Pheu! pheu!*" an exclamation which among the tragedians expresses grief and anguish, but which here signifies *Psha, psha*. Now it is evident that Comatas had attempted to make Lacon jealous, by telling him how sorry the girl was that he should milk the goats himself without anybody to help him. Lacon in return is ready to show that he also had his good fortune. There is reason therefore to suspect that the name Λάχων should be Δάμων; because from all that precedes we may suppose that Lacon was never possessed of such wealth, and that Comatas would have turned him into ridicule if he had boasted of it. "Psha! psha! you are a grand personage with your twin-bearing goats, no doubt! but you milk them yourself: now Damon is richer than you are: he fills pretty nearly twenty hampers with cheeses."

This seems indubitable from the following speech of Lacon. Not to be teased any more after he had been taunted by Comatas, that Clearista, although he was a goatherd, threw apples at him, and began to sing the moment he drove his herd by her, Lacon, out of patience at last, says, "Cratidas makes me wild with that beautiful hair about the neck." There could have been no room for this if he had spoken of himself, however insatiable. For, in a later verse, Cratidas seems already to have made room for another.

'Αλλ' ἐγὼ Εὐμήδευς ἔραμαι μέγα.

Finding Damon here in Theocritus, we may account for his appearance in Virgil. No Greek letters are more easily mistaken one for the other than the capital Λ for Δ, and the small χ for μ. In the one hundred and fifth verse, Comatas boasts of possessing a cup sculptured by Praxiteles. This is no very grave absurdity in such a braggart: it suits the character: Virgil, who had none to support for his shepherd, makes him state that his is only "*divini* opus Alcimedontis."

It may be remarked, in conclusion, that no other Idyl contains so many pauses after the fourth foot, which Hermann calls bucolic: nearly half of the verses have this cadence.

Idyl VI. This is dramatic, and is addressed to Aratus. The shepherds Damœtas and Daphnis had driven their flocks into one place, and, sitting by a fountain, began a song about Polyphemus and Galatea. Daphnis acts the character of Galatea, Damœtas of Polyphemus. The various devices of the gigantic shepherd to make her jealous, and his confidence of success in putting them into practice, are very amusing. His slyness in giving a secret sign to set the dog at her, and the dog knowing that he loved her in his heart, and pushing his nose against her thigh instead of biting her, are such touches of true poetry as are seldom to be found in pastorals. In the midst of these our poet has been thought to have committed one anachronism. But where Galatea is said to have mistaken the game, when

> φεύγει φιλέοντα καὶ οὐ φιλέοντα διώκει
> Καὶ τὸν ἀπὸ γραμμᾶς κινεῖ λίθον,

> . . Seeks him who loves not, him who loves, avoids:
> And makes false moves,

she herself is not represented as the speaker, nor is Polyphemus, but Daphnis. It is only at the next speech that either of the characters comes forth in person: here Damætas is the Polyphemus, and acts his part admirably.

Idyl VII. The last was different in its form and character from the five preceding: the present is more different still. The poet, on his road to Alexandria with Eucritus and Amyntas, meets Phrasidamus and Antigenes, and is invited to accompany them to the festival of Ceres, called Thalysia. He falls in with Lycidas of Cidon, and they relate their love-stories. This Idyl closes with a description of summer just declining into autumn. The invocation to the Nymphs is in the spirit of Pindar.

Idyl VIII.* The subject is a contest in singing between Menalcas and Daphnis, for a pipe. Here are some verses of exquisite simplicity, which Virgil has most clumsily translated. '

> Ego hunc vitulum, ne *forte* recuses, &c.
> De grege non ausim quidquam deponere tecum,
> Est mihi namque domi pater, est *injusta* noverca,
> Bisque die numerant ambo *pecus* . . *alter et hœdos.*

It is evident that Virgil means by *pecus* the sheep only ; *pecora*

---

* The two first lines are the least pleasant to the ear of any in this melodious poet.

> Δάφνιδι τῷ χαρίε | ν τι . . . . συνήντετο βουκολέο | ν τι
> Μᾶλα νέμων ὡς φα ¦ ν τί, &c.

'Ὼς φαντί is found in all editions; but Pierson has suggested Διόφαντε. Diophantus was a friend of Theocritus, addressed in Idyl XXI.

at this day means a *ewe* in Italian. Virgil's Menalcas had no objection to the robbery, but was afraid of the chastisement.

The Menalcas of Theocritus says, " I will never lay what belongs to my father ; but I have a pipe which I made myself ; " and according to his account of it, it was no ordinary piece of workmanship. Damætas, it appears, had made exactly such another, quite as good, and the cane of which it was made cut his finger in making it. They carry on the contest in such sweet hexameters and pentameters as never were heard before or since : but they finish with hexameters alone. The prize is awarded to Daphnis by the goatherd who is arbitrator. He must have been a goatherd of uncommonly fine discernment : the match seems equal : perhaps the two following verses turned the balance :—

'Αλλ' ὑπὸ τᾷ πέτρᾳ τᾷδ' ᾄσομαι, ἀγκὰς ἔχων τυ,
Σύννομα μᾶλ' ἐσορῶν, τὰν Σικελὰν ἐς ἅλα.

Of these, as of those above, we can only give the meaning : he who can give a representation of them, can give a representation of the sea-breezes.

> It never was my wish to have possest
>   The land of Pelops and his golden store ;
> But only as I hold you to my breast,
>   Glance at our sheep and our Sicilian shore.

Idyl IX.   Again Menalcas and Daphnis ; but they must both have taken cold.

Idyl X.   Milo and Battus are reapers. Milo asks Battus what ails him, that he can neither draw a straight furrow nor reap like his neighbours. For simplicity none of the pastorals is more delightful, and it abounds in rustic irony.

Idyl XI. is addrest to Nikias of Miletus, and appears to have been written in Sicily, by the words ὁ Κύκλωψ ὁ παρ' ἁμῖν. It describes the love of Polyphemus for Galatea, his appeal to her, his promises (to the extent of eleven kids and four bear-cubs), and his boast that, if he can not have her, he can find another perhaps more beautiful ; for that many are ready enough to play with him, challenging him to that effect, and giggling (κιχλίζοντι) when he listens to them. Virgil's imitation of this Idyl is extremely, and more than usually, feeble. The last verse, however, of Theocritus is somewhat flat.*

IDYL XII. We now arrive at the first of those Idyls of which the genuineness has been so pertinaciously disputed.† And why? Because forsooth it pleased the author to compose it in the Ionic dialect. Did Burns, who wrote mostly in the Scottish, write nothing in the English? With how much better reason has the competitor of Apollonius and Callimachus deserted the Doric occasionally! Meleager, and other writers of inscriptions, mix frequently Ionic forms with Doric. In fact, the most accurate explorers must come at last to the conclusion, that even in the pastoral portion of these Idyls, scarcely a single one is composed throughout of unmingled Doric. The ear that is accustomed to the exuberant flow of Theocritus, will never reject as spurious this melodious and graceful poem. Here, and particularly toward the conclusion, as very often elsewhere, he writes in the style and spirit of Pindar, while he celebrates the loves extolled by Plato.

IDYL XIII. is addrest to Nikias, as the eleventh was. It is not a dialogue: it is a narrative of the loss of Hylas. The same story is related by Propertius in the most beautiful of his elegies.

IDYL XIV. is entitled Cynisca's Love, and is a dialogue between her husband Æschines and his friend Thyonichus. Cynisca had taken a fancy to Lucos. At an entertainment given by Æschines, a very mischievous guest, one Apis, sings about a wolf (Λύκος), who was quite charming. Æschines had

---

* ῥᾷον δὲ διᾶγ᾽ ἢ χρυσὸν ἔδωκεν.

"*He lived more pleasantly than if he had given gold for it.*"

This is barely sense; nor can it be improved without a bold substitution,

ἢ χρυσὸν ἔχων τις.

Such terminations are occasionally to be found in our poet; for example.

Idyl 1. ἀλλὰ μάχευ μοι. Idyl 2. ὄσσον ἐγὼ δήν. Idyl 3. εἰ φιλεεις, με, and three lines further on, οὔνεκ᾽ ἐγὼ μὲν, &c.

† The title of this is *Aites*, which among the Thessalians was what, according to the poet in v. 13, εἴσπνηλος was among the Spartans: the one παρὰ τὸ τὸν ἐρώμενον εἰσαίειν, the other from εἰσπνεῖν τὸν ἔρωτα τῷ ἀγαπῶντι.

had some reason for jealousy before. Hearing Cynisca sigh at the name of Lucos, he can endure it no longer, and gives her a slap in the face, then another, and so forth, until she runs out of the house, and takes refuge with her Lucos day and night. All this the husband relates to Thyonichus; and the verses from the thirty-fourth to thirty-eighth, θάλπε φίλον, are very laughable. Thyonichus advises that so able a boxer should enter the service of Ptolemy.

IDYL XV. The Syracusan Gossips. Never was there so exact or so delightful a description of such characters. There is a little diversity, quite enough, between Praxinoë and Gorgo. Praxinoë is fond of dress; conceited, ignorant, rash, abusive in her remarks on her husband, ambitious to display her knowledge as well as her finery, and talking absurdly on what she sees about her at the festival of Adonis. Gorgo is desirous of insinuating her habits of industry. There are five speakers: Gorgo, Praxinoë, Eunoë, an old woman and a traveller, besides a singing girl, who has nothing to do with the party or the dialogue. " *Gorgo :* Don't talk in this way against your husband while your baby is by. See how he is looking at you. *Praxinoë :* Sprightly, my pretty Zopyrion! I am not talking of papa. *Gor :* By Proserpine! he understands you. Papa is a jewel of a papa." After a good deal of tattle, they are setting out for the fair, and the child shows a strong desire to be of the party. " *Gor :* I can't take you, darling! There's a hobgoblin on the other side of the door; and there's a biting horse. Ay, ay, cry to your heart's content. Do you think I would have you lamed for life? Come, come; let us be off." Laughter is irrepressible at their mishaps and exclamations in the crowd. This poem, consisting of one hundred and forty-four verses, is the longest in Theocritus, excepting the heroics on Hercules. The comic is varied and relieved by the song of a girl on Adonis. She notices everything she sees, and describes it as it appears to her. After an invocation to Venus, she has a compliment for Berenice, not without an eye to the candied flowers and white pastry, and the pretty little baskets containing mossy gardens and waxwork Adonises, and tiny Loves flying over,

Οἷοι ἀηδονιδῆες ἐφεζόμενοι ἐπὶ δένδρων
Πωτῶνται, πτερύγων πειρώμενοι ὄζον' ἀπ' ὄζω.

> Like the young nightingales, some nestling close,
> Some plying the fresh wing from bough to bough.

Idyl XVI. The Graces. Here Hiero is reminded how becoming is liberality in the rich and powerful; and here is sometimes a plaintive under-song in the praise. The attributes of the Graces were manifold; the poet has them in view principally as the distributors of just rewards. We have noticed the resemblance he often bears to Pindar: nowhere is it so striking as in this and the next. The best of Pindar's odes is not more energetic throughout: none of them surpasses these two in the chief qualities of that admirable poet; rejection of what is light and minute, disdain of what is trivial, and selection of those blocks from the quarry which will bear strong strokes of the hammer and retain all the marks of the chisel. Of what we understand by sublimity he has little; but he moves in the calm majesty of an elevated mind. Of all poets he least resembles those among us whom it is the fashion most to admire at the present day. The verses of this address to Hiero by Theocritus, from the thirty-fourth to the forty-seventh, are as sonorous and elevated as the best of Homer's: and so are those beginning at the ninety-eighth verse to the end.

Idyl XVII. This has nothing of the Idyl in it, but is a noble eulogy on Ptolemy Philadelphus, son of Ptolemy Lagus and Berenice. Warton is among the many who would deduct it from the works of our poet. It is grander even than the last on Hiero, in which he appears resolved to surpass all that Pindar has written on the earlier king of that name. It is only in versification that it differs from him : in comprehensiveness, power, and majesty, and in the manner of treating the subject, the same spirit seems to have guided the same hand.

Idyl XVIII. The Epithalamium of Helen. There were two species of epithalamium : the κοιμητικόν, such as this, and such likewise as that of Catullus, sung as the bride was conducted to her chamber; and the ἐγερτικόν, sung as she arose in the morning. The poet, in the first verses, introduces twelve Spartan girls crowned with hyacinths, who sing and dance about Menelaus. " And so you are somewhat heavy in the knees, sweet spouse ! rather fond of sleep, are you ? You ought to have gone to sleep at the proper time, and have let a young maiden play with other young maidens at her mother's until long after daybreak." Then follow the praises of Helen, wishes for her prosperity, and promises to return at the crowing of the cock.

Idyl XIX. Kariocleptes, or the Hive-stealer, contains but eight verses. It is the story of Cupid stung by a bee: the first and last bee that ever stung *all* the fingers (Δάκτυλα πάνθ' ὑπένυξεν) of both hands: for it is not χειρός but χειρῶν. Having said in the first verse that the bee stung him, as he was plundering the hive, we may easily suspect in what part the wound was inflicted; and, among the extremely few things we could wish altered or omitted in Theocritus, are the words

ἄκρα δὲ χειρων.
Δάκτυλα πάνθ' ὑπένυξεν. 'Ο δ' ἄλγεε.

All the needful and all the ornamental would be comprised in

Κηρίον ἐκ σίμβλων συλεύμενον, ὃς χέρ' ἔφυσσε, &c.

Idyl XX. The Oxherd. He complains of Eunica, who holds his love in derision and finds fault with his features, speech, and manners. From plain downright contemptuousness she bursts forth into irony.

ὡς ἄγρια παίσδεις
'Ωs τρυφερὸν λαλέεις, ὡς κωτίλα ῥήματα φράσδεις. &c.

How rustic is your play!
How coarse your language! &c.

He entertains a very different opinion of himself, boasts that every girl upon the hills is in love with him, and is sure that only a *townlady* (which he thinks is the same thing as a *lady of the town*) could have so little taste. There is simplicity in this Idyl, but it is the worst of the author.

Idyl XXI. The Fisherman. Two fishermen were lying stretched on seaweed in a wattled hut, and resting their heads against the wall composed of twigs and leaves. Around them were spread all the implements of their trade, which are specified in very beautiful verse. They arose before dawn, and one said to the other, " They speak unwisely who tell us that the nights are shorter in summer when the days are longer; for within the space of this very night I have dreamt innumerable dreams.

Have you ever learnt to interpret them?" He then relates how he dreamt of having caught a golden fish, how afraid he was that it might be the favourite fish of Neptune or Amphitrite. His fears subsided, and he swore to himself that he would give up the sea for ever and be a king. "I am now afraid of having sworn any such oath," said he. "Never fear," replied the other: "the only danger is, of dying with hunger in the midst of such golden dreams."

IDYL XXII. This is the first heroic poem in Theocritus: it is in two parts. First is described the fight of Polideukes and Amycus: secondly, of Castor and Lynceus. Of Amycus the poet says that "his monstrous chest was *spherical:*" ἐσφαίρωτο. Omitting this, we may perhaps give some idea of the scene.

> In solitude both wandered, far away
> From those they sail'd with. On the hills above,
> Beneath a rocky steep, a fount they saw
> Full of clear water; and below were more
> That bubbled from the bottom, silvery,
> Crystalline. In the banks around grew pines,
> Poplars, and cypresses, and planes, and flowers
> Sweet-smelling; pleasant work for hairy bees
> Born in the meadows at the close of spring.
> There, in the sunshine, sat a savage man,
> Horrid to see; broken were both his ears
> With cestuses, his shoulders were like rocks
> Polisht by some vast river's ceaseless whirl.

Apollonius and Valerius Flaccus have described the fight of Amycus and Polydeukes: both poets are clever, Valerius more than usually: Theocritus is masterly.

IDYL XXIII. Dyseros, or the Unhappy Lover. The subject of this is the same as the Corydon of Virgil: but here the statue of Cupid falls on and crushes the inflexible.

IDYL XXIV. Heracliskos, or the Infant Hercules. There are critics of so weak a sight in poetry as to ascribe this magnificent and wonderful work to Bion or Moschus. Hercules is cradled in Amphitryon's shield. The description of the serpents, of the supernatural light in the chamber, and the prophecy of Tiresias, are equal to Pindar and Homer.

IDYL XXV. Hercules the Lion-Killer. This will bear no comparison with the preceding. The story is told by Hercules himself, and the poet has taken good care that it should not be beyond his capacity.

IDYL XXVI. The Death of Pentheus. Little can be said for this also ; only that the style is the pure antique.

IDYL XXVII. Daphnis and the Shepherdess, has been translated by Dryden. He has given the Shepherdess a muslin gown bespangled. This easy and vigorous poet too often turns the country into the town, smells of the ginshop, and staggers toward the brothel. He was quite at home with Juvenal, imitating his scholastic strut, deep frown, and loud declamation : no other has done such justice to Lucretius, to Virgil, to Horace, and to Ovid : none is so dissimilar to Theocritus. Wherever he finds a stain, he enlarges its circumference, and renders it vivid and indelible. In this lively poem we wish the sixty-fifth and sixty-sixth verses were omitted.

IDYL XXVIII. Neither this nor any one of the following can be called an Idyl. The metre is the pentameter choriambic, like Catullus's " *Alphene immemor, &c.* "

IDYL XXIX. Expostulation against Inconstancy. The metre is the dactylic pentameter, in which every foot is a dactyl, excepting the first, which is properly a trochee : this however may be converted to a spondee or an iambic, enjoying the same licence as the Phaleucian. In the twentieth verse there is a false quantity, where κς is short before ζ.

IDYL XXX. The death of Adonis. Venus orders the Loves to catch the guilty boar and bring him before her. They do so : he makes his defence against the accusation, which is, that he only wished to kiss the thigh of Adonis ; and he offers his tusk in atonement, and, if the tusk is insufficient, his cheek. Venus pitied him, and he was set at liberty. Out of gratitude and remorse, he went to a fire and burnt his teeth down to the sockets. Let those who would pillage Theocritus of his valuables, show the same contrition : we then promise them this poem, to do what they will with.

The Inscriptions, which follow, are all of extreme simplicity and propriety. These are followed by the poems of Bion and Moschus. Bion was a native of Smyrna, Moschus (his scholar) of Syracuse. They are called authors of Idyls, but there is nothing of idyl or pastoral in their works. The worst of them, as is often the case, is the most admired. Bion tells us that the boar bit the thigh of Adonis with his *tusk ;* the *white thigh with the white tusk ;* and that Adonis grieved Venus by breathing *softly* while the blood was running. Such faults as these are rarely to be detected in Greek poetry, but frequently on the revival of Pastoral in Italy.

Chaucer was born before that epidemic broke out which soon spread over Europe, and infected the English poetry as badly as any. The thoughts of our poets in the Elizabethan age often look the stronger because they are complicated and twisted. We have the boldness to confess that we are no admirers of the Elizabethan *style.* Shakespeare stood alone in a fresh and vigorous and vast creation : yet even his first-born were foul offenders, bearing on their brows the curse of a fallen state. Elsewhere, in every quarter, we are at once slumberous and restless under the heaviness of musk and benzoin, and sigh for the unattainable insipidity of fresh air. We are regaled with dishes in which no condiment is forgotten, nor indeed anything but simply the meat ; and we are ushered into chambers where the tapestry is all composed of dwarfs and giants, and the floor all covered with blood. Thomson, in the *Seasons,* has given us many beautiful descriptions of inanimate nature ; but the moment any one speaks in them the charm is broken. The figures he introduces are fantastical. The *Hassan* of Collins is excellent : he however is surpassed by Burns and Scott : and Wordsworth, in his *Michael,* is nowise inferior to them. Among the moderns no poet, it appears to us, has written an Idyl so perfect, so pure and simple in expression, yet so rich in thought and imagery, as the *Godiva* of Alfred Tennyson. Wordsworth, like Thomson, is deficient in the delineation of character, even of the rustic, in which Scott and Burns are almost equal. But some beautiful Idyls might be extracted from the *Excursion,* which would easily split into *laminæ,* and the residue might, with little loss, be blown away. Few are suspicious that they may be led astray and get benighted by following simplicity too far. If there are pleasant fruits growing on the ground, must we therefore cast aside, as unwholesome, those which have required the pruning-knife to correct and the ladder to reach them ? Beautiful thoughts are seldom disdainful of sonorous epithets : we find them continually in the Pastorals of Theocritus : sometimes we see, coming rather obtrusively, the wanton and indelicate ; but never (what poetry most abhors) the mean and abject. Widely different from our homestead poets, the Syracusan is remarkable for a facility that never draggles, for a spirit that never flags, and for a variety that never is exhausted. His reflections are frequent, but seasonable ; soon over, like the shadows of spring clouds on flowery meadows, and not hanging heavily upon the scene, nor depressing the vivacity of the blythe antagonists.

THE POEMS OF CATULLUS.

DOERING's first edition of Catullus came out nearly half a century before his last edition. When he returned to his undertaking, he found many things, he tells us, to be struck out, many to be altered and set right. We believe we shall be able to show that several are still remaining in these predicaments.

They who in our days have traced the progress of poetry, have pursued it generally not as poets or philosophers, but as hasty observers or cold chronologists. If we take our stand on the Roman world, just before the subversion of its free institutions, we shall be in a position to look backward on Greece, and forward on Italy and England : and we shall be little disposed to pick up and run away with the stale comments left by those who went before us ; but rather to loiter a little on the way, and to indulge, perhaps too complacently, in the freshness of our own peculiar opinions and favourite speculations.

The last poet who flourished at Rome, before the extinction of the republic by the arms of Julius Cæsar, was Catullus ; and the last record we possess of him is about the defamatory verses which he composed on that imperishable name. Cicero, to whom he has expressed his gratitude for defending him in a lawsuit, commends on this occasion the equanimity of Cæsar, who listened to the reading of them in his bath before dinner. There is no reason to believe that the poet long survived his father's guest, the Dictator : but his decease was unnoticed in those times of agitation and dismay ; nor is the date of it to be ascertained. It has usually been placed at the age of forty-six, four years after Cæsar's. Nothing is more absurd than the supposition of Martial, which however is but a poetical one.

> Si forsan tener ausus est Catullus
> Magno mittere *Passerem* Maroni.

(It is scarcely worth a remark by the way, that *si forsan* is not Latin; *si forte* would be: *si* and *an* can have nothing to do with each other.) But allowing that Virgil had written his *Ceiris* and *Culex*, two poems inferior to several in the Eton school-exercises, he could not have published his first Eclogues in the lifetime of Catullus: and if he had, the whole of them are not worth a single Phaleucian or scazon of the vigorous and impassioned Veronese.

But Virgil is not to be depreciated by us, as he too often has been of late, both in this country and abroad; nor is he at all so when we deliver our opinion that his pastorals are almost as inferior to those of Theocritus as Pope's are to his. Even in these, there not only are melodious verses, but harmonious sentences, appropriate images, and tender thoughts. Once or twice we find beauties beyond any in Theocritus: for example,

> Ite, capellæ!
> Non ego vos posthac viridi projectus in antro
> Dumosâ pendere procul de rupe videbo.

Yet in other places he is quite as harsh as if he had been ever so negligent. One instance is,

> Nunc victi, tristes, quoniam Fors omnia *versat*,
> Hos illi (quod nec bene *vertat*) mittimus hædos.

> But now we must stoop
> To the worst in the troop.
> And must do whatsoever that vagabond wills:
> I wish the old goat
> Had a horn in his throat,
> And the kids and ourselves were again on the hills.

Supposing the first of the Eclogues to have appeared seven years after the death of Catullus, and this poet to have composed his earliest works in the lifetime of Lucretius, we can not but ponder on the change of the Latin language in so short a space of time. Lucretius was by birth a Roman, and wrote in Rome; yet who would not say unhesitatingly, that there is more of what Cicero calls *urbane* in the two provincials, Virgil and Catullus, than in the authoritative and stately man who leads Memmius from the camp into the gardens of Epicurus. He complains of poverty in the Latin tongue; but his complaint is only on its insufficiency in philosophical terms, which Cicero also felt twenty years later, and called in Greek auxiliaries. But in reality the language never exhibited such a profusion of richness as in the comedies of Plautus, whose style is the just admiration of the Roman orator.

Cicero bears about him many little keepsakes received from this quarter, particularly the diminutives. His fondness for them borders on extravagance. Could you believe that the language contains in its whole compass a hundred of these? could you believe that an orator and philosopher was likely to employ a quarter of the number? Yet in the various works of Cicero we have counted and written down above a hundred and sixty. Catullus himself has employed them much more sparingly than Cicero, or than Plautus, and always with propriety and effect. The playful Ovid never indulges in them, nor does Propertius, nor does Tibullus. Nobody is willing to suspect that Virgil has ever done it; but he has done it once in

Oscula libavit natæ.

Perhaps they had been turned into ridicule, for the misapplication of them by some forgotten poet in the commencement of the Augustan age. Quintilian might have given us information on this: it lay in his road. But whether they died by a natural death or a violent one, they did not appear again as a plague until after the deluge of the Dark Ages; and then they increased and multiplied in the slime of those tepid shallows from which Italy in few places has even yet emerged. In the lines of Hadrian,

Animula, vagula, blandula,

they have been greatly admired, and very undeservedly. Pope has made sad work of these. Whatever they are, they did not merit such an *experimentum crucis* at his hands.

In Catullus no reader of a poetical mind would desire one diminutive less. In Politian and such people they buzz about our ears insufferably; and we would waft every one of them away, with little heed or concern if we brush off together with them all the squashy insipidities they alight on.

The imitators of Catullus have indeed been peculiarly unsuccessful. Numerous as they are, scarcely five pieces worth remembrance can be found among them. There are persons who have a knowledge of latinity, there are others who have a knowledge of poetry, but it is not always that the same judge decides with equal wisdom in both courts. Some hendecasyllabics of the late Serjeant Lens, an excellent man, a first-rate scholar, and a graceful poet, have been rather unduly praised; to us they appear monotonous and redundant. We will transcribe only the first two for particular notice and illustration.

> Grates insidiis tuis dolisque
> Vinclis jam refero lubens solutis.

Never were words more perplext and involved. He who brings them forward as classical, is unaware that they are closely copied from a beautiful little poem of Metastasio, which J. J. Rousseau has translated admirably.

> Grazie agli inganni tuoi
> Alfin respiro, O Nice!

How much better is the single word *inganni* than the useless and improper *insidiis*, which renders *dolis* quite unnecessary. A better line would be

> Vincla projicio libens soluta.

Or,

> Tandem projicio soluta vincla.

In fact, it would be a very difficult matter to suggest a worse. The most-part of the verses may be transposed in any way whatsoever: each seems to be independent of the rest: they are good, upright, sound verses enough, but never a sentence of them conciliates the ear. The same objection is justly made to nearly all the modern hendecasyllabics. Serjeant Lens has also given us too many lines for one Phaleucian piece: the metre will admit

but few advantageously: it is the very best for short poems.
This might be broken into three or four, and almost in any place
indifferently. Like the *seta equina*, by pushing out a head and a
tail, each would go on as well as ever.

In how few authors of hendecasyllabics is there one fine
cadence! Such, for instance, as those in Catullus:

> Soles occidere et redire possunt,
> Nobis quum semel occidit brevis lux
> Nox est perpetua una dormienda.

And those,

> Quamvis candida millies puella
> Euntem revocet, manusque collo
> Ambas injiciens roget morari.

And twenty more. In the former of these quotations, Catullus
had before him the best passage in Moschus, which may be thus
translated:

> Ah! when the mallow in the croft dies down,
> Or the pale parsley or the crisped anise,
> Again they grow, another year they flourish;
> But we, the great, the valiant, and the wise,
> Once covered over in the hollow earth,
> Sleep a long, dreamless, unawakening sleep.

The original verses are as harmonious as almost any in the
language. But the epithet which the poet has prefixed to *parsley*
is very undistinguishing. Greek poets more frequently than
Latin, gave those rather which suited the metre than those which
conveyed a peculiar representation. Neither the χλωρά, applied
to parsley, is in any of its senses very appropriate, nor are the
εὐθαλές and οὖλον to anise, but rather to burrage.

Catullus has had innumerable imitators in the Phaleucian, but
the only dexterity displayed by them, in general, is in catching a
verse and sending it back again like a shuttlecock. Until our
own times, there is little thought, little imagination, no passion, no
tenderness, in the modern Latin poets. Casimir shows most
genius and most facility: but Casimir, in his best poem, writes

> Sonora buxi filia *sutilis*.

Was ever allegory treated with such indignity? What becomes
of this tight-laced daughter of a box-tree? She was hanged.

Where? On a high poplar. Wherefore? That she might be the more easily come at by the poet. Pontanus too has been praised of late: but throughout his thick volume there is scarcely a glimpse of poetry. There are certain eyes which, seeing objects at a distance, take snow for sunshine.

Two verses of Joannes Secundus, almost the only two he has written worth remembering, outvalue all we have imported from the latter ages. They would have been quoted, even from Catullus himself, as among his best.

> Non est suaviolum dare, lux mea, sed dare tantum
> Est desiderium flebile suavioli.

The Six of Bembo on Venice are admirable also. And there are two from two French authors, each worth two Pontanuses. The first is on the Irish.

> Gens *ratione furens* et mentem pasta chimæris.

The second (but this is stolen from Manilius) on Franklin, his discoveries in electricity, and his energy in the liberation of his country.

> Eripuit cœlo fulmen sceptrumque tyranno.

Another has been frequently quoted from a prize poem by Canning. Such as it is, it also is stolen; and with much injury (as stolen things often are) from the *Nutricia* of Politian, among whose poems one only, that on the death of Ovid, has any merit. This being the only one which is without metrical faults, and the rest abounding in them, a reasonable doubt may arise whether he could have written it: he who has written by the dozen such as the following:

> Impedis amplexu,

intending *impedis* for a dactyl:

> Quando expĕdiret inseris hexametro,

for a pentameter:

> Mutare domi-num dŏm-us hæc nescit suum,

for an iambic:

> Lucreti fuit hoc, et Euripĭdis,

for a Phaleucian : and in whom we find *Plutarchus* short in the first syllable ; *Bis-ve semelve ;* and *Vaticani* long in the second syllable twice.

Milton has been thought like Politian in his hexameters and pentameters.   In his Elegies he is Ovidian ; but he is rather the fag than the playfellow of Ovid.   Among his Latin poems the scazon *De Hominus Archetypo* is the best.   In those of the moderns there is rarely more than one thing missing ; namely, the poetry ; which some critics seem to have held for a matter of importance.   If we may hazard a conjecture, they are in the right.   Robert Smith is the only one who has ascended into the higher regions.   But even the best scholars, since they receive most of their opinions from tradition, and stunted and distorted in the crevices of a quadrangle, will be slowly brought to conclude that his poetry is better (and better it surely is) than the greater part of that which dazzles them from the luminaries of the Augustan age.   In vigour and harmony of diction, in the selection of topics, in the rejection of little ornaments, in the total suppression of playful prettinesses, in solidity and magnitude of thought, sustained and elevated by the purest spirit of poetry, we find nothing in the Augustan age of the same continuity, the same extent.   We refer to the poem entitled *Platonis Principia,* in which there are a hundred and eleven such verses as are scarcely anywhere together in all the realms of poetry.

The alcaic ode of the same writer, *Mare Liberum,* is not without slight blemishes.   For instance, at the beginning,

> Primo Creator spiritus halitu
> Caliginosi regna silentii
> Turbavit.

In latinity there is no distinction between *spiritus* and *halitus ;* and, if theology has made one, the *halitus* can never be said to proceed from the *spiritus.*   In the second verse the lyric metre requires *silentj* for *silentii.*   Cavilers may also object to the elision of *quà* at the conclusion.

> Et rura *quà* ingentes Amazon
> Rumpit aquas, violentus amnis.

It has never been elided unless at the close of a polysyllable ; as, among innumerable instances,

Obliquâ invidia stimulisque agitabat amaris.

This fact is the more remarkable, since *quæ* and *præ* are elided ; or, speaking more properly, coalesce.

Et tibi præ invidiâ Nereides increpitarent.   Propertius.
Quæ omnia bella devorastis.   Catullus.
Quæ imbelles dant prælia cervi :
Quæ Asia circum.   Virgil.

But what ode in any language is more animated or more sublime ?

In reading the Classics we pass over false quantities, and defer to time an authority we refuse to reason.   But never can time acquit Horace of giving us false measure in *palus aptaque remis*, nor in *quomodo*.   Whether you divide or unite the component parts of *quomodo*, *quo* and *modo*, the case is the same.   And as *palus* is *palūdis* in the genitive case, *salus salūtis*, no doubt can exist of its quantity.   Modern Latin poets, nevertheless, have written *salŭber*.   Thomas Warton, a good scholar, and if once fairly out of latinity, no bad poet, writes in a Phaleucian

Salŭberrimis et herbis.

There is also a strange false quantity in one of the most accurate and profound grammarians, Menage.   He wrote an inscription, in one Latin hexameter, for Mazarin's college, then recently erected.

Has Phœbo et Musis Mazarinus consecrat ædes.

Every vowel is long before z.   He knew it, but it escaped his observation, as things we know often do.   We return from one learned man to another, more immediately the object of our attention, on whom the same appellation was conferred.

Catullus has been called the *learned :* and critics have been curious in searching after the origin of this designation.   Certainly both Virgil and Ovid had greatly more of archæology, and borrowed a great deal more of the Greeks.   But Catullus was, what Horace claims for himself, the first who imported into Latin poetry any vast variety of their metres.   Evidently he translated from the Greek his galliambic on Atys.   The proof is, that

Tympanum tubam Cybeles

would be opposite to, and inconsistent with, the metre. He must have written *Typanum*, finding τύπανον before him. But as, while he was in the army, he was stationed some time in Bithynia and Phrygia, perhaps he had acquired the language spoken in the highlands of those countries: in the lowlands it was Greek. No doubt, his curiosity led him to the temple of Cybele: and there he heard the ancient hymns in celebration of that goddess. Nothing breathes such an air of antiquity as his galliambic, which must surely have been translated into Greek from the Phrygian. Joseph Warton, in the intemperance of admiration, prefers it not only to every work of Catullus, but to every one in the language. There is indeed a gravity and solemnity in it, a fitness and propriety in every part, unequalled and unrivalled. Poetry can, however, rise higher than these " templa serena," and has risen higher with Catullus. No human works are so perfect as some of his, but many are incomparably greater. Among the works of the moderns, the fables of La Fontaine come nearest to perfection; but are there none grander and higher?

This intemperance of admiration has been less excusable in some living critics of modern Latin poetry. Yet when we consider how Erasmus, a singularly wise and learned man, has erred in his judgment on poetry, saying, while he speaks of Sidonius Apollinaris, " Let us listen to our Pindar," we are disposed to be gentle and lenient even in regard to one who has declared his opinion, that the elegies of Sannazar " may compete with Tibullus."* If they may, it can only be in the number of feet; and there they are quite on an equality. In another part of the volume which contains so curious a decision, some verses are quoted from the *Paradise Regained* as " perhaps the most musical the author ever produced." Let us pause a few moments on this assertion, and examine the verses referred to. It will not be without its use to exhibit their real character, because, in coming closer to the examination of Catullus, we shall likewise be obliged to confess that, elegant and graceful as he is, to a degree above all other poets in the more elaborate of his compositions, he too is by no means exempt from blemishes in his versification. But in

* Mr Hallam, in the first volume of his *Introduction to the Literature of Europe*, p. 597.

Milton they are flatnesses; in Catullus they are asperities; which is the contrary of what might have been expected from the characters of the men.

There is many a critic who talks of harmony, and whose ear seems to have been fashioned out of the callus of his foot. "Quotus enim quisque est," as Cicero says, "qui teneat artem numerorum atque modorum!" The great orator himself, consummate master of the science, runs from rhetorical into poetical measure at this very place.

Numerorum atque modorum

is the same in time and modulation as the verses in Horace,

Miserarum est neque amori
Dare ludum neque dulci, &c.

Well; but what "are perhaps the most musical verses Milton has ever produced?" They are these (si diis placet!):

> Such forces met not, nor so wide a camp,
> When Agrican with all his northern powers
> Besieged Albracca, *as romances tell,*
> The city of Gallaphrone, *from thence to win*
> *The fairest of her sex Angelica*
> *His daughter, sought by many prowest knights,*
> Both Paynim and the peers of Charlemagne.

There is a sad hiatus in "Albracca as." On the whole however, the verses, thus unluckily hit upon for harmony, are fluent; too fluent; they are feeble in the extreme, and little better than prose, either in thought or expression: still, it is better to praise accidentally in the wrong place than to censure universally. The passage which is before them leads us to that magnificent view of the cities and empires, the potentates and armies, in all their strength and glory, with which the Tempter would have beguiled our Redeemer. These appear to have left no impression on the critic, who much prefers what every schoolboy can comprehend, and what many undergraduates could have composed. But it is somewhat, no doubt, to praise that which nobody ever praised before, and to pass over that which suspends by its grandeur the footstep of all others.

There is prodigious and desperate vigour in the Tempter's reply to our Saviour's reproof:

> All hope is lost
> Of my reception into grace: what worse?
> For when no hope is left, is left no fear.
> If there be worse, the expectation more
> Of worse torments me than the feeling can.
> I would be at the worst: worst is my port,*
> My harbour, and my ultimate repose;
> The end I would attain, my final good.

Yet Milton, in this *Paradise Regained,* seems to be subject to strange hallucinations of the ear; he who before had greatly excelled all poets of all ages in the science and display of harmony. And if in his last poem we exhibit his deficiencies, surely we never shall be accused of disrespect or irreverence to this immortal man. It may be doubted whether the Creator ever created one altogether so great; taking into our view at once (as much indeed as can at once be taken into it) his manly virtues, his superhuman genius, his zeal for truth, for true piety, true freedom, his eloquence in displaying it, his contempt of personal power, his glory and exultation in his country's.

Warton and Johnson are of opinion that Milton is defective in the sense of harmony. But Warton had lost his ear by laying it down on low and swampy places, on ballads and sonnets; and Johnson was a deaf adder coiled up in the brambles of party prejudices. He was acute and judicious, he was honest and generous, he was forbearing and humane: but he was cold where he was overshadowed. The poet's peculiar excellence, above all others, was in his exquisite perception of rhythm, and in the boundless variety he has given it, both in verse and prose. Virgil comes nearest to him in his assiduous study of it, and in his complete success. With the poetical and oratorical, the harmony is usually in proportion to the energy of passion. But the numbers may be transferred: thus the heroic has been carried into the Georgics. There are many pomps and vanities in that fine poem, which we would relinquish unreluctantly for one touch of nature; such as

* A daring critic might suggest *fort* for *port*, since *harbour* makes that word unnecessary.

It tristis arator
Mœrentem abjungens fraterna morte juvencum.

In sorrow goes the ploughman, and leads off
Unyoked from his dead mate the sorrowing steer.

Here however the poet is not seconded by the language. The ploughman can not be going on while he is in the act of separating the dead ox from its partner, as the word *it* and *abjungens* signify.

We shall presently show that Catullus was the first among the Romans in whose heroic verse there is nothing harsh and dissonant. But it is not necessary to turn to the grander poetry of Milton for verses more harmonious than those adduced ; we find them even in the midst of his prose. Whether he is to be censured for giving way to his genius, in such compositions, is remote from the question now before us. But what magnificence of thought is here! how totally free is the expression from the encumbrances of amplification, from the crutches and cushions of swollen feebleness!

When God commands to take the trumpet
And blow a shriller and a louder blast,
It rests not in Man's will what he shall do,
Or what he shall forbear.

This sentence in the *Treatise on Prelaty* is printed in prose: it sounds like inspiration. "It rested not in Milton's will" to crack his organ-pipe, for the sake of splitting and attenuating the gush of harmony.

We will now give the reason for the *falling sickness* with which several of his verses are stricken. He was too fond of showing what he had read : and the things he has taken from others are always much worse than his own. Habituated to Italian poetry, he knew that the verses are rarely composed of pure iambics, or of iambics mixed with spondees, but contain a great variety of feet, or rather of subdivisions. When he wrote such a line as

In thĕ bosŏm of bliss and light of light,

he thought he had sufficient authority in Dante, Petrarca, Ariosto, and Tasso, who wrote

> Questă selvă selvaggia.　Dante.
> Tra lĕ vanĕ speranze.　Petrarca.
> Con lă gentĕ di Francia.　Ariosto.
> Cantŏ l' armĭ pietose.　Tasso.

And there is no verse whatsoever in any of his poems for the metre of which he has not an Italian prototype.

The critic who knows any thing of poetry, and is resolved to select a passage from the *Paradise Regained*, will prefer this other far above the rest; and may compare it, without fear of ridicule or reprehension, to the noblest in the nobler poem.

> And either tropic now
> 'Gan thunder, and both ends of heaven: the clouds,
> From many a horrid rift, abortive poured
> Fierce rain with lightning mixt, water with fire,
> In ruin reconciled: nor slept the winds
> Within their stony caves, but rushed abroad
> From the four hinges of the world, and fell
> On the vext wilderness, whose tallest pines,
> Though rooted deep as high, and sturdiest oaks,
> Bowed their stiff necks, loaden with stormy blasts
> Or torn up sheer.　Ill wast thou shrouded then,
> O patient son of God! yet only stoodst
> Unshaken!　Nor yet stayed the terrour there:
> Infernal ghosts and hellish furies round
> Environed thee: some howled, some yelled, some shrieked,
> Some bent at thee their fiery darts; while thou
> Satst unappall'd in calm and sinless peace.

No such poetry as this has been written since, and little at any time before.　But Homer would not have attributed to the *pine* what belongs to the *oak*.　The tallest pines have superficial roots; they certainly are never "deep as high:" oaks are said to be; and if the saying is not phytologically true, it is poetically; although the oak itself does not quite send

> radicem ad Tartara.

There is another small oversight.

> Yet only *stoodst*
> Unshaken.

Below we find

Satst unappalled.*

But what verses are the following!

> And made him bow to the gods of his wives. . .
> Cast wanton eyes on the daughters of men. . .
> After forty days' fasting had remained. . .
> And with these words his temptation pursued. . .
> Not difficult if thou hearken to me.

It is pleasanter to quote such a description as no poet, not even Milton himself, ever gave before, of Morning,

> Who with her radiant finger stilled the roar
> Of thunder, chased the clouds and laid the winds
> And grisly spectres, which the Fiend had raised
> To tempt the son of God with terrors dire.

In Catullus we see morning in another aspect; not personified: and a more beautiful description, a sentence on the whole more harmonious, or one in which every verse is better adapted to its peculiar office, is neither to be found nor conceived.

> Heic qualis flatu placidum mare matutino
> Horrificans zephyrus proclivas incitat undas,
> Aurorâ exoriente vagi sub lumina solis,
> Quæ tarde primum clementi flamine pulsæ
> Procedunt, leni resonant plangore cachinni,
> Post, vento crescente, magis magis increbescunt,
> Purpureâque procul nantes a luce refulgent.

Our translation is very inadequate:

* But Milton's most extraordinary oversight is in *L'Allegro*.

> Hence loathed Melancholy!
> Of Cerberus and blackest Midnight born.

Unquestionably he meant to have written Erebus instead of Cerberus, whom no imagination could represent as the sire of a goddess. *Midnight* is scarcely to be converted into one, or indeed into any allegorical personage: and the word "*blackest*" is far from aiding it. Milton is singularly unfortuuate in allegory; but nowhere more so than here. The daughter of Cerberus takes the veil, takes the

> Sable stole of *Cyprus* lawn,

and becomes, now her father is out of the way,

> A nun devout and pure.

> As, by the Zephyr wakened, underneath
> The sun's expansive gaze the waves move on
> Slowly and placidly, with gentle plash
> Against each other, and light laugh ; but soon,
> The breezes freshening, rough and huge they swell,
> Afar refulgent in the crimson east.

What a fall is there from these lofty cliffs, dashing back the waves against the winds that sent them ; what a fall is there to the " wracks and flaws " which Milton tells us

> Are to the main as inconsiderable
> And harmless, if not wholesome, as a *sneeze*.

In the lines below, from the same poem, the good and bad are strangely mingled : the poet keeping in his verse, however, the firmness and majesty of his march.

> So saying, he caught him up, and, *without wing*
> *Of hippogrif*, bore through the air sublime,
> Over the wilderness—*and o'er the plain :*
> Till underneath them fair Jerusalem.
> The holy city, lifted high her towers,
> And higher yet the glorious temple—*rear'd*
> *Her pile*, far off appearing like a mount
> Of alabaster, topt with golden *spires*.

Splendid as this description is, it bears no resemblance whatsoever to the temple of Jerusalem.　　It is like one of those fancies in which the earlier painters of Florence, Pisa, Lucca, and Siena, were fond of indulging ; not for similitude, but for effect.　The poets of Greece and Rome allowed themselves no such latitude. The Palace of the Sun, depicted so gorgeously by Ovid, where imagination might wander unrestricted, contains nowhere an inappropriate decoration.

No two poets are more dissimilar in thought and feeling than Milton and Catullus ; yet we have chosen to place them in juxtaposition, because the Latin language in the time of Catullus was nearly in the same state as the English in the time of Milton. Each had attained its full perfection, and yet the vestiges of antiquity were preserved in each.　　Virgil and Propertius were, in regard to the one poet, what Dryden and Waller were in regard to the other.　　They removed the archæisms ; but the herbage grew up rarer and slenderer after those extirpations.　If so consummate a master of versification as Milton is convicted of faults so numerous and so grave in it, pardon will the more easily be granted to Catullus. Another defect is likewise common to both ; namely the disposition or ordinance of parts. It would be difficult to find in any other two poets, however low their station in that capacity, two such signal examples of disproportion as are exhibited in *The Nuptials of Peleus and Thetis* and in *The Masque of Comus*. The better part of the former is the description of a tapestry ; the better part of the latter are three undramatic soliloquies. In other respects, the oversights of Catullus are fewer : and in Comus there is occasional extravagance of expression such as we never find in Catullus, or in the playful Ovid, or in any the least correct of the ancients. For example, we read of

The sea-girt isles,
That, like to rich and various gems, inlay
The unadorned bosom of the deep.

How *unadorned*, if inlaid with *rich and various gems ?* This is a pendant to be placed exactly opposite :

The silken vest Prince Vortigern had on,
Which from a naked Pict his grandsire won.

We come presently to

The sounds and *seas*.

Sounds are parts of seas. Comus, on the borders of North Wales, talks of

A green mantling vine,
That crawls along the side of yon small hill ;

and of

Plucking ripe clusters.

Anon we hear of "*stabled wolves*." What wolves can those be ? The faults we find in the poet we have undertaken to review we shall at the same time freely show.

Carmen I. *Ad Cornelium Nepotem*. In verse 4, we read

Jam tum *cum* ausus es.

We believe the poet, and all the writers of his age, wrote

quum. *Quoi* for *cui* grew obsolete much earlier, but was always thus spelt by Catullus. The best authors at all times wrote the adverb *quum.*

Carmen II. *Ad Passerem Lesbiæ.* In verse 8 we read "acquiescat;" the poet wrote "adquiescat," which sounds fuller.

Carmen III. *Luctus in Morte Passeris.* This poem, and the preceding, seem to have been admired, both by the ancients and the moderns, above all the rest. Beautiful indeed they are. Grammarians may find fault with the hiatus in

O factum male! O miselle passer!

poets will not.

We shall now, before we go farther, notice the metre. Regularly the Phaleucian verse is composed of four trochees and one dactyl: so is the Sapphic, but in another order. The Phaleucian employs the dactyl in the second place; the Sapphic employs it in the third. But the Latin poets are fonder of a spondee in the first. Catullus frequently admits an iambic; as in

Meas esse aliquid putare nugas.
Tuâ nunc operâ meæ puellæ. &c.

Carmen IV. *Dedicatio Phaseli.* This is a senarian, and composed of pure iambics. Nothing can surpass its elegance. The following bears a near resemblance to it in the beginning, and may be offered as a kind of paraphrase.

'The vessel which lies here at last
Had once stout ribs and topping mast,
And, whate'er wind there might prevail,
Was ready for a row or sail.
It now lies idle on its side,
Forgetful o'er the waves to glide.
And yet there have been days of yore
When pretty maids their posies bore
'To crown its prow, its deck to trim,
And freight it with a world of whim.
A thousand stories it could tell,
But it loves secrecy too well.
Come closer, my sweet girl! pray do!
'There may be still one left for you.

Carmen V. *Ad Lesbiam.* It is difficult to vary our expression of delight at reading the three first poems which Lesbia and her sparrow have occasioned. This is the last of them that is fervid and tender. There is love in many of the others, but impure and turbid, and the object of it soon presents to us an aspect far less attractive.

Carmen VI. *Ad Flavium.* Whoever thinks it worth his while to peruse this poem, must enclose in a parenthesis the words "Nequicquam tacitum." *Tacitum* is here a participle: and the words mean, "It is in vain that you try to keep it a secret."

Carmen VII. *Again to Lesbia.* Here, as in all his hendeca-syllabics, not only are the single verses full of harmony, a merit to which other writers of them not unfrequently have attained, but the sentences leave the ear no "aching void," as theirs do.

Carmen VIII. *Ad seipsum.* This is the first of the scazons. The metre in a long poem would perhaps be more tedious than any. Catullus, with admirable judgment, has never exceeded the quantity of twenty-one verses in it. No poet, uttering his own sentiments on his own condition in a soliloquy, has evinced such power in the expression of passion, in its sudden throbs and changes, as Catullus has done here.

In Doering's edition we read, verse 14,

> At tu dolebis, cum rogaberis nullâ.
> Scelesta ! nocte.

No such pause is anywhere else in the poet. In Scaliger the verses are,

> At tu dolebis, quum rogaberis nulla.
> Scelesta rere, quæ tibi manet vita.

The punctuation in most foreign books, however, and in all English, is too frequent: so that we have snatches and broken bars of tune, but seldom tune entire. Scaliger's reading is probably the true one, by removing the comma after *rere :*

> Scelesta rere quæ tibi manet vita !
> (*Consider* what must be the remainder of your life !)

Now certainly there were many words obliterated in the only copy of our author. It was found in a cellar, and under a wine-barrel. Thus the second word in the second line appears to have left no traces behind it; otherwise, words so different as *nocte* and *rere* could never have been mistaken. Since the place is open to conjecture, therefore, and since every expression round about it is energetic, we might suggest another reading:

> At tu dolebis quum rogaberis *nullo,*
> Scelesta! *nullo.* Quæ tibi manet vita?
> Quis nunc te adibit? quoi videberis bella?
> Quem nunc amabis? quojus esse diceris?
> Quem basiabis? quoi labella mordebis?
> At tu, Catulle! destinatus obdura.

Which we will venture to translate:

> But you shall grieve while none complains,
> None, Lesbia! None. Think, what remains
> For one so fickle, so untrue!
> Henceforth, O wretched Lesbia! who
> Shall call you dear? shall call you his?
> Whom shall you love? or who shall kiss
> Those lips again? Catullus! thou
> Be firm, be ever firm, as now.

The angry taunt very naturally precedes the impatient expostulation. The repetition of *nullo* is surely not unexpected. *Nullus* was often used absolutely in the best times of latinity. "Ab *nullo* repetere," and "*nullo* aut paucissimis præsentibus," by Sallust. "Qui scire possum? *nullus* plus," by Plautus. "Vivis his incolumibusque, liber esse *nullus* potest," by Cicero.

It may as well be noticed here that *basiare, basium, basiatio,* are words unused by Virgil, Propertius, Horace, Ovid, or Tibullus. They belonged to Cisalpine Gaul more especially, although the root has now extended through all Italy, and has quite supplanted *osculum* and its descendants. *Bellus* has done the same in regard to *formosus,* which has lost its footing in Italy, although it retains it in Spain, slightly shaken, in *hermoso.* The *saviari* and *savium* of Plautus, Terence, Cicero, and Catullus, are never found in the poets of the Augustan age, to the best of our recollection, excepting once in Propertius.

Carmen IX. *Ad Verannium.* Nothing was ever livelier or more cordial than the welcome here given to Verannius on his return from Spain. It is comprised in eleven verses. Our poets,

on such an occasion, would have spread out a larger table-cloth
with a less exquisite desert upon it.

Carmen X. *De Varri Scorto.* Instead of expatiating on this,
which contains, in truth, some rather coarse expressions, but is
witty and characteristical, we will subjoin a paraphrase, with a
few defalcations.

Varrus would take me t' other day
   To see a little girl he knew,
Pretty and witty in her way,
   With impudence enough for two.

Scarce are we seated, ere she chatters
   (As pretty girls are wont to do)
About all persons, places, matters . .
   " And pray, what has been done for *you?* "

" Bithynia, lady ! " I replied,
   " Is a fine province for a pretor,
For none (I promise you) beside,
   And least of all am I her debtor."

" Sorry for that ! " said she.   " However
   You have brought with you, I dare say,
Some litter bearers : none so clever
   In any other part as they.

" Bithynia is the very place
   For all that's steady, tall, and straight ;
It is the nature of the race.
   Could you not lend me six or eight ? "

" Why, six or eight of them or so,"
   Said I, determined to be grand,
" My fortune is not quite so low
   But these are still at my command."

" You'll send them ? "   " Willingly ! " I told her,
   Altho' I had not here or there
One who could carry on his shoulder
   The leg of an old broken chair.

" Catullus ! what a charming hap is
   Our meeting in this sort of way !
I would be carried to Serapis
   To-morrow."   " Stay, fair lady, stay !

" You overvalue my intention.
   Yes, there *are* eight . . there may be nine .
I merely had forgot to mention
   That they are Cinna's, and not mine."

Catullus has added two verses which we have not translated, because they injure the poem.

> Sed tu insulsa male et molesta vivis
> Per quam non licet esse negligentem.

This, if said at all, ought not to be said to the lady. The reflection might be (but without any benefit to the poetry) made in the poet's own person. Among the ancients however, when we find the events of common life and ordinary people turned into verse, as here for instance, and in the *Praxinoë* of Theocritus, and in another of his where a young person has part of her attire torn, we never are bored with prolixity and platitude, in which a dull moral is our best relief at the close of a dull story.

Carmen XI. *Ad Furium et Aurelium.* Furius and Aurelius were probably the comrades of Catullus in Bithynia. He appears to have retained his friendship for them not extremely long. Here he entrusts them with a message for Lesbia, which they were fools if they delivered, although there is abundant reason for believing that their modesty would never have restrained them. He may well call these

> Non bona dicta.

But there are worse in reserve for themselves, on turning over the very next page. The last verses in the third strophe are printed

> Gallicum Rhenum horribiles*que* ulti-
> Mosque Britannos.

The enclitic *que* should be changed to *ad*, since it could not support itself without the intervention of an aspirate,

> Gallicum Rhenum horribileis *ad* ulti-
> mosque Britannos.

and the verse " Cæsaris visens," &c., placed in a parenthesis. When the poet wrote these Sapphics, his dislike of Cæsar had not begun. Perhaps it was occasioned long afterward, by some inattention of the great commander to the Valerian family on his last return from Transalpine Gaul. Here he writes,

> Cæsaris visens monimenta *magni.*

Very different from the contemptuous and scurril language with which he addressed him latterly.

Carmen XII. *Ad Asinium Pollionem.* Asinius Pollio and his brother were striplings when this poem was written. The worst, but most admired of Virgil's Eclogues, was composed to celebrate the birth of Pollio's son, in his consulate. In this Eclogue, and in this alone, his versification fails him utterly. The lines afford one another no support. For instance, this sequence,

> Ultima Cumæi venit jam carminis ætas.
> Magnus ab integro sæclorum nascitur ordo,
> Jam redit et virgo, redeunt Saturnia regna.

Toss them in a bag and throw them out, and they will fall as rightly in one place as another. Any one of them may come first; any one of them may come last; any one of them may come intermediately; better that any one should never come at all. Throughout the remainder of the Eclogue, the ampulla of Virgil is puffier than the worst of Statius or Lucan.

In the poem before us it seems that Asinius, for whose infant the universe was to change its aspect, for whom grapes were to hang upon thorns, for whom the hardest oaks were to exude honey, for whom the rams in the meadows were to dye their own fleeces with murex and saffron . . this Asinius picked Catullus's pocket of his handkerchief. Catullus tells him he is a blockhead if he is ignorant that there is no wit in such a trick, which he says is a very dirty one, and appeals to the brother, calling him a smart and clever lad. He declares he does not mind so much the value of the handkerchief, as because it was a present sent to him out of Spain by his friends Fabullus and Verannius, who united (it seems) their fiscal forces in the investment. This is among the lighter effusions of the volume, and worth as little as Virgil's Eclogue, though exempt from such grave faults.

Carmen XIII. *Ad Fabullum.* A pleasant invitation to dinner.

Verse 8.   Plenus sacculus est aranearum.

It is curious that Doering, so sedulous in collecting scraps of similitudes, never thought of this in Plautus, where the idea and expression too are so alike.

Ita inaniis sunt oppletæ atque araneis.

Let us offer a paraphrase:

> With me, Fabullus, you shall dine,
>   And gaudily, I promise you,
> If you will only bring the wine,
>   The dinner, and some beauty too.
>
> With all your frolic, all your fun,
>   I have some little of my own;
> And nothing else: the spiders run
>   Throughout my purse, now theirs alone.

He goes on rather too far, and promises his invited guests so sweet a perfume, that he shall pray the gods to become *all nose;* that is, we may presume, if no one should intervene to correct or divert in part a wish so engrossing.

CARMEN XIV. *Ad Calvum Licinium.* The poet seems in general to have been very inconstant in his friendships: but there is no evidence that he was ever estranged from Calvus. This is the more remarkable as Calvus was a poet, the only poet among his friends, and wrote in the same style. At the close of the poem here addressed to him, properly ending at the twenty-third verse, we find four others appended. They have nothing at all to do with it: they are a worthless fragment: and it is a pity that the wine-cask, which rotted off and dislocated so many pieces, did not leak on and obliterate this, and many similar, particularly the two next. We should then, it may be argued, have known less of the author's character. So much the better. Unless, by knowing the evil that is in any one, we can benefit him, or ourselves, or society, it is desirable not to know it at all.

CARMEN XVII. *Ad Coloniam.* Here are a few beautiful verses in a very indifferent piece of poetry. We shall transcribe them, partly for their beauty, and partly to remove an obscurity.

> Quoi quum sit viridissimo nupta flore puella,
> Et puella tenellulo delicatior hædo,
> Asservanda nigerrimis diligentiùs uvis;
> Ludere hanc sinit ut lubet, nec pili facit uni,
> Nec se sublevat ex suâ parte; sed velut alnus
> In fossâ Liguri jacet suppernata securi,
> Tantundem omnia sentiens quam si nulla sit usquam,
> Talis iste meus stupor nil videt. nihil audit,
> Ipse qui sit, utrum sit, an non sit, id quoque nescit.

This is in the spirit of Aristophanes, and we may fancy we hear his voice in the cantilena. *Asservanda* should be printed *adservanda ;* and *suppernata, subpernata. Liguri* is doubtful. Ligur*is* is the genitive case of Ligur. The Ligurians may in ancient times, as in modern, have exercised their industry out of their own country, and the poorer of them may have been hewers of wood. Then *securis Ligur*is would be the right interpretation. But there are few countries in which there are fewer *ditches*, or fewer *alders*, than in Liguria ; we, who have travelled through the country in all directions, do not remember to have seen a single one of either. It would be going farther, but going where both might be found readily, if we went to the *Liger*, and read " In fossâ Liger*is*."

Carmina XVIII., XIX., XX. *Ad Priapum.* The first of these three is a Dedication to the God of Gardens. In the two following the poet speaks in his own person. The first contains only four lines. The second is descriptive, and terminates with pleasantry.

> O pueri ! malas abstinete rapinas !
> Vicinus prope dives est, negligensque Priapus ;
> Inde sumite ; semita hæc deinde vos feret ipsa.

In the third are these exquisite verses :

> Mihi corolla picta vere ponitur,
> Mihi rubens arista sole fervido,
> Mihi virente dulcis uva pampino.
> Mihique glauca duro oliva frigore.
> Meis capella delicata pascuis
> In urbem adulta lacte portat ubera,
> Meisque pinguis agnus ex ovilibus
> Gravem domum remittit ære dexteram,
> Teneraque matre mugiente vaccula
> Deûm profundit ante templa sanguinem.

We will attempt to translate them.

> In spring the many-colour'd crown,
> The sheafs in summer, ruddy-brown,
> The autumn's twisting tendrils green,
> With nectar-gushing grapes between,
> Some pink, some purple, some bright gold,
> Then shrivel'd olive, blue with cold,

> Are all for me: for me the goat
> Comes with her milk from hills remote,
> And fatted lamb, and calf pursued
> By moaning mother, sheds her blood.

The third verse, as printed in this edition and most others, is contrary to the laws of metre in the pure iambic.

> Agellulum hunc, sinistrā, *tute* quam vides.

And *tute* is inelegant and useless.   Scaliger proposed "sinistera *ante* quem vides."   He was near the mark, but missed it; for Catullus would never have written "sinistera."   It is very probable that he wrote the verse

> Agellulum hunc sinistrà, *inante* quem vides.
> On the left hand, just before you.

Inante and *exante* were applied to time rather than place, but not exclusively.

Carmen **XXII.**   *Ad Varrum.*   This may be advantageously contracted in a paraphrase.

> Suffenus, whom so well you know,
> My Varrus, as a wit and beau,
> Of smart address and smirking smile,
> Will write you verses by the mile,
> You can not meet with daintier fare
> Than title-page and binding are;
> But when you once begin to read
> You find it sorry stuff indeed,
> And you are ready to cry out
> Upon this beau, *Ah! what a lout!*
> No man on earth so proud as he
> Of his own precious poetry,
> Or knows such perfect bliss as when
> He takes in hand that nibbled pen.
>   Have we not all some faults like these?
> Are we not all Suffenuses?
> In others the defect we find,
> But can not see our sack behind.

Carmen **XXV.** *Ad Thallum.*   It is hardly safe to steal a laugh here, and yet it is difficult to refrain from it.   Some of the verses must be transposed.   Those which are printed

> Thalle! turbidâ rapacior procellâ,
> *Cum de viâ* mulier aves ostendit oscitantes,
> Remitte pallium mihi, meum quod involâste,

ought to be printed

> Thalle! turbidâ rapacior procellâ,
> Remitte pallium mihi, meum, quod involâste
> *Quum* "devias" mulier aves ostendit oscitantes.

This shows that Thallus had purloined Catullus's cloak while he was looking at a nest of owls; for such are *devia aves*, and so they are called by Ovid. It is doubtful whether the right reading is *oscitantes*, "opening their beaks," or *oscinentes*, which is applied to birds that do not sing; by Valerius Maximus to crows, by Livy to birds of omen. In the present case we may believe them to be birds of augury, and inauspicious, as the word always signifies, and as was manifest in the disaster of Catullus and his cloak. In the eleventh verse there is a false quantity:

> Inusta turpiter tibi flagella conscribillent.

Was there not such a word as *contribulo?*

CARMEN XXIX. *Ad Cæsarem.* This is the poem by which the author, as Cicero remarks, affixes an eternal stigma on the name of Cæsar, but which the most powerful and the best tempered man in the world heard without any expression of anger or concern. The punctuation appears ill-placed in the sixteenth and seventeenth verses.

> Quid est? ait sinistra liberalitas:
> Parum expatravit. An parum helluatus est?

We would write them,

> Quid est? ain? Sinistra liberalitas
> Parum expatravit? &c.

"Where is the harm? do you ask? What! has this left-handed liberality of his," &c.

CARMEN XXX. *Ad Alphenum.* A poem of sobs and sighs, of complaint, reproach, tenderness, sad reflection, and pure poetry.

CARMEN XXXI. *Ad Sirmionem Peninsulam.* Never was a return to home expressed so sensitively and beautifully as here. In the thirteenth line we find

Gaudete vosque Lydiæ lacûs undæ.

The "Lydian waves of the lake" would be an odd expression. Although, according to a groundless and somewhat absurd tradition,

Gens *Lyda* jugis insedit Etruscis,

yet no *gens Lyda* could ever have penetrated to these Alpine regions.   One of the Etrurian nations did penetrate so far, whether by conquest or expulsion is uncertain.   But Catullus here calls upon Sirmio to rejoice in his return, and he invites the waves of the lake to laugh.   Whoever has seen this beautiful expanse of water, under its bright sun and gentle breezes, will understand the poet's expression; he will have seen the waves laugh and dance.   Catullus, no doubt, wrote

Gaudete vosque " *ludiæ* " lacûs undæ!
Ye revellers and dancers of the lake!

If there was the word *ludius*, which we know there was, there must also have been *ludia*.

Carmen **XXXIV.**   *Ad Dianam.*   A hymn, of the purest simplicity.

Carmen **XXXV.**   *Cæcilium invitat.*   It appears that Cæcilius, like Catullus, had written a poem on Cybele.   Catullus invites him to leave Como for Verona :

Quamvis candida millies puella
Euntem revocet, manusque collo
Ambas injiciens roget morari.

Which may be rendered :

Although so passing fair a maid
Call twenty times, be not delayed ;
Nay, do not be delayed although
Both arms around your neck she throw.

For it appears she was desperately in love with him from the time he had written the poem.   Catullus says it is written so beautifully, that he can pardon the excess of her passion.

Carmen **XXXIX.**   *In Egnatium.*   This is the second time he has ridiculed Egnatius, a Celtiberian, and overfond of displaying his teeth by continually laughing.   Part of the poem is destitute of merit, and indelicate : the other part may be thus translated, or paraphrased rather :

> Egnatius has fine teeth, and those
> Eternally Egnatius shows.
> Some criminal is being tried
> For murder ; and they open wide ;
> A widow wails her only son ;
> Widow and him they open on.
> 'Tis a disease, I'm very sure,
> And wish 'twere such as you could cure,
> My good Egnatius ! for what's half
> So silly as a silly laugh ?

We can not agree with Doering that we should read

> Aut *porcus* Umber aut obesus Etruscus.   *Verse* 11.

First, because the *porcus* and *obesus* convey the same meaning without any distinction ; and secondly, because the distinction is necessary both for the poet and the fact.   The Etrurians were a most luxurious people ; the Umbrians a pastoral and industrious one.   He wishes to exhibit a contrast between these two nations, as he has done in the preceding verse between what is *urbane* and what is *Sabine.*   Therefore he wrote,

> Aut " *parcus* " Umber aut obesus Hetruscus.

Carmen XL. *Ad Ravidum.*   The sixth verse is printed improperly

> Quid vis ? quâ lubet esse notus optas ?

Read

> Quid vis ? qua lubet esse notus ? opta.

" *Opta,*" make your *option.*

Carmen XLII. *Ad Quandam.*   We should not notice this " *Ad Quandam* " were it not to correct a mistake of Doering. " Ridentem canis ore *Gallicani.*"   His note on this expression is, " Epitheton *ornans,* pro *quovis* cane venatico cujus rictus est latior."   No, the canis *gallicus* is the *greyhound,* whose *rictus* is indeed much *latior* than that of other dogs ; and Catullus always uses words the most characteristic and expressive.

Carmen XLV. *De Acme et Septimio.* Perhaps this poem has been admired above its merit. But there is one exquisitely fine passage in it, and replete with that harmony which, as we have already had occasion to remark, Catullus alone has given to the Phaleucian metre.

> At Acme leviter caput reflectens,
> Et dulcis pueri ebrios ocellos
> Isto purpureo ore suaviata,
> " Sic," inquit, " mea vita Septimille !
> Huic uni domino usque serviamus."

Carmen XLVI. *De Adventu Veris.* He leaves Phrygia in the beginning of spring, and is about to visit the celebrated cities of maritime Asia. What beauty and vigour of expression is there in

> Jam mens prætrepidans avet vagari,
> Jam læti studio pedes vigescunt.

There is also much tenderness at the close in the short valediction to his companions, who set out together with him in the expedition, and will return (whenever they do return) by various roads into their native country.

Carmen L. *Ad Licinium.* On the day preceding the composition of this poem, he and Licinius had agreed to write together in different metres, and to give verse for verse. Catullus was so delighted with the performances of Licinius, that he could never rest, he tells us, until he had signified it by this graceful little poem.

Carmen LI. This is a translation from Sappho's ode, and perhaps is the first that had ever been attempted into Latin, although there is another which precedes it in the volume. Nothing can surpass the graces of this, and it leaves us no regret but that we have not more translations by him of Sappho's poetry. He has copied less from the Greek than any Latin poet had done before Tibullus.

The adonic at the close of the second strophe is lost. Many critics have attempted to substitute one. In the edition before us we find,

> Simul te
> Lesbia ! adspexi, nihil est super mi
> *Vocis in ore.*

A worse can not be devised.

Quod loquar amens

would be better.   The ode ends, and always ended with

Lumina nocte.

CARMEN LIII.   *De Quodam et Calvo.*   Calvus, as well as Cicero, spoke publicly against Vatinius.   It will be requisite to write out the five verses of which this piece of Catullus is composed.

Risi nescio quem modo in coronâ
Qui quum mirifice Vatiniana
Meus crimina Calvus explicasset,
Admirans ait hæc manusque tollens,
Dî magni! *salaputium* disertum!

Doering's note on the words is this : " Vox nova, ridicula et, ut videbatur, *plebeia* (*Salaputium*).   Catullum ad hos versus scribendos impulit."   He goes on to put into prose what Catullus had told us in verse, and adds, " Catullus a risu sibi temperare non potuit."   Good Herr Doering does not *see where's the fun.* It lies in the fact of Calvus being a very little man, and in the clown hearing a very little man so eloquent, and crying out, " Heavens above! what a clever little *cockie !* "   The word should not be written " salapuńium," but " salapuſium."   The termination in *um* is a signification of endearment ; as *deliciolum* for *deliciæ:* and correspondently the *ov* in Greek ; παιδιον, for instance, and παιδαριον.   It can not be *salepygium*, as some critics have proposed, because the third syllable in this word (supposing there were any such) would, according to its Greek origin, be short.   Perhaps the best reading may be " saliρusium," from *sal* and *pusius.*   Rustic terms are unlikely to be compounded with accuracy.   In old Latin the word, or words, would be *sali* (for *salis*) *pusium.*   But *t* is equivalent to *s :* and the modern Italian, which is founded on the *most* ancient Latin, has *putto.*

CARMEN LIV.   *Ad Cæsarem.*

Fuffitio seni *recocto.*

On this is the note " Homo *recoctus* jam dicitur qui in rebus *agendis* diu multumque *agitatus*, versatus, exercitatus, et quasi *percoctus*, rerum naturam penitus perspexit," &c.

Surely these qualities are not such as Catullus or Cæsar ought to be displeased with. But "senex *recoctus*" means an old dandy boiled up into youth again in Medea's caldron. In this poem Catullus turns into ridicule no other than personal peculiarities and defects, first in Otho, then in Libo, lastly in Fuffitius.

CARMEN LVII. *In Mamurram et Cæsarem.* If Cæsar had hired a poet to write such wretched verses as these and swear them to Catullus, he could never in any other way have more injured his credit as a poet. The *Duo Cæsaris Anti-Catones,* which are remembered as having been so bulky, could never have fallen on Cato so fatally as this Anti-Catullus on Catullus.

CARMEN LXI. *De Nuptiis Juliæ et Manlii.* Never was there, and never will there be probably, a nuptial song of equal beauty. But in verse 129 there is a false quantity as now printed, and quite unnoticed by the editor.

Desertum domini audiens.

The metre does not well admit a spondee * for the second foot: it should be a trochee; and this is obtained by the true reading, " Des*i*tum."

CARMEN LXII. Another nuptial song, and properly an Epithalamium, in heroic verse, and very masterly. It seems incredible however that the last lines, beginning

At tu ne pugna,

were written by Catullus. They are trivial: and beside, the young singing men never have sung so long together in the former parts assigned to them. The longest of these consists of *nine* verses, with the choral

Hymen, O Hymenæe!

and the last would contain *eleven* with it, even after rejecting these *seven* which intervene, and which, if admitted, would double the usual quantity. We would throw them out because there is no room for them, and because they are trash.

* Yet here, in 235 verses, nine begin with it.

Carmen LXIII. This has ever been, and ever will be, the admiration of all who can distinguish the grades of poetry.

The thirty-ninth verse is printed,

> Piger his labantes languore oculos sopor operit.

The metre will not allow it. We must read, "labante languore," although the construction may be somewhat less obvious. The words are in the ablative absolute, "Sleep covers their eyes, a languor dropping over them."

Verse 64 should be printed "gymnasj," not gymnasii. The seventy-fifth and seventy-sixth lines must be reversed, and instead of

> Geminas " Deorum " ad aures nova nuncia referens
> Ibi juncta juga resolvens Cybele leonibus
> Lævumque pecoris hostem stimulans,

read

> Ibi juncta juga resolvens Cybele leonibus,
> Geminas " eorum " ad aureis nova nuncia referens, &c.

Carmen LXIV. *Nuptiæ Pelei et Thetidis.* Among many excellences of the highest order, there are several faults and inconsistencies in this heroic poem.

> Verse 15. Illâque haudque aliâ, &c.

It is incredible that Catullus should have written " haud*que*."

> Verse 37. Pharsaliam coeunt, Pharsalia rura frequentant.

No objection can be raised against this reading. " Pharsaliam " is a trisyllable. The *i* sometimes coalesces with another vowel, as *a* and *o* do. In Virgil we find

> Stell*io* et lucifugis.
> Aure*â* composuit spondâ.
> Unâ eâdemque viâ.
> Uno *eo*demque igni.
> Perque ære*a* scuta.

Verses 58 and the following are out of their order. They stand thus :

> Rura colit nemo : mollescunt colla juvencis :
> Non humilis curvis purgatur vinea rastris :

> Non glebam prono convellit vomere taurus:
> Non falx attenuat frondatorum arboris umbram:
> Squalida desertis robigo infertur aratris.

The proper and natural series is, together with the right punctuation,

> Rura colit nemo: mollescunt colla juvencis,
> Non glebam prono convellit vomere taurus;
> Squalida desertis robigo infertur aratris.
> Non humilis curvis purgatur vinea rastris,
> Non falx attenuat frondatorum arboris umbram.

Because here the first, the second, and the third, refer to the same labour, that of ploughing: the fourth and fifth to the same also, that of cultivating the two kinds of vineyard. In one kind the grapes are cut low, and fastened on poles with bands of withy, and raked between: in the other they are trained against trees: formerly the tree preferred was the elm; at present it is the maple, particularly in Tuscany. The branches are lopt and thinned when the vines are pruned, to let in sun and air. By ignorance of such customs in agriculture, many things in the classics are mistaken. Few people know the meaning of the words in Horace,

> Cum *duplice* ficu.

Most fancy it must be the purple fig and the yellow. But there is also a green one. The Italians, to dry their figs the more expeditiously, cut them open and expose them on the pavement before their cottages. They then stick two together, and this is *duplex ficus*.

We now come to graver faults (and faults certainly the poet's) than a mere transposition of verses. In the palace of Peleus there is a piece of tapestry which takes up the best part of the poem.

> Hæc vestis *priscis* hominum variata figuris,

exhibits the story of Theseus and Ariadne. Their adventures could not have happened five-and-twenty years before these nuptials. Of the Argo, which carried Peleus when Thetis fell in love with him, the poet says, as others do,

> Illa rudem cursu *prima* imbuit Amphitriten.

But, in the progress of sixty lines, we find that vessels had been sailing to Crete every year, with the Athenian youths devoted to the Minotaur. Castor and Pollux sailed in the Argo with Peleus; and Helen, we know, was their sister: she was about the same age as Achilles, and Theseus had run away with her before Paris had. But equal inconsistencies are to be detected in the Æneid, a poem extolled, century after century, for propriety and exactness. An anachronism quite as strange as this of Catullus, is in the verses on Acragas, Agrigentum.

> Arduus inde Acragas ostentat maxima longe
> Mœnia, magnanimum *quondam* generator equorum.

Whether the city itself was built in the age of Æneas is not the question; but certainly the breed of horses was introduced by the Carthaginians, and improved by Hiero and Gelon. The breed of the island is small, as it is in all mountainous countries, where the horses are never found adapted to chariots, any more than chariots are adapted to surfaces so uneven.

Verse 83, for " *Funera* Cecropiæ," &c., we must read " *Pubis* Cecropiæ."

Verse 119. " Quæ misera," &c., is supposititious.

> Verse 178. *Idomeneos-ne* petam montes? at gurgite lato, &c.

Idomeneus was unborn in the earlier days of Theseus. Probably the verses were written,

> *Idam ideone* petam? Montes (ah gurgite vasto
> Discernens!) ponti truculentum dividit æquor.

Verse 191. Nothing was ever grander or more awful than the adjuration of Ariadne to the Eumenides.

> Quare facta virûm multantes vindice pœnâ
> Eumenides! quarum anguineo redimita capillo
> *Frons expirantes præportat pectoris iras,*
> Huc, huc adventate!

Verse 199. Doering explains,

> Vos nolite pati nostrum *vanescere* luctum,

" *Impunitum* manere." What? her grief? Does she pray that her grief may not remain *unpunished?* No, she implores that the prayers that arise from it may not be in vain.

Verse 212.   Namque ferunt olim [classi cum mœnia Divæ]
            Linquentem, natum, ventis concrederet Ægeus,
            Talia complexum juveni mandata dedisse.

The mould of the barrel has been doing sad mischief there. We must read

        Namque ferunt, natum ventis quum crederat Ægeus.
Verse 250.   At parte ex aliâ.

This scene is the subject of a noble picture by Titian, now in the British Gallery. It has also been deeply studied by Nicolas Poussin. But there is a beauty which no painting can attain in

       Plangebant alii proceris tympana palmis,
       Aut tereti tenues tinnitus ære ciebant.

Soon follows that exquisite description of morning on the sea-side, already transcribed, and placed by the side of Milton's personification.

Verse 340.   Nascetur vobis expers terroris Achilles,
            Hostibus haud tergo sed forti pectore notus,
            Qui persæpe vagi victor certamine cursûs
            Flammea prævertet celeris vestigia cervi.

It is impossible that Catullus, or any poet whatever, can have written the second of these. Some stupid critic must have done it, who fancied that the " expers terroris " was not clearly and sufficiently proven by urging the car over the field of battle, and had little or nothing to do in outstripping the stag.

     Verse 329.   Rarely have the Fates sung so sweetly as in these to Peleus.

       Adveniet tibi jam portans optata maritis
       Hesperus, adveniet fausto cum sidere conjux,
       Quæ tibi flexanimo mentem perfundat amore
       Languidulosque paret tecum conjungere somnos,
       Lævia substernens robusto brachia collo.

Carmen LXV. *Ad Hortalum.* He makes his excuse to Hortalus for delaying a compliance with his wishes for some verses. This delay he tells him was occasioned by the death of his brother, to whom he was most affectionately attached, and whose loss he laments in several of his poems. In this he breaks forth into a very pathetic appeal to him:

Alloquar? audiero numquam tua facta loquentem?
    Nunquam ego te, vitâ frater amabilior,
Adspiciam posthac!   At certe semper amabo,
    Sempermæsta tuâ carmina morte canam.

The two following lines are surely supposititious.   Thinking with such intense anguish of his brother's death, he could find no room for so frigid a conceit as that about the Daulian bird and Itylus.   This is almost as much out of place, though not so bad in itself, as the distich which heads the epistle of *Dido to Æneas* in Ovid.

Sic, ubi Fata vocant, udis abjectus in herbis
    Ad vada Mœandri concinit *albus olor*.

As if the Fates were busied in "calling white swans!"   Ovid never composed any such trash.   The epistle in fact begins with a verse of consummate beauty, tenderness, and gravity.

Verse 21.   Quod miseræ oblitæ molli sub veste locatum,
        Dum adventu matris prosilit, excutitur.

These require another punctuation.

Quod miseræ (oblitæ molli sub veste locatum).

The Germans, to whom we owe so much in every branch of learning, are not always fortunate in their punctuation : and perhaps never was any thing so subversive of harmony as that which Heyne has given us in a passage of Tibullus.

Blanditiis vult esse locum Venus ipsa.

Who could ever doubt this fact? that even Venus herself will admit of blandishments!   But Tibullus laid down no such truism. Heyne writes it thus, and proceeds,

                  querelis
Supplicibus, miseris fletibus, illa favet.

The tender and harmonious poet wrote not "Blanditiis" but "Blanditis."

Blanditis vult esse locum Venus ipsa querelis ;
    Supplicibus, miseris, flentibus, illa favet.

Here the "blanditiæ" are quite out of the question; but the "*blanditæ querelæ*" are complaints softly expressed and *coaxingly* preferred.

To return to Catullus.   The following couplet is,

> Atque illud prono præceps agitur decursu ;
> Huic manat tristi conscius ore rubor.

Manat can hardly be applicable to *rubor*.   We would prefer,

> *Huic manet in* tristi conscius ore rubor

the opposite to "*agitur*" *decursu.*

They whose ears have been accustomed to the Ovidian elegiac verse, and have been taught at school that every pentameter should close with a dissyllable, will be apt to find those of Catullus harsh and negligent.   But let them only read over, twice or thrice, the twelve first verses of this poem, and their ear will be cured of its infirmity.   By degrees they may be led to doubt whether the worst of all Ovid's conceits is not his determination to give every alternate verse this syllabic uniformity.

Carmen LXVI.   *De Comâ Berenices.*   This is imitated from a poem of Callimachus, now lost.   Probably it was an early exercise of our poet, corrected afterward, but insufficiently.   The sixth verse, however, is exquisite in its cadence.

> Ut Triviam furtim sub Latmia saxa relegans
> *Dulcis amor gyro devocat aerio.*
> Verse 27.   Anne bonum oblita es facinus, quo regium adepta es
> Conjugium, quod non fortior ausit *alis.*

Berenice is said to have displayed great courage in battle.   To render the second verse intelligible, we must admit *alis* for *alius,* as *alid* is used for *aliud* in Lucretius.   Moreover, we must give *fortior* the expression of *strength,* not of *courage,* as *forte* throughout Italy at the present time expresses never courage, always strength.   The sense of the passage then is, " Have you forgotten the great action by which you won your husband ? an action which one much stronger than yourself would not have attempted." For it would be nonsense to say, " You have performed a brave action which a *braver* person would not have dared."   In the sense of Catullus are those passages of Sallust and Virgil,

Neque a "fortissimis" *infirmissimo* generi resisti posse.
" Forti " fidis equo.
Verse 65.   Virginis, *et* sævi contingens *namque* Leonis Lumina.

Namque may be the true reading.   The editor has adduced two examples from Plautus to show the probability of it, but fails.

> Quando hæc innata est nam tibi.   Pers. ii. 5, 13.
> Quid tibi ex filio nam ægre est.   Bacch. v. I. 20.

He seems unaware that *nam*, in the first, is only a part of *quid-nam*, the *quid* being separated ; *quando-nam*, the same for *ecquando* (*ede* quando) " tell me when," *quianam*, &c.: but *namque* is not in the like condition, and in this place it is awkward.   The *nam* added to the above words is always an interrogative.

Carmen LXVII.   *Ad Januam, &c.*

> Verse 31.   Atqui non solum se dicit cognitum habere
>   Brixia, Cycnææ supposita speculæ,
> *Fluvus quam molli percurrit flumine Mela,*
>   Brixia Veronæ mater amata meæ.

Why should the sensible Marchese Scipione Maffei have taken it into his head that the last couplet is spurious ? What a beautiful verse is that in italics !

Carmen LXVIII. *Ad Manlium.* A rambling poem quite unworthy of the author. The verses from the beginning of the twenty-sixth to the close of the thirtieth appertain to some other piece, and break the context. Doering has given a strange interpretation to

> Veronæ turpe Catullo, &c.

The true meaning is much more obvious and much less delicate. In the sixty-third we must read " *At* " for " *Ac :* " this helps the continuity. After the seventy-third, we must omit, as belonging to another place, all, until we come to verse 143. Here we catch the thread again. The intermediate lines belong to *two* other poems ; both perhaps addressed to Manlius ; one relating to the death of the poet's brother, the other on a very different subject : we mean the fragment just now indicated,

> Quare quod scribis, Veronæ turpe Catullo, &c.
> Verse 145.   Sed furtiva dedit mirâ munuscula nocte,
>   Ipsius ex ipso demta viri gremio.

The verses are thus worded and punctuated in Doering's edition and others, but improperly. " *Mirâ* nocte " is nonsense. We must read the lines thus:

> Sed furtiva dedit *mirè* munuscula nocte
> Ipsius ex ipso, &c.

Or thus:

> Sed furtiva dedit *mediâ* munuscula nocte
> Ipsius ex ipso demta viri gremio.

Verse 147.   Quare illud satis est, si nobis is datur unus,
Quem lapide illa diem candidiore notat,

Doering thus interprets:

Quare jam illud mihi satis est, si illa vel *unum diem, quem mecum vixit*, ut diem faustum felicemque albo lapide insigniat.

That the verses have no such meaning is evident from the preceding:

> Quæ tamen etsi uno non est contenta Catullo
> Rara verecundæ furta feremus heræ.

This abolishes the idea of one single day contenting him, contented as he professes himself to be with little aberrations and infidelities. Scaliger has it:

> Quare illud satis est, si nobis *id* datur *unis :*
> Quod lapide illa dies candidiore notat.

And it appears to us that Scaliger has given the first line correctly; but not the punctuation. We should prefer,

> Quare illud satis est, si nobis id datur unis
> Quo lapide illa diem candidiore notet.
> " Quo," *ob quod.*

Verses 69, 70.   Trito fulgentem in limine plantam
Innisa argutâ constitit *in soleâ.*

The slipper could not be *arguta* while she was standing in it. Scaliger reads " constit*uit* soleâ." The one is not sense: the other is neither sense nor Latin, unless the construction is *constituit plantam;* and then all the other words are in disarray. The meaning is, " she placed her foot against the door, and, *without speaking*, rapped it with her sounding slipper: " then the words would be " argutâ *conticuit* soleâ."

Verse 78. Nil mihi tam valde placeat, Rhamnusia virgo,
Quod temere invitis suscipiatur heris.

In Scaliger it is :

Quàm temere, &c.

The true reading is neither, but

Quàm *ut* temere.

Such elisions are found in this very poem and the preceding :

Ne amplius a misero.
and,
Qui ipse sui gnati.

CARMEN LXXI. *Ad Virronem.* Doering thinks, as others have done, that the poem is against *Virro.* On the contrary, it is a facetious consolation to him on the punishment of his rival.

Mirifice est *a te* nactus utrumque malum,

means only "*for his offence against you.*" We have a little more to add on this in CXV.

CARMEN LXXV. *Ad Lesbiam.* Here are eight verses, the rhythm of which plunges from the ear into the heart. Our attempt to render them in English is feeble and vain.

> None could ever say that she,
> Lesbia ! was so loved by me.
> Never all the world around
> Faith so true as mine was found :
> If no longer it endures
> (Would it did !) the fault is yours.
> I can never think again
> Well of you : I try in vain :
> But . . be false . . do what you will . .
> Lesbia ! I must love you still.

CARMEN LXXVI. *Ad seipsum.* They whose ears retain only the sound of the hexameters and pentameters they recited and wrote at school, are very unlikely to be greatly pleased with the versification of this poem. Yet perhaps one of equal earnestness and energy was never written in elegiac metre. *Sentences* must be read at once, and not merely distichs ; then a fresh harmony will spring up exuberantly in every part of it, into which many discordant verses will sink and lose themselves, to produce a part of the effect.   It is, however, difficult to restrain a smile at such expressions as these from such a man.

Si vitam puriter egi,
O Dii! reddite mî hoc pro pietate meâ!

CARMEN LXXXV.   *De Amore suo.*

Odi et amo.   *Quare id faciam, fortasse requiris :*
Nescio, sed fieri sentio et excrucior.

The words in italics are flat and prosaic : the thought is beautiful, and similar to that expressed in LXXV.

I love and hate.   Ah! never ask why so!
I hate and love . . and that is all I know.
I see 'tis folly, but I feel 'tis woe.

CARMEN XCII.   *De Lesbia.*   The fourth verse is printed,

Quo signo? quasi non totidem *mox* deprecor illi
Assidue.

Mox and *assidue* can not stand together.   Jacobs has given a good emendation.

Quasi non totidem *mala* deprecer, illi, &c.

CARMEN XCIII.   *In Cæsarem.*   Nothing can be imagined more contemptuous than the indifference he here affects toward a name destined in all after ages to be the principal jewel in the highest crowns : and, thinking of Cæsar's genius, it is difficult to see without derision the greatest of those who assume it.   Catullus must have often seen, and we have reason to believe he personally knew, the conqueror of Gaul when he wrote this epigram.

I care not, Cæsar, what you are,
Nor know if ye be brown or fair.

CARMEN XCV.   *De Smyrnâ Cinnæ Poetæ.*   There is nothing of this poem, in which Cinna's *Smyrna* is extolled, worth notice, excepting the last line ; and that indeed not for what we read in it, but for what we have lost.

Parva mei mihi sunt cordi monumenta . .

The word "mon*u*menta" is spelt improperly: it is "mon*i*-menta." The last word in the verse is wanting: yet we have seen quoted, and prefixed to volumes of poetry:

Parva mei mihi sunt cordi monumenta laboris.

But Catullus is not speaking of himself: he is speaking of Cinna: and the proper word comes spontaneously "sodalis."

CARMEN XCIX. *Ad Juventium.*

Multis diluta labella
Guttis *abstersisti omnibus articulis.*

How few will this verse please! but how greatly those few!

CARMEN CI. *Inferiæ ad Frateris Tumulum.* In these verses there is a sorrowful but a quiet solemnity, which we rarely find in poets on similar occasions. The grave and firm voice, which has uttered the third, breaks down in the fourth.

Multas per gentes et multa per æquora vectus
Adveni has miseras, frater, ad inferias,
Ut te postremo donarem munere mortis
Et mutum nequidquam alloquerer cinerem.

Unusual as is the cadence, the cæsura, who would wish it other than it is? If there were authority for it, we would read, in the sixth, instead of

Heu *miser* indigne frater ademte mihi!
Heu *nimis,* &c.

Because just above we have,

Adveni has *miseras,* frater, ad inferias.

CARMEN CX. *Ad Aufilenam.* Doering says, " Utrum poetæ an scribarum *socordiæ* tribuenda sit, qua ultimi hujus carminis versus laborant, obscuritas, pro suo quisque statuat arbitrio. Tolli quidem potest hæc obscuritas, sed *emendandi genere liberrimo.*" We are not quite so sure of that: we are only sure that we find no obscurity at all in them. The word *factum* is understood, and would be inelegant if it could have found for itself a place in the verse.

Carmen CXV.   It is requisite to transcribe the verses here to show that Doering is mistaken in two places: he was, at LXXI., in one only.

> Prata arva, ingentes sylvas saltusque paludesque
> Usque ad Hyperboreos et mare ad Oceanum.
> Omnia magna hæc sunt, tamen ipse est *maximus ultor*.

He quotes LXXI., forgetting that that poem is addressed to Virro, and this to Mamurra, under his old nickname: Mamurra, whatever else he might be, was no *maximus ultor* here. The context will show what the word should be. Mamurra, by his own account, is possessor of meadow ground and arable ground, of woods, forests, and marshes, from the Hyperboreans to the Atlantic. "These are great things," says Catullus, "but he himself is great *beyond them all;*" "ipse est maximus, ultra:" sc. Hyperboreas et Oceanum.

In how different a style, how artificially, with what infinite fuss and fury, has Horace addressed Virgil on the death of Quintilius Varus. Melpomene is called from a distance, and several more persons equally shadowy are brought forward; and then Virgil is honestly told that, if he could sing and play more blandly than the Thracian Orpheus, he never could reanimate an empty image which Mercury had drawn off among his "black flock."

In selecting a poet for examination, it is usual either to extol him to the skies, or to tear him to pieces and trample on him. Editors in general do the former: critics on editors more usually the latter. But one poet is not to be raised by casting another under him. Catullus is made no richer by an attempt to transfer to him what belongs to Horace, nor Horace by what belongs to Catullus. Catullus has greatly more than he; but he also has much; and let him keep it. We are not at liberty to indulge in forwardness and caprice, snatching a decoration from one and tossing it over to another. We will now sum up what we have collected from the mass of materials which has been brought before us, laying down some general rules and observations.

There are four things requisite to constitute might, majesty, and dominion, in a poet: these are creativeness, constructiveness, the sublime, the pathetic. A poet of the first order must have formed, or taken to himself and modified, some great subject. He must be creative and constructive. Creativeness may work upon old materials: a new world may spring from an old one. Shakespeare found Hamlet and Ophelia; he found Othello and Desdemona: nevertheless he, the only universal poet, carried this, and all the other qualifications, far beyond the reach of competitors. He was creative and constructive, he was sublime and pathetic, and he has also in his humanity condescended to the familiar and the comic. There is nothing less pleasant than the smile of Milton; but at one time Momus, at another the Graces, hang upon the neck of Shakespeare. Poets whose subjects do not restrict them, and whose ordinary gait displays no indication of either greave or buskin, if they want the facetious and humorous, and are not creative, nor sublime, nor pathetic, must be ranked by sound judges in the secondary order, and not among the foremost even there.

Cowper, and Byron, and Southey, with much and deep tenderness, are richly humorous. Wordsworth, grave, elevated, observant, and philosophical, is equidistant from humour and from passion. Always contemplative, never creative, he delights the sedentary and tranquillizes the excited. No tear ever fell, no smile ever glanced, on his pages. With him you are beyond the danger of any turbulent emotion at terror, or valour, or magnanimity, or generosity. Nothing is there about him like Burns's *Scots wha ha'e wi' Wallace bled*, or Campbell's *Battles of Copenhagen and Hohenlinden*, or those exquisite works which, in Hemans, rise up like golden spires among broader but lower structures, *Ivan* and *Casabianca*. Byron, often impressive and powerful, never reaches the heroic and the pathetic of these two poems: and he wants the freshness and healthiness we admire in Burns. But an indomitable fire of poetry, the more vivid for the gloom about it, bursts through the crusts and crevices of an unsound and hollow mind. He never chatters with chilliness, nor falls overstrained into languor; nor do metaphysics ever muddy his impetuous and precipitate stream. It spreads its ravishes in some places, but it is limpid and sparkling everywhere. If no story is well told by him, no character well delineated, if all resemble one another by their beards and Turkish dresses, there is however the first and the second and the third requisite of eloquence, whether in prose or poetry, vigour.   But no *large* poem of our days is so animated, or so truly of the heroic cast, as *Marmion.*   Southey's *Roderick* has less nerve and animation: but what other living poet has attempted, or shown the ability, to erect a structure so symmetrical and so stately?   It is not enough to heap description on description, to cast reflection over reflection: there must be development of character in the development of story; there must be action, there must be passion; the end and the means must alike be great.

The poet whom we mentioned last is more studious of classical models than the others, especially in his *Inscriptions.*   Interest is always excited by him, enthusiasm not always.   If his elegant prose and harmonious verse are insufficient to excite it, turn to his virtues, to his manliness in defence of truth, to the ardour and constancy of his friendships, to his disinterestedness, to his generosity, to his rejection of title and office, and consequently of wealth and influence.   He has laboured to raise up merit in whatever path of literature he found it; and poetry in particular has never had so intelligent, so impartial, and so merciful a judge. Alas! it is the will of God to deprive him of those faculties which he exercised with such discretion, such meekness, and such humanity.

We digress; not too far, but too long: we must return to the ancients, and more especially to the· author whose volume lies open before us.

There is little of the creative, little of the constructive, in him: that is, he has conceived no new varieties of character; he has built up no edifice in the intellectual world; but he always is shrewd and brilliant; he often is pathetic; and he sometimes is sublime.   Without the sublime, we have said before, there can be no poet of the first order: but the pathetic may exist in the secondary, for tears are more easily drawn forth than souls are raised.   So easily are they on some occasions, that the poetical power needs scarcely be brought into action; while on others the pathetic is the very summit of sublimity.   We have an example of it in the *Ariadne* of Catullus: we have another in the *Priam* of Homer.   All the heroes and gods, debating and fighting, vanish before the father of Hector in the tent of Achilles, and before the storm of conflicting passions his sorrows and prayers excite. But neither in the spirited and energetic Catullus, nor in the masculine and scornful and stern Lucretius, no, nor in Homer, is there anything so impassioned, and therefore so sublime, as the last hour of Dido in the Æneid. Admirably as two Greek poets have represented the tenderness, the anguish, the terrific wrath and vengeance of Medea, all the works they ever wrote contain not the poetry which Virgil has condensed into about a hundred verses: omitting, as we must, those which drop like icicles from the rigid lips of Æneas ; and also the similes which, here as everywhere, sadly interfere with passion. In this place Virgil fought his battle of Actium, which left him poetical supremacy in the Roman world, whatever mutinies and conspiracies may have arisen against him in Germany or elsewhere.

The *Ariadne* of Catullus has greatly the advantage over the *Medea* of Apollonius : for what man is much interested by such a termagant? We have no sympathies with a woman whose potency is superhuman. In general, it may be apprehended, we like women little the better for excelling us even moderately in our own acquirements and capacities. But what energy springs from her weaknesses ! what poetry is the fruit of her passions ! once perhaps in a thousand years bursting forth with imperishable splendour on its golden bough. If there are fine things in the *Argonautics* of Apollonius, there are finer still in those of Catullus. In relation to Virgil, he stands as Correggio in relation to Raffael : a richer colourist, a less accurate draughtsman ; less capable of executing grand designs, more exquisite in the working-out of smaller. Virgil is depreciated by the arrogance of self-sufficient poets, nurtured on coarse fare, and dizzy with home-brewed flattery. Others, who have studied more attentively the ancient models, are abler to show his relative station, and readier to venerate his powers. Although we find him incapable of contriving, and more incapable of executing, so magnificent a work as the Iliad, yet there are places in his compared with which the grandest in that grand poem lose much of their elevation. Never was there such a whirlwind of passions as Virgil raised on those African shores, amid those rising citadels and departing sails. When the vigorous verses of Lucretius are extolled, no true poet, no sane critic, will assent that the seven or eight examples of the best are equivalent to this one : even in force of expression, here he falls short of Virgil.

When we drink a large draught of refreshing beverage, it is only a small portion that affects the palate.   In reading the best poetry, moved and excited as we may be, we can take in no more than a part of it.   Passages of equal beauty are unable to raise enthusiasm.   Let a work in poetry or prose, indicating the highest power of genius, be discoursed on ; probably no two persons in a large company will recite the same portion as having struck them the most forcibly.   But when several passages are pointed out and read emphatically, each listener will to a certain extent doubt a little his own judgment in this one particular, and hate you heartily for shaking it.   Poets ought never to be vext, discomposed, or disappointed, when the better is overlookt, and the inferior is commended.   Much may be assigned to the observer's point of vision being more on a level with the object. And this reflection also will console the artist, when really bad ones are called more simple and natural, while in fact they are only more ordinary and common.   In a palace we must look to the elevation and proportions ; whereas a low grotto may assume any form and almost any deformity.   Rudeness is here no blemish ; a shell reversed is no false ornament ; moss and fern may be stuck with the root outward ; a crystal may sparkle at the top or at the bottom ; dry sticks and fragmentary petrifactions find everywhere their proper place ; and loose soil and plashy water show just what nature delights in.   Ladies and gentlemen who at first were about to turn back, take one another by the hand, duck their heads, enter it together, and exclaim, " What a charming grotto ! "

In poetry, as in architecture, the Rustic Order is proper only for the lower story.

They who have listened, patiently and supinely, to the catarrhal songsters of goose-grazed commons, will be loth and ill-fitted to mount up with Catullus to the highest steeps in the forests of Ida, and will shudder at the music of the Corybantes in the temple of the Great Mother of the Gods.

FRANCESCO PETRARCA.

Scarcely on any author, of whatever age or country, has there so much been written, spoken, and thought, by both sexes, as on the subject of this criticism, Petrarca.

The compilation by Mr Campbell is chiefly drawn together from the French. It contains no criticism on the poetry of his author, beyond a hasty remark or two in places which least require it. He might have read Sismondi and Ginguené more profitably; the author of the *Introduction to the Literature of Europe* had already done so; but neither has *he* thrown any fresh light on the character or the writings of Petrarca, or, in addition to what had already been performed by those two judicious men, furnished us with a remark in any way worth notice. The readers of Italian, if they are suspicious, may even suspect that Mr Campbell knows not very much of the language. Among the many apparent causes for this suspicion, we shall notice only two. Instead of *Friuli*, he writes the French word *Frioul*; and, instead of the *Marca* di Ancona, the *Marshes*. In Italian, a *marsh* is *palude* or *padule*: whereas *marca* is the origin of *marchese*: the one a *confine*; the other a *defender* of a *confine*, or lord of such a territory.

Whoever is desirous of knowing all about Petrarca, will consult Muratori and De Sade: whoever has been waiting for a compendious and sound judgment on his works at large, will listen attentively to Ginguené: whoever can be gratified by a rapid glance at his works and character, will be directed by the clear-sighted follower of truth, Sismondi; and whoever reads only English, and is contented to fare on a small portion of recocted criticism in a long excursion, may be accommodated by Mrs Dobson, Mr Hallam, and Mr Campbell.

It may seem fastidious and affected to write, as I have done, his Italian name in preference to his English one; but I think it better to call him as he called himself, as Laura called him, as he was called by Colonna and Rienzi and Boccaccio, and in short by all Italy: for I pretend to no vernacular familiarity with a person of his distinction, and should almost be as ready to abbreviate Francesco into Frank, as Petrarca into Petrarch.

Beside, the one appellation is euphonious, the other quite the reverse.

We Englishmen take strange liberties with Italian names. Perhaps the human voice can articulate no sweeter series of sounds than the syllables which constitute *Livorno :* certainly the same remark is inapplicable to *Leghorn.* However, we are not liable to censure for this depravation : it originated with the Genoese, the ancient masters of the town, whose language is extremely barbarous, not unlike the Provensal of the Troubadours. With them the letter *g,* pronounced hard, as it always was among the Greeks and Romans, is common for *v :* thus *lagoro* for *lavoro.*

I hope to be pardoned my short excursion, which was only made to bring my fellow-labourers home from afield. At last we are beginning to call people and things by their right names. We pay a little more respect to Cicero than we did formerly, calling him no longer by the appellation of Tully : we never say Laurence, or Lal de Medici, but Lorenzo. On the same principle, I beg permission to say Petrarca and Boccaccio, instead of Petrarch and Boccace. These errors were fallen into by following French translations : and we stopt and recovered our footing only when we came to *Tite-live* and *Aulugelle.* It was then indeed high time to rest and wipe our foreheads. Yet we cannot shake off the illusion that *Horace* was one of us at school, and we continue the friendly nickname, although with a whimsical inconsistency we continue to talk of the *Horatii* and Curiatii. *Ovid,* our earlier friend, sticks by us still. The ear informs us that Virgil and Pindar and Homer and Hesiod suffer no worse by defalcation than fruit-trees do : the sounds indeed are more euphonious than what fell from the native tongue. The great historians, the great orators, and the great tragedians of Greece, have escaped unmutilated ; and among the Romans it has been the good fortune, at least as far as *we* are concerned, of Paterculus, Quintus Curtius, Tacitus, Catullus, Propertius, and Tibullus, to remain intact by the hand of *onomaclasts.* Spellings, whether of names or things, should never be meddled with, unless where the ignorant have superseded the learned, or where analogy has been overlooked by these. The courtiers of Charles II. chalked and charcoaled the orthography of Milton. It was thought a scandal to have been educated in England, and a worse to write as a republican had written. We were the subjects of the French king, and we borrowed at a ruinous rate from French authors: but not from the best. Eloquence was extinct; a gulf of ignominy divided us from the genius of Italy; the great Master of the triple world was undiscovered by us; and the loves of Petrarca were too pure and elevated for the sojourners of Versailles.

Francesco Petrarca, if far from the greatest, yet certainly the most celebrated of poets, was born in the night between the nineteenth and twentieth day of July, 1304. His father's name was Petracco, his mother's Eletta Canigiani. Petracco left Florence under the same sentence of banishment as his friend Dante Alighieri, and joined with him and the other exiles of the Bianchi army in the unsuccessful attack on that city, the very night when, on his return to Arezzo, he found a son born to him: it was his first. To this son, afterward so illustrious, was given the name of Francesco di Petracco. In after life the sound had something in it which he thought ignoble; and he converted it into Petrarca. The wise and virtuous Gravina, patron of one who has written much good poetry, and less of bad than Petrarca, changed in like manner the name of Trapasso to Metastasio. I can not agree with him that the sound of the Hellenized name is more harmonious: the reduplication of the syllable *tas* is painful: but I do agree with Petrarca, whose adopted form has only one fault, which is, that there is no meaning in it.

When he was seven months old he was taken by his mother from Arezzo to Incisa, in the Val-d'Arno, where the life so lately given was nearly lost. The infant was dropt into the river, which is always rapid in that part of its course, and was then swollen by rain into a torrent. At Incisa he remained with her seven years. The father had retired to Pisa; and now his wife and Francesco, and another son born after, named Gherardo, joined him there. In a short time however he took them to Avignon, where he hoped for employment under Pope Clement V. In that crowded city lodgings and provisions were so dear, that he soon found it requisite to send his wife and children to the small episcopal town of Carpentras, where he

often went to visit them. In this place Francesco met Con-
venole, who had taught him his letters, and who now undertook
to teach him what he knew of rhetoric and logic. He had attained his tenth year when the father took him with a party of
friends to the fountain of Vaucluse. Even at that early age his
enthusiasm was excited by the beauty and solitude of the scene.
The waters then flowed freely: habitations there were none but
the most rustic : and indeed one only near the rivulet. Such was
then Vaucluse ; and such it remained all his lifetime, and long
after. The tender heart is often moulded by localities. Perhaps
the purity and singleness of Petrarca's, his communion with it on
one only altar, his exclusion of all images but one, result from
this early visit to the gushing springs, the eddying torrents, the
insurmountable rocks, the profound and inviolate solitudes, of
Vaucluse.

The time was now come when his father saw the necessity of
beginning to educate him for a profession : and he thought the
canon law was likely to be the most advantageous. Consequently
he was sent to Montpelier, the nearest university, where he resided
four years ; not engaged, as he ought to have been, among the
jurisconsults, but among the classics. Information of this per-
versity soon reached Petracco, who hastened to the place, found
the noxious books, and threw them into the fire : but, affected by
the lamentations of his son, he recovered the Cicero and the
Virgil, and restored them to him, partially consumed. At the
age of eighteen he was sent from Montpelier to Bologna, where
he found Cino da Pistoja, to whom he applied himself in good
earnest, not indeed for his knowledge as a jurisconsult, in which
he had acquired the highest reputation, but for his celebrity as a
poet. After two more years he lost his father: and the guardians,
it is said, were unfaithful to their trust. Probably there was little
for them to administer. He now returned to Avignon, where,
after the decease of Clement V., John XXII. occupied the
popedom. Here his Latin poetry soon raised him into notice,
for nobody in Avignon wrote so good ; but happily, both for
himself and many thousand sensitive hearts in every age and
nation, he soon desired his verses to be received and understood
by one to whom the Latin was unknown.

Benedetto sia il giorno, e 'l mese, e l'anno !

Blest be the day, and month, and year!

Laura, daughter of Audibert de Noves, was married to Hugh de Sade; persons of distinction. She was younger by three years than Petrarca. They met first on Good Friday, in the convent-church of St Claire, at six in the morning. That hour she inspired such a passion, by her beauty and her modesty, as years only tended to strengthen, and death to sanctify. The incense which burnt in the breast of Petrarca before his Laura, might have purified, one would have thought, even the court of Avignon; and never was love so ardent breathed into ear so chaste. The man who excelled all others in beauty of person, in dignity of demeanour, in genius, in tenderness, in devotion, was perhaps the only one who failed in attaining the object of his desires. But cold as Laura was in temperament, rigid as she was in her sense of duty, she never was insensible to the merits of her lover. A light of distant hope often shone upon him, and tempted him onward, through surge after surge, over the depths of passion. Laura loved admiration, as the most retired and most diffident of women do: and the admiration of Petrarca drew after it the admiration of the world. She also, what not all women do, looked forward to the glory that awaited her, when those courtiers, and those crowds, and that city should be no more, and when of all women, the Madonna alone should be so glorified on earth.

Perhaps it is well for those who delight in poetry that she was inflexible and obdurate; for the sweetest song ceases when the feathers have lined the nest. Incredible as it may seem, Petrarca was capable of quitting her: he was capable of believing that absence could moderate, or perhaps extinguish, his passion. Generally the lover who can think so, has almost succeeded; but Petrarca had contracted the habit of writing poetry; and now writing it on Laura, and Laura only, he brought the past and the future into a focus on his breast. All magical powers, it is said, are dangerous to the possessor: none is more dangerous than the magic of the poet, who can call before him at will the object of his wishes; but her countenance and her words remain her own, and beyond his influence.

It is wonderful how extremely few, even of Italian scholars, and natives of Italy, have read his letters or his poetry entirely

through.   I am not speaking of his Latin; for it would indeed
be a greater marvel if the most enterprising industry succeeded
there.   The thunderbolt of war . . "Scipiades fulmen belli" . .
has always left a barren place behind.   No poet ever was fortunate
in the description of his exploits; and the least fortunate of the
number is Petrarca.   Probably the whole of the poem contains
no sentence or image worth remembering.   I say *probably :* for
whosoever has hit upon what he thought the best of it, has hit
only upon what is worthless, or else upon what belongs to another.
The few lines quoted and applauded by Mr Campbell, are taken
partly from Virgil's *Æneid,* and partly from Ovid's *Metamorphoses.*
I can not well believe that any man living has read beyond five
hundred lines of *Africa :* I myself, in sundry expeditions, have
penetrated about thus far into its immeasurable sea of sand.   But
the wonder is that neither the poetry nor the letters of Petrarca
seem to have been, even in his own country, read thoroughly and
attentively; for surely his commentators ought to have made
themselves masters of these, before they agitated the question,
some whether Laura really existed, and others whether she was
flexible to the ardour of her lover.   Speaking of his friends,
Socrates and Lælius, of whose first meeting with him I shall
presently make mention, he says,

> Con costor colsi 'l glorioso ramo
> Onde forse anzi tempo ornai le tempie,
> In memoria di quella ch' io tant' amo :
> Ma pur di lei che il cuor di pensier m' empie
> Non potei coglier mai ramo nè foglie;
> Si fur' le sue radici acerbe ed empie.

I can not render these verses much worse than they actually
are, with their " *tempo* " and " *tempie,*" and their " radici *empie,*"
so let me venture to offer a translation :

> They saw me win the glorious bough
> That shades my temples even now,
> *Who never bough nor leaf could take*
> From that severe one, for whose sake
> So many sighs and tears arose . .
> Unbending root of bitter woes.

There is a canzone to the same purport, to be noticed in its
place ; and several of his letters could also be adduced in evidence.

We may believe that, although he had resolved to depart from Avignon for a season, he felt his love increasing at every line he wrote. Such thoughts and images can not be turned over in the mind and leave it perfectly in composure. Yet perhaps when he had completed the most impassioned sonnet, the surges of his love may have subsided under the oil he had poured out on his vanity. For love, if it is a weakness, was not the only weakness of Petrarca : and, when he had performed what he knew was pleasing in the eyes of Laura, he looked abroad for the applauses of all around.

Giacomo Colonna, who had been at the university of Bologna with him, had come to Avignon soon after. It was with Colonna he usually spent his time ; both had alike enjoyed the pleasures of the city, until the day when Francesco met Laura. To Giacomo was now given the bishopric of Lombes, in reward of a memorable and admirable exploit, among the bravest that ever has been performed in the sight of Rome herself. When Lewis of Bavaria went thither to depose John XVIII., Giacomo Colonna, attended by four men in masks, read publicly, in the Piazza di San Marcello, the bull of that emperor's excommunication and dethronement, and challenged to single combat any adversary. None appearing, he rode onward to the stronghold of his family at Palestrina, the ancient Preneste. His reward was this little bishopric. When Petrarca found him at Lombes, in the house of the bishop he found also two persons of worth, who became the most intimate of his friends : the one a Roman, Lello by name, which name the poet latinized to Lælius ; the other from the borders of the Rhine, whose appellation was probably less tractable, and whom he called Socrates. Toward the close of autumn the whole party returned to Avignon.

In the bosom of Petrarca love burnt again more ardently than ever. It is censured as the worst of conceits in him that he played so often on the name of Laura ; and many have suspected that there could be little passion in so much allusion. A purer taste might indeed have corrected in the poetry the outpourings of tenderness in the name ; but surely there is a true and a pardonable pleasure in cherishing the very sound of what we love. If it belongs to the heart, as it does, it belongs to poetry, and is not easily to be cast aside. The shrub recalling the idea of Laura was planted by his hand ; often, that he might norture it, was the pen laid by ; the leaves were often shaken by his sighs, and not unfrequently did they sparkle with his tears. He felt the comfort of devotion as he bent before the image of her name. But he now saw little of her, and was never at her house : it was only in small parties, chiefly of ladies, that they met. She excelled them all in grace of person and in elegance of attire. Probably her dress was not the more indifferent to her on her thinking whom she was about to meet : yet she maintained the same reserve : the nourisher of love, but not of hope.

Restless, for ever restless, again went Petrarca from Avignon. He hoped he should excite a little regret at his departure, and a desire to see him again soon, if not exprest to him before he left the city, yet conveyed by letters or reports. He proceeded to Paris, thence to Cologne, and was absent eight months. On his return, the bishop, whom he expected to meet, was neither at Avignon nor at Lombes. His courage and conduct were required at Rome, to keep down the rivals of his family, the Orsini. Disappointed in his visit, and hopeless in his passion, the traveller now retired to Vaucluse ; and here he poured in solitude from his innermost heart incessant strains of love and melancholy.

At Paris he had met with Dionigi de' Ruperti, an Augustine monk, born at Borgo San Sepolcro, near Florence, and esteemed as one of the most learned, eloquent, philosophical and religious men in France. To him Petrarca wrote earnestly for counsel ; but before the answer came he had seen Laura. A fever was raging in the city, and her life was in danger. Benedict XII., to whom he addressed the least inelegant of his Latin poems, an exhortation to transfer the Roman See to Rome, conferred on him, now in the thirtieth year of his age, a canonry at Lombes. But the bishop was absent from the diocese, and again at Rome. Thither hastened Petrarca, and was received at Capraniccia, a castle of the Colonnas, not only by his diocesan, but likewise by Stefano, senator of Rome, to which city they both conducted him. His stay here was short ; he returned to Avignon ; but, inflamed with unquenchable love, and seeking to refresh his bosom with early memories, he retired to Vaucluse. Here he purchased a poor cottage and a small meadow ; hither he transferred his books; and hither also that image which he could nowhere leave behind. Summer, autumn, winter, he spent among these solitudes; a fisherman was his only attendant, but occasionally a few intimate friends came from Avignon to visit him. The Bishop of Cavaillon, Philippe de Cabassoles, in whose diocese was Vaucluse, and who had a villa not far off, here formed with him a lasting friendship, and was worthy of it. During these months the poet wrote the three canzoni on the eyes of Laura, which some have called the "Three Graces," but which he himself called the "Three Sisters." The Italians, the best-tempered and the most polite of nations, look rather for beauties than faults, and imagine them more easily. A brilliant thought blinds them to improprieties, and they are incapable of resisting a strong expression. Enthusiastic criticism is common in Italy, ingenious is not deficient, correct is yet to come.

About this time Simone Memmi of Siena, whom some without any reason whatsoever have called a disciple of Giotto, was invited by the pope to Avignon, where he painted an apartment in the pontifical palace, just then completed. Petrarca has celebrated him, not only in two sonnets, but also in his letters, in which he says, "Duos ego novi pictores egregois: Joctium Florentinum civem, cujus inter modernos fama ingens est, et Simonem Senensem."

Had so great an artist been the scholar of Giotto, it would have added to the reputation of even this illustrious man, a triumvir with Ghiberti and Michel-Agnolo. These although indeed not flourishing together, may be considered as the first triumvirate in the republic of the arts; Raffael, Correggio, and Titian the second. There is no resemblance to Giotto in the manner of Simone; nor does Ghiberti mention him as the disciple of the Florentine. No man knew better than Ghiberti how distinct are the Siennese and the Florentine schools. Simone Memmi, the first of the moderns who gave roundness and beauty to the female face, neglected not the graceful air of Laura. Frequently did he repeat her modest features in the principal figure of his sacred compositions; and Petrarca was alternately tortured and consoled by the possession of her portrait from the hand of Memmi. It was painted in the year 1339, so that she was thirty-two years old; but, whether at the desire of her lover, or guided by his own discretion, or that in reality she retained the charms of youth after bearing eight or nine children, she is represented youthful, and almost girlish, whenever he introduces her.

With her picture now before him, Petrarca thought he could reduce in number and duration his visits to Avignon, and might undertake a work sufficient to fix his attention and occupy his retirement. He began to compose in Latin a history of Rome, from its foundation to the subversion of Jerusalem. But, almost at the commencement, the exploits of Scipio Africanus seized upon his enthusiastic imagination, and determined him to abandon history for poetry. The second Punic war was the subject he chose for an epic. Deficient as the work is in all the requisites of poetry, his friends applauded it beyond measure. And indeed no small measure of commendation is due to it; for here he had restored in some degree the plan and tone of antiquity. But to such a pitch was his vanity exalted, that he aspired to higher honours than Virgil had received under the favour of Augustus, and was ambitious of being crowned in the capitol. His powerful patrons removed every obstacle; and the senator of Rome invited him by letter to his coronation. A few hours afterward, on the 23rd of August 1340, another of the same purport was delivered to him from the University of Paris. The good king Robert of Naples had been zealous in obtaining for him the honour he solicited: and to Naples he hastened, ere he proceeded to Rome.

It was in later days that kings began to avoid the conversation and familiarity of learned men. Robert received Francesco as became them both; and, on his departure from the court of Naples, presented to him the gorgeous robe in which, four days afterward, he was crowned in the capitol. At the close of his life he lamented the glory he had thus attained, and repined at the malice it drew down on him. Even in the hour of triumph he was exposed to a specimen of the kind. Most of those among the ancient Romans to whom in their triumphal honours the laurel crown was decreed, were exposed to invectives and reproaches in their ascent. Fescennine verses, rude and limping, interspersed with saucy trochaics, were generally their unpalatable fare. But Petrarca, the elect of a senator and a pope, was doomed to worse treatment. Not on his advance, but on his return, an old woman emptied on his laurelled head one of those mysterious vases which are usually in administration at the solemn hour of night. Charity would induce us to hope that her venerable age was actuated by no malignity. But there were strong surmises to the contrary: nor can I adduce in her defence that she had any poetical vein, by which I might account for this extraordinary act of incontinence. Partaking, as was thought by the physicians, of the old woman's nature, the contents of the vase were so acrimonious as to occasion baldness. Her cauldron, instead of restoring youth, drew down old age, or fixed immovably its odious signal. A projectile scarcely more fatal, in a day also of triumph, was hurled by a similar enemy on the head of Pyrrhus. The laurel decreed in full senate to Julius Cæsar, although it might conceal the calamity of baldness, never could have prevented it: nor is it probable that either his skill or his fortune could have warded off efficaciously what descended from such a quarter. The Italians, who carry more good humour about them than any other people, are likely to have borne this catastrophe of their poet with equanimity, if not hilarity. Perhaps even the gentle Laura, when she heard of it, averted the smile she could not quite suppress.

I will not discuss the question, how great or how little was the glory of this coronation; a glory which Homer and Dante, which Shakespeare and Milton, never sought, and never would have attained. Merit has rarely risen of itself, but a pebble or a twig is often quite sufficient for it to spring from to the highest ascent. There is usually some baseness before there is any elevation. After all, no man can be made greater by another, although he may be made more conspicuous by title, dress, position, and acclamation. The powerful can only be ushers to the truly great; and in the execution of this office, they themselves approach to greatness. But Petrarca stood far above all the other poets of his age; and, incompetent as were his judges, it is much to their praise that they awarded due honour to the purifier both of language and of morals. With these indeed to solicit the wife of another may seem inconsistent; but such was always the custom of the Tuscan race; and not always with the same chastity as was enforced by Laura. As Petrarca loved her,

Id, Manli ! non est turpe, magis miserum est.

Love is the purifier of the heart ; its depths are less turbid that its shallows.   In despite of precepts and arguments, the most sedate and the most religious of women think charitably, and even reverentially, of the impassioned poet.   Constancy is the antagonist of frailty, exempt from the captivity and above the assaults of sin.

There is much resemblance in the character of Petrarca to that of Abeillard.   Both were learned, both were disputatious, both were handsome, both were vain ; both ran incessantly backward and forward from celebrity to seclusion, from seclusion to celebrity ; both loved unhappily ; but the least fortunate was the most beloved.

Devoted as Petrarca was to the classics, and prone as the Italian poets are to follow and imitate them, he stands apart with Laura ; and if some of his reflections are to be found in the sonnets of Cino da Pistoja, and a few in the more precious reliquary of Latin Elegy, he seems disdainful of repeating in her ear what has ever been spoken in another's.   Although a cloud of pure incense rises up and veils the intensity of his love, it is such love as animates all creatures upon earth, and tends to the same object in all.   Throughout life we have been accustomed to hear of the Platonic : absurd as it is everywhere, it is most so here. Nothing in the voluminous works of Plato authorizes us to affix this designation to simple friendship, to friendship exempt from passion.   On the contrary, the philosopher leaves us no doubt whatever that his notion of love is sensual.*   He says expressly

---

* A mysterious and indistinct idea, not dissipated by the closest view of the original, led the poetical mind of Shelley into the labyrinth that encompassed the garden of Academus.   He has given us an accurate and graceful translation of the most eloquent of Plato's dialogues.   Consistently with modesty he found it impossible to present the whole to his readers ; but as the subject is entirely on the nature of love. they will discover that nothing is more unlike Petrarca's.   The trifles, the quibbles, the unseasonable jokes, of what is exhibited in very harmonious Greek. and in English nearly as harmonious, pass uncensured and unnoticed by the fascinated Shelley.   So his gentleness and warmth of heart induced him to look with affection on the poetry of Petrarca ; poetry by how many degrees inferior to his own !   Nevertheless, with justice and propriety he ranks Dante higher in the same department, who indeed has described love more eloquently than any other poet, excepting (who always must be excepted) Shakespeare.   Francesca and Beatrice open all the heart, and fill it up with tenderness and with pity.

what species of it, and from what bestowers, should be the reward of sages and heroes.

Dii meliora piis!

Beside Sonnets and Canzoni Petrarca wrote "Sestine;" so named because each stanza contains six verses, and each poem six stanzas, to the last of which three lines are added. If the terza-rima is disagreeable to the ear, what is the sestina, in which there are only six rhymes to thirty-six verses, and all these respond to the same words! Cleverness in distortion can proceed no further. Petrarca wearied the popes by his repeated solicitations that they would abandon Avignon: he never thought of repeating a sestina to them: it would have driven the most obtuse and obstinate out to sea; and he never would have removed his hands from under the tiara until he entered the port of Civita-Vecchia. While our poet was thus amusing his ingenuity by the most intolerable scheme of rhyming that the poetry of any language has exhibited, his friend Boccaccio was occupied in framing that very stanza, the ottava-rima, which so delights us in Berni, Ariosto, and Tasso. But Tasso is most harmonious when he expatiates most freely, "numerisque fertur lege solutis:" for instance, in the *Aminta*, where he is followed by Milton in his *Lycidas*.

We left Petrarca not engaged in these studies of his retirement, but passing in triumph through the capital of the world. On his way toward Avignon, where he was ambitious of displaying his fresh laurels, he stayed a short time at Parma with Azzo da Correggio, who had taken possession of that city. Azzo was among the most unprincipled, ungrateful, and mean, of the numerous petty tyrants who have infested Italy. Petrarca's love of liberty never quite outrivalled his love of princes: for which Boccaccio mildly expostulates with him; and Sismondi, as liberal, wise, and honest as Boccaccio, severely reprehends him. But what other, loving as he loved, would have urged incessantly the return to Italy, the abandonment of Avignon? At times, beyond a doubt, he preferred his imperfect hopes to the complete restoration of Italian glory; but he shook them like dust from his bosom, and Laura was less than Rome. Shall we refuse the name of patriot to such a man? No; those alone will do it who have little to lose or leave. Sismondi, who never judges harshly, never hastily, passes no such sentence on him.

So pleased was he with his residence at Parma, that he purchased a house in the city, where he completed his poem of "Africa." He was now about to rejoin at Lombes his friend and diocesan, whom he saw in a dream, pale as death. He communicated this dream to several persons; and twenty-five days afterwards he received the intelligence of its perfect truth. Another friend, more advanced in years, Dionigi di Borgo San Sepolcro, soon followed. Before the expiration of the year he was installed archdeacon of Parma. Soon after this appointment, Benedict XII. died, and Clement VI. succeeded. This pontiff was superior to all his predecessors in gracefulness of manners and delicacy of taste; and at his accession, the corruptions of the papal court became less gross and offensive. He divided his time between literature and the ladies: not quite impartially. The people of Rome began to entertain new and higher hopes that their city would again be the residence of Christ's vicegerent. To this intent they delegated eighteen of the principal citizens, and chose Petrarca, who had received the freedom of the city on his coronation, to present at once a remonstrance and an invitation. The polite and wary pontiff heard him complacently, talked affably and familiarly with him, conferred on him the priory of Migliorino; but, being a Frenchman, thought it gallant and patriotic to remain at Avignon. Petrarca was little disposed to return with the unsuccessful delegates. He continued at Avignon, where his countryman Sennuccio del Bene, who visited the same society as Laura, and who knew her personally, gave him frequent information of her, though little hope.

Youth has swifter wings than Love. He had loved her sixteen years; but all the beauty that had left her features had settled on his heart, immovable, unchangeable, eternal. Politics could however at all times occupy him; not always worthily. He was induced by the pope to undertake a mission to Naples, and to claim the government of that kingdom on the part of his Holiness. The good king Robert was dead, and had bequeathed the crown to the elder of his two granddaughters. Giovanna, at nine years of age, was betrothed to her cousin Andreas of Hungary, who was three years younger. She was beautiful, graceful, gentle, sensible, and fond of literature : he was uncouth, ferocious, ignorant, and governed by a Hungarian monk of the same character, Fra Rupert. It is deplorable to think that Petrarca could ever have been induced to accept an embassy, of which the purport was to deprive of her inheritance an innocent and lovely girl, the grand-daughter of his friend and benefactor. She received him with cordiality, and immediately appointed him her private chaplain. His departure, he says, was hastened by two causes : first, by the insolence of Fra Rupert, which he has well described ; and secondly, by an atrocious sight, which also he has commemorated. He was invited to an entertainment, of which he gives us to understand he knew not at all the nature. Suddenly he heard shouts of joy, and *" turning his head,"* he beheld a youth of extraordinary strength and beauty, covered with dust and blood, expiring at his feet. He left Naples without accomplishing the dethronement of Giovanna, or, what also was entrusted to him, the liberation from prison of some adherents of the Colonnas : robbers, no doubt, and assassins, who had made forays into the Neapolitan territory ; for all persons of that description were under the protection of the Colonnas or the Orsini. His failure was the cause of his return, and not the ferocity of a monk and a gladiator.

He went to Parma on his way back to Avignon : the roads were dangerous ; war was raging in the country. His friend Azzo had refused to perform the promise he made to Lucchino Visconti, by whose intervention he had obtained his dominion, which he was to retain for five years, and then resign. Azzo he found had taken refuge with Mastino della Scala, at Verona ; and he embarked on the Po for that city. His friends hastened him forward to Avignon ; some by telling him how often the pope had made enquiries about him ; and others, that Laura looked melancholy. On his return Clement offered him the office of Apostolic secretary : it was a very laborious one, and was declined.

Laura, pleased by his return to her, was for a time less rigorous. Within the year, Charles of Luxemburg, soon after made emperor, went to Avignon. Knowing the celebrity of Laura, and finding her at a ball, he went up to her and kissed her forehead and her eyes. " This sweet and strange action," says her lover, " filled me with envy." Surely, to him at least, the sweetness must have been somewhat less than the strangeness. She was now indeed verging on her fortieth year: but love is forgetful of arithmetic. The following summer, Francesco for the first time visited his only brother Gherardo, who had taken the monastic habit in the Chartreuse of Montrieu. On his return he went to Vaucluse, where he composed a treatise *De Otio Religiosorum*, which he presented to the monastery.

Very different thoughts and feelings now suddenly burst upon him. Among the seventeen who accompanied him in the deputation, inviting the pope to Rome, there was another beside Petrarca chosen for his eloquence. It was Cola Rienzi. The love of letters and the spirit of patriotism united them in friendship. This extraordinary man, now invested with power, had driven the robbers and assassins, with their patrons the Orsini and Colonnas out of Rome, and had established (what rarely are established together) both liberty and order. The dignity of tribune was conferred on him; by which title Petrarca addressed him, in a letter of sound advice and earnest solicitation. Now the bishop of Lombes was dead he little feared the indignation of the other Colonnas, but openly espoused and loudly pleaded the cause of the resuscitated commonwealth. The cardinal was probably taught by him to believe that, by his influence with Rienzi, he might avert from his family the disaster and disgrace into which the mass of the nobility had fallen. "No family on earth," says he, "is dearer to me; but the republic, Rome, Italy, are dearer."

He took leave of the prelate, with amity on both sides undiminished: he also took leave of Laura. He could not repress, he could not conceal, he could not moderate his grief, nor could he utter one sad adieu. A look of fondness and compassion followed his parting steps; and the lover and the beloved were separated for ever. He did not think it; else never could he have gone; but he thought a brief absence might be endured once more, rewarded as it would be with an accession to his glory; and, precluded from other union with him, in his glory Laura might participate.

Retired, and thinking of her duties and her home, sat Laura; not indifferent to the praises of the most celebrated man alive (for her heart in all its regions was womanly) but tepidly tranquil, or moved invisibly, and retaining her purity amidst the uncleanly stream that deluged Avignon. We may imagine that she sometimes drew out, and unfolded on her bed, the apparel long laid apart and carefully preserved by her, in which she first had captivated the giver of her immortality; we may imagine that she sometimes compared with him an illiterate, coarse, morose husband; and perhaps a sigh escaped her, and perhaps a tear, as she folded up again the cherished gown she wore on that Good Friday.

On his arrival at Genoa, Petrarca heard of the follies and extravagances committed by Rienzi, and, instead of pursuing his journey to Rome, turned off to Parma. Here he learnt that the greater part of the Roman nobility, and many of the Colonnas, had been exterminated by order of the tribune. Unquestionably they had long deserved it; but the exercise of such prodigious power unsettled the intellects of Rienzi. In January the poet left Parma for Vienna, where on the 25th (1348) he felt the shock of an earthquake. In the preceding month a column of fire was observed above the pontifical palace. After these harbingers of calamity came that memorable plague, to which we owe the immortal work of Boccaccio; a work occupying the next station, in continental literature, to the *Divina Commedia*, and displaying a greater variety of powers. The pestilence had now penetrated into the northern parts of Italy, and into the southern of France; it had ravaged Marseilles; it was raging in Avignon. Petrarca sent messenger after messenger for intelligence. Their return was tardy; and only on the 19th of May was notice brought to him that Laura had departed on the 6th of April, at six in the morning; the very day, the very hour, he met her first. Beloved by all about her for her gentleness and serenity, she expired in the midst of relatives and friends. But did never her eyes look round for one who was away? And did not love, did not glory tell him, that in that chamber he might at least have died?

Other friends were also taken from him. Two months after this event he lost Cardinal Colonna; and then Sennuccio del Bene, the depository of his thoughts and the interpreter of Laura's.

The Lord of Mantua, Luigi Gonzaga, had often invited him

to his court, and he now accepted the invitation. From this residence he went to visit the hamlet of Pietola, formerly Andes, the birthplace of Virgil. At the cradle of her illustrious poet the glories of ancient Rome burst again upon him ; and, hearing that Charles of Luxemburg was about to cross the Alps, he addressed to him an eloquent exhortation, *Dê pacificandâ Italiâ*. After three years the emperor sent him an answer. The testy republican may condemn him, as Dante was condemned before, for inviting a stranger to become supreme in Italy ; but how many evils would this step have obviated! Recluses, and idlers, and often the most vicious, had been elevated to the honours of demigods ; and incense had been wafted before the altar, among the most solemn rites of religion, to pilferers and impostors. As the Roman empire, with all the kingdoms of the earth, was sold under the spear by the Pretorian legion, so now, with title-deeds more defective, was the kingdom of Heaven knocked down to the best bidder. It was not a desire of office and emolument, it was a love of freedom and of Roman glory, which turned the eyes of Petrarca, first in one quarter, then in another, to seek for the deliverance and regeneration of his native land.

No preferment, no friendship, stood before this object. In the beginning he exhorted Rienzi to the prosecution of his enterprise, and augured its success. But the vanity of the tribune, like Buonaparte's, precipitated his ruin. Both were so improvident as to be quite unaware, that he who continues to play at *double or quits* must at last lose all. Rienzi, different from that other, was endowed by nature with manly, frank, and generous sentiments. Meditative but communicative, studious but accessible, he would have followed, we may well believe, the counsels of Petrarca, had they been given him personally. Cautious but not suspicious, severe but not vindictive, he might perhaps have removed a D'Enghien by the axe, but never a L'Ouverture by famine. He would not have banished, he would not have treated with insolence and indignity, the greatest writer of the age, from a consciousness of inferiority in intellect, as that other did in Madame de Stael. With that other, similarity of views and sentiments was no bond of union : he hated, he maligned, he persecuted, the wisest and bravest who would not serve his purposes : patriotism was a ridicule, honour was an insult to him, and veracity a reproach. The *heart* of Rienzi was not insane. Instead of ordering the murder, he would have condemned to the gallows the murderer, of such a man as Hofer. In his impetuous and eccentric course he carried less about him of the middle ages, than the pestilent meteor that flamed forth in ours. Petrarca had too much wisdom, too much virtue, to praise or countenance him in his pride and insolence; but his fall was regretted by him, and is even still to be regretted by his country. It is indeed among the greatest calamities that have befallen the human race, condemned for several more centuries to lie in chains and darkness.

In the year of the jubilee (1350) he went again to Rome. Passing through Florence, he there visited Boccaccio, whom he had met at Naples. What was scarcely an acquaintance grew rapidly into friendship; and this friendship, honourable to both, lasted throughout life, unbroken and undiminished. Both were eloquent, both richly endowed with fancy and imagination; but Petrarca, who had incomparably the least of these qualities, had a readier faculty of investing them with verse, in which Boccaccio, fond as he was of poetry, ill succeeded. There are stories in the *Decameron* which require more genius to conceive and execute than all the poetry of Petrarca, and indeed there is in Boccaccio more variety of the mental powers than in any of his countrymen, greatly more deep feeling, greatly more mastery over the human heart, than in any other but Dante. Honesty, manliness, a mild and social independence, rendered him the most delightful companion and the sincerest friend.

Petrarca, on his road through Arezzo, was received with all the honours due to him, and among the most delicate and acceptable to a man of his sensibility was the attendance of the principal inhabitants in a body, who conducted him to the house in which he was born, showing him that no alteration had been permitted to be made in it. Padua was the place to which he was going: on his arrival he found that the object of his visit, Giovanni da Carrara, had been murdered: nevertheless, he remained there several days, and then proceeded to Venice. Andrea Dandolo was doge: and war was about to break out between the Venetians and the Genoese. Petrarca, who always wished most anxiously the concord and union of the Italian States, wrote a letter to Dandolo, powerful in reasoning and eloquence, dissuading him from hostilities. The poet on this occasion showed himself more provident that the greatest statesman of the age. On the 6th of April, the third anniversary of Laura's death, a message was conveyed to him from the republic of Florence, restoring his property and his rights of citizen. Unquestionably he who brought the message counselled the measure, and calculated the day : Boccaccio again embraced Petrarca.

It was also proposed to establish a university at Florence, and to nominate the illustrious poet its rector. Declining the office, he returned to Vaucluse, but soon began to fancy that his duty called him to Avignon. Rome and all Italy swarmed with robbers. Clement, from the bosom of the Vicomtesse de Turenne, consulted with the cardinals on the means of restoring security to his dominions. Petrarca too was consulted, and, in the most elaborate and most eloquent of his writings, he recommended the humiliation of the nobles, the restoration of the republic, and the enactment of equal laws.

The people of Rome however had taken up arms again, and had elected for their chief magistrate Giovanni Cerroni. The privileges of the Popedom were left untouched and unquestioned ; not a drop of blood was shed ; property was secure ; tranquillity was established. Clement, whose health was declining, acquiesced. Petrarca, disappointed before, was reserved and silent. But his justice, his humanity, his gratitude, were called into action elsewhere.

Ten years had elapsed since his mission to the court of Naples. The King Andreas had been assassinated, and the Queen Giovanna was accused of the crime. Andreas had alienated from him all the Neapolitans, excepting the servile, which in every court form a party, and in most a majority. Luigi of Taranto, the Queen's cousin, loved her from childhood, but left her at that age. Graceful, and gallant as he was, there is no evidence that she placed too implicit and intimate a confidence in him. Never has any great cause been judged with less discretion by posterity. The Pope, to whom she appealed in person, and who was deeply interested with all the cardinals and all the judges, unanimously and unreservedly acquitted her of participation, or connivance, or knowledge. Giannone, the most impartial and temperate of historians, who neglected no sources of information, bears testimony in her behalf. Petrarca and Boccaccio, men abhorrent from every atrocity, never mention her but with gentleness and compassion. The writers of the country, who were nearest to her person and her times, acquit her of all complicity. Nevertheless she has been placed in the dock by the side of Mary Stuart. It is as certain that Giovanna was *not* guilty as that Mary *was*. She acknowledged before the whole Pontifical Court her hatred of her husband; and in the simplicity of her heart, attributed it to magic. How different was the magic of Othello on Desdemona! and this too was believed.

If virtuous thoughts and actions can compensate for an irrecoverable treasure which the tomb encloses, surely now must calm and happiness have returned to Petrarca's bosom. Not only had he defended the innocent and comforted the sorrowful, in Giovanna, but, with singular care and delicacy, he reconciled two statesmen whose disunion would have been ruinous to her government; Acciajoli and Barili. Another generous action was now performed by him, in behalf of a man by whom he, and Rome, and Italy, had been deceived. Rienzi, after wandering about for nearly four years, was cast into prison at Prague, and then delivered up to the Pope. He demanded to be judged according to law: which was refused. The spirit of Petrarca rose up against this injustice, and he addressed a letter to the Roman people, urging their interference. They did nothing. But it was believed at Avignon that Rienzi, the correspondent and friend of Petrarca, was not only an eloquent and learned man, but (what Petrarca had taught the world to reverence) a poet. This caused a relaxation in the severity of his confinement, subsequently his release, and ultimately his restoration to power.

Again the office of apostolic secretary was offered to Petrarca; again he declined it; again he retired to Vaucluse. Clement died; Innocent was elected; so illiterate and silly a creature, that he took the poet for a wizard, because he read Virgil. It was time to revisit Italy. Acciajoli had invited him to Naples, Dandolo to Venice: but he went to neither. Giovanni Visconti, Archbishop of Milan, had succeeded his brother Lucchino in the sovranty. Clement, just before his decease, sent a nuncio to him, ordering him to make choice between the temporal and spiritual power. The duke-archbishop made no answer; but on the next

Sunday, after celebrating pontifical mass in the cathedral, he took in one hand a crozier, in the other a drawn sword, and "Tell the Holy Father," said he, " here is the spiritual, here the temporal : one defends the other." Innocent was unlikely to intimidate a prince who had thus defied his predecessor. Giovanni Visconti was among the most able statesmen that Italy has produced ; and Italy has produced a greater number of the greatest than all the rest of the universe. Genoa reduced to extremities by Venice had thrown herself under his protection ; and Venice, although at the head of the Italian league, guided by Dandolo, and flushed with conquest, felt herself unable to contend with him. Visconti who expected and feared the arrival of the Emperor in Italy, assumed the semblance of moderation. He engaged Petrarca, whom he had received with every mark of distinction and affection, to preside in a deputation with offers of peace to Dandolo. The doge refused the conditions ; and Visconti lost no time in the prosecution of hostilities. These were so successful, that Venice was in danger of falling ; and Dandolo died of a broken heart. In the following month died also Giovanni Visconti. The emperor Charles, who had deceived the hopes of the Venetians by delaying to advance into Italy, now crossed the Alps : and Petrarca met him at Mantua. Finding him, as usual, wavering and avaricious, the poet soon left him, and returned to the nephews and heirs of Visconti. He was induced by Galeazzo to undertake an embassy to the emperor. Ill disposed as was Charles to the family, he declared that he had no intention of carrying his arms into Italy. On this occasion he sent to Petrarca the diploma of Count Palatine, in a golden box, which golden box the Count Francesco returned to the German chancellor : and he made as little use of the title.

He now settled at Garignano, a village three miles from Milan, to which residence he gave the name of Linterno, from the villa of Scipio on the coast of Naples. Fond as he was of the great and powerful, he did not always give them the preference. Capra, a goldsmith of Bergamo, enthusiastic in admiration of his genius, invited him with earnest entreaties to honour that city with a visit. On his arrival, the governor and nobility contended which should perform the offices of hospitality toward so illustrious a guest : but he went at once to the house of Capra, where he was treated by his worthy host with princely magnificence, and with delicate attentions which princely magnificence often overlooks. The number of choice volumes in the library, and the conversation of Capra, were evidences of a cultivated understanding and a virtuous heart. In the winter following (1359) Boccaccio spent several days at Linterno, and the poet gave him his Latin Eclogues in his own handwriting. On his return to Florence, Boccaccio sent his friend the *Divina Commedia*, written out likewise by himself, and accompanied with profuse commendations.

Incredible as it may appear, this noble poem, the glory of Italy, and admitting at that time but one other in the world to a proximity with it, was wanting to the library of Petrarca. His reply was cold and cautious : the more popular man, it might be thought, took umbrage at the loftier. He was jealous even of the genius which had gone by, and which bore no resemblance to his own, excepting in the purity and intensity of love : for this was a portion of the genius in both. He was certainly the very best man that ever was a very vain one : and vanity has a better excuse for itself in him than in any other, since none was more admired by the world at large, and particularly by that part of it which the wisest are most desirous to conciliate, turning their wisdom in full activity to the elevation of their happiness. Laura, it is true, was sensible of little or no passion for him ; but she was pleased with his ; and stood like a beautiful Cariatid of stainless marble, at the base of an image on which the eyes of Italy were fixt.

Petrarca, like Boccaccio, regretted at the close of life, not only the pleasure he had enjoyed, but also the pleasure he had imparted to the world. Both of them, as their mental faculties were diminishing, and their animal spirits were leaving them apace, became unconscious how incomparably greater was the benefit than the injury done by their writings. In Boccaccio there are certain tales so coarse that modesty casts them aside, and those only who are irreparably contaminated can receive any amusement from them. But in the greater part, what truthfulness, what tenderness, what joyousness, what purity ! Their levities and gaieties are like the harmless lightnings of a summer sky in the delightful regions they were written in. Petrarca, with a

mind which bears the same proportion to Boccaccio's as the
Sorga bears to the Arno, has been the solace of many sad hours
to those who probably were more despondent.   It may be that,
at the time when he was writing some of his softest and most
sorrowful complaints, his dejection was caused by dalliance with
another, far more indulgent than Laura.   But his ruling passion
was ungratified by her ; therefore she died unsung, and, for aught
we know to the contrary, unlamented.   He had forgotten what
he had declared in Sonnet 17.

> E. se di lui forse altra donna spera,
>   Vive in speranza debile e fallace,
>   Mio, perche sdegno ciò ch' a voi dispiace, &c.

> If any other hopes to find
>   That love in me which you despise,
> Ah ! let her leave the hope behind :
> I hold from all what you alone should prize.

It can only be said that he ceased to be a visionary : and we
ought to rejoice that an inflammation, of ten years' recurrence,
sank down into a regular fit, and settled in no vital part.   Yet I
can not but wish that he had been as zealous in giving instruction
and counsel to his only son, a youth whom he represents in one
of his letters to have been singularly modest and docile, as he
had been in giving it to princes, emperors, and popes, who exhibited very little of those characters.   While he was at his
villa at Linterno, the unfortunate youth robbed the house in
Milan, and fled.   We may reasonably suppose that home had
become irksome to him, and that neither the eye nor the heart
of a father was over him.   Giovanni was repentant, was forgiven,
and died.

The tenderness of Petrarca, there is too much reason to fear,
was at all times concentrated in self.   A nephew of his early
patron Colonna, in whose house he had spent many happy hours,
was now deprived of house and home, and, being reduced to
abject poverty, had taken refuge in Bologna.   He had surely
great reason to complain of Petrarca, who never in his journeys
to and fro had visited or noticed him, or, rich as he was in benefices by the patronage of his family, offered him any succour.
This has been excused by Mr Campbell : it may be short of
turpitude ; but it is farther, much farther, from generosity and

from justice. Never is mention made by him of Laura's children, whom he must have seen with her, and one or other of whom must have noticed with the pure delight of unsuspicious childhood his fond glances at the lovely mother. Surely in all the years he was devoted to Laura, one or other of her children grieved her by ill-health, or perhaps by dying: for virtue never set a mark on any door so that sickness and sorrow must not enter. But Petrarca thought more about her eyes than about those tears that are usually the inheritance of the brightest, and may well be supposed to have said, in some inedited canzone,

> What care I what tears there be,
> If the tears are not for me?

His love, when it administered nothing to his celebrity, was silent. Of his two children, a son and a daughter, not a word is uttered in any of his verses. How beautifully does Ovid, who is thought in general to have been less tender, and was probably less chaste, refer to the purer objects of his affection!

> Unica nata, mei justissima causa doloris, &c.

Petrarca's daughter lived to be the solace of his age, and married happily. Boccaccio, in the most beautiful and interesting letter in the whole of Petrarca's correspondence, mentions her kind reception of him, and praises her beauty and demeanour. Even the unhappy boy appears to have been by nature of nearly the same character. According to the father's own account, his disposition was gentle and tractable: he was modest and shy, and abased his eyes before the smart witticisms of Petrarca on the defects his own negligence had caused. A parent should never excite a blush, nor extinguish one.

Domestic cares bore indeed lightly on a man perpetually busy in negotiations. He could not but despise the emperor, who yet had influence enough over him to have brought him into Germany. But bands of robbers infested the road, and the plague was raging in many of the intermediate cities. It had not reached Venice: and there he took refuge. Wherever he went, he carried a great part of his library with him: but he found it now more inconvenient than ever, and therefore he made a present of it to the republic, on condition that it neither should be sold nor separated. It was never sold, it was never separated; but it was suffered to fall into decay, and not a single volume of the collection is now extant. While he was at Verona, his friend Boccaccio made him another visit, and remained with him three summer months. The plague deprived him of Lælius, of Socrates, and of Barbato. Among his few surviving friends was Philip de Cabassoles, now patriarch of Jerusalem, to whom he had promised the dedication of his treatise on "Solitary Life," which he began at Vaucluse.

Urban V., successor to Innocent, designed to reform the discipline of the church; and Petrarca thought he had a better chance than ever of seeing its head at Rome. Again he wrote a letter on the occasion, learned, eloquent, and enthusiastically bold. Urban had perhaps already fixed his determination. Despite of remonstrances on the side of the French king, and of intrigues on the side of the cardinals, whose palaces and mistresses must be left behind, he quitted Avignon on the 30th of April, 1367, and, after a stay of four months at Viterbo, entered Rome. Before this event Petrarca had taken into his house, and employed as secretary, a youth of placid temper and sound understanding, which he showed the best disposition to cultivate. His name was Giovanni Malpighi, better known afterward as Giovanni da Ravenna. He was admitted to the table, to the walks, and to the travels of his patron, enjoying far more of his kindness and affection than, at the same time of life, had ever been bestowed upon his son. Petrarca superintended his studies, and prepared him for the clerical profession. Unexpectedly one morning this youth entered his study, and declared he would stay no longer in the house. In vain did Petrarca try to alter his determination: neither hope nor fear moved him: and nothing was left but to accompany him as far as Venice. Giovanni would see the tomb of Virgil: he would visit the birthplace of Ennius: he would learn Greek at Constantinople. He went however no farther than Pavia, where Petrarca soon followed him, and pardoned his extravagance.

Urban had no sooner established the holy see at Rome again, than he began to set Italy in a flame, raising troops in all quarters, and directing them against the Visconti. The Emperor too in earnest had resolved on war. But Bernabo Visconti, who knew his avarice, knew how to divert his arms. He came into Italy, but only to lead the Pope's palfrey and to assist at the empress's coronation. Urban sent an invitation to Petrarca; and he prepared, although in winter, to revisit Rome. Conscious that his health was declining, he made his will. To the Lord of Padua he bequeathed a picture of the Virgin by Giotto; and to Boccaccio fifty gold florins for a cloak to keep him warm in his study. Such was his debility, he could proceed no farther than Ferrara, and thought it best to return to Padua. For the benefit of the air he settled in the hamlet of Arquà, where he built a villa, and where his daughter and her husband Francesco di Brossano, came to live with him. Urban died, and was succeeded by Gregory XI., who would have added to the many benefices held already by Petrarca: and the poet in these his latter days was not at all averse to the gifts of fortune. His old friend the bishop of Cabassoles, now a cardinal, was sent as legate to Perugia: Petrarca was desirous of visiting him, and the rather as the prelate's health was declining: but before his own enabled him to undertake the journey, he had expired.

One more effort of friendship was the last reserved for him. Hostilities broke out between the Venetians and Francesco da Ferrara, aided by the king of Hungary, who threatened to abandon his cause unless he consented to terms of peace. Venice now recovered her advantages, and reduced Francesco to the most humiliating conditions. He was obliged to send his son to ask pardon of the republic. To render this less intolerable, he prevailed on Petrarca to accompany the youth, and to plead his cause before the senate. Accompanied by a numerous and a splendid train, they arrived at the city; audience was granted them on the morrow. But fatigue and illness so affected Petrarca that he could not deliver the speech he had prepared. Among the many of his compositions which are lost to us, is this oration. Happily there is preserved the friendly letter he wrote to Boccaccio on his return; the last of his writings. During the greater part of his lifetime, though no less zealous than Boccaccio himself in recovering the works of the classics, he never had read the *Divina Commedia*; nor, until this period of it, the *Decameron*; the two most admirable works the continent has produced from the restoration of learning to the present day. Boccaccio, who had given him the one, now gave him the other. In his letter of thanks for it, he excuses the levity of his friend in some places, attributes it to the season of life in which the book was written, and relates the effect the story of Griseldis had produced, not only on himself, but on another of less sensibility. He even learnt it by heart, that he might recite it to his friends; and he sent the author a Latin translation of it. Before this, but among his latest compositions, he had written an indignant answer to an unknown French monk, who criticised his letter to Urban, and had spoken contemptuously of Rome and Italy. Monks generally know at what most vulnerable part to aim the dagger: and the Frenchman struck Petrarca between his vanity and his patriotism. A greater mind would have looked down indifferently on a dwarf assailant, and would never have lifted him up, even for derision. The most prominent rocks and headlands are most exposed to the elements; but those which can resist the violence of the storms are in little danger from the corrosion of the limpets.

On the 18th of July, 1374, Petrarca was found in his library, his brow upon a book he had been reading: he was dead.

There is no record of any literary man, or perhaps of any man whatsoever, to whom such honours, honours of so many kinds, and from such different quarters and personages, have been offered. They began in his early life; and we are walking at this hour in the midst of the procession. Few travellers dare to return from Italy until they can describe to the attentive ear and glistening eye the scenery of the Euganean hills. He who has loved truly, and, above all, he who has loved unhappily, approaches, as holiest altars are approached, the cenotaph on the little columns at Arqua.

The Latin works of Petrarca were esteemed by himself more highly than his Italian.* His Letters and his Dialogues "De Contemptu Mundi," are curious and valuable. In the latter he converses with Saint Augustin, to whom he is introduced by

---

* It is incredible that Julius Cæsar Scaliger, who has criticised so vast a number of later poets quite forgotten, and deservedly, should never have even seen the Latin poetry of Petrarca. His words are: " Primus, quod equidem sciam, Petrarca ex lutulentâ barbarie os cœlo attollere ausus est, *cujus*, quemadmodum diximus alibi, *quòd nihil videre licueret*, ejus viri castigationes sicut et alia multa, relinquam studiosis." *Poet.* l. vi., p. 769.

Truth, the same personage who appears in his *Africa*, and whom Voltaire also invokes to descend on his little gravelly Champ de Mars, the *Henriade*. The third dialogue is about his love for Laura, and nobly is it defended. He wrote a treatise on the ignorance of one's self and others (*multorum*), in which he has taken much from Cicero and Augustin, and in which he afterward forgot a little of his own. "Ought we to take it to heart," says he, "if we are ill spoken of by the ignorant and malicious, when the same thing happened to Homer and Demosthenes, to Cicero and Virgil?" He was fond of following these two; Cicero in the number of his epistles, Virgil in eclogue and in epic.

Of his twelve eclogues, which by a strange nomenclature he also called bucolics, many are satirical. In the sixth and seventh Pope Clement is represented in the character of Mitio. In the sixth Saint Peter, under the name of Pamphilus, reproaches him for the condition in which he keeps his flock, and asks him what he has done with the wealth intrusted to him. Mitio answers that he has kept the gold arising from the sale of the lambs, and that he has given the milk to certain friends of his. He adds that his spouse, very different from the old woman Pamphilus was contented with, went about in gold and jewels. As for the rams and goats, they played their usual gambols in the meadow; and he himself looked on. Pamphilus is indignant, and tells him he ought to be flogged and sent to prison for life. Mitio drops on a sudden his peaceful character, and calls him a faithless runaway slave, deserving the fetter and the cross. In the twelfth eclogue, under the appellations of Pan and Arcticus, are represented the kings of France and England. Arcticus is indignant at the favours Pan receives from Faustula (Avignon). To king John the Pope had remitted his tenths, so that he was enabled to continue the war against England, which ended in his captivity.

Petrarca in all his Latin poetry, and indeed in all his Latin compositions, is an imitator, and generally a very unsuccessful one; but his versification is more harmonious, and his language has more the air of antiquity, and more resembles the better models, than any had done since Boethius.

We now come to his Italian poetry. In this he is less deficient in originality, though in several pieces he has imitated too closely Cino da Pistoja. "Mille dubj in un dì," for instance, in his seventh canzone.   Cino is crude and enigmatical : but there is a beautiful sonnet by him addressed to Dante, which he wrote on passing the Apennines, and stopping to visit the tomb and invoke the name of Selvaggia.   Petrarca, late in life, made a collection of sonnets on Laura ; they are not printed in the order in which they were written.   The first is a kind of prologue to the rest, as the first ode of Horace is.   There is melancholy grace in this preliminary piece.   The third ought to have been the second ; for, after having in the first related his errors and regrets, we might have expected to find the cause of them in the following ; we find it in the third.   "Di pensier in pensier," "Chiare dolci e fresche acque," "Se il pensier che mi strugge," "Benedetto sia il giorno," "Solo e pensoso," are incomparably better than the "Tre Sorelle," by which the Italians are enchanted, and which the poet himself views with great complacency.   These three are upon the eyes of Laura.   The seventh canzone, the second of the " Sorelle," or, as they have often been styled, the "Grazie," is the most admired of them.   In this however the ear is offended at " *Qual all' alta*."   The critics do not observe this sad cacophony.   And nothing is less appropriate than

Ed al fuoco *gentil* ond' io *tutt' ardo*.

The close is,

Canzon ! l'una Sorella è poco inanzi.
E l' altra sento in quel medesmo albergo
Apparecchiarsi, *ond' io più carta vergo*.

This ruins the figure.   What becomes of the *Sorella*, and the *albergo*, and the *apparecchiarsi* ?   The third is less celebrated than the two elder sisters.

Muratori, the most judicious of Italian commentators, gives these canzoni the preference over the others : but it remained for a foreigner to write correctly on them, and to demonstrate that they are very faulty.   I find more faults and graver than Ginguené has found in them : but I do not complain with him so much that the commencement of the third is heavy and languid, as that serious thoughts are intersected with quibbles, and spangled with conceits.   I will here remark freely, and in some detail, on this part of the poetry of Petrarca.

Sonetto 21. It will be difficult to find in all the domains of poetry so frigid a conceit as in the conclusion of this sonnet,

> E far delle sue braccie a se stess' ombra.

Strange that it should be followed by the most beautiful he ever wrote :

> Solo e pensoso, &c.

Canzone 1.

> Ne mano ancor m' agghiaccia
> L' esser coperto poi di bianche piume,
> Ond' io presi col suon color di cigno !

How very inferior is this childish play to Horace's ode, in which he also becomes a swan.

Canzone 3. Among the thousand offices which he attributes to the eyes is *carrying the keys.* Here he talks of the *sweet eyes* carrying the keys of his *sweet thoughts.* Again he has a peep at the keyhole in the seventh.

> Quel cuor ond' hanno i begli occhi la chiave.

He also lets us into the secret that he is really *fond* of complaining, and that he *takes pains* to have his eyes always full of tears.

> Ed io son un di quei ch' il pianger *giova,*
> E par ben ch' io m' *ingegno*
> Che di lagrime pregni
> Sien gli occhi miei.

Sonetto 20. Here are Phœbus, Vulcan, Jupiter, *Cæsar*, Janus, Saturn, Mars, Orion, Neptune, Juno, and a chorus of *Angels :* and they have only fourteen lines to turn about in.

Canzone 4. The last part has merit from " E perche un poco."

Sonetto 39. In this beautiful sonnet, as in almost every one, there is a redundancy of words : for instance,

> Benedetto sia il giorno, e 'l mese, e l' anno,
> *E la stagion, e 'l tempo.*

Sonetto 40 is very serious. It is a prayer to God that his

heart may be turned to other desires, and that it may remember how on that day He was crucified.

Sestina 3. With what derision would a poet of the present day be treated who had written such stuff as,

> E *nel bel* petto l' *indurato* ghiaccio
> Che trae del mio si *dolorosi venti.*

Sonetto 44. "L'aspetto sacro" is ingenious, yet without conceits.

Canzone 8. As far as we know it has never been remarked (nor indeed is an Italian Academia worth a remark) that the motto of the Academia della Crusca, " Il più bel fior ne coglie " is from

> E, le onorate
> Cose cercando, il più bel fior ne coglie.

Sonetto 46. Here he wonders whence all the ink can come with which he fills his paper on Laura.

Sonetto 51. In the fourteenth year of his passion, his ardour is increasing to such a degree, that, he says, " Death approaches . . *and life flies away.*"

> Che la morte s'appressa . . . . . *e 'l viver fugge.*

We believe there is no instance where life has resisted the encounter.

Sonetto 59. This is very different from all his others. The first part is poor enough: the last would be interesting if we could believe it to be more than imaginary. Here he boasts of the impression he had made on Laura, yet in his last Canzone he asks her whether he ever had. The words of this sonnet are,

> Era ben forte la nemica mia,
> E lei viddi io ferita in *mezzo'l core.*

But we may well take all this for ideal, when we read the very next, in which he speaks of being free from the thraldom that had held him so many years.

Sonetto 66. The conclusion from " Ne mi lece ascoltar," is

very animated: here is greatly more vigour and incitation than usual.

Canzone 9. It would be difficult to find anywhere, except in the rarest and most valuable books, so wretched a poem as this. The rhymes occur over and over again, not only at the close, but often at the fifth and sixth syllables, and then another time. Metastasio has managed best the redundant rhymes.

Sonetto 73. The final part, " L' aura soave," is exquisitely beautiful, and the harmony complete.

Sonetto 84. " Quel vago impallidir " is among the ten best.

Canzone 10. In the last stanza there is a lightness of movement not always to be found in the graces of Petrarca.

Canzone 11. This is incomparably the most elaborate work of the poet, but it is very far from the perfection of " Solo e pensoso." The second and third stanzas are inferior to the rest; and the *fera bella e mansueta* is quite unworthy of the place it occupies.

Canzone 13 is extremely beautiful until we come to

Pur tì medesmo assido,
Me freddo, *pietra morta in pietra viva.*

Sonetto 95. " Pommi ovi 'l Sol," is imitated from Horace's " Pone me pigris," &c.

Sonetto 98. Four verses are filled with the names of rivers, excepting the monosyllables *non* and *e*. He says that all these rivers can not slake the fire that is the anguish of his heart: no, nor even ivy, fir, pine, beech, or juniper. It is by no means a matter of wonder that these subsidiaries lend but little aid to the exertions of the fireman.

Sonetto 110.

O anime gentili ed amorose

has been imitated and improved upon by Redi, in his

Donne gentili, divote d' amore.

Sonetto 111. No extravagance ever surpassed the invocation to the rocks in the water, requiring that henceforward there would not be a single one which had neglected to learn how to burn with his flames. He himself can only go farther in

Sonetto 119, where he tells us that Laura's eyes can burn up the Rhine when it is most frozen, and crack its hardest rocks.

Sonetto 132. In the precarious state of her health, he fears more about the disappointment of his hopes in love than about her danger.

Sonetto 148. His descriptions of beauty are not always distinct and correct: for example,

> Gli occhi sereni e le *stellanti* ciglia
> La bella bocca angelica . . de perle
> *Pienâ*, e di rose . . e di dolci *parole*.

In this place we shall say a little about *occhi* and *ciglia*. First, the sense would be better and the verse equally good, if, transposing the epithets, it were written

> Gli occhi stellanti e le serene ciglia.

The Italian poets are very much in the habit of putting the *eyelashes* for the *eyes*, because *ciglia* is a most useful rhyme. The Latin poets, contented with *oculi*, *ocelli*, and *lumina*, never employ *cilia*, of which indeed they appear to have made but little account. Greatly more than a hundred times has Petrarca inserted eyes into the first part of his sonnets; it is rarely that we find one without its *occhi*. They certainly are very ornamental things; but it is not desirable for a poet to resemble an Argus.

Canzone 15. The versification here differs from the others, but is no less beautiful than in any of them. However, where Love appears in person, we would rather that Pharaoh, Rachel, &c., were absent.

Sonetto 157. He tells us on what day he entered the labyrinth of love.

> Mille trecento ventisette *appunto*
> Sull' ora prima il dì sesto d' Aprili.

This poetry has very unfairly been taken advantage of, in a book

> Written by William Prynne Esquier, the
> Year of our Lord sixteen hundred thirty-three.

Sonetto 158. He has now loved twenty years.

Sonetto 161. The first verse is rendered very inharmonious by the cesura and the final word having syllables that rhyme. Tuto 'l dì *piango*, e per la notte *quando*, lagri*mando*, and consu*mando*, are considered as rhymes, although rhymes should be formed by similarity of sound and not by identity. The Italians, the Spaniards, and the French, reject this canon.

Sonetto 187, on the present of two roses, is light and pretty.

Sonetto 192. He fears he may never see Laura again. Probably this was written after her death. He dreams of her saying to him, "do you not remember the last evening, when I left you with your eyes in tears? Forced to go away from you, I would not tell you, nor could I, what I tell you now. *Do not hope to see me again on earth.*" This most simple and beautiful sonnet has been less noticed than many which a pure taste would have rejected. The next is a vision of Laura's death. There are verses in Petrarca which will be uttered by many sorrowers through many ages. Such, for instance, are

> Non la connobbe il mondo mentre l' ebbe,
> Conobbi la io chi a pianger qui rimasi.

But we are hard of belief when he says

> Pianger cercai, *non già dal pianto onore*.

There are fourteen more Sonnets, and one more Canzone in the first series of the *Rime;* but we must here close it. Of the second, third, and fourth series we must be contented with fewer notices, for already we have exceeded the limits we proposed. They were written after Laura's death, and contain altogether somewhat more than the first alone. Many of the poems in them are grave, tender, and beautiful. There are the same faults, but fewer in number, and less in degree. He never talks again, as he does in the last words of the first, of carrying a laurel and a column in his bosom, the one for fifteen, the other for eighteen years.

Ginguené seems disinclined to allow a preference to this second part of the Canzoniere. But surely it is in general far more pathetic, and more exempt from the importunities of petty fancies. He takes the trouble to translate the wretched sonnet

(33, part 2) in which the waters of the river are increased by the poet's tears, and the fish (as they had a right to expect) are spoken to.   But the next is certainly a most beautiful poem, and worthy of Dante himself, whose manner of thinking and style of expression it much resembles.   There is a canzone in dialogue which also resembles it in sentiment and feeling ;

> Quando soave mio fido conforto, &c.

The next again is imitated from Cino da Pistoja : what a crowd of words at the opening !

> Quel antico mio dolce empio signore.

It is permitted in no other poetry than the Italian to shovel up such a quantity of trash and triviality before the doors.   But rather than indulge in censure, we will recommend to the especial perusal of the reader another list of admirable compositions. "Alma felice," "Anima bella," "Ite rime dolenti," "Tornami a mente," "Quel rossignol," "Vago augelletto," "Dolce mio caro," "Gli angeli," "Ohime! il bel viso," "Che debbo io far," "Amor! se vuoi," "O aspettata," "Anima, che dimostra," "Spirto gentil," "Italia mia."   Few indeed, if any, of these are without a flaw ; but they are of higher worth than those on which the reader, unless forewarned, would spend his time unprofitably. It would be a great blessing if a critic deeply versed in this literature, like Carey, would publish the Italian poets with significant marks before the passages worth reading ; the more worth, and the less.   Probably it would not be a mark of admiration, only that surprise and admiration have but one between them, which would follow the poet's declaration in Can. 18, that "if he does not melt away it is because fear holds him together."   After this foolery he becomes a true poet again, "O colli!" &c., then again bad, "You see how many colours love paints my face with."

Nothing he ever wrote is so tender as a reproach of Laura's, after ten years' admiration, "You are *soon* grown tired of loving me!"

There is poetry in Petrarca which we have not yet adverted

to, in which he has changed the chords και την λυρήν απασαν: such as " Fiamma del ciel," " L' avara Babilonia," " Fontana di dolor." The volumes close with the " Trionfi." The first, as we might have anticipated, is " Il Trionfo d' Amore." The poem is a vile one, stuffed with proper names. The " Triumph of Chastity " is shorter, as might also be anticipated, and not quite so full of them. At the close, Love meets Laura, who makes him her captive, and carries him in triumph among the virgins and matrons most celebrated for purity and constancy. The " Triumph of Death " follows.

This poem is truly admirable. Laura is returning from her victory over Love ; suddenly there appears a black flag, followed by a female in black apparel, and terrible in attitude and voice. She stops the festive procession, and strikes Laura. The poet now describes her last moments, and her soft sleep of death, in which she retains all her beauty. In the second part she comes to him in a dream, holds out her hand, and invites him to sit by her on the bank of a rivulet, under the shade of a beech and a laurel. Nothing, in this most beautiful of languages, is so beautiful, excepting the lines of Dante on Francesca, as these.

> E quella man' già tanto desiata,
> *A me, parlando e sospirando, porse.*

Their discourse is upon death, which she tells him should be formidable only to the wicked, and assures him that the enjoyment she receives from it, is far beyond any which life has to bestow. He then asks her a question, which he alone had a right to ask her, and only in her state of purity and bliss.

> She sigh'd, and said, " No; nothing could dissever
> My heart from thine, and nothing shall there ever.
>   If, thy fond ardour to repress,
> I sometimes frown'd (and how could I do less ?)
> If, now and then, my look was not benign,
>   'Twas but to save my fame, and thine.
> And, as thou knowest, when I saw thy grief,
>   A glance was ready with relief."

> Scarce with dry cheek
> These tender words I heard :   speak.
> " Were they but true ! " I cried.   She bent the head,
> Not unreproachfully, and said,
> " Yes, I did love thee ; and whene'er
> I turn'd away mine eyes, 'twas shame and fear ;
> A thousand times to thee did they incline.
> But sank before the flame that shot from thine."

He who, the twentieth time, can read unmoved this canzone, never has experienced a love which could not be requited, and never has deserved a happy one.

INDEX.